GW01454204

Her/Story

By Thomas Harrison

First Publication 2025

Published by Amazon Kindle Direct Publishing

Also by Thomas Harrison

The Glass Man (2024)

Praise for *The Glass Man*:

"... compelling characters rendered me unable to put it down..."

"... A thought provoking and insightful debut novel...."

"... this book still haunts me..."

"... A raw and honest portrayal of someone struggling with mental illness..."

Her/Story

Thomas Harrison

Her/Story

I know what it means when people say that actions have consequences. Because I am one.

There's a reason it's known as *his*tory.

So - I wanted to write a story, a *her*story I suppose, where a woman doesn't turn to a man to be saved, where she doesn't shy away from her problems but embraces them; where she acknowledges that she doesn't deserve to be treated badly by a man just because that is what time and *his*tory dictates should happen.

I made myself a to-do list.

It's what I always do when I feel the need to get some control back in my life. It's an easy win so I can feel good about myself; if I tick something off then I have achieved. I can be an adult. I am successful. The only problem with tick-lists and to-do lists is that they can be never ending. It is easy to add something else then something else then another idea or task that must completed and if you don't do it then you're just as useless and shit as you've always thought you were. The little voice inside whines at you again. You wait for it like one of Pavlov's dogs.

I circle round and round these thoughts in the hallway of my house. It takes me five minutes to decide whether to take my coat off first or my shoes, write another to-do list, or pull out the envelopes to Billy I have hoarded away. This constant second guessing and uncertainty and anxiety, it's... exhausting.

My grief counsellor said it's something I can retrain. I can unlearn. *Keep going, keep going,* I tell myself: a mantra, a cycle, keep going like spokes on a wheel.

But I'm not so sure. I'm not certain that the guilt I feel over what I've done will ever go away.

-

PART ONE

"His fingernails."

I could see the light dimming through the windows. There were lines streaked across each of the windowpanes, telling me they'd been cleaned, not very well, granted, but cleaned at least. Inside or outside though I couldn't tell. It was past seven. My shift ended at six but Mrs Lullin was taking her time tonight. Not that I minded. It saved me having to go home. The bedspread would need to be changed again tomorrow - the pillows she liked to keep even when they were a little ripe - but the sheets she agreed to. She wasn't like a lot of the other people here, she didn't necessarily need the one-to-one care some required throughout the day (feedings, changings, reminding them of where they were and who they had as family members) but someone had felt strongly enough to place her here. I caught myself wondering sometimes - in the mirror brushing my teeth before work, cutting flowers to place in vases around the home to "spruce the place up" as Lizzie would say, pouring cup after cup of tea during games of bingo - if it would be easy for someone to make that decision about you: to send you somewhere to be cared for, less of a burden. To die? I wasn't sure if I'd want to end up somewhere like this myself one day. Maybe I wouldn't have a choice in the matter. Mrs Lullin didn't seem to.

"What do you mean his fingernails? Who misses someone's fingernails?"

I was painting her nails. Tonight was karaoke in the living room, and she wanted to look her best. Every Wednesday like clockwork. "Sorry Mrs Lullin. I was concentrating on your hands. I've never been able to multitask. You wanted to know what I miss most about him?"

"Yes dear. I mean, I miss my husband's eyes the most. I miss his ears. Don't know why. They were huge like Mickey Mouse. But they made me smile whenever I saw him."

"Ah. So that's how you met. You fell in love at Disneyland Paris. No, let me guess... it was at the foot of the Disney Palace that you first saw him... in his Mickey Mouse costume and you were... a summer temp there too as Minnie... and the rest is history."

"Michelle, you do talk nonsense," Mrs Lullin laughed, an old smoker's laugh despite the fact that she'd never smoked. That was her husband's vice. "But I like your stories. I wish that was true. No, no. We met at church. The only way really in our day." She opened and closed the hand that I wasn't painting, as though trying to grasp at something, gone. "He asked me for my landline the first time we met. I was 19."

I smirked at 'landline'. I loved hearing about the different courtships and events and stories of the people here. Their stories were better than anything I could tell, or would have been able to invent and write. Some of the stories would make you blush. Some were sweet. Some were just plain sad.

"Did they have phones back then Mrs Lullin?"

"I know I'm a septarian, but I can still fight for myself when needed." Mrs Lullin raised her head in a mock regal manner, chin up, eyes raised, then laughed like the silly schoolgirl it was easy to imagine that she once was. That's what I loved about the people here: their faces, their skin; it told fragments of their history within a couple of movements. The home was filled with moving pictures. "And for the love of God, please stop calling me Mrs Lullin. You've known me far too long and cleaned up far too many of my messes to be so formal. And I've always hated that name. It makes me sound like I'm having a constant and very slow stroke." The irony of her comment wasn't lost on either of us. "It was the only thing that put me off marrying him. But I did it anyway." Her free hand grasped again. "Happiest day of my life."

I rounded off her left-hand thumb with the polish. "Well," wanting to brighten the mood, "if you win tonight then this day might come a close second." I took her other hand and squeezed it. Our eyes met for a moment. "And these will dazzle the other competitors off the stage." She held up her right hand and admired my artistry. "Not bad?" I asked. She smiled back with her eyes. "Not bad."

She passed me the pot of green polish. "So, what *do* you miss about him then?"

I didn't answer straight away. How do you answer a question like that? Can you only miss one thing about a person? Could you just say the very person themselves?

"Time," I say.

"Time?" Mrs Lullin cocked her head. Her old eyes, wrinkled, wise, studied me. "You wish you'd had more of it with him." Not a question, but a declarative. A truth.

"Yes. I miss the time we had. The time we should have had."

"Well, that's natural," she blew on her nails as she spoke, "we all wish we had more time with those we love. I wish I still had my husband. At my age you realise how much you took for granted."

I didn't tell her that time is also my greatest fear – not just what I miss. I fear the hours ahead of me. The blank time I have left, alone. The seemingly endless cycle of time.

"You know," I say, attempting to change the tone of our talk, "I think I was right the first time. It's his fingernails. Well, his fingers. His hands in general. They were just always moving. Cooking or typing. Writing. I loved watching him write. He had these great little sayings that he'd write down too, you know cheesy things you'd see on fridge magnets and such but... he could write about anything. He could improve anything anyone sent to him. He was the best."

"Well, that's why your business was so successful. It still could be." She paused. "Have you thought about carrying on with the business at all?"

"No, I... I tried to at first, but it didn't feel right somehow. Didn't seem to..." now it was my turn to grasp at something, gone, "work. I still do some freelance stuff just to keep my toes in."

"Fingers in, dear. Just to keep your fingers in, that's the expression."

"I'm the writer here. I think I know." For a moment I could have sworn I felt his fingers interlaced with mine. His hand on my hip.

"And I'm about triple your age. So I know."

"And I can smudge the rest of your winning secret weapon across your hands if you continue to argue."

"Please. My *voice* is my secret weapon."

I finished the last nail and screwed the lid of the bottle on tight. I let it roll down the bedspread away from our weight. Mrs Lullin blew on her nails and wafted them away from her.

"What are you singing tonight anyway?"

"Oh God knows. I'll see what I fancy when I get in there."

The main room of the care home was spacious with a high ceiling and a wide carpeted floor, but it always felt oddly close due to the sheer volume of furniture. Chairs upon chairs upon sofas upon bookcases upon various flotsam and jetsam that had somehow drifted its way into the building over the years; from the patients' own collections they didn't want to leave behind, to items donated from family members. It had the strange look of a house of cards, as if one false move, which was quite common with people who weren't too solid on their feet, could cause it all to come toppling down. A bonfire ready to be lit.

I left just as the karaoke started. The room had become even more dense with the mingling bodies of the elderly and the overpowering scents of potpourri perfumes and Old Spice. When the flirting started that was my cue to exit. I could hear the first warbles as I walked down the path to the main road. The moon behind the building giving it a halo effect. 'Rosewood Assisted Living' shone above the front door in a cursive neon sign. I recognised the window cleaner's ladder propped up by the growing vines and trellises. I saw the diagonal smudges on the windowpanes.

Maybe I should have told her that what I missed the most were the love letters and daft romantic notes he'd write to me for no reason. I should have told her that today was actually our anniversary. I should have told her that what I missed was the baby. The time we'd lost together as a family.

-

Today you got up and went to work.

-

I ignored his bar on the walk home. I ignored the plaque drilled to the wall nearby. It had started to rain and the umbrella over my head helped me to avoid having to see much of anything. I didn't smell the pasta and spices pumping out of the building's funnels. I didn't notice the fairy lights that were now blue rather than the pink of last month. I didn't see any couples inside, especially those sat by the front door in the loveseat sipping wine, laughing and looking longingly at each other. I ignored the swell inside my stomach, the bloated anxiety. Instead, I went into my local supermarket and picked up the usual: boxed stir fry ingredients, some fruit that would be rotten in my fruit bowl in a few days, a bottle of wine. The rain had stopped by the time I got back onto the street and I could hear music coming from the pubs and restaurants that littered my road. For a moment I lingered on the curb, one foot lolling over the edge, unsure whether to turn home or not. I considered going to see him but knew he'd be busy on a Friday night. I headed home.

My husband always said I was 'quirky' because of the simple things I found amusing, the minute details I noticed about people and places. How I called him Billy Goat after Billy Goat's Gruff. How many sips of coffee he still had to take before he'd finish the cup, whether the carpet had been vacuumed when I was out (it never had been). If he'd shut the gate when leaving the house. He would sometimes speak to me in crossword clues: 'Four along, three letters. A hot drink' - that was his way of asking me to make him a cup of tea.

I want your fingertips to run along my spine again, I want your palm to cup my chin before you kiss me again. I want, I want I want...

The gate was wide open. The postman must have had been. He never remembered to close it. I was expecting, well, hoping for, a letter from one of the magazines I had been sending freelance pieces to. I had written fluff pieces about working in a care home for various magazines for women, most of them published, but I was bored of that. It was easy. It made me feel like I was still writing but it was just repetitive; there are only so many times you can rewrite an article on how thrilling karaoke is for the elderly. I'd been trying to write some short stories, entering a few poetry contests. But nothing. Maybe I was a better editor than a writer, the irony of critiquing someone's writing when your own pieces can't even get into a woman's monthly magazine, well...

My hand was on my wrist. Again. A criticism and that's where my body goes. A punishment. A Chinese burn to remind me just how little I deserve. *You won't get published. Why even bother writing? And you actually think you can tell others that they're not good enough?* I take my hand from my wrist. I put both hands in my pockets. Safe.

I notice the same diagonal shaped smears on my windows as those at work. The voice whispers *like the window-cleaner equivalent of men always leaving skid marks.* I grip my right wrist again. Count to five. The voice is always there, commenting.

My husband said I was quirky, that was what drew him to me. The first time we met he said he liked the sadness in my eyes. When I was with him, I didn't grip my wrist as much. When I was with him the voices didn't intrude as often. I had done well that last year or so we were together; one or two wrist grabs a day wasn't too bad at all, trying to exorcise whatever demon the inner voices were trying to conjure up. I try to push the gate shut with a clang louder than the voices. Like the care home, my home was buffeted by moonlight from behind, so it had a ghostly sheen around it.

Inside, I leave the hallway light off. I can make out the shapes of furniture. The post-it note I attached to the hallway mirror this morning flutters as outside air trickles in. The dark night air calms me.

-

That night I made myself another to-do list. It's what I always do when I feel the need to get some control back in my life. Lists are what my counsellor calls an 'easy win' because you can make yourself feel like you are achieving and successful by doing small, manageable tasks. Lists and a cup of coffee. That's what mature, functioning adults do and achieve on a daily basis. *Yes.* For someone who is anxiety prone like me though, tick-lists have a tendency to become a never-ending spinning wheel, stuck on a cycle: it is far too easy to keep adding and adding and adding to what initially started as a short list of quick tasks... and what's worse is that if you *don't* do them all then you're just as pathetic and terrible as everyone has always known you are and you deserve to feel that way about yourself because –

I pause. Breathe. *Remember the breathing exercises* I tell myself. In and out. Centre yourself. You don't need to do all the jobs on the list right now, just making a start is enough. You're enough. You're okay. You can go to bed and leave the jobs until tomorrow. You can. You *can.*

Bravely, as ridiculous as that sounds, I leave today's written list in the kitchen. The simple household tasks can wait. They *can.* I am not a failure just because I haven't put the bin out yet. Out of the corner of my eye I see some black, ink-like smudges on the living room door handle. I close my eyes and look again - they are gone. It isn't until I turn to lock the front door that I notice an envelope on the doormat. I turn it over in my hand. My address is handwritten on the front, but there's no return address on the back.

-

We can always hire a cleaner if you want, Billy says.

Oh yeah. I can just imagine what my left-wing brother would say about that, I say.

It isn't capitalist to have a cleaner, Billy says.

You don't know my brother very well then, I say.

Billy just rolls his eyes.

-

The kettle clicked and steam started to billow out from under the kitchen cupboards. I decided to stay up and go through the week's mail. I could tick it off my to - do list. *Easy win*, I could hear my counsellor saying. I know, deep down, it's just to keep the little voice inside at bay, that doing even one job that could have waited until tomorrow just makes life easier. Trust me.

I stirred milk and coffee and hot water together as I sifted through the mail. A bill, an oversized shiny sheet from a new takeaway, an income update from the freelance website I work for, letting me know I'd get my next payment of £264 in a week or so. I don't know why they always wrote to me to tell me what I'd get paid; I knew myself from how much work I'd decided to take on that month, and it was always the 27th of the month on which I got paid. Dates and knowing when things happen makes me feel a little calmer, more in control. Empty time can be an anxious trigger. Looking back at the invoice and letter from the magazine, when most things are done by email or text, getting a letter is oddly human, especially when it's signed at the bottom. It's nice that some people still take the time to write letters.

LETTER ONE

This was their last chance. Their last chance to fit in and be normal. To start again. Their last chance to feel like they belonged.

I don't believe it! This is it! The first day of the rest of my life.

I can't believe I'm finally hear in my dorm room. I have a mixture of both excitement and absolute dread though... what if I don't understand the classes? What if no one likes me? What if... what if... I could go on. These questions have bounced around in my mind for the past God knows how many days and weeks and months... I've tried to *not* think about this but here it is again. When I brush my teeth or go to the cinema... 'What if...' like some spectre haunting me. My mum always said I was good with hyperbole and I suppose this is exactly what she means. I do tend to exaggerate but what can I say? It's the writer in me. It's the language lover in me. I'm sure it will come in handy when I'm trying to impress someone someday. I'm excited for my creative writing course. I've read about it online and the tutor seems brilliant. He's published (which I very much hope to be too one day!) and even if he decimates my writing I will take it constructively. I will always look for the good. This I solemnly swear.

See, I'm being more positive already.

I think dad has found this harder than mum, which is to break stereotype - something I'm *definitely* for in today's society. He kept smiling and helped with the packing and boxing stuff up but every now and again I'd catch him holding something of mine - last night it was a stuffed teddy - and he just seems to freeze, like he's trying to hold onto something: me, the past I guess. It's sweet really. Mum told me just to "let him be." She's the more stoic one of the two. I wrote a short story once about a girl who was cut in half when a circus trick went wrong. If I was cut in half I'd have half mum, planned and methodical, and half dad, reflective and thoughtful. I think they complement each other well, opposites attracting and such. The circus act gone wrong was the story I submitted as part of my entry essays to get onto this course. I got a letter a few weeks ago telling me that in the first seminars we would be analysing our peer's short stories, those initially submitted and those we'll write in the first couple of weeks and would start to learn how to be editors as well as writers. I suppose it's some clever reversal point of view method writing technique (I have no idea what I'm saying, clearly!) that will help us with our own writing style. I don't think I could sound more naïve if I tried.

I used to try and write about all sorts of random stuff: magic animals and people with various diseases that were metaphors for this and that; a newlywed's new home with a ghost that tried to represent the wife's loss of self or something... I wrote myself into loops. I tried to put all these wonderfully subtle styles and ideas I'd seen or read elsewhere and cram them into my own prose but they just never quite... worked. They'd spill over like a glass of water with too many ice cubes and it would never work on the page. Then my lecturer at college told me to just write something more honest, to just get to the point - not lose my reader's interest by overegging description. So I wrote a story about a girl getting cut in half. An accident. A short tale. I guess it must've been okay, good enough to get into university anyway. I just hope I am good enough. I don't want to be amazing. I don't want to be a bestselling author. I just want to be decent. I want to be read and enjoyed.

So, this is it: the first day of the rest of my life. My room will be... small but homely. My classmates will be... welcoming and have stories and drink. My classes will be... intimidating but informative... no, *inspirational*. My first night out in the capital will... been drunken and have dancing. And boys. Well, you never know!

I turn over this strange letter in my hands. I have no idea what it was about or who it was from. It seemed like a letter to a friend or family member, but then it also had qualities of a diary entry, almost a stream of consciousness as if it has been transcribed from a recording. I thought to take it to my neighbour in the morning and see if it made sense to them; perhaps a niece writing to them about their first few weeks at university. I turned the envelope over several times, no name, just my address, holding it above my cup of coffee imagining steaming the seal open to discover the secrets within it. I guess I'd already ruined that illusion by opening and reading it. But that was when I thought it was for me. I unfolded the pages again and found the dogeared page I had read up to. The pages were typed but had several scribblings out as if it had been proofread and corrected before being posted. It seemed quite sweet, the idea that someone who would check and edit a letter before posting - it reminded me of a novel where the protagonist has to scrawl in the letters that don't work on their typewriter. A hangover from my teenager reading days. *Misery*. If I read a bit more of the letter, I reasoned, then perhaps I'll know who it's meant for.

LETTER ONE

My first night out will... been drunken and have dancing. And boys. Well, you never know!

You don't know what will happen though. That's the only certain thing, I'm trying to find the positives of this place but it's hard to see the moon and stars through the stamp sized window or appreciate the calm silent learning atmosphere when your walls are paper thin. I swear my roommate has been listening to the same dance track for the past two hours. It started almost as soon as my parents left me in my dormitory. My mum gave me a hug and wiped down one last surface for me. My dad plugged lots of things in and set up my laptop. He tried not to meet my eyes. I hugged him, hard. He whispered into my left ear. Then, they were gone.

The most awful moment came when I ventured out into the hallway. It loomed away from me on both sides like a snake slithering, yet dull and brown where sparkling scales should be. The only thing that shone was an erratically popping light above my head. It made me feel a little dizzy. I walked away from it towards what I thought was the kitchen or TV room. Everywhere seemed empty. The banging music of my neighbour hadn't started just yet and for a moment I thought I had been set up on a reality show, like this was a televised joke and everyone would suddenly appear from their rooms and yell and laugh and we'd all go for drinks. Surely this can't be the first night of the best years of my life? I turned a corner and immediately walked into someone.

"Sorry! I wasn't looking where I was going at all. That was my fault." To be honest I was just happy to have bumped into someone.

"It's quiet up here isn't it? But everyone is down at the bar. The student bar?" It wasn't an invite, more of a pitying question about why I wasn't already there.

Already I didn't fit in. Or that's how it felt.

"It's freshers' week so, or *night* I should say, so everyone is signing in and getting name tags and... getting to know each other." She turned away from me and messed with her handbag, brushed her hair behind her ear. I just stood there, too embarrassed to say I knew nothing about the bar - I was on my way down, I should have said. *Of course,* I knew it was fresher's night! I was just getting ready! I was too weak to ask to walk down with her, for fear she'd say no. But then, she turned back around: "Listen, you can come down... with me? If you'd like?" I knew she didn't really want to ask me. She just felt bad for me. "Look, come down when you're ready and pick up your name badge and just, you know, start to talk to a few people. It doesn't matter if you don't remember them tomorrow."

"Thanks, I'll just get my things. My purse."

"I'm-" but I didn't get to hear her name as the door down the hall slammed open as two boys jumped and chased each other past us, grabbed "I'm" by the wrist and dragged her with them. I stood in the hallway with the one light flickering over me like a sad shooting star. I scraped my left shoe along my right ankle.

Despite feeling less than confident, I headed down to the bar after all. Why not? At the very least I'd sign in and sign up to whatever awful events I probably wouldn't attend and get a drink. I queued patiently, as was the English way, to write my name on a piece of paper; I was told I'd get an email in the next few days about upcoming events. As I filled in a name badge, someone behind me pushed me into the table. A couple next to me laughed with each other as if they'd known each other for years and not just the two minutes it took to wait in line. I shook my head. No – I'd been told about this. Don't loop and spiral and look only for the negatives: people can trip (it doesn't mean you are a lesser person), people can laugh with a new friend (it doesn't mean they're laughing at you), people can just be doing their job handing out badges (they're not dismissive of you, they're busy).

I caught myself in the mirror, smiled and realised I didn't look that bad. At the bar I ordered a red wine, small, and tried to find... someone, somewhere to sit or at least pretend to be looking for someone. I got my phone out and scrolled through some messages. A few from friends back home: *Good luck* 😊*, Have a great first evening!, Wish I'd gone now and wasn't stuck here working...,* and from dad *Don't forget to lock your door.*

This is fine. I can do this. I can meet new people and chat and flirt and forget their names tomorrow just like *"I'm-"* told me to.

The jukebox machine was free so I scrolled through a few songs, deciding what to add to the queue - then walk away quickly so no one would judge me for my choices. I ran my finger along the sticky screen.

"No, no, no. No such music will be played in here."

"Excuse me?"

"Mate, you pick a bad song tonight and you will be the laughingstock of your peers for the next three years." Three years – that hit me in the stomach with a blow. Three years of... *this.* "Trust me, just go for something simple. Something people won't really notice in the background." He took the coin from my hand and put it in the machine and keyed in a selection. It wasn't until later I thought about how rude that was - at the time I took it for flirting. "Let me get you a drink. You can come and meet some of my friends and by *friends* I mean people I met ten minutes ago whose names I don't know yet but who I'm trying to impress by buying them all drinks." Half of his mouth smiled as he said this. Flirting. "Red wine for..." he cocked his head, and I moved my hair from my name badge. "Lovely. Wait here."

I waited. And I waited. I waited until I realised he had probably found someone else to offer a drink to, someone who had better conversation. Maybe someone go to bed with and wake up with tomorrow and lie to them too when offering to go get morning coffee and never coming back. It was probably some initiation game with a group of male friends; how many girls can you chat up and make wait for you? I waited long enough for it to be embarrassing. I didn't see him or *"I'm"* nor anyone I vaguely recognised the rest of the night.

The song I'd paid for came and went. I heard it again later that night when it had started to be cranked up next door to me. Either it was a cruel coincidence, mocking me, or I'd found out who my neighbour was.

Heading back to my dorm room, I saw something familiar: the popping white light in the hallway. It was oddly comforting.

I locked my door. I washed my face. I sat on the small window ledge looking out of my small window at the small patch of nothing I could twist my neck to see. The windowpane was dirty. I ignored the flashing lights coming from the student bar over the field. *They're all lairs*, I thought to myself. I decided to drink some of the wine my parents had given to me as a gift. I'm pretty sure they expected me to have cracked it open with some new acquaintances but oh well - if I can't drink with the rest of them I might as well do it alone. No point in being left out altogether. Maybe tomorrow will be different. Yes... positive positive change change happy happy me me. Tomorrow *will* be different. I held my wine glass, drinking to keep myself from rubbing my ankle.

I thought about what my dad had whispered to me before he left: "Kiddo. Chin up. Feet down."

- Anne.

It was after twelve by the time I finished reading. My coffee had gone cold. I hadn't noticed the time. I'd moved the wine bottle closer toward me over the kitchen table but hadn't opened it.

My mind was buzzing. I had no clue what this was that I was reading. I was certain though it was just a letter, something addressed to me by mistake. I'd take it to my neighbour in the morning and it would be sorted out. But it read like a narrative of some kind rather than a letter. It felt somewhat voyeuristic enjoying reading the emotions of someone I'd never met. As I got into bed, rubbing my stomach, my mind floated around two things: one of my fridge magnets downstairs, and the three mistakes I'd noticed as I'd been reading the letter.

-

You managed to sleep for six hours.

-

"Hey, sorry I'm a bit late."

Cups clattered, the bell above the doorway jangled. There's something comforting in the noise of a café, something in the bustle and calm chaos that lets you know you're alive. Those other people are just like you: running late for work, picking something up for a friend, catching up with someone, having a moment to read or attempt a crossword. A breather. 'Two down, four letters. A culinary hobby.' That was his way of telling me that I needed to learn to bake. Or cook in general. The smell of grinding coffee beans are always soothing, something I know my brother would find 'terribly millennial' and have a 'First World' comment to make. I can imagine his sarcastic comment: "Well no wonder you find it all very serene and zen. You're not being blown up or sold off into some slave trade."

"Would I expect anything else?"

"I was up late finishing this report and then… whatever. Doesn't matter. You hungry?"

"No, coffee's fine."

"Okay, two minutes."

Sometimes, you don't always notice the people around you who've been in your life the longest. They sit outside of your eyeline, so present and constant that you don't need reminders that they're there - they just are. Donna is one of these people. She floated on the periphery always, safe, there and present. An anchor. My father was constantly in my eyeline like a train bulleting right at me, his eyes angry and bright and red like level crossing lights. His arms were the barriers. His voice scared animals.

"So, Sherry, how's things? You in work later?"

I snapped back into the present. "Yeah. Yes, a late Saturday morning start at work which is nice." I could feel Donna's eyes on me as I lowered my head and brushed my hair back. I already knew the question(s) she wanted to ask and brewed up my answers.

"Are you free on Sunday next week? There's an outdoor cinema showing in the park if you fancy it?" (Oh, maybe not the questioned I had predicted then.) "It could be a chance to meet someone." (Ah, there we go.) "Not just for *you*," she held up her hands in mock protest to placate me and elongated the "you" childishly, "I need it too. I need to stop staying in all the time."

Despite my reservations, I took the bait. "Sure. Just text me when and where and whatever."

"*Whatever*? Enthusiasm."

"I know I'm a grouch sometimes."

"*Sometimes*?" Her lips curled.

"Very funny. Listen to my laughter - I was just up later than I meant to be last night that's all."

"All okay?" (Here it comes.) "I know last night was, well…"

"Anniversary, yeah. Look it's fine. We can talk about it. I've been told to. It's meant to help." Does talking about something you don't want to talk about really help though?

"So, what did you do? I would've come over if you'd wanted anyone."

"I know. No, I needed to just have some time. I just… pottered about. Couldn't settle."

"Did you-" now that the preamble was over, she would probably ask one of five possible questions:

1. "-drink?"
2. "-try and talk to Tony?"
3. "-hear from the parents?"
4. "-look at the scan again?"
5. "-get around to putting up the rest of the mirrors and clocks in the house?"

"No. I didn't. I'll be honest with you I bought a bottle but no. The lid stayed firmly on. Oddly it's less of a temptation if it's just sitting there. At least then I can see it, say *no*, and leave the room. It works for me."

"And what about…"

"No to that too. I thought about it but… I didn't."

"Maybe you should've done. Might have cleared the air." She took a sip of her drink.

"No. I force myself to walk on the other side of the road. You know it's not just Tony. It's that plaque on the wall. I hate it there."

"Anymore thoughts on moving?"

"I know I should. Deep down I know that but it's just… I need to sort through his things still, you know? I feel like… that I still need to miss him."

Donna reached her hand over the table and put it on top of mine. "We all do. All the time. No one more so that you. And you… you take whatever time you need."

I nodded. Shame and embarrassment and pride are strange emotions, especially when all bundled up together. "Anyway, I caught the start of Old Age Karaoke. It was… interesting."

"Oh Jesus, *please* invite me to the next one."

"You can be the host if you wish. The guest speaker."

"Yes! I would *love* that. Can you imagine me with all those old folks? They'd adore me."

"They love anyone that speaks to them. They just like attention. It's quite sad actually."

"So, is it all power ballads and propaganda ditties from World War Two?"

"Not quite."

The door of the café opened, signalled by the little clang of bells. From the look on Donna's face, I could tell that whoever had entered had immediately irritated her: a sigh, a tapping of fingers.

"Here they fucking come."

"Who?" I had no idea who could have made her so irate so quickly.

"Oh, yes," she said, sarcastically surprised, "and not just one but *four* of them. What a shock."

I turned to see four women standing at the counter, all with prams. A waiter struggled to get past, twisting his body and moving his arms up and down like a seesaw. I could tell from his expression that he was doing his best not to appear put out by the room the four women had taken up; they were customers after all.

"I mean, come on. If you want to meet up and trade stories about nappy rash or whatever, fine. But please do it where," Donna held up a finger, "you don't take up the whole fucking room," and a second, "you don't get in the way of other childless, less invasive folk," then a third, "where people who don't want to hear about breast feeding or your vagina don't have to listen against their will, and…" a final, fourth finger was held up, "you aren't going to distract someone working, or reading, or enjoying some well-deserved quiet time with… *that*." As if on cue one baby started to cry, promptly followed by another. If looks could kill, Donna would have been responsible for the very bloody massacre of four mothers and their offspring.

The four friends had managed to get a table in the corner. They moved chairs around to accommodate the prams, one of the mothers lifting their baby out and starting to rock them gently against her chest. I could feel the atmosphere of the room change: people were turning and looking, some with intrigued faces, smiling, pointing at something funny one of the babies may have done; others were doing the same as Donna, quietly tutting, casting annoyed glances, pulling faces whenever one of the women moved a chair that made a screeching sound on the floor. Two of the babies were still crying.

"See, that's what happens. Crying dominoes. One starts and another one does it straight away. If I owned a café, I would ban mothers with prams and groups over two."

"You'd ban mothers? From being sociable?" I raised my eyebrow, knowing that Donna was only half serious, but definitely no less than half.

"If we can ban smokers then we should be able to ban gaggles of women who have forgotten what life was like before they gave birth. In my café you would only be allowed in if you promised to discuss something *other* than whether your child has taught itself to shit on a potty or not. I. Don't. Care."

"Aren't we lucky we aren't in Nazi Germany."

Donna tore her frustrated gaze away from the parents to look at me, smiling. "Very funny. But you know what I mean."

"Do I? Donna, you're like the enemy of feminism."

She sipped her coffee, then continued her rant. "Please. I am the epitome of feminism. Don't want kids? Don't have them then. Who the fuck cares? Do what you like." She puts her drink down more forcefully than needed. "But can I tell you what *really* pisses me off?"

She pauses, as if I have a chance of asking her not to.

"It's the countless female members of the society like *that*," she stresses *that*, just to clarify she is talking about the mothers, "who add to the stereotype that a) women have to have children and b) you can't have a brain once you do have children. And", she continues, without even pausing for breath, "Facebook is the worst. The *worst*. If I have to unfriend one more person who puts up some mindless post or photo or thoughtful statement like '90% of being a parent is wondering when I can next sit down' I swear I will only have *you* left on there. If you want to sit down then sit the fuck down. Your kid will be fine. But you've obviously had the time to post about your *lack* of time so you can't be that bloody pressured or busy. Fuck. Off."

She speaks with such venom that, if I didn't know her, I would genuinely worry for the safety of the women and their children. They were ordering drinks from the same waiter who had squeezed past them minutes earlier.

"'Shall I have decaf? You know Tommy doesn't sleep well but I can't have any more caffeine today.' 'No, you shouldn't but you aren't breastfeeding now are you, so you should be fine.' 'Ouch, my vagina still hurts whenever I sit down because of the stitches.'"

"Donna. They might hear you." I put a hand over the side of my face, embarrassed but also amused, by Donna's impressions of the women talking. I take a sip of my coffee and for a moment I imagine myself with those mothers, being one of them. How would I feel, knowing I annoyed some people by just being present, by just being a mother? How would I react to that feeling of inconvenience which seemed to be pushed upon these women, just for doing and being what was meant to come most naturally to a woman: being a mother. Would I even be aware? Are these women conscious of the glances, the intakes of breath, caused by them just being there? I looked around the room and was surprised by the reactions of both men and women - an irritation that crossed genders, seemed to cross age and race, wealth too.

"Why do people get so annoyed at mothers?"

"Because of *that*." Donna was referring again to the low rumbling of the whimpering babies.

"No, what I mean is, why *mothers* specifically? If four fathers came in here, pushchairs and buggies, bags filled with nappies and toys, no one would care. If anything, women, including you Donna, would swoon at the notion of four men meeting to socialise and spend time with their kids. And other fathers would either be jealous that they don't have that free time away from family responsibilities to meet friends, or they would be impressed by the

Instagram new-age *dad-ness* of it. But when *women* do it… well, look." I let Donna think about what I said, allowing her a minute to look at the room, and gage the reactions of those inside. Her face did soften a little. "Trust me. If the exact same situation happened tomorrow but with dads instead of mothers no one would bat an eyelid. In fact, people would be impressed. But when four *women* do it everyone just gets impatient. Because God forbid a woman leave the house."

We were silent for a few moments. I wasn't sure who I was annoyed with. Donna, myself, or society itself.

"Look, I know," Donna started, "I didn't mean to-"

Suddenly, my right arm jolted forward and the remainder of my coffee splashed onto the table. Our table number took a tumble in the process.

"Oh, I'm so sorry. Shit. I don't believe it! I… Michelle?"

For a second I thought I was in a dream or that perhaps I'd woken from a nightmare. I could have sworn it was him. His voice. That gentle Irish twang.

I turned around. I felt in between waking and a sleep. I looked into her eyes. "Shit, I'm sorry. Let me buy you another. And for your friend. What were you having? Do you want anything to eat too?" Her hands were pulling wipes from a handbag.

"Jenni? Jenni! No, oh no, no. Don't worry," I replied, "Jenni, it's fine. We were nearly finished anyway." It took everything for me not to use his name instead of hers. I'd never realised it before just how much they looked alike. The eyes.

"Are you sure?" She was still pulling baby wipes out of a packet and trying to clean up the table. "Oh well. At least I know how to make an entrance."

"What are you doing here?" I asked. "Aren't you based up north still?" *Don't look at the eyes, don't look at the eyes.*

"Yeah. Well, I'm away for a couple of weeks on business but I've come back down just to see mum and dad for a few days for the… you know."

The difficulty of two people meeting who don't really know each other, apart from an unpleasant connection: it's verbal wordplay and silent whackamole as to who will say it first. "It's been a year, so we decided to all get together." Her first, kind of. "Mum and dad had me stay last night. They're thinking of moving back to Ireland soon actually. I was on my way to his office, well your office, I mean… I wasn't sure if you'd be there."

"You could have called first."

I spun around to Donna and just stared at her. She gave me a hard stare.

"What she means is," I turned back to Jenni, "is that you could have called me, and we could have met up or I would have made sure someone was in the office block for you. To be honest most of what you'd need would be at ours… at mine… I…" I paused for a moment.

"He mostly worked from home. The office pretty much drained us of money as we hardly used it."

"Are you still…"

"Working with dying old people? Yes." She was taken aback, clearly unsure whether to laugh or not, and then gave this bizarre cackle that seemed totally out of place coming from her manicured lips. "Michelle. I never quite got your sense of humour. Guillotine humour."

"Gallows humour."

"You know when you've always had a phrase or song lyric wrong?"

"No," said Donna, a little too loudly to pretend to have said it under her breath.

"Well," Jenni continued, "I'm glad you're working though. Whatever the work is I'm sure that it helps."

I could feel steam rising from Donna. "It helps," I say. "It's been great up until now, so I can't complain. I still do a bit of freelance on the side."

"Editing?"

"Yeah. Some. Some writing too, when I can."

"Well if you get anything good make sure to send it my way. We need something good on the shelves. It's all wizards and death trials and kids with cancer and women trapped in various vehicles. My editor said the next bestseller is going to be called something like 'Terminal Girl on a Bike in the Magic Games' or… whatever. I don't like them. They're all the same women shaming rubbish, you know? Women making a man's life hell whilst drunk out of their faces. We need something new." Again, I could imagine the face Donna was pulling. "But I *should* have called you're right. I'm sorry. It was last minute. You know mum and dad, they're never well prepared. I'm off again soon anyway. What about next week maybe? We could meet for a drink?"

"You're back around here again? I mean, you're not working from your own offices?"

"Like I said, mum and dad are thinking of moving so they keep bloody calling for advice. Tell you what, next week when I'm back from this publishing conference and I won't have to see the old people as much, we should definitely make time to catch up. How does that sound? And I do need to get into that office of yours."

"Sure. Yeah, that would be nice. And give my best to your mum and dad."

"I will. Sorry again for the drinks. Nice to meet you…"

"…Donna."

"Donna. Okay, have a good day." She put her hands to her face in mock embarrassment and promptly left the coffee shop.

Donna and I were silent for a moment.

"You were related to her?"
"She's not that bad."

"We've met plenty of times. She knows my name."

"She's busy."

"'Whatever the work is?' 'I'm sure that it helps?' Helps with *what*? How fucking condescending."

"You're taking it too personally."

"You're not taking it personally *enough*. I never liked her. I mean didn't she vote *against* a woman's right to abortion?"

I almost snort. "Donna, what on earth does that have to do with her being my sister in law?"

"She just complained about the woman shaming literature she's having to peddle out - no offense to your company - but then doesn't support women in the biggest vote for women's rights this decade. She's a misogynist."

"Oh come on... Donna, that's a bit harsh. I mean, there's a lot going on with... well... First of all, how on earth do you know if she voted for or against legalising abortion? *I* don't even know what she decided! And there's so much weight on that issue. She's from the same family as Billy, remember. Extremely Catholic. And look, I know she's a little... just hard to read sometimes. She's not highly strung but then she is. She's not rude but then she is. She's not flouncy but then sometimes she is. She's... different."

"No, *different* people are interesting and mysterious. Attractive. She's just a dick."

"She's had a tough time."

"You've *all* had a tough time. You don't go around not inviting her to family gatherings though." She looked at me through her long fringe, eyes boring holes into mine.

"I did notice that, too. But she said they're moving. It's not exactly a cause for a reunion, is it? Jenni was great at the time. She helped with the business. She was great about me stepping out for a while and she helped with... everything. Paperwork, signing stuff over, money. She's someone who kept calm through it all. She didn't have to give me an open window to come back."

"And work for her."

"Well the company had to go to someone. She *is* his sister." I caught myself. "*Was* his sister. She was. And she had to grieve too. I think working is how she does it.""

"And it's not for you?"

"That's different. I needed money, I had to work Donna. Just not... there."

"Yes, so you went to where you are constantly surrounded by the possibility of death."
Pause. "You don't have to keep in contact with her because she reminds you of him." A
beat. "You won't just *forget* him, you know. That's impossible."

"I never said that. Donna, look - people act in different ways in response to... Christ, now I
sound like one of the grief counsellors." I pause. "She looks so much like him. I forgot."

We had a few moments of quiet, just watching others coming and going. Silent time
between friends makes you realise how good friends you really are with someone - no need
to fill every silence. Just be.

Some of the babies gurgled across the room. Donna checked her phone. I thought about
Jenni, about whether she was as confident as she appeared to be. I couldn't get over how
alike they were. I'd not noticed when we were married but somehow all my senses became
heightened after he'd died. I began to notice him in other people: his mum's lilting Irish
accent; his father's ears, one oddly larger than the other; his sister's eyes, brown and
welcoming. A year is not a long time. Maybe I should have reached out to her by now.
Maybe I should be the first one to do so now - invite her out for a drink, we could be friends
or at the very least someone we both could have to talk to occasionally. The thought made
me feel a little warmer. Maybe it was the notion of seeing his eyes up close again.

"Will you go and see Tony tonight?"

I opened my handbag and got out my purse. "And on that note, I now need to go to work."

We hugged at the door. She told me to message her later if I needed anything. As I walked
down the road, I could smell the morning scents of bacon and eggs coming from various
bars and restaurants; the wafts from Tony's place seemed stronger than the others. It
turned my stomach. The image of the plaque throbbed in my head. My stomach turned. I
kept my head straight down, willing myself not to be sick. It was then that I realised how
odd it was for Jenni to still have baby wipes in her handbag.

-

You held a conversation.

-

Luckily, the phantom nausea left when I started work. Mrs Lullin was having one of her off days. Most of the time she's fine, sharp as a tack, brilliant wit and memory. Then she has the odd day or two when she just isn't herself; she loses things, thinks she's lost something, can't remember a name. It's the main reason, she says, that her son had her placed in the home. With her husband gone and no family near enough for daily visits it was the only option as far as he could see. It's a difficult decision to make; one I can't judge anyone for. Could you make it work if you wanted, really wanted, a family member to live with you? Is it wrong to send them somewhere you at least know they will have someone on call all day every day? No. Many of the people here, patients and staff, feel it's an easy option to cast the forgetful and ailing old person off to a "pre-hospice to die" (an actual description from one resident here) but I don't see it that way. Maybe losing Billy makes me see death differently.

It still shocks me to hear his name so casually inside my own thoughts sometimes. I stop what I'm doing. Usually work is helpful, keeping busy. It preoccupies my thoughts away from... Billy... but, thinking his name twice is almost too much. Trying *not* to think is almost as hard... what we could have had together. Of what I made us lose.

I take a seat on the edge of the bed. Meredith is in and out of a medicated sleep. She'd woken up this morning talking about "him", that "he" had been here in the night and that "he" had wanted to know what had happened to "her". No one could make sense of what she was trying to explain. By the time I arrived she was somewhat calmer than I'd been told she'd been but as soon as she saw me she grabbed my hand, talking in some stream of consciousness that "He was here again last night. I wanted to know why he was here but he only told me to answer questions and not ask them. He wanted to know what had happened to me and why I was here." Somewhere in the dialogue she started to repeat what this supposed guest had told her "What are you here for? Why are you here with these old people? Shouldn't you get your old life back?"

She was sedated soon after. I think the nurses waited until I arrived to help soothe her. I was her favourite and everyone knew it. I think I am the only one who can stand her, which I've never understood as she's not the worst in here by far. She doesn't need changing for one thing. People perhaps find her occasional racism offensive but, despite my better judgement and angel on my right shoulder of a brother, I do find the left over and mostly unintentional racism of the older generation quite funny. It is the total disregard for social norms that makes me wish sometimes we were all a little less politically correct. And the literary side of me sees their language as a trip to past, when terms were used differently, when words we now find inappropriate were the acceptable descriptions. I tried to explain this once to an orderly here who refused to clean Meredith's room until she learned the difference between the descriptions of people as 'black' and 'brown'. I tried to explain that 'black' was once the offensive term. They never did come back to clean her room. I do it now.

"So who you do think the 'he' was?"

"There wasn't anyone here Michelle."

"Yes, but what I mean is who do we think she was referring to? Did she say a name?"

"No. Not that anyone's heard. We've written the incident up as protocol but it's another one of her turns. I wouldn't worry."

"I know. It's just... if she's talking about her husband or her son then we might know what to say to her next time. How to calm her before she has to be sedated."

Mrs Lullin was snoring behind me, lost in whatever memory she was reliving. I hoped it was a happy one, whether it was with her son or husband, or both. I continued to tidy up her room, picked up the odd picture she'd knocked over, mopped the tea upset over her dresser. There were a few pages torn from some magazines and newspapers on the floor as well: TV listings, a half-completed crossword, an agony aunt section. The focus of the agony aunt page seemed to be about parenting. There was one letter from a reader about suffering a miscarriage. I found myself unfolding it. It was torn and most of the article was missing but I could see the pain, the confusion, the guilt felt by the writer.

Words jolt out from the page, little ink daggers, that seep deep into my skin, quickly, reminding me of how it felt to be pregnant. *Joy. Hope. Finally! Scan.*

When I had recovered from losing the baby, I tried to write about it. First it was just some diary style scribbles, a couple of paragraphs about longing, about wanting. The blackness. I tried some short stories. I wrote in role as a mother. Then as a baby. I think I wanted some evidence, even if just for me, just in writing that no one would ever read, that the baby *had* existed. That I hadn't made this all up. I wanted a small piece of proof that I had been a mother. I don't know why. It's impossible to explain. To justify.

I spent time reading up on miscarriages and ectopic pregnancies, abortions and pro-life protests in Ireland and America. I even bought some pregnancy magazines, thinking it would make me realise how I had made the right decision; that I couldn't possibly have dedicated myself to another human being the way these magazines suggested you would need to, that I couldn't care for and raise a child to become a decent person like the smiling and glowing mothers in those pages - that what had happened was for the best. But it was just another form of self-harm. When I wasn't squeezing my wrist, when I wasn't drinking, I was cutting myself with these paper-thin razors: turn the page and feel like shit, turn the page and accept that you're a slut, turn the page and realise you've taken away something another woman would die for. *You've lost one and killed another.*

I blinked, finding myself back in Mrs Lullin's room. I had screwed the magazine cuttings into a ball. Along with the other random pages on the floor, I tossed the article into the bin by the door. She wouldn't remember much of this later anyway; she wouldn't be bothered with some random magazines being chucked away. I wouldn't mention it if she didn't. I thought about going to read the incident sheet to perhaps find out more about what had happened with her but, before I knew it, I was on lunch duty and bingo duty and washroom duty and then it was the end of my shift.

How many children do you want? Billy says.

Don't get too ahead of yourself, I say.

I want one of each, Billy says.

If you're lucky, I say.

Billy puts his arms around me.

On the way home my mind continued to drift, something I would usually welcome, but I wanted to come to a decision about Jenni: to meet or not to meet? Was I thinking about it too much? Was Donna right about her? Could it be a trigger to meet up with her not so long after...

I was just about to cross the street to avoid the restaurant and bars and head into my local shop - "Hello Miss, how was your day at work? The usual? You could just call ahead, and we'll have it all ready for you" - but I saw Tony standing outside of his restaurant. I found myself stopping, unable to walk, trapped in amber and unable to move. Time seemed to stop. I had no idea what to do, whether to go and try and explain myself, try to play the other night off as a drunken nothing and a forgotten slurring conversation or... I felt embarrassment rise up from my toes and get redder and redder until my face was crimson.

I turned, turned again, got out my umbrella although it wasn't raining and rushed across the street away from him hoping against hope he hadn't seen me. I passed the corner shop and didn't take my eyes away from my feet until I got to my front gate. Then, I breathed. I lowered the needless umbrella. I shook my head, found my spare hand grasping my wrist and snapped: *No, don't go back to that again.* The same had happened last night when I got home. *That's what this place does to you. It makes you twist and hurt yourself again. It makes you crazy.*

I shook my head for the second time, ignoring the voice. I twirled my hands in the air like little propellers, keeping them busy, pushed through the gate. Next door didn't have their lights on. I thought about knocking and asking about yesterday's letter, seeing if it was perhaps meant for them. Instead, I took a scrap of paper and pen from my handbag and scribbled a short note-

This is Michelle from next door. I tried to catch you but don't think you were in - just a note to say that I received a letter yesterday from a girl called Anne. She was writing about her first few days at university. It has been sent to me by mistake, but if it sounds familiar to you then just knock and I'll pass it to you. x

It dropped through the letter box with a swoosh. I heard it pat onto the carpet inside. It wasn't until I bent down to take my shoes off inside my house that I noticed another envelope, with the same cursive handwriting as the previous day's letter, waiting patiently for me. This time however, my name was on it.

LETTER TWO

Graduation day. I can't even try to explain how awful that day was. Has been. Imagine being wrapped inside a body bag and forced to walk in it in front of hundreds of people you don't know, who didn't take the time to get to know you, students and lecturers alike. My parents were so excited building up to the big day, and it took everything in me not to… not to tell them how I'd flunked the coursework, the exams, the dissertation. My dad's words had echoed around in my head for days, months, bashing back and forth as I'd waited to get the results. One voice inside my head told me to tell someone, tell my mum and dad how I'd been feeling, what had happened, how defenceless I'd been. The other voices told me I was bad, I was deserving of this failure, I was living up to what everyone had always known.

My ankle was red raw.

The morning of graduation I could smell the cooked breakfast that my housemates were making for themselves floating up through the ceiling and into my room. Housemates… I'd scribbled in my diary pictures of empty rooms and stick men… buildingpeople, roomhumans… that's what this arrangement was. I was just a bill-paying and renting student. Nothing more to them. They laughed and joked and hugged in the hallway, driving off to lectures together, road trips at the weekend, drunken stumbles in the middle of the night, hushed giggles. I don't know what I did wrong.

I remember housing day, or whatever it was called. I skipped my first two lectures and scoured over the board of available rooms and houses in the Student Union. I felt tiny next to groups of friends calling each other, texting and arranging house viewings, speaking to parents about rents and what was acceptable for a house on this road or a flat on that street. I spent what felt like hours searching for a one bedroom somewhere. I red page after page stuck up on the noticeboard. I'd not made many friends during the first year. I'd not been invited to live with anyone. Close to returning for my second year, I'd seen an advert on the student housing website: a house of girls with a spare room after one of them had dropped out. I never did find out why. I emailed. I got a reply a few hours later asking me to go around for an 'informal' chat – since when do you have to interview for a room in a house share at university?

I'd told my parents that I had managed to move into a place with some friends from my course. I couldn't tell them I might be relegated to halls again. I'd been too ashamed. If this interview went well then at least I'd be able to tell them the names of my 'friends' and not just fudge around it: "She's away with her family this weekend… They've got a part time job so there's no one else in at the moment dad… It's her parents' anniversary, so they've met up for a family meal…" It was exhausting. Maybe now I could start to tell some truths.

I touched up my makeup, straightened my hair. I threw on dress after dress. What did you wear to meet a group of girls who you might be living with, who could decide if you were going to have a place to live or not? On the bus ride over excuses and reasons formed in the steam of my breath on the windows, shoe rubbing away on my ankle the whole time:

maybe living by yourself will be okay *(Yeah because no one else wants anything to do with you, you sad bitch)*; maybe I'll meet a fresher this year and we can move in together next year *(As if you might have to stay in student halls for a second year! No wonder even your friends from back home don't call anymore)*; staying in halls will be okay, last year was alright, at least then I'm closer to the lecture halls and the library and what matters *(But you'll fail anyway just like you've failed being here. Don't know why you came back)*; these girls will be nice, they'll like me, they'll make me laugh *(They'll fucking hate you because you're weird, they'll smell it on you)*. I limped from the bus stop to the front door.

I was met by two girls. Soft skinned, each shaped faces. They offered me a coffee. I said 'No' and instantly worried I'd been rude by turning something down and only using one word rather than 'No, thank you'. I was so anxious about every word I said, so hardly said anything. I didn't want to appear grabbing by taking something from them straightaway. I felt like I had a clipboard hovering above my head and with each thing I got wrong I got an enormous X scratched across it. I could almost hear the pen on paper making a violent X each time I spoke:

They asked me what I thought I was like as a housemate – I said I was quiet and tidy.

X Boring! X

They asked me if I minded house parties and other people coming over – I said that was fine as I was used to being the sober, sensible one anyway.

X Loser! X

They asked me what I wanted to achieve when I was at university – I said I wanted to get a 1st class degree and then a job.

X WTF X

One asked me what home comforts I would bring with me. She told me that her room was covered with stuffed toys, her favourite being a farmyard animal her grandfather gave to her when she was little. I laughed and said that sounded sweet.

X People pleaser X

One of them told me that her boyfriend was coming over later. I didn't catch his name. They asked me what boys I liked around campus and in my lectures – I giggled and made up someone's name. I'm pretty sure it was the names of two actors put together.

X Liar X

One or two other girls came in and out of the living room during the interview. I felt they were judging me. It seemed they had their own language and could talk about me without me knowing.

My head rested on the windowpane for the whole bus journey home, my steamed excuses now gone and replaced by drips, just damp glass wetting my hair. I tried humming a song to keep thoughts at bay. That stupid song from my first night here nearly a year ago was stuck in my head. Odd what your mind latches onto. I never did find out who my neighbour was. They only ever seemed to play that one bloody song though.

Somehow, I got the room. Maybe they just needed the rent. Maybe they wanted someone to do the chores for them. I remember one Sunday morning coming downstairs and one of the girls (I could say Melissa but I'm not certain that was her name) just passing me a mop and bucket on her way from the bathroom and nodding to some sick. I caught the glimpse of a boy's naked torso on her bed before her door closed. At least when my mum rang I could tell her that "Shannon's just upstairs doing some work" and "Leanne has some friends over, they're in the living room" – it wasn't a lie... I just didn't know for certain it was Leanne and not Sarah. But I was a housemate at least, there was truth in that.

Now, in bed, I can almost taste the fried eggs and bacon and the burnt toast as it penetrates my room. Nearly two years later and they've still never asked me to join them for breakfast. I've never asked to join them either. I roll over. I know this is my fault. I know I deserve to be the odd one out. I feel tears prick at the back of my eyeballs as I remember my dad's words from that first morning: "Kiddo. Chin up. Feet down." I can do this. That's what I'll do today, that's what I'll do on that stage. Then I can get the hell out of here. Back home... catch up with friends... look for a job.

My parents will be so disappointed in me.

"Oh love. You look gorgeous. We're so proud." My mum hugs me and it feels nice. "I wish we'd have come up to see you more often. I feel like we don't really know this place." 'Neither do I', I think to myself. I move out of her arms. The graduation hall feels too big. I don't belong here. I shouldn't be here with everyone else who has done and will do brilliant things. I feel both thin and heavy under this gown, as if I could crumble and combust at the same time, just disappear under its weight - this black cloak. It feels like night around me, with the moon cut and coloured into a sharp back hat placed upon my head. I sit waiting for my name to be called and can feel the gaze of my parents burrowing into the back of my skull, but not just their looks: the weight of their expectations; the smirks of the girls I've lived with; the bumps from students who've not even seen me walking past them in the corridors; the glass of wine I didn't get that first night still splinters and cuts into my head... I imagine sometimes taking a knife or piece of glass and standing in front of a mirror and slicing down the back of my head, right into the fleshy part at the base of the skull, and reaching in to pull out the blackness, the dirt inside my head that makes me so different, so uncertain, so wrong, so filled with little voices *(I hope you trip, I hope you fall on your face, I hope your parents find out how badly you've done at university - not today, not tomorrow, but that the worry of them finding out lingers over you for days and weeks and months to come like a sword of Damocles, I hope your gown gets pulled up and shows your disgusting ankle you freak, pulled up again like when he-)*

My names is called. I don't remember much else, apart from the satisfying throb and trickle of blood down my foot.

-   Ann.

P.S Thank you for reading my two pieces of writing so far. I apologise for the somewhat unorthodox way in which I have submitted them to you. If you would be interested in receiving any further parts of my manuscript, then please let me know. I would be so thrilled and honoured for you to read them and give me your thoughts. I do appreciate though that you will be very busy with your business and, from experience, I know that it can take months for a reply. That's why I've gone a little 'outside of the box' by using this manner of communication. Hopefully it will pay off.

Please feel free to email me on:

caprahircus@livemail.com

I read the letter in one sitting. I had no idea what it was that I was reading. Was it a confession to something, a cry for help? A diary entry or a letter sent to me by mistake? It even crossed my mind that it was some longwinded suicide note. It was a relief when I got to the end and found the real reason behind the two letters. The drop in my stomach that I felt when I saw the envelope there again had been an unusual sensation; it wasn't dread as such, more an uncertainty about who and what and why. It was compounded by the fact that this time the envelope had my name above the address. At least now I know the writing *is* meant for me.

I clicked the kettle on.

Well, it makes sense now doesn't it? They know I'm a freelance editor and writer, and I've been sent a manuscript. A little unorthodox sure, but it certainly did get my attention. I remember reading about a young writer a few years ago who dug up their front garden as a stunt to get an agent interested in their murder mystery trilogy. I don't know if it paid off, I hope it did though after all that effort. I put the writing to one side and picked up my phone. Every time I press the home button and see the screen's background a pang shoots through me. It's odd... I know it's there, that picture, but I also seem to forget that it will be flashing up before me, even though I chose it, even though I snapped and cropped and placed it there as a... reminder? I'm not sure what to call it. It feels like it's from another life.

Quickly, ignoring the feeling the picture creates again, I scroll and find the link to our webpage: *Tulip and Thorn Publishing – Looking for the best in new literary talent.* The editor side of me feels excited, something I've not felt for a while. These two letters potentially had something, something different. Perhaps I was flattered because I was the foci of them, in a way. Maybe their epistolary nature reminded me of some other texts.

My mind continued to wander around and within the pages as I drank my coffee, took a bath, dried my hair, dressed for bed; the words, an odd mixture of handwritten and typed again, seemed to float in the steam of my bathroom. I had questions: about them getting my contact details; the continued errors in the writing; if anyone else was being sent the texts; where was the story going and were the extracts in chronological order? I decided that having these questions was a good sign - maybe a new project was just what I needed. Before going to bed I decided to compose an email to the writer.

To: caprahircus@livemail.com

From: mthorn@livemail.com

Subject: Letters

Dear Ann(e?),

I have received both your letters. Thank you for sending them to me and for taking the time at the end of your second letter to explain the reason for submitting them in the first place.

I will say that after working as an editor for a number of years, your method of submission is a little unusual compared to what I have been accustomed to but I would be lying if I said it hasn't at least caught my attention. There are a few points I would like to make regarding the manuscript, despite having only seen several pages, and your method of communication.

First of all, I would like to know your general outline for the story. Where is it going? Is there a vision for the narrator's journey? Are the letters that you have sent mere extracts and therefore out of order or are you employing the currently very popular and commercial fragmented narrative and unreliable narrator technique? I am also intrigued about whether the mistakes, of which there are several (such as homophone errors and missing words), are intentional – if so, does this form part of a bigger plotline?

I also have to mention the more professional side of writing and of contacting any agent or publisher. It is common practice to submit a covering letter, outline of the plot and sometimes the opening three chapters via a website link or suggested email approved by the agent or publishing house. I have just checked the webpage for Tulip and Thorn and the company not only prefers email submissions, but the postal address is different to my own, so I have to ask how you came to send the letters to this particular location. Finally, although submitting parts of a manuscript one letter at a time (if your text is only made up of this medium) is certainly an interesting ploy, I have to ask if there are any other publishers or agents who are currently receiving your extracts in the same method.

I apologise for the perhaps brusque tone of this letter however with the volume of submissions we receive at Tulip and Thorn, and the 'different' manner in which you have submitted yours, I would like the above queries clarified.

Thank you in advance,

Ms Thorn.

I considered taking the section out about how 'Ann/e' had got my address. I realised that they themselves may have had it on file or saved for future reference when we'd initially run the company from my home. It had only recently changed and been taken from the website in the months after Jenni took over from Billy and I, and she moved all contact to her own place and the tiny office we rented across town. It made me realise just how vulnerable you are when everything is online. I made a mental note to message Jenni and let her know, just in case.

-

You told yourself not to feel bad about yourself.

-

It is morning. No one else is here. The ground is always wet. No matter how warm the weather has been, how long we've had without rain, the grass and dirt is forever damp.

I tidy the clumps of grass away from the base of the stone and pour some water over the head. I run a cloth along the edges, trace each letter with my forefinger. I take my time, making sure the gold lettering shines through just as brightly as it did a year ago. Over a year ago now. There's no one else around. Usually there's one or two other people tending to the gravestones of a loved one, a few melancholic teenagers sat on a bench talking about death; sometimes a homeless man is asleep on one instead. I look at the dates, then his name, the inscription that wasn't my choice: I left that up to his parents who left it up to his sister. 'His absence is a silent grief'. I can't decide if that is respectful or not, beautiful or just miserable. He would think it ambiguous and literary and pretentious - and would therefore love it. It shows that Jenni knew him. For the second time in as many days my mind has drifted back to her. Perhaps she was someone I needed around me right now, someone to help me continue to get through this.

"I think you'd be proud of me," I say.

When I first visited, I just sat and looked at the stone. I couldn't touch it let alone speak to it. How do you speak to a block? Why would you? It can't do anything back... it can't wink or smile or play with its ear when it gets nervous or bite its lip when impatient. After spending so long looking at the thing I started to see his face in it: his balding *(receding thank you very much, he'd say)* hairline where the curved top is; the odd bump in his nose *(character building, looks like I've been in a fight, he'd say)* in some of the Bs and Ds of gold lettering; his pale eyes *(green not grey, he'd say)* where the marble meets the ground.

"I've been doing better. Doing well, I think". Now it gives me some relief. "It's been a year. Can you believe it? A year. I can't even begin to think how I'll survive another year. What will I do with the time I have left without you? I get through day to day, but..."

A soft wind rustles the leaves on the trees above me. The grass moves in rhythm. In response.

"I still avoid the bar like the plague. It's a shame though, we used to like going there didn't we? With Donna and our friends, and seeing Tony..." I pause. A beat. "And I don't want to see that awful plaque. Can you imagine your name on a plaque? What would your crossword clue be for that? 'Ten across, six letters. Another word for a sign.' It's dated and everything. Well, you probably could imagine it actually - you were always vain enough. I haven't drunk in a few months. I still go to counselling each week. Jenni's still working to keep the business going. She's been really good actually. I should ask her to come here with me, might be an odd bonding thing. I saw her the other day – she was down seeing your parents, wanting to look over some stuff. And no, your parents didn't invite me over but I'm sure that wouldn't surprise you. You should've seen Donna's face when Jenni let that slip. But I think I should spend some time with her, I can tell she's still hurting. Work is interesting. It's different but it'll do for now until I get back into writing again. I want to, I do, I just... don't know how to if you're not there."

I lay tulips at the bottom of the grave. "Our flowers," he always said - the first flowers he ever bought me.

I take a step back and feel tears forming, my bottom lip begins to sag. I wave my arms and breathe out. Turn, put my hands on my hips. Closing my eyes, I lift my head up to the sky. The breeze is cool, comforting. I could just cry if I wanted to, there would be no shame in that, not here. Instead, I turn around and take in his face, his hair, his nose, his teeth. His everlasting stone body.

"I'm so sorry. I'm so sorry for what happened. I know it was my fault. All of it. I'll never forgive myself for what I did to you, for what I lost. I'll never forgive myself for being the reason you're not here anymore."

I kiss the fingers on my right hand and place them on his head.

"I love you," I said.

-

If you weren't a writer, what job would you have done instead? Billy says.

Teaching maybe. Working with people, I say.

I don't think I could do anything else. I don't know what I'd be good at, Billy says.

That's because of the two of us, you're the writer, I say.

Billy just tuts at me.

-

"She's ready for you now Michelle."

I'd arrived at work early and helped in the kitchen. The scent of soap suds had permeated through into my skin, and I could still faintly smell lemons on my way to Meredith's room. She hadn't been awake long. "She slept through breakfast this morning. We thought it best to let her rest."

"Has her son been informed?"

He had and would be coming down at some point in the week to try and sort some things out. I didn't know what these 'things' were and I didn't really want to; they were either just tick box questions to make sure that the care home kept family members in the loop, or they were going to ask that Mrs Lullin be moved elsewhere. I hoped that wasn't the case. She really was no worse than any other resident here. Even now, nearly a year after starting to work here, I still think sometimes of the people here as 'patients' and have to stop myself. My grief counsellor said it was because of the place having a similar atmosphere to a hospital which conjured the word: the sensation of illness, the constant coughing, the smell of worry. They weren't patients though. They were people. The bedsheets sometimes made the sleeping elderly look like body bags.

She was sat up in bed when I knocked on her door and popped my head around.

"Aw, Michelle. Come in, come in. Sit, sit." She patted the edge of the bed next to her. "I'm so sorry about yesterday."

I sat where she had patted and smiled at her. "Mrs L – Meredith – why are you apologising? Nothing happened."

"The alarm clock might think differently." She pointed at the now cracked glass face, the hands still ticking away below. "I was such a fool. An old fool."

"No you're not. You get confused. You know that. There's nothing to be ashamed of or worried about. It's why you're here, so people can help you."

"Because some people don't want to take care of me."

It hung in the air for a moment before I asked; "Have you heard from him? Do you know when he's coming to see you?"

"*If* he's coming you mean."

"One of the nurses just told me he was coming down at some point this week."

"Oh yes. That's just lip service, mark my words. He only comes here as it's mainly female nurses he has to deal with. It's not a coincidence that there are hardly any male nurses or orderlies here. He comes here to flirt and look good in front of a skirt or two, no offense, whilst he faffs over me with them looking. Men." She tutted, and I found myself fighting a smile. "Don't you laugh at me! All men are the same. They take whatever they can get."

I knew that mood changes were common with illnesses like Mrs Lullin had; loss of memory and mood swings and irrational acting out. She seemed like a pedantic angry housewife today whereas just the other day she was still so deeply in her love with her husband, a 'man'.

"Do you remember anything from the other night? What you were asking and talking about?"

She grimaced and her face seemed to crunch up in a way that would squeeze out a memory, a drop of what had happened. Her hands clenched slightly. She avoided meeting my eyeline.

"Oh, it's just embarrassing. The ravings of a forgetful old woman. I wish I could forget I had this-" she waved one hand above her head, as if batting away an invisible cloud, "-thing inside my head... dragging all my memories away."

"Not all of them. You have your husband still. You were talking so passionately about him to me the other day."

"Would you like to see a picture of him? A good old black and white photo?"

I'd seen her one and only picture many times, but it made her happy to show me. And they had made a handsome pairing. "Of course," I said. I knew exactly where to find the photograph - "Second drawer down on the right hand side, underneath the birthday and Christmas cards" - but she told me anyway.

"I was certain there was a man in the room with me, Michelle. And when I told the nurse about it she just said it was impossible. Like I said, hardly any men work here do they?"

"You thought a man was in here?"

"You too? 'Thought' there was a man."

"Sorry. Just a turn of phrase" I pulled the drawer open. "There was a man in here with you? What did he say?"

"They were asking about a baby, or their daughter. She'd gone missing. For some reason they thought to look here. But... I do get confused. It was so dark. I remember it was dark. I'd been asleep."

"Did he say anything else? A name?"

"No. I mean, *why* would he be looking for a daughter here? We're all older than time itself."

"Could it be one of the nurses perhaps? How old was the man?"

"By the voice, maybe... in their thirties."

I sat back down with her on the bed and held the photograph. Her eyes immediately softened and smiled. "There he is," she said, "my one and only."

"See. You do still have memories. Good ones. Ones that matter." She sighed, looked down at her hands and then back at the picture. "You really do remember someone being in here, don't you?"

"I think I do, yes."

I tapped the photo on my thigh, thinking - about what I wasn't sure, but I felt that I needed to ask around just to put her mind at ease. Maybe it was a male visitor, or a resident here that just wandered into the wrong room?

"And you can't remember a name?"

She shook her head.

I made her a cup of tea, tidied up a little bit for her. I found the remote control under the chair in the corner of the room, another item she'd carelessly flung around in her rage the other evening ('I wondered where that had gone. I missed the news last night') and reminded her about Games Night later that afternoon. Even though it was called Games Night it actually ran from 4pm to 6pm so the clientele wouldn't be too tired to think of the answers, something that Donna found hilarious when I told her about it and something that *again* she asked to attend when she was next free. She'd actually fit in here, she'd make everyone laugh.

"Right. I'm off. My time here is done."

"You know you should probably spend time with other patients around here at some point."

"Firstly, you're not a patient, and if you *were* one, you'd be my favourite. I get all my other jobs done quickly so that I can shoot the shit with you."

"Shoot the shit. I haven't heard that in years."

I picked up my bag and made to leave. I thought back to her photograph and that little memory preciously tucked up and protected. "Meredith, would you like to see a picture of my husband?"

I heard her exhale, and her eyes were smiling again. "Oh Michelle. I'd love to. I've never wanted to ask."

"Well, I think we know each other well enough now don't we?"

I kept several pictures of him in my purse. Silly photo booth ones. Our honeymoon. With family, or just of him. For a moment I held all four in my hand, one of top of the other like a small pack of playing cards. His eyes beamed up at me, grinning and holding a beer as I, behind the camera, snapped a moment now frozen: my Billy with the ocean behind him, the sunset startlingly red and orange, glowing. His teeth bright. Our marriage was three days old. I tucked that picture away, I wasn't ready to share that one with anyone else just yet. I passed Meredith the picture of our two families together.

"This is all of us. We are in the middle, his sister next to him and then his parents. On the other side are my parents and a few friends behind us."

"Where is this?" she asked, squinting.

"A family birthday. His mum's a few years ago. They're celebrating St. Patrick's Day too, hence all the green clothing."

She turned the photograph over once, twice. I wasn't quite sure what she was doing. She ran a forefinger over the two rows of faces in the picture as if looking for someone, or perhaps making sure she didn't miss a single face.

"Who are these again?"

I leant over and saw her pointing at Billy and Jenni.

"That's my husband next to me. And that's his sister."

She continued to tap their faces for a moment and then ran her finger over everyone else one more time before handing it back. I tucked the photograph back in my purse, in front of the others and behind the scan picture I knew was there too; the tiny black and white dot that I'd never let anyone see.

"He's very handsome. You made a handsome couple."

"I thought the same about you. You made a handsome pair with your husband. I'd not told anyone about his fingernails before." She didn't reply. She just let me speak. "He was obsessed with crosswords. The first time we met he was doing a crossword. I was behind him in a queue at a coffee shop on the university campus and I leaned over his shoulder to give him the answer to one word he couldn't figure out. From then on, he used to speak to me in crossword clues. Like he'd say 'Three down, four letters. An alcoholic beverage.' which was his way of asking me to get him another beer from the fridge. He knew it wound me up but he kept doing it. Especially when he'd leave his little ink-smudged fingerprints all over the house. I'd find the inky remnants of his crossword puzzles on door handles, toilet roll, milk cartons in the fridge." I paused, realising I was smiling. "I don't think I've spoken about him for this long since he died."

"Make sure you hold onto those memories. They'll keep you going when you're my age."

"I bet you have lots of anecdotes."

"Did I ever tell you about Thursday?" I shake my head. "The goat I had as a pet when I was little?"

"A goat? Since when did people ever have goats for pets? Where did you live?"

"My mother and father had some land but, granted, not enough to really house a living and kicking goat. And believe you me, it kicked." She chuckled to herself.

"So why call it Thursday?"

"That was the day we saved it from being sent to slaughter. My father worked on a farm and the goat was considered too old. Useless. So they were going to send it away. My father, heaven knows why as the goat was a miserable old, well, goat, felt guilty about it and rescued the elderly creature. Thursday." She smiled again, her eyes crinkling. "And that's how he got his name."

"I like that story." I take a deep breath, let it out. "You're right," I say, "stories like that are important. I need to remember more of them."

"Then write them down. You told me you're a writer, so write them down. Even if they are just snippets of conversations or parts of memoires... it's better to try and hold onto them than to just let them go."

"More than anything, I worry..." I pause. She nods at me, supporting what I want to try and say. "I worry that I'll forget what we *talked* about. The sound of his voice. I have pictures of him, things around the house that remind me of him like his clothes or his pens... but his *voice*, his words. I worry I'll lose the sound of him one day."

"Then that's what you need to write. Any conversations you remember having with him. Anything at all. No matter how mundane it might seem. It'll help you. It'll help him too, no doubt."

I told her I would be back in the morning. I told her to make sure that she got a good sleep that night. I was just leaving her room when she spoke again:

"Sam."

I stopped.

"Sam."

"Who?" I turned around to face her.

"Who was in here with me the other night. Sam. They said their name was Sam."

-

You went to visit him. It is okay to miss him.

-

I was trembling.

I didn't know why. Why did the name Sam send chills through me? I didn't know anyone called Sam, not that I could remember. Walking home, I felt the urge to head into my corner shop. Something I had started doing to make me feel more in control was to buy a bottle of wine and merely have it in my kitchen. I wouldn't drink it, I wouldn't even open it. I would merely have it there, spin it, have it in my eyeline when watching something on television or reading a newspaper after work. But it made me feel powerful to know I could control that urge.

After we lost the baby I found it harder and harder to sleep and at first having a slight buzz just took the edge off the insomnia that had started to creep in. It was one of the few things Billy and I ever argued about. To begin with I think he was unsure how to broach the topic – how do you talk to your wife who is mourning a miscarriage that she might be drinking too much? I didn't think I ever drank too much - it soon became a habit. I remember raising with him and Donna (in what I think was a pre-intervention-intervention they'd organised) that having one glass of wine before bed to help you get to sleep was surely no different than a couple who regularly polish off a bottle of wine together with dinner after the kids had gone to bed, or the guy who necks five cans whilst watching his favourite sports. We agreed to disagree. Then came our trouble getting pregnant again. Then came the doctor appointments and passive aggressive references to my drinking. Then came the concern that my drinking could affect me being able to conceive. Then came my guilt, swirling around inside the glass of red wine that mirrored the blood of the babies I'd lost… what I'd done.

For some reason it feels felt safer to have a bottle of wine in the house. It sounds odd I know, like having a safety net that isn't actually going to protect you but just let you fall instead. I spent many nights looking up local AA meetings on my phone but I never went to one. Grief counselling is enough for now. After talking with Meredith, I felt this tug from my naval dragging me with an invisible line towards the store, the bottles, the counter, the wine glass at home. I pulled on all my usual tricks to avoid this temptation: walk on the other side of the road; hands in my pockets, hunched shoulders to make myself feel cold, the need to rush home; get home quicker and then you can check your phone to see whatever that buzz just was in your coat; rub my wrist to distract myself from one sensation with another. Thoughts were rumbling and rambling through my mind, from Meredith's husband to her son and if he would actually come and see her, to Jenni and her wanting to collect some of Billy's things, then this new writer and their odd book of sorts I was being sent, wondering if it was a sign I needed to work again or just a waste of my time, and back to this 'Sam' - somewhere I thought that the name meant something to me but I couldn't find it – I was worrying about the confused memories of a woman with early onset dementia, after all.

Suddenly, I felt the pain of the Chinese burn gripping my flesh and stopped. I paused in the street. I took a breath. My thoughts had run from one to the other like a waterfall, like they did when allowed. I remembered my breathing exercises from grief counselling. I stop for what is no more than five seconds. Everything seems to slow down. I feel myself blink. I run my tongue over my lips. These short seconds of calm I give myself which are unnoticeable to anyone around me.

'Eleven down, eight letters. The aftermath of drinking.' I could hear him saying one of his clues to me, could feel the judgemental tone. *Hangover.*

I felt an odd sense of anticipation as I walked up to the front door, expecting the next instalment of this girl, this student struggling with friends and self-esteem. There was something about the entries that made me want to read on. Tonight though, there was nothing waiting for me. I turned on the lights in the hallway and kitchen, dropped my bag and keys on the table. I bent over the counter and let out a long, loud sigh. I raised my head to the ceiling. 'Stop,' I tell myself. 'Just stop.'

"Just tell yourself to stop harassing yourself." I could hear Donna as if she were right beside me. "If you need to, just tell yourself off for being such a dick to yourself all the time." She was right. I let out another sigh.

I felt another buzz from my phone in my pocket. There was a message on the screen, an email:

From: caprahircus@livemail.com

Re: Letters

Dear M

Unsure what to expect, I swiped the screen.

EMAIL ONE

From: caprahircus@livemail.com

Re: Letters

Dear Ms Thorn,

Thank you so much for your reply. I have to admit that after sending the first extract I was concerned that I had perhaps overstepped, that by not going through the proper channels I would just be slapped most certainly with a 'thanks but no thanks' copy and paste reply, as you get from so many publishers and agents. I use 'you' in reference to us writers who are constantly ignored by the people we send our work to. I have been writing for many, many years now and have even worked in the industry for a short time. I have perhaps become cynical and frustrated with how the system works. I have sat in meetings as an intern where manuscripts are cast to one side if the writer's name doesn't excite, or the first sentence isn't quite there yet – it was as if the people had never heard of, or didn't see the irony in, judging a book by its cover. I hoped that working behind the scenes - for free I might add! - would help me get a foot in the proverbial door. But nothing.

I don't want to sound angry – I realise this reply has now become somewhat of a rant – but there are only so many rejections you can take and still have the energy, belief, to put pen to paper. Each empty reply and rejection is like getting a paper cut from the pages that you have written, your own babys. Fine. Play it safe then, I told myself. Try to write to their mould. But there are only so many short story and poetry competitions you can enter to make you still 'feel' that you're a writer. It begins to feel rather empty. The most vacuous of words are always used in replies from agents and publishers, if you are lucky enough to get one at all. My favourite phrases are how my writing has "potential" but that with current publishing trends it doesn't "sit" or "fit" well, or it wouldn't be "prudent" to take my manuscript further. They just made me feel like an outcast. All of them. Like I was some sort of freakishly bad writer belonging in an anthology of freakshow stories to be made fun of. Therefore, after years of rejections, I thought I'd do something different with my writing and when trying to get someone's attention.

In answer to the questions you raised in your email: yes, I am sending this to a few different agents and publishers, I don't see the harm in that personally. However, I would happily be exclusive to anyone who expressed an interest: I apologise for sending my work to an incorrect address, but this was the address listed on your website most recently, so therefore I presumed that was the correct one to use. Please let me know where best to send future extracts and correspondence. Finally, the story does have an 'end game' for want of a better phrase. I don't know about you but I am sick and tired of the current trend in fiction for stories to be told by women - that's not my issue; we live in a #metoo world that I fully support – women who are always drunk or embittered due to a secret, or always ignore what's in front of them with a friend or a phone or a missing key or something seemingly benign. These books have become thriller-by-numbers in my point of view, and also woman shaming, even though they're meant to show females being dominant. Just think about it: how many of these nonlinear or fragmented narrative tales which line every supermarket, with their predictable titles of 'Feminine pronoun, preposition, vehicle and/or place', just drag the female protagonist down into a pit of alcohol or sex or shame for not being perfect? Women more than that surely? Does every story have to end with a death?

I am very much interested in epistolary novels. The likes of 'Dracula' are so rich and layered that they draw a reader into another world of real people, real penmanship, real lifes. I am aware, trust me, that I am not up to that standard, yet it's a style I enjoy writing in. It leaves you wanting more, wanting to get the next letter as though you are the powerless recipient of whatever the postman delivers.

I would be more than happy to supply a covering letter and overview of the story or send further extracts if you would like to read those to.

Again, thank you for your reply and taking the time to respond to my writing. It means a great deal to actually receive some written communication for a change!

Yours,

Andy.

I leant back in my chair. I felt part intrigued, part admonished child. Did this person, Andy, think this was the best way to catch a publisher's attention, to almost chastise the entire industry they were trying to crack? Despite this, it annoyingly engaged me, made me want to reply 'yes' to getting more extracts of his writing. Maybe this passive aggressive method of contacting a publisher was the way forward? I rubbed my eyes, laughing at the thought. There was an odd, uncomfortable feeling though that I had about the email. I couldn't shake it. The fridge magnet seemed to throb at me from across the kitchen. Surely that was just a coincidence - cheesy sayings and fridge magnets are a dime a dozen. You can *Google* all sorts of uplifting sayings, and *Instagram* is nothing but... I'm reading too much into the letters, that's all. My eyes drifted from one fridge magnet to another: one a cartoon ceramic goat, the Billy Goat.

I logged onto my computer, accessed the email and printed it off. With a red pen I ran through the writing as I would when editing or considering a book proposal. Where were the errors? Where were the missteps? Where were the questions that needed to be raised?

I have been writing for many, many years now and have even worked in the industry – could I try and find out where he'd been a writer? That might help me discover more about him. Maybe he'd been asked to leave or not given a full-time job and held some anger at the publishing world in general. I made a note to ask that in my reply email.

yes I am sending this to a few different agents and publishers, I don't see the harm in that personally, – the arrogance here made me laugh out loud when reading it the first time. But again, oddly, it intrigued me... the usual contact letters you get from wannabe writers are so formal they verge on sickening. Maybe his brash tone would appeal to readers and a market?

but this was the address listed on your website most recently so therefore I presumed that was the correct one to use – I am certain that it had been removed a little while ago. It's an innocent mistake if he just had the old address saved somewhere. I made another note, this time to text Jenni to change it on the website if needed.

oddly woman shaming even though they're meant to show females being dominant – this I kind of agreed with. We'd published one or two of these in the past. They sell well. Jenni had just mentioned something similar the other day too. Maybe we did need to be braver with our next publication. But he hadn't answered my question about the plot at all – he had sent no outline, no further extract even. Did he even have a plotline or was this all just an angry rant at the first publisher to properly contact him? But why would he do that?

I am so interested in epistolary novels – what a rapid change of tone this was in his letter. Ironic, considering how much he seems to dislike fragmented narratives made popular in current fiction. His email was all over the place. And the last extract he sent to me didn't flow chronologically from the first either. But again, despite my reservations, it made me interested to read and hear more. I paced around the kitchen as I re-read the email and made my marks and notes. I found myself tapping my right fingers on the single wine bottle in the kitchen. I got my phone and replied.

-

To: caprahircus@livemail.com

Re: Re: Letters

Dear Andy,

Thank you for your reply. I understand some of your frustrations; this industry is very hard to break. It takes a lot of time, patience and more often than not just some luck. The right manuscript at the right time.

I am more than happy to continue reading your work for the time being. This is not an invitation to an exclusive reading nor an offer to publish - let me be clear on that - but I am interested to see where your writing goes. At present I am working freelance and only part time. If, as you say, you are pursuing something to break the mould of the current literary trend then I am intrigued.

Email is best for me, or if you want to continue sending hardcopies then please do so to the updated addressed on our company's website. I have attached the link below:

www.tulipandthornagency.co.uk

Thank you in advance,

Ms Thorn.

-

Short and to the point. I didn't want to pander to him.

In bed, I text Jenni about changing the website contact address if she hasn't done so already. I ask her if she is free for a drink when next in town. Then, I remember one other thing the writer didn't clarify in his response: were all the errors in the writing purposeful? Either he was embarrassed I had noticed or they were there for a reason; a sub plot for a reader to figure out. I turned on my bedside lamp and pulled the first two letters out from the drawer next to me where I had placed them after reading. I scanned the letters again for those simple errors, homophones and wrong tenses. I read over them twice just to be sure.

I wrote them down on the back of one of the pages:

Letter 1 errors – *hear, been, lairs*. This I rewrote, I presumed, as *here be liars*.

Letter 2 errors – *red, each, names*. This I rewrote as *read peach name*. But 'peach' was the correct word about the girls' faces so 'each' was in fact the error.

Here be liars. Read each name.

I picked up my phone. I scanned through his recent email to see if this was more than just a coincidence. One paragraph, then another. I wrote them down as I found them.

Email errors – *babys*, the phrase 'Women more than that surely?' was missing 'are', lifes, to. This I rewrote as *babies are lives too*.

Here be liars. Read each name. Babies are lives too.

If these were deliberate and the writer, Andy, was trying to get the reader to crack a code, then it was working. It was all I thought of as I lay in bed trying to sleep. My mind kept rearing up the fridge magnet too - the ceramic Billy Goat.

-

You did not buy something that you did not need.

-

"What the fuck Michelle?"

Donna. I knew she'd have an opinion.

"Surely you aren't going to continue reading any stuff he sends you? He sounds insane."

"Well it's not like I have to meet him or anything. I've asked for further pieces of writing to be *emailed* now anyway, so there's no harm."

"No harm? He's leaving you codes and hidden messages in his writing."

"That's part of the novel. It's quite clever actually."

"Even in his emails? That's not part of the book."

"Maybe he's just testing me to see if I actually pay attention to what he's writing."

"Hold on, hold on. Since when do you let a shitty writer be in charge? Isn't one of the perks of being on the other side of the page, that you can just snub anyone you want to?"

"Did you actually read the email? That's exactly what he's complaining about."

"Yeah, because he's been refused so many times, he's gone so crazy with jealousy that he's plotting revenge against random agents. I bet he's writing a true crime. I bet you're the girl in the book."

"But I'm not at university. And I didn't graduate with a bad degree."

"You know what I mean. This has stalker written all over it."

"I think you're overreacting."

"No, you're *under*reacting. Hold on, let me just find and quote my favourite part." I can hear Donna on the other end of the line scrolling through her emails on her phone, putting me on speaker; "Oh yes, here it is: *It leaves you wanting more, you wanting to get the next letter as if you are the powerless recipient of whatever the postman delivers.* He sounds tapped."

"I know..."

"Are you listening?"

"Yeah. Yes. I did second guess that part myself." There's a slight pause. "Donna?"

"It's you I'm worried about. He knows where you live."

"Because of the website. Jenni text me back and said it's definitely been changed now anyway. You should be pleased that she had the same reaction as you."

"You told her?"

"Well I kind of had to; she wanted to know why I wanted the company address changed. To be honest I thought it already had been but... anyway she's agreed to be part of any further communication with him. I just need to copy her into any further emails. Anything he posts now *should* go to the office space we rented. Rent. Well, Jenni rents."

"Hmmm."

"Stop being so judgemental of her. And jealous."

"I am not jealous of her!"

She sounded so incredulous I had to laugh. "Look, she's away at a conference or something she said so the other day didn't she, and she still took the time to message me back. I'm not even properly working for her, and she still makes time for me. She's not that bad."

"And you are related. Don't forget that. So she should be nice to you."

"And me to her then, yes?"

"Is it just work stuff at the offices? Like manuscripts and things?"

"Mostly. Some paperwork from the house, letters and stuff we just wanted to move out of here. I can't remember the last time I went through any of it."

"Are your doors locked?"

"Donna! You're meant to keep me calm not freak me out even more." Despite myself, I'm laughing. "And it's nothing, honestly. I actually quite like what he writes. It's not especially well written but there's... something."

"Something fucking weird. Call Tony. Can I call Tony?"

"No! God no. I don't need to see *him*."

A flash of his bar. Several drinks. I am laughing and Billy is there but I see Tony behind him, behind the bar.

"Have you still not spoken to him? He really didn't care. He doesn't."

"No, no," I put my head in my free hand, "it's too embarrassing."

"Michelle. You got drunk. You chatted him up. He's cute. He's nearby. He owns a pub. What's the problem?"

"Because I'm still going to grief counselling? For my husband who died a year ago? Because I'm not working at a proper job at the moment? Because -"

"You might like him."

I wasn't sure if it was a question or statement. I paused. I didn't know what I thought about him, about anything. We'd just gone for a few drinks, Donna and I, the night her nephew was born a couple of months ago. It was impromptu but fun with some of her friends and family. I only had a few glasses of wine but it quickly went to my head, I hadn't drunk in so long. I felt comfortable with friends, with Donna, and he was kind to me. He was kind to me just as he always had been, and was with everyone.

"It's nice to see you back in here," he'd said, "I haven't known what to say. I didn't know whether to send a card, pop round or…"

As he'd spoken, I had felt a hand run up my neck. A shiver. A ghost.

"Well, you've waited long enough to talk to me about it." I joked. I tried to smile, keep things normal.

"I blame you anyway," I say to Donna now, "you always wanted to me stop drinking and then there you were watching me get hammered."

"Okay, first of all you make it sound like Billy and I-" the tell-tale pause when someone mentions his name, isn't sure if they've done something wrong, but tries to carry on without it being too noticeable, "- that I created an *intervention* or something. It wasn't that and you know it. It was more about your mood and your sleeping. Secondly, drinking socially is fine. We were having a good time. I've never suggested you stop *that*. Finally, you weren't hammered. You were tipsy. Funny. You made him laugh. He made you laugh."

"I know but… it felt… it feels…" I don't know what to say. I couldn't tell her the truth. I couldn't face it. Not yet.

"It will do. For a long time. But being in the company of friends, even the odd flirt with a nice guy who we both know – it isn't going to change anything. I mean, this is Tony who we've known for years. It doesn't make you a bad person."

She stops but I can tell there's something else she means to say. I wait.

"It doesn't mean you're forgetting Billy."

She's right. I know she is. She's right. I put the phone to my forehead. I think for a moment.

"I know. I know. Thank you. I'm sorry."

"You've nothing to apologise for. It's a shitty, shitty time and a shitty, shitty thing for anyone to have to deal with. Just promise me a few things?"

"What's that?" I sigh again.

"Copy Jenni into any emails you receive and send. Please?"

"Okay."

"I know I'm exaggerating but it's just given me the creeps. That email from him."

"Okay. Will do. What else?"

"Talk to Tony. Just say hello. Anything. It'll be like ripping off a plaster: quick, a little pain, and then done with."

"Okay. I promise."

Sat in my living room, the conversation with Donna over, I wonder whether I should go and talk to Tony? But Donna has no idea how difficult it is, how painful seeing him is though. It's *me* doing this though - overplaying things in my head over and over, again and again. He's only down the road. The past is the past.

Then, the conversation with Mrs Lullin pops into my mind... writing about Billy. Writing down sections of conversations I can remember. I stretch my hands out, as though preparing for a sporting event I haven't competed in for a while. A retired athlete.

I look around for a pen, some paper. The printed email from Andy catches my eye. I have a sudden thought. I flip open my laptop and decide it might be a good idea to email an old friend of mine, someone I used to work with before Billy and I set up our own company. I want a second opinion on the writing, just to see what they think of it, if it has any merit. If it's a waste of my time or not. I can scan the extracts over to her. I won't include the emails or anything, there's no need for them, just the manuscript so far. If she says it's nonsense, I'll take that as my sign to leave well alone and perhaps just suffer the wrath of the embittered emails I'll inevitably get when he realises I'm not interested in any further portions of his book. He's right though - the publishing world can be cold.

I find her email address. Leesha. The name feels ancient on my tongue. Contacting an old friend will feel good, and not just because of dealing with Andy in a more professional way; it warms me to see her name. Like I'm reclaiming something thought lost.

-

I get ready for work. Donna must have really felt passionate about the email I'd forwarded to her to call me this early; she's not normally awake before double figures. In the hallway there's a piece of paper on the mat; it's from next door, just saying that they've no idea who 'Anne' is and they don't know anyone at university. Well, I know the letters were never for them anyway now. I consider writing a note back to explain but I decide there's not really any point - it's not like next door need to know I'm getting an unsolicited manuscript dropped off.

It isn't until I put my coat on that I notice them: black marks on the cuff of my coat. They look like ink stains from a pen, or where someone with ink from a fountain pen on their fingers has left a mark. In the living room I swear I can see Billy sat down, running his index finger over the morning newspaper's crossword puzzle.

-

You can watch films and listen to music that reminds you of him.

-

My mind is spiralling from one thought strand to another: Tony, Andy, the ink stains, the emails, the letters posted to my door, drink, Donna worrying, Jenni being my boss... I can't seem to separate one thought from the other. By the time I get to work I am consciously squeezing my wrist, adding to the red rings that are already there which I must have made in my sleep, or when on the phone to Donna. It worries me that I can't always remember when I do it. I was doing so well. just need a straightforward busy day at work, that's all. I just need to take my mind off... my mind.

Inside the care home however, the situation is anything but calm. The front desk is unmanned. A number of staff are rushing about. I wonder if they've caught wind of an inspection. One has been looming for a while. Ever since care homes and the like have been given ratings by Ofsted everyone has been on tenterhooks for 'the phone call' as it's referred to. I head to the desk and answer the phone that's been ringing for the past thirty seconds.

"Oh, sorry Michelle, I've been run off my feet this morning." Lizzie, the receptionist, appears behind me looked harried.

"What's up? Am I late or... are we short staffed today?"

"No, no. We're just tidying up. One of the patients had a fall this morning. We've been making sure the staircase is safe. We had to cordon it off for a little while. Mayhem. Honestly, you'd think we'd left half of them up there with no access to water or food. It was for an hour at most."

"God... what happened? Was anyone hurt?"

"One of the old dears tripped down the stairs. It must've been the carpet. I don't know. They're meant to use the bloody stairlift. I don't why she didn't."

"Who was it? Are they okay?"

"Yeah they're fine. They've been taken to hospital just to be checked over. Concussion. No broken bones or anything I don't think, but she'll probably bruise. They're all so fragile here aren't they?" She pauses for a second, then tells me who had the accident: "It was Meredith. Mrs Lullin. She's one of yours, isn't she?"

"And you didn't tell me this straight away? Lizzie! Shit!"

Immediately, I spin around and race to her room. 'One of *yours*?' I think to myself. These people don't *belong* to anyone. They need our care, and not be judged or seen as annoying problems as some of the staff view them. I march into the middle of a conversation between a nurse I've seen once or twice, she's new, and Dr Hopkins who must be overseeing the home today. They stop talking when I enter the room.

"Sorry to interrupt, er..." I look at the nurse but can't remember her name. "I've just heard about Meredith. What happened?"

Mark - Dr Hopkins - nods to the young girl who leaves the room with a small stack of papers. Mark looks at me which I appreciate. Often when something happens that's unpleasant, like an accident or when one of the elderly here is moved to hospice care, no one ever looks at you when they tell you – it's as if they're embarrassed and scared it will catch. It's silly to me to be worried about aging in a place built to care for it. Mark doesn't break eye contact as he tells me.

"She was upstairs playing bingo with one of her acquaintances here. She must have tripped when coming down the stairs. She's fine. Nothing's broken. We checked her over thoroughly but we've sent her to hospital to be doubly safe. We've contacted her son. He should be here soon."

"He was contacted the other day. He should already be here." I can't hide my exasperation towards him, the son.

"About the incident the other day?"

"Yes. Her 'outburst' I suppose you could call it. Do you think these two things are related?"

"Well old people get confused. They forget things. Meredith has the early stages of dementia so she is prone to mood swings, not being sure of who she's seen or what she's done. She might have even forgotten that she's meant to use the stairlift."

"Oh god. I feel like this is my fault. I should have been here."

"Michelle, you have nothing to feel bad about. You do your shifts here. You care for who you can when you're here. That's the job. She was looked after, don't worry. And her son will be here tomorrow."

"Well at least he's coming now."

"Listen, I've got to go and see to a few other things. Just carry on as normal. You've got other people to tend to, it's just a normal day. I'll let you know the minute I hear anything else about her, alright?"

Alone in her room I hold myself, put my arms around my waist. My eyes run over the various items and objects of Meredith's, the flotsam and jetsam of her past: her jewellery stand with earrings and necklaces, although she only rotates wearing two or three pieces; the dogeared books on her bedside table; the television remote that was hidden under her chair just the other day. It seems strange to think that so much has happened in just a few short days... some confused rant about a visitor, things being thrown around, falling down the staircase, and amidst it all we shared some real truths, real feelings about our husbands, ourselves. Out of her window I watch the traffic, slowly humming past. I run my hands through my hair. My eyes drift to a photograph of her and her husband.

I see two figures outside of my front door. I hear the knock. Then, I remember the sensation of my phone buzzing in my hand, hearing my mother's voice, distant but still there. I remember the private hospital room door opening. I see policemen in the dark, damp from the drizzling rain we'd been having that day - they had more questions about Billy's accident. That night was just a flashbulb of pain and waiting rooms and waking up and wanting Billy, contacting Jenni, his mother tucking me into bed like I was child again when I came home from hospital a few days later, a cup of tea that I let get cold by the bedside lamp, hearing people talking downstairs about what had happened, what would have to happen to him - the funeral, the arrangements, the guilt and shame swirling around my head down to my stomach that felt bloated and kicking with empty air that breathed names in wisps... Billy... Donna.... Baby... Tony... Mother...

I was silent for a week. Laying still, just there. Listening. Nodding. Agreeing to arrangements.

When I lost our baby, I was the one who comforted Billy.

I let out a deep breath. Nothing makes sense. It never did.

I realise I've been alone in Meredith's room now for several minutes. I need to go and tend to other people, carry on as normal. It's just another day at work. People have accidents, people get ill. Just as I'm straightening her bedding I notice something poking out from a drawer, the one where she keeps her photographs. I open it and pull out a small, crumpled piece of paper. It's been ripped, the top half jagged. Due to the words being torn I can't fully make them out - but there's one word that is clear and intact at the end of the page:

Sam.

-

On my walk home I wasn't sure whether to take Donna's advice or not. I walk past Tony's bar twice a day, to and from work. I tend to walk on the other side of the road: I try to avoid his place, head into my local shop. The day's events were still whirring around in my mind, and I didn't think I looked my best after hours of folding sheets, making beds and cleaning bathrooms. I didn't want to see Tony looking like this. The corner store was drawing me in, an invisible hand waving, beckoning. I grab my wrist. The pain of a Chinese burn, the twist of skin, snaps me away from the voice inside my head.

The hospital had been in contact to say that Mrs Lullin was fine but had a fractured hip and ankle. She would be out in a few days and to do nothing but rest. I asked Mark if she'd need a hip replacement but he said he hadn't been told.

The name Sam kept reappearing in front of me as I walked home: in the letters of an advert on the side of a bus, in a word I heard someone say as they passed me. I couldn't shake the feeling that there was a reason the rest of the note was missing. I just kept reminding myself that this wasn't a book and new bestseller, this wasn't a manuscript that I was editing and reminding my writer to drop little red herrings every so often to fool a reader. This was just an accident and a piece of paper. Nothing more. It's just a letter or part of a card that got caught in the drawer, accidentally ripped – that the piece of paper had just fallen in with the rest of the drawer's contents.

I flinched slightly when I turned my wrist to open my front door; my already bruised wrist enflamed from the day's work. I saw a couple of letters on the hallway floor: two bills, a reminder about a credit card offer, and the handwriting I now knew to be Andy. My writer. I wasn't sure whether to open it. We had agreed to only communicate now via email. I flipped the letter in the air for a moment, decided to text Jenni that another piece of writing had been delivered. I'd scan and email it over for her to look at.

I guess he was right in what wrote he wrote earlier – the postman and the recipient, left wanting more.

I sit down in my living room and open the envelope.

LETTER THREE

That stupid fucking song. I thought I'd heard enough of it when I was back in halls but it's the only damn song that my housemates seem to want to play now as well. I don't know whether I'm being a snob about music or if people my age (maybe just those I live with) are devoid of any interests that don't involve pop music and reality TV - especially pop music that just remixes old classics, like this bullshit I'm having to listen to. Last night I sat in my room and just listened to them laughing and talking over the television in the living room – it's above my bedroom so I can hear everything they say and do. Sometimes they bitch about me and think I cant hear them. Maybe they know I can and just say it on purpose, or maybe they don't care either way: my clothes, how much I work, how I actually *attend* lectures. *Loser, geek, saddo.* I sit here in my room, in the dark, and I can feel those words crawling along my skin like tattoos sliced with a knife. They move from my arms down my sides and thighs to my ankles, one of which is red raw as usual. There's a shaking sensation in my body that I've never felt before; a tremor that sits below my skin, humming. Electric.

The lightbulb in my room went out yesterday and after lectures I stopped off to buy a new one. I was on my chair screwing it into place when one of girls ran past my room so quickly, being chased no doubt by her ape of a boyfriend, that it spooked me and I dropped the bulb. It smashed on the floor. Luckily, I had another in the pack but I couldn't quite turn it into place. I made to gently drop it onto my bed so I could try and figure out the problem with the socket but the bulb bounced off the bed and it too shattered onto the floor. I stood there, on my chair in the middle of the room, and felt my body just hang - as if I was hanging from the light above me. I felt limp. A doll that no one wanted to play with. I saw two of the girls (I'm ashamed to say I don't honestly know their names) walk past and stop for a moment to look into my room. I heard them giggle, I saw them nudge each other with their elbows – how funny, the odd girl is miming hanging herself, glass broken at her feet. No, don't offer to at all. Why would you?

I tiptoed around my room, careful not to cut my feet on the glass. In the bathroom I found a dustpan and brush but stood for a moment in front of the mirror and for the first time in I can't remember how long, I looked at myself. I really looked at my reflection. *Pale, thin, tissue paper.* All these words seemed to sneak over my face, felling from my eyebrows to above my lips, describing what I was seeing.

More laughter from somewhere in the house.

Why, why do we not support each other? Why do girls not care for one another more? Why always pick one out, why always form a pack and circle around one as the prey? I'd spent the last three years studying literature where women were strong and fierce - *The Age of Innocence, The Wings of the Dove, Les Liaisons Dangereuses, The House of Mirth* – but with one common theme: women against women, woman against woman, scandal taking innocence, female destroying female. A predator and prey. 'Why, why do we shame each other?' I wanted to scream, 'Why after years and centuries of rule and rape and powerlessness do we still turn on each other?'

I hated the girls in my house at that moment, I hated them. I hated them and hated myself for becoming one of those women hating women too – for turning against my own sex. I grabbed a towel and bellowed into it, felt the fabric inside my mouth. I let out a howl, a howl that was against every person who'd ignored me, friends who'd not responded to a letter or email, parents who couldn't see how fucking lost I was right infront of them.

It took me nearly an hour to gather all the shards of glass that had shattered over my carpet. Thin and papery but lethal if stepped on. I had managed to, walking carefully around the room like I was on hot coals, avoid cutting my feet or toes and then – a quick and subtle nip into the skin. A warm buzz along flesh. I looked down and saw a well of blood ooze up between two toes on my right foot. I didn't swear, I didn't wince. I spent a few moments just looking at the red swelling out from the tiny prick and then sliding, sliding down between my toes and down the bottom of my foot, to a slow drip onto the carpet.

I hobbled over to the bed trying not to get any blood on the floor and cradled my foot whilst wrapping my toes in tissue. I closed my eyes. It was unusually silent in the house. The pack must have ventured out for the night. My eyes were drawn to my wardrobe, where my bottles of wine were hidden. Well, if I didn't go out and drink with 'friends' I could still drink, couldn't I? Isn't that what university is about? I could imagine their stupid status updates the next day proclaiming *best night ever luv my girls* or some such drivel.

My hand had started to rub my stomach. A flashbulb of a waiting room, the stab of a needle, a hollow ache in my gut, a throbbing pain between my thighs. I felt queasy. I tried to stand but couldn't. I placed my head between my legs and breathed slowly, in and out, in and out. Breathing exercises which I had been told to use whenever and wherever I needed to - in a shop, during a lecture, walking on a busy street. In and out. Calm. Centre.

And then that fucking song started again.

Annie.

The writing had changed again. I sat with my head resting against the couch and looked up at the ceiling, imagining where this piece fitted in with the rest. This was *after* the interview to move in with the girls during her second year at university, but *before* the description of her graduation. And then there was the reference to self-harm, not explicit but implied with the broken glass - a metaphor for emotional pain? Psychological pain? Or was the broken glass just broken glass? Was it about her broken youth, her shattered dreams for what university should have been - lost hopes, friends never heard from again, her failure as a student? And then, that last section... an illness or something more serious, more sinister?

I was both engaged and concerned. I'd been sent more graphic and violent stories in my time, but the sudden altered tone felt more disconcerting. I had to hand it to Andy; he knew how keep a reader guessing. The manuscript seemed to start as some kind coming of age story, then drifted into a series of angsty regrets, and now turned sharply into a rant, rage and abuse of some kind - a statement about women shaming other women, women not helping their own allies.

It occurred to me that I hadn't noticed the errors that were typically there in his writing. I took a pen from my handbag and scanned through, circling and then writing down any I found:

The word *help* was missing in one sentence; *Infront* should have been 'in front' separately.

Help in or *Help front* I wrote down, but neither made sense.

I kept looking and noticed the missing apostrophe in *cant* and then, after *help*, the wrong use of *felling* in the description of the bathroom mirror, which should have been *falling*.

Can't help falling in... in what?

Then it hit me. A nauseous feeling trickled down the back of my neck, down my throat, warm and sickly, into my stomach. The final misspelt word was *luv*.

Can't help falling in love.

That must have been the song the girl kept hearing being played in her halls of residence and her rented house, the one that annoyed her being played so loud.

Can't help falling in love.

My head was swimming.

I reached back into my handbag and pulled out my purse. I unfolded the photograph I had shown Mrs Lullin – me with Billy and the rest of our families. Together.

Can't Help Falling in Love had been the song we had chosen as our first wedding dance.

-

You separated your day into manageable chunks.

-

The next morning, I got up early and went swimming. I needed to be alone and with the cool water. The last year I have just been trying to survive and get through a day, a week, a month, so that things I did and took for granted – time to swim, time to read, time to properly socialise – have just slipped by the wayside. It was sometimes enough just to dress or get up in the morning. Any notion of doing something 'normal' seemed… a waste of time. Why bother with exercise, why bother with a book, why bother chatting to someone when we all know the end outcome, that the end game for all of us is death? And for some it comes sooner than expected, sooner than it should. My head would spin and loop around this for hours on end, trapped in a cycle of anxiety. But swimming this morning felt good; I felt the buzz in my limbs afterwards, the warmth. It was almost as though I was pushing through questions, trying to find answers, as I was slicing through the water.

Last night, when I went to bed, I could feel the slow despair creeping in, like black honey oozing over my mind. I know the feeling well: when I just know the next morning will be dark and heavy, no matter the picture outside my bedroom window. I lay in bed with the molten lead feeling humming inside my head and prepared myself for the worst, my wrist in a vice like grip for most of the night. Whilst turning through the water, I thought about what to say about the latest letter. Would I sound insane if I said what I was *really* thinking and worrying about? Even hoping? I could imagine Donna's response; a mixture between anger and sarcasm. I thought about telling Jenni but I hadn't heard back from her since I'd text her. Instead, I decided to try and talk to someone tonight. That's what the group is for after all.

Work dragged. I asked Mark about Mrs Lullin and he just said she'd be out in a day or two. Her son had called ahead to say he would be coming in later today at some point. I hung around as long as I could to try and meet him and catch a glimpse of him but by the time my shift had ended he'd still not arrived.

"Maybe he's at the hospital. It would make more sense for him to just go and be with his mum there wouldn't it?"

I did my best to be civil to Lizzie as I passed reception on my way out, but I was still irritated at her for the other day. Like Donna, I am something of a grudge holder. When I first started working here I wrote a couple of freelance pieces for a woman's magazine. Filler pieces about the lighter, happier side of retirement homes. Care homes in which the patrons laugh and giggle over tea or bingo, something that middle-aged housewives lap up in their weekly magazine fix. Stories of last rites, cancer and dementia however do not fit in with a magazine which includes how-to guides on knitting and making soup from scratch. I did try once to write a more realistic piece, but the editor sent it back. Return to sender. No thanks. I got bored of writing the same beige pieces after a while, so I stopped altogether. I wondered, looking at Lizzie, if I could do a piece on her for a magazine. The day in the life of a receptionist. *The Front Lines of Elderly Care*. A no holds barred expose on how the NHS are stretched to capacity caring for the aged in our society. I couldn't see any of the magazines I freelanced for opting for it. An article on the latest quilt being stitched however…

Walking from work to the group session I saw Tony. He was outside his bar rewriting a sign with colourful chalk. He has weekly drinks offers, usually, as he told me once, for the drinks that are closest to going out of date or that he'd ordered too much of and needed to get rid of. "The trick" he told me, "is just to make people think they're getting more for less. Then people will pay anything," I remember he scratched the back of his neck, embarrassed, "or at least, that's what I take from watching *The Apprentice*. So, I'm sure it'll work in my dead-end pub, right?" I considered walking over to him, just a quick 'hello' on my way past but before I built up the courage he had disappeared back inside. I text Donna, thinking it might get her off my back or at least make her laugh: *Nearly spoke to Tony. Tried to cross the street on way to session but he'd gone back in before I could. At least I tried!* She was less than impressed and just sent back an unhappy face. If only she knew... what an effort doing just that had been.

I picked up some biscuits in a corner shop on the way, ignored the pull to the wine aisle, and rushed to the community centre. It was just when I was going into the hall that I felt my phone vibrate. A long text from Jenni:

That stupid fucking letter! Michelle, I'll be back in a few days, but let me handle this for you. If you get any more post from him just ignore it and I'll collect it all when I come back. Don't bother faxing over the latest, I can't be bothered pretending to read the damn thing. He can't write for shit anyway whoever he is... Andy, Annie or whatever. Forward me any emails you get. I don't care if this bloke turns out to be the next J.K. Rowling... he's never getting published with us if he can't follow a few simple professional requests! Hope you're well. It's good to hear from you, whatever the circumstances. J x

I smiled, amused by her unusually aggressive tone. It was quite sweet, that she was so annoyed for, and defensive of, me. It was after I slipped the phone back into my pocket that something irked me, something subtle that I couldn't put my finger on... something about her message. I quickly read over it again and shook the thought from my head.

-

We each take turns to speak. We can speak for however long we want to, about whatever we choose to: our partner, our family, their family, something good from the week, a memory. A concern for the coming week. I go every fortnight. For me that is plenty. It was Donna that persuaded me to go to my first session. I took some cajoling - why did I need to go and talk about being sad and lonely with other people who were sad and lonely? She came with me to two sessions, the very first one I sat in silence just listening, too nervous to speak. I didn't know what I'd reveal, what I'd say without meaning to and what I'd let slip without realising. I heard from the others there how they'd blamed themselves, a blamed family member, the other driver, the doctor, even the deceased... I didn't know what I wanted to say, what I *could*. What if I just cried? It wasn't until my third meeting, this time without Donna, that I felt ready to speak. I think it made it easier that she wasn't there: talking to people that I didn't really know felt freeing, that I was less likely to be judged, and felt less like I was walking on eggshells. Talking to people you know and who knew the deceased, to the people who knew both Billy and I, just never felt comfortable. I worried I was being rude or cruel, crying too little or too much, taking up too much time, being nagging, being annoying, not 'getting over it'. But saying just a few words to people who knew nothing about Billy, or myself, actually felt good. It surprised me. So, I've kept going back, every two weeks, just for a 'top up' as one person calls it: a 'top up' of feeling good about yourself, being with people who know exactly how you feel. Tonight, I'm last to speak.

"I feel like it's been a busy two weeks. I've seen my sister-in-law for the first time in months. We didn't arrange to meet or anything, we just bumped into each other in a café. It was strange, strained at first. I think we were both unsure of the etiquette... do we hug, do we be false friendly, do we go back to not really knowing each other like we did when Billy was alive? I mean, she's always been nice, cordial, but we were never close. But she's been good to me, helping with our business and taking it over while I'm just dealing with... anyway, we've been texting and it feels, I don't know, normal? I mean, it's been about work, a new writer, but it's nice to have someone to chat to. We've arranged to meet up when she's here next. Or we've arranged to arrange at least. The funny thing is what's forced us to be back in contact. I've been getting some submissions from this writer and I've been asking Jenni for advice. I'm rambling this evening. I'm not making much sense I know. I guess I just... for me it's been a *good* thing to be in contact with someone, to speak to someone new. Someone else who knew Billy. It's made me feel a little bit more connected to him I suppose. In a way. New but old. That's... all."

Later, by the coffee and biscuits we bring, the session leader, Phillip, came over to speak to me.

"Michelle, you doing okay?"

"Yeah. Sorry about before. I know I sounded a bit out of it."

"It's okay. You just seemed, I don't know... not your usual self."

"Depressed and sceptical?"

He smiles. "Less coherent, perhaps."

"I know how I sounded. Trust me. But... you'll think I'm crazy."

"Michelle you know this is a safe place. Crazy is welcomed here. Come on." He motions to a few empty chairs away from the other coffee drinkers.

"Okay. Promise not to judge me?" He makes mock sign of the cross at me. "As I mentioned, I've been getting some writing sent to me. Well, it's been in the form of letters. One at time, like an epistolary novel or something, being sent to me the last few days. It's weird because it's so different from how submissions typically work, I don't even run the editing business from my home and the address isn't even on the website anymore - it moved to the tiny office we used to rent to meet clients. I haven't done anything other than the odd freelance piece for magazines in months, but there's something interesting about the writing: it's engaging, it's angry but intelligent, has a strong female voice, it tries to raise some important issues about how women treat women but… there's something about it that I can't shake."

I pause, and Phillip asks, "Something good or bad?"

"There are parts of the writing that seem to do more than just speak to me. They seem to almost *be* me. Or *about* me, at least."

"What do you mean?" By his tone I can tell that Phillip doesn't think I'm losing my mind, he's just interested.

"Well, each letter seems to have purposeful mistakes that a reader has to figure out. Or, I think they do. The latest one spelt out the song Billy and I had for our first dance at our wedding. The character mentioned a saying that their father says which is word for word what a magnet says on my fridge. And the character has a predilection to rub her ankle when she's stressed just like I… well, you know."

He takes a moment to respond. I can tell he is picking his words carefully.

"Is that still an issue for you?" He nods to my wrist.

"No" I lie. I pull my sleeves down.

"So what is it you think is happening?"

"What, with the writing?"

"And the writer, yes."

"Honestly, I don't know. I've gone from thinking I have a stalker to I'm just reading into coincidences to… what if Billy is alive?"

Phillip smiles a sad, not condescending, but understanding smile at me. "I think you're reading into it what you want to. And that's fine. That's understandable. That's not, to use your word, 'crazy' at all."

"So what do you think?"

"Have you told anyone?"

"Not about my thoughts, my worries… no. I've forwarded Jenni the emails I sent to the writer about submitting work properly. My fiend Donna told me to change my locks. She likes drama."

"Well, I maybe wouldn't go that far. But I would perhaps limit your communication with whoever this person is if it's bringing up uncomfortable feelings for you. Only you know that though. But personally, I think it's mere coincidence. Let's test it."

"What do you mean?"

He takes his phone out of his pocket. "I'm going to type into my phone 'Popular wedding songs' and see what comes up."

It's not a 'wedding song' in the story though, is it? I think to myself. He continues to search in his phone and then hands it to me.

"What do you see?"

I scan the *Google* page and sure enough on the list is the song: *Can't Helping Falling in Love*.

"Anyone can search anything and by chance pick something that relates to another person. And how many stores and supermarkets up and down the county do you think sell similar magnets with corny phrases on? And we both know, sadly, how common self-harm is." He puts his phone back in his pocket and places a hand on mine. "What I'm saying Michelle is that this is just a couple of random similarities and nothing more. I wouldn't worry."

I'm too ashamed to tell him that I'm almost hurt he's right. It means it's not Billy after all. Something, of course, deep down I knew. I feel tears running down my cheeks.

"I'm sorry" I say, "I don't know where this is coming from."

"Michelle, it's been a year. *Only* a year. Give yourself time." He hugs me. "Michelle, I have to ask... how's the drinking?"

"I haven't drunk alone for a while now. I drink socially with friends but that's not very often. I think... I think I'm good."

"Good. I'm glad to hear it. Are you still buying a bottle to have in the house?"

"Yes. It works. I know it seems like a danger, having the temptation right there but honestly, it's easier to say no to it if I can see it. If it's not in the kitchen, the fridge or wherever... it makes me want to seek it out. It's hard to explain."

"Michelle," he puts a hand on my shoulder, "you don't have to explain anything. Only know that you have people you can turn to at any time. Okay?"

A few stray tears continue to roll down my cheeks. I'm not sure whether they are due to embarrassment, relief, or that even the *smallest* chance of Billy being alive has now slipped away.

-

You didn't think about drowning yourself.

-

Picking up my coat, I overheard someone mentioning a holiday.

"We've got the visas and everything, the money and we're all packed and ready to go. I can't wait!" The person speaking punctuated "can't. wait" in a manner that emphasised their excitement. I put my coat on and turned around to see one of the younger women talking to an older man. "It's been so long since we've been away."

"Don't forget to get your injections too."

"Injections?"

"Yeah, you never know what you'll pick up over there."

"In America?"

"Yeah, you might come back gun wielding and woman hating," the man joked. "Next meeting you'll be all 'fake news' and pro-Trump."

"I very much doubt it. But I'll keep it in mind."

"Whereabouts are you going? I've never to been to the States." She turned to me, gave me a quick look up and down; we'd never spoken. "My husband and I had planned to go there on our tenth anniversary." It surprised me how easily I had just been able to mention Billy – the magic of talking to neutral people.

"Oh, we're planning to drive Route 66. Cringy I know. But, it's something he's wanted to do since he was a teenager, so…"

"That was his plan too. I mean, Billy's plan… my husband's." I pause. Suddenly, I feel the hot prick of tears. "I vetoed that though. I can't sit still for that long." As others were leaving, the chilly air from outside came in through the front door. "Well, I hope you have a great time. You deserve to have fun. Everyone here does."

I swipe my phone to check the time and notice a missed call and a voicemail. It's from the care home. I slide across the screen and put the phone to my ear:

"Michelle. It's Mark. I am ringing with some bad news I'm afraid. I'm sorry to have to tell you over the phone but I didn't want you to find out after everyone else at work tomorrow. It's about Mrs Lullin. There seems to have been some complication at the hospital and her injuries got worse very quickly. She died earlier this evening. I'm so, so very sorry and please…"

I don't hear the rest of the message. My arm drops to my side. Mark's voice continues somewhere in the distance, lost in the darkness around me.

-

"Mum?"

"Hello? Who is it?"

"Mum, it's me Michelle."

"Michelle? Your voice doesn't sound the same. Are you okay?"

This is what I didn't say:

"No Mum. No, I'm not okay. You don't recognise my voice because I've been crying. Why have I been crying? Because a lady that was kinder to me than you ever were has just died. It was an accident. A stupid, pointless accident and now she's gone. Now she's not there when I needed someone, something constant in my life. Is this something that'll keep happening to me? Is this something that I will just have to get used to? I can't have people continuing to die around me Mum. What's the point in getting to know someone, to love them, if they just leave? If everyone just… leaves. And you don't recognise my voice because you don't call me. You don't come to see me. Even after everything that has happened you don't check on me or ask if I'm okay… you don't even try to see me and *not* ask questions but at least *help* me fill my time… this endless void of fucking time. It was *his* mother who comforted me after what happened. She had her own grief to deal with and yet she was there for me more than you were. My own mother! If only you knew what had happened. What I've done. I know I let you down, I know I'm a disappointment, I know I'm not the fucking doctor or surgeon or medical whatever that I went to university to be, but …"

This is what I did say:

"Sorry. Wrong number."

It's much easier for the both of us to believe that.

-

I walk the long way home from my meeting. It's raining. I don't care.

How can she be dead?

It was just an accident. Didn't the hospital say she'd be out soon? I didn't want to contact the hospital myself. The idea of dialling that number, seeing those rooms inside my head, hearing his voice panicked on the phone, being told... being told...

I stop walking. I close my eyes.

Hadn't her son *just* arranged to come and see her? I could already feel my head getting heavy under the weight of thoughts, questions, anger. I knew people would be looking at me, wondering who I was, if I was okay, if they should try and help me. I knew I was zigzagging across the street, probably not making much sense when I muttered apologies to people I bumped into. But my head... I could feel that tension, the lead weight, coming back into and onto and over my head. It laughs, snaps its fingers, enjoys it...

I am squeezing and scratching my wrist but I don't care. This is a kind of intoxication that drink never gives. This self-induced pain is thrilling. It feels wrong to do it in public, voyeuristic, knowing that I am making my wrist red and raw and sore as people walk past. The sharp twinges help to pull attention away from how awful I feel: Billy, people leaving me, how useless and pointless I really am. Why bother going to a grief counselling session only to be told someone else you care about has kicked the bucket? How can she just be dead? I can't handle this, I can't handle the disappointment of losing someone that I spent time with, cared about, invested in – "invested" – the word appears before me... bright, dashed and quickly fading in the night, the way a child writes words with a sparkler at a Bonfire... is that how I see people? Is that how they see *me*? Something to view with the same trepidations as with a business model, a business partner: the risks, the challenges, that you need to put something in to get something out? I know I am reeling and try to stop the spinning thoughts from getting worse. I keep hold of my wrist, for balance, for something tangible to help me walk and get home. I try to pause for a moment to complete my breathing exercises. But it's dark. But it's raining. But it's cold. I want to get home and drink. I want a fucking drink.

I turn in the street, turn again. I try to get my bearings, but the rain is hard and sharp, and it cuts across my face. I catch my reflection in a shop window and I look like I'm drowning standing up. Dishevelled, alone. Then the twinge of my wrist, tight from being held in a vice like grip, sizzles up at me when some droplets of rain hit the exposed skin under my jacket. In the brief shootings of pain, I see an arm around my back, lips on my neck, but they're not Billy's and suddenly my stomach feels weighed down again, heavy. No one cares. No one's looking. No one-

"Michelle? Michelle! Are you okay?"

I turn around and see a figure approaching me, holding a newspaper over their head for cover from the lashing rain. I can't make out who it is.

"Michelle? Hey, what are you doing stood in the rain?"

Tony. Fucking typical.

"I... I'm on my way back from..." I stammer.

"Bloody hell mate, you look freezing. Are you okay? Do you want to come inside and dry off?"

"Tony? How did you know it... how did you see me?"

He takes a moment to answer; he seems unsure about what I've said – what *did* I say?

"I was taking in the menus and stuff from the outside tables and I just spotted you... standing there."

He doesn't say anything else. He doesn't need to. It hangs there for a few seconds, this acknowledgement of how much of a mess I am. I can see my tipsy self of just a few weeks ago bashing into him again, slurring something embarrassing. I can't stay here and talk to him. I can't go inside, get dry and warm, make small talk with him. My wrist is hissing at me and telling me to go home.

"I... I'm fine. I just need to get home before I.... say something I shouldn't... I can't see you again like this..."

Without looking back or saying anything else, I quickly dash across the street. I don't turn around once the whole way home, but I replay the conversation over and over in my head.

"...see you again"

The panic in the sentence floats in front of me like the steam rising from the pavement.

"...see you again"

The words shout up at me from my wrist, *"...see you again"*, and mock me for being so incapable of talking to another person. The words yell at me from the rain that is still crashing down, *"...see you again!"*, and spits scornfully for even trying to talk to another man who isn't Billy. The words slink down my skin like ice cold rainwater, *"...see you again"*, telling me how pointless my life is, a seasick nausea, that I should just go inside and do to myself whatever it takes to make sure no will ever *"...see you again"*. Because what's the point of anything else? Even Meredith is fucking dead.

I slam the front door shut. I feel the whole building shake. Under my shoe I can see part of an envelope, my drenched and muddy shoeprint dirtying the now recognisable handwriting. I bend over and hold it up. Parts of my name and address are covered in brown sludge. I turn it over and see a message: "Email me back this time." I can feel my face contort in rage, not fear or shock, but pure anger. I want to scream at whoever this person is who thinks their stupid, middle of the road, will-never-be-a-bestseller writing can make demands like that. Who do they think they are? Don't they know what I am going through? I feel my hands trembling, my fingers twitching... to email them in outrage or to call Jenni in a crackling, sobbing voice or to storm into the kitchen and crack open that bottle of wine... to no longer just look at it, pick it up and feel strong for not tasting it, but damn well knock the bottle back and enjoy every single drop.

I honestly couldn't tell you how long I stood there for in the darkness, in the damp night. *Stand here and just let yourself drown*, the voice says to me. It laughs.

My brain is on fire.

-

It's something we have to talk about. I can't keep ignoring it. Neither can you, Billy says.

Jesus, Billy. I swear, if you're planning some sort of intervention I will kill you, I say.

You're dreaming. You're dreaming if you think this isn't becoming a problem, Billy says.

Oh go back to Donna... go and have another one of your little chats about me with her, I say.

Billy puts both his hands down on the kitchen table, and just stares at me.

-

My head thunders. Objects blur, out of place. Slowly, like painful molasses, last night sinks in: starting at the very top of my head and then trickling down to my forehead, behind my eyes and then wrapping around the base of my skull. The foggy sensation of a hangover: sleepy, almost warm in its approach, dry inside the mouth. I open my eyes and rub my face with both hands. Maybe I ate something past its sell by date – *'undigested beef'* wafts into my mind from an English lesson years ago... Perhaps I've picked up a cold from someone at work. The patients, like young children, always forget to cover their mouths when they sneeze. But this isn't a cold. My head aches in response to the frantic, erratic panic of the evening.

My brain had been on fire.

And I know this feeling by now. Drowsy and slow to start after something like last night, when my head seems to buckle under the pressure of anxiety and that heavy metal plate crushes down and down inside my skull until I just need to, have to, sleep. It gets to a point where I can't untangle my thoughts and I just have to stop – to lie down, not talk, try not to think, and sleep engulfs me. How long did I stand in the hallway for? I picture the wet footprints on the carpet. The mark on the wall where a clock used to be. I know I'll need painkillers to get me through the day. I don't want to go to work but I want to find out what happened to Meredith. *'undigested beef'*... maybe I'm being visited by my own Christmas Ghost. Maybe I deserve to be. Maybe her son will stop by to speak to the staff who cared for her. Maybe he won't. Maybe.

I need a shower. I need coffee. I need to slowly plan my day. A to-do list. I *can* be.

I stumble out of bed, head downstairs, and catch my wrist on the end of the banister. The memory of Tony bursts suddenly in front of my eyes. I stop at the bottom of the stairs. Pain, guilt, dread just flood over me.

'You're a bloody embarrassment.' The voice.

What Tony must think of me... stood in the dark, in the rain, staring at myself, looking like an abandoned pet. Just *wait* until Donna hears about this from Tony. I can hear the conversation, worried quick statements about "She looked so confused", "She was just stood there", "I'm surprised no one else stopped to helped her", "Do you think she needs to go back to the doctor?" I rub my face again, shake my head to try and get rid of any and all thoughts of last night, and drag myself into the kitchen.

It is then that I see the open wine bottle.

The lid is on the countertop. There's no wine glass though. I approach the bottle with caution, as though nearing an unexploded mine. I stop just short of it and peer over into the sink. No wine glass there either. I inspect the bottle and make out the level of wine at the neck; if I did drink anything then it was a sip at most. I am on the verge of tears, whether grateful or scared tears, I can't tell. Quickly, I pick up the lid, screw it back on and place the bottle on the wine rack. I step away, hands by my sides. I feel as though I have just safely defused a bomb and I'm waiting, waiting for the inevitable explosion after cutting the wrong wire. My heart is racing. I can feel my pulse. I keep my eyes on the bottle of wine as I start to move over to the kettle, click, and take a mug from the cabinet, clink, and close the fridge door after taking some milk, thud, pour in some milk, splash. I eye it like an enemy, like a despicable foe. I can't remember opening the bottle. I'm certain I went straight to bed and crashed out. I remember being irate from the letter. I can't remember reading it though - maybe I got drunk on one sip of red wine and tore through the letter, emailed back an aggressive retort at four in the morning.

Just to put my mind at ease I dash to the front door (envelope still there, unopened) and check my phone (no messages or emails, sent or received). I flick through my handbag and my purse... nothing seems to be have been moved or taken. I breathe a sigh of relief. But it's short lived and stilted. I genuinely don't understand how the wine bottle got opened during the night.

-

I shower and dress. I ignore the unopened letter for now, not picking it up on my way out of the house. It can wait and he can wait. Walking down the main street, I send Jenni a short email letting her know that another letter has arrived. This postal submission stunt is starting to grate. It's more than I need right now. I'll wait and see what Jenni chooses to do about it. The traffic lights change, and I'm forced to wait before I can cross the road; that's when I get another short flashback of last evening: Tony, the rain, my stuttering. My fingers tap my waist, in beat to a decision: *for* on one leg, *against* on the other. I imagine two versions of Donna on my shoulders.

The bar hasn't opened yet for breakfast, but the door is partly open. Perhaps he's waiting for a delivery. I step inside and the smell of food and drink, that scent of meals and alcohol that seeps into the frames of all pubs, welcomes me. I've had so many good times here. My fingers trace a table where Billy, Donna and I once played cards, laughing into the night. I remember kissing him by the pool table. Tony appears from behind the bar. He looks shocked for a second, and then his face splits into a smile.

"Michelle. Morning mate. How are you feeling?"

The question, although well intended, embarrasses me immediately. It implies that I haven't been well, but when I shamefully recall last night I am certain I *didn't* look at my best... He comes around the bar and walks over to me.

"I was a bit worried when I saw you last night. You were just stood in the rain."

A shiver runs down my neck. Suddenly it feels wrong being here. I shouldn't be here again. *'No you shouldn't. Slut.'*

"Yeah, I..." I brush my hair back, feel the urge the grab my wrist, "I wasn't really myself, I'll be honest. I think I was just a bit... all over the place. I'd just had some bad news."

"Have you got a few minutes? Do you want a tea or a coffee? Just a quick catch up?" He seems genuinely interested in talking. It's sweet, and I feel a small grin start to form. But it is matched with a throb than beats under the skin of my wrist. Words circle my mind telling me how dangerous this is, how all these problems started because of conversations like this. I blink. I *can't* let this control me. I keep the grin held, frozen. The clock over the bar lets me know I have some time before work starts. I really should put the clocks back up around the house.

"Sure" I say, *'You shouldn't be here'* it says.

"So how's the business going?" I say. *'Don't flirt. It's embarrassing'* it says.

"Really well. *Really* well actually. It's a great location. It's picked up around here in the last few years hasn't it? New schools and houses. It's just a busy little place now which is great for all us businesses. There's always a lot to do but I can't complain."

I forgot that Tony has a tendency to meet your eye and then look up and away for moments as he speaks to you. He always seems to talk to his fringe. His own nervous tic. *'How's the wrist?'* it says. I jolt with a memory of his arm around me.

"And what about you? How's your agency going?" I falter a little and he says; "Oh, sorry. That was a stupid question."

"No, no," I say, putting my hand up, "The publishing business? Erm…" I laugh a little, "it's not being run by me at the moment. The main point of contact is the office space we rent across town. I mean, we only ever went there to meet with clients; Billy and I were often so busy it was easier just to work from home. But Jenni has stepped in. She's been great."
'Because you're nothing but shit,' it says.

"Jenni?" he asks.

"Jenni, Billy's sister. She's taken over for a little bit. *(Liar. You're never going back.)* She's been great." I hope he can't hear my other voice while I talk to him. I grab my wrist for balance even though I'm sat down.

"Ah that's good of her. Is it busy? I mean does she have her own job too?"

"Yeah. She's just been away for a conference this week actually. I won't lie, I don't know *exactly* what she does," I try a laugh again - *Don't laugh. You don't deserve to* – and a sharp pain shoots through my head. *'Please, please stop,'* I ask it, myself. "But, she's been a great help," I feel I'm repeating myself, "we're not taking on any new clients at the moment, not until I decide to go back full time, but she has some general stuff to oversee for me, so I can't thank her enough. She'll be back in town in a week or so hopefully to catch up properly."

"Well I'm glad you're thinking of going back to it. You were good at it."

"How do you know?"

"Hey, I *read*! I read that one you guys published."

"That *one*?" I mock. I am trying. I am trying to hold a conversation, despite the dull ache inside my head that will not dissipate.

"Yeah, that one about the woman who gets stuck in an elevator? She only has the intercom to use for help and finds out that the person she's speaking to on the other end knows more about her than they initially let on. Like... they're not the building's caretaker or something but they know her somehow? Her mother, maybe?"

"Who she thought was dead. Yeah. *The Woman in the Lift*. It sold well for us." I remember what was written in one of Andy's letters about the copycat titles of most novels these days. He was right.

"Well, I liked it. Even if it seems I can't remember it very well!"

"It's popular fiction. It doesn't set the world on fire."

"But people read it and talked about it. I saw the writer on a chat show."

He asks me about where I'm working now. I feel guilty for having forgotten about Meredith for a few minutes.

"It's just for now. I needed something to keep me busy. And I like working with people, and it's nearby. I just... I needed to get away from our business for a little bit."

The word 'our' hangs between Tony and I. It hovers as a reminder of who I have been in this bar with, the home I have just left, who I really wish I was sat having morning coffee with. When Tony starts chatting again, offers me another coffee which I decline as I really do have to get to work, and he greets a waitress who has arrived for her shift, I remember that yes, Tony is kind, but that Tony can't be anything more. I can't let him be anything more. I don't want him to be, and he hasn't been.

This I repeat to myself. *He hasn't been.*

I know Donna just wants me to move on, be less anxious around new people, around men. But looking at Tony now, I realise that I can't date or even think about another man in that way. *'You need to leave,' it says.*

"It was my fault," I say. "What happened. To Billy. It was my fault."

Tony doesn't move, doesn't come closer or put a hand on mine. He doesn't need to make a gesture to show me he is listening. He just lets me continue talking and say what I need to. I'm not sure why exactly I feel the need to say this right now, at this moment, but it feels right somehow, almost cathartic.

"He was coming to see me. I'd been away at a publishing conference for a few days and on the journey home I fell ill. I was rushed straight to hospital *(Lying bitch lying bitch)* I was in the hospital for... and he rushed from work and... he didn't see it coming..." *'Because your lies got him knocked over,' it says.*

My wrist throbs.

"...see you again."

Tony continued to hold a distance between us that didn't feel neglectful or cold but respectful, calm. Not pressuring me. I dabbed my eyes.

"It's just the sheer randomness of it all. You can't plan for anything like that. With an illness you can look ahead and know what could happen, where you might be in a few years but with this... with what ... and he was coming to see me because I..." I looked up, trying to stop anymore tears from falling, from incriminating myself, from saying what the real *truth* was – why Billy was rushing to see me that day. I blinked. I need to hold it together. "Fuck, this is just what you need," I dab my eyes again. I smile at him. I grapple for something different to say and talk about. "Are you seeing anyone at the moment?"

"What?" Tony can't hide his surprise.

I have no idea why I asked him that.

"Sorry. That's none of my business. I don't know why on earth I just asked that!" I say by way of an apology.

He moves awkwardly on his chair.

"I've been on a few dates. Nothing major though."

"Well, dating some is good at least." I'm surprised at how this news makes my stomach feel. "Anyone we know?"

"No. She's just come in here a few times. More so recently. Samantha. She's nice. Travels for work quite a lot, so it's nothing serious." He pauses. "Listen, Michelle. I can see you're upset. Don't go into work today. You look tired. Stay here even, just hang out."

"It's nothing Tony. Really, don't worry. It's nothing. You don't need this. And I need to get to work. I'll be fine."

I thank him for the coffee. He walks me to the door and waves me out, asking me to come back anytime, perhaps for another morning chat when I feel like it. There's no pressure there, no ulterior motive from him, I can sense it. That makes everything worse. I am a terrible person. *'You're a whore. You're fucking disgusting. Go - go see the plaque next to the bar. It should be a red lettered A.'*

Tony goes back inside.

My wrist, my wrist, my wrist.

"*...see you again.*"

Billy's face bullets through my mind's eye.

'You killed a baby. Tell him. Tell him!'

My wrist bursts with pain.

-

At least you haven't cut yourself.

-

There is a police car outside of the care home. Lizzie is at the front desk.

"Oh, it's just so odd Michelle. I'm sure you'd be allowed in though. I told them you'd be in after ten."

I asked what had happened that meant a police car was needed.

"It's Meredith's room. You should probably just walk down and see for yourself. Are you okay, by the way? I know she was one of your patients."

I mumble something like "I'm fine" as I walk through the main hall and communal room, not really seeing who is in there playing backgammon or watching TV, and head straight to Meredith's room. I see Mark standing just inside the door and when I get closer, I see there are two policemen inside. It takes me a minute to recognise this is actually Meredith's room. All her belongings are strewn over the floor: her flowery dresses have been tossed around and dragged out of her cupboard, shoes kicked over the carpet; books and pages from a newspaper just left loose over her bed and chair; each drawer pulled open, contents hanging out. I must have the wrong room. This is the room of someone else.

"What's happened?" I manage to ask.

"We were called here about an hour ago," one policeman said, not necessarily to me, just to the situation in general.

"It was one of the cleaners. They reported it to the front desk and we decided it was best to call the police," Mark said.

"Has there been some kind of break in?"

"It could be," the same policeman replies, "but it could also have been one of the patients here. You don't lock the doors to the rooms do you?"

"No," Mark replied.

"Has anything been taken?"

"I was hoping you might be able to help us with that, Michelle." I turned to Mark. "You worked with Meredith the most, would you be able to tell if something was missing?"

"I... I can try. I don't know what anyone would *want*. I mean... she was just..."

"Anything you can do," the same police officer said. "Just be careful not to move too much around, okay?"

"Sure. I'll have a look around."

The officers and Mark step outside. I could hear them talking about the rooms, who has keys and who doesn't, whether the windows are ever opened, visitor logs and other things. My eyes roamed over the chaos. Who would do this? Why would someone want to tear apart the bedroom of an old lady? She had only just passed away... I hadn't even really had time to think about that, to grieve a little, and now her earthly possessions, her memoires, were scattered like pieces of a dropped jigsaw. Surely this was a misunderstanding. Surely this was just one of the other elderly people here having got confused and angry and... I couldn't make sense of it. I picked up the odd dress and coat, folded the newspaper pages together to make the room look less chaotic. Maybe I didn't know her as well I hoped I did. The room looked off kilter. It wasn't just because of the items that had been thrown around but more to do with the feel of the room itself. The angles all felt wrong, invaded and off centre. One wall looked longer than another, the corners where they met seemed slanted, the floor felt at once both on an incline and decline. I had the sudden sickly sensation of being seasick. Warm and nauseous.

"Michelle, sorry to interrupt." Mark's voice was gentle. "Anything?"

I turned to face him, stood in the middle of the debris. Shipwreck. "Nothing that I can see. I'm sorry. It's too much of a mess."

"What can you tell me about Mrs Lullin?" The same police officer stood just inside the room again, now poised with a pen and pad. It was almost like something from a novel I'd work on; I'd tell my writer not to be so old fashioned, surely a modern-day policeman wouldn't make notes that way.

"I've told them that Meredith had just had an accident. That she," here, Mark avoided eye contact with me, "passed away last night. Her son arrived just in time to see her at the hospital."

"Anything else out of the ordinary lately?"

"Well," I began, trying to ignore the sensation of being at sea, the room's angles changing, "she'd been getting more confused of late. She'd needed calming down a few nights ago after getting angry."

"Angry? Because of what?"

"She had dementia. It's something that happens. Getting confused and stressed."

"Did the patient say anything to anyone? Did she tell anyone what had got her so worked up?"

I felt my fist clench at his ignorance. The people here didn't just get 'worked up'. They were old, and ill, and people, and needed care and time and support. They needed better than this.

"I spoke to her when she'd had time to settle down. She couldn't really remember much, she just seemed confused. She did mention though that someone had been in her room."

The officer raised his head raised. "Who? Did she say?"

"I wrote it up in my notes at the end of my shift as we're meant to do. It's all there in her care file. You can just ask at the front desk for them."

"I will, thank you," the officer replied. "Did she say who this person was?"

"She just said 'he' at first, and then 'Sam'. Nothing else. But to be honest she could have been imagining her husband, her son. We'd only been talking about them the day before." Without thinking I turned and pointed at the set of drawers. "I did find though..."

"Yes, Miss...?"

"It's Michelle." I walked over to the drawers, all yanked open like jagged teeth. "The other day I found a note, or part of a note, poking out of the drawer here," I tapped the top of the cabinet. "It had been ripped in half though. I could only make out a few letters and who it was from. It was from someone named Sam. I presumed it was a family member."

"Is that all? Anything else?"

"No. I don't suppose that's useful. Sorry."

"Well, it is common for the people who stay here to keep letters, cards, keepsakes like that to remind them of family and friends. It's probably just a letter from a family member." I nodded my head at Mark. He was right. "Her son's name is Matthew I believe, but I'll double check. When the room is properly tidied then who knows... maybe the rest of it will turn up."

"Are you going to be looking through the room?"

The officer had put away his notepad and pen, looking like he was ready to end this part of his time here. "Most likely yes, just in case something turns up. We'll have to look over some security footage too." He was talking to Mark now. "We might need to interview the staff here last night as well. Just to cover all bases. But I'm sure it will turn out to be nothing malicious." Just before walking down the corridor, he asked Mark for the contact details of Meredith's son. Then, out of nowhere, he faced me and said: "I'm sorry for your loss."

I stay for a little longer. I close my eyes and take deep breaths, calming the restless waters of the room. I know I shouldn't tidy up or move things around, but I can't stand just leaving it in this state. It seems so unfair. I don't like the idea of her memories being cast aside, broken. I haven't even been able to ask anyone yet about what happened with Meredith at the hospital. I want to ask "How? What happened? Why?" but I didn't know who to speak to, even if I should. I'm not family after all. I walk around the room a few more times and lift the odd book and photo frame. I don't know what I'm expecting to find, but I stop in my tracks when I notice something black and white, chequered, poking out from under her bureau. I bend down and pull out a crumpled crossword puzzle. It's blank, none of the clues filled in. I can't put my finger on why but it sends cold ripples through my body.

After a few minutes I head to the front desk.

Lizzie is speaking to the other police officer, the one I didn't talk to, handing him what I presume are some notes or files on Meredith, maybe some visitor logs. When he leaves I see another man standing just behind him. He smiles at Lizzie, a little emptily, takes a few pieces of paper as well and heads out the front doors with the police.

"Who was that?" I ask Lizzie.

"That was Mrs Lullin's son. Poor guy. He arrived just in time to see her last night at the hospital before she…" she trailed off. Everyone is so afraid of death. Everyone who hasn't experienced it, anyway. "And now he's turned up just in time to see the police."

"What happened to her? To Meredith. Do you know?"

"Not really Michelle, no. You'd need to ask whoever was on call here last night. We were the first point of call, after her son obviously, but he was already there. I think it was just her fall."

"But she seemed okay at first. Mark said she'd be out and probably just needed a hip replacement."

"Maybe it was too much for her. Everyone here is so frail. A fall is so dangerous for them."

I could tell she was trying to be thoughtful, sensitive in her own way, but she wasn't helping. I thought about trying to catch her son before he left the home, but I thought it might seem a little strange. I didn't know him. I had no right to go and ask him questions about his mother's death.

I worked the rest of the day. Tidying and serving. Making small talk without really paying attention. I walked home, taking desperate gasps of fresh air, trying to clear the oppressive rocking boat sensation still lodged in the back of my throat; the overpowering sensation of illness that seemed to permeate Mrs Lullin's old room.

-

"So you didn't manage to properly see him then?"

"No, I mean it would've been a bit weird for me to start questioning him about his mum. She'd only just died."

"You could've asked him about the note. Whether it was from him or not."

"Yes but he would want to know why, quite rightly, I was reading notes in his mother's room. Secondly, it's none of my business what he may have written to her about. I don't think the police were that interested anyway. They'll ask me about it again if they are."

"Was he hot?"

"Donna!"

"Not for you, for *me*!"

"Oh okay, so now I'm meant to be spotting potential suitors for you at work as well in any shop, bar, cinema I go into. Well I'm sorry but you're only likely to meet the man of your dreams at the care home if you've got a thing for octogenarians."

"They might leave me money in their will."

Donna's deadpan delivery lost none of its wit over Skype. She was the only person, apart from Billy, who could make me laugh whatever my mood. I carry my laptop, talking at the screen and Donna's slightly blurry face, from the living room to the kitchen.

"Are you okay though? I mean, about the lady that died?"

I pause. "It was a shock. And then with her room being all... I don't know. Anyway, you'll be pleased to know that I finally spoke to Tony. Twice in less than twenty-four hours, I'll have you know."

"I know. He texted me."

"What?" I say it much louder than I intend to but can't help the indignation from appearing in my voice. "How on earth do you two keep such close tabs on me? You two should just go out with each other."

"Calm down," Donna replied in a mock soothing tone, the one she knows annoys me, "he just text to say that you seemed okay. You chatted. You seemed fine. He just worries, we all do. And I know, I know," I see her put her hands up in defence, "we don't need to, but we do. Sorry. We're your friends. Guilty."

"No, no... it's nice. It is. Knowing you guys have my back. It's just... well for one, chatting to him this morning let me know I definitely *can't* have any romantic interest in anyone right now. I just can't. And honestly, I don't think I want to. I just want to... get through another month, few months, a year and... see where I am. How I'm doing."

"That's smart." I set my laptop, and Donna, down on the counter. "And you know what, it's probably healthier for you just to have another person in your life. Someone else to just hang out with."

"When I get bored with you, you mean?"

"Very funny. As if you could ever get bored of me."

"You're right though. I don't know why I was so nervous to speak to him." *'Yes, you do'* it says.

"I think that's mostly my fault. I just wanted you to speak to someone and have... it's too soon for you to date, I know that - I just don't like the idea of you being alone."

"But I'm not."

There's a beat before Donna speaks again, and I can tell the pause marks a change in the conversation; something in her breathing, in how she moves her bottom lip before speaking.

"Listen. I just wanted to apologise for what I went on about in the café the other day."

"What?"

"You know, going on about those mothers coming in with their prams and babies and all. It wasn't right."

"I don't mind. I'm used to your rants by now."

"I know," she laughs, "but that's just it. It's *another* one of my rants. I should hold my tongue sometimes. Or at least reign it in a bit."

I can't help feeling that there's more she wants to say, that she's hedging a deeper conversation.

"Donna, if I wanted you to reign in your opinions we would have lost touch as friends a long time ago. I'm just glad Jenni didn't overhear your thoughts on motherhood."

"Jesus, I know. Then she really would have a reason to hate me. Another reason, I mean."

"Your rows and debates are fine. They're good. It's what keeps my brain from turning into mush. I miss learning. I miss writing."

"Aren't you still writing some bits though?"

"If you count lazy puff pieces about the care home for magazines read by bored housewives, then yeah. It's hardly scintillating. Or what I got into this business for."

"Well, what do you *want* to write about?"

"I don't know. Just… something…" The sentence hangs there, incomplete. I don't know whether to admit how interested I am in these extracts I have been receiving. How the topics raised have intrigued me. "Just writing that means something. That gets people talking. However odd these pieces are that have been sent to me, the argument there about women, men, how girls treat each other… it's current."

"Maybe I should meet with them," I can tell by her tone that Donna is again being sarcastic, "they'd love my feminist views on motherhood."

"The thing is though what we spoke about the other day links to the type of issues this text is trying to raise. How do women see each other? Do we add to each other's social rejections? Are women sexist against women?"

"I know I can be. I don't mean to be. I think, for me, it's groups; it's groups of women that annoy me." Then Donna checks herself by quickly adding "- sometimes."

"But it goes deeper than that. I mean, just today I read an article in the newspaper about how differently men and women respond to sexual assault or harassment claims." Donna nods, sipping her tea. She doesn't offer an opinion - yet. "It said that when told about a sexual harassment claim by a woman, up to 82% of men felt more empathy for the man accused than for the female victim."

"What? Why?" Donna sounds both shocked and irritated. "What reasons did they give?"

"That," I could feel myself smiling as I spoke, "the man's advances may have been misconstrued and weren't meant to be harassment at all, just flirtatious. It's the 'Me Too' backlash. Men are afraid to give a compliment in case they get accused of assault."

"That's bullshit. You know how you can stop yourself getting accused of assault? Don't assault someone."

I laugh. "You don't need to tell me! But it's more than that… if women still criticise each other so publicly, like, I'm sorry, but slagging off mothers just for being mothers," I pause, to show I am allowing Donna a chance to give her input if she wants to, but she lets me continue, "then how on earth can we stand up and tell men what is wrong in how they treat women? Women need to be kinder to other women."

The conversation hovers between us, over the electricity connecting us. I can almost see the sparks, feel something in my veins. I am passionate about this topic, I realise; *more* than I realised before. Do I have these manuscript extracts to thank? Donna then does what she does best, and quickly turns the focus of the conversation. She swaps the topic back to Tony, how he's a catch for someone out there who's not me; I try to encourage Donna to ask him out, she declines but doesn't explain why; we each make another cup of tea and drink them over Skype together like an old couple. Then I tell her about the wine bottle.

"None of it had been drunk though."

"And you can't remember opening it?"

"No. Nothing."

"Anymore weird letters from writer guy? I did tell you to change your locks. Maybe he's sneaking in at night and opening wine bottles to freak you out."

"Okay, that's not helpful. And yes, I had a letter yesterday but I haven't read it yet. And no, I don't think he's creeping in at night."

"Are you going to read whatever it is he's sent? Remember, he's the postman and you are his captive audience or whatever he wrote."

"Good effort at remembering his analogy," I laugh, "but you know what, something he said made sense. I was talking to Tony today about a book he read that we published, and a lot of what's out there is very similar. A woman, a secret, a location, a fragmented narrative. I think one of the reasons I don't want to go back to work straight away is because I'm bored with it. These books that make *women* out to be unhinged or weak because of something a *man* has done to them. There's so much shame surrounding women in the media all the time, but these books, whilst *trying* to make strong female protagonists, they actually end up doing the opposite: making them drunks or addicts or unable to move on from a relationship. I want something new, something challenging. Find a new trend to get onto the shelves. Part of me feels guilty that I added to the market of women attacking each other." As a half serious after thought I add; "Maybe I have too much of a conscience for the publishing world."

There's a pause before Donna speaks. "I think that's a good thing though. It shows you care about your work. That you want a fresh voice, something new for readers." I nod. "Just please don't tell me that the 'something new' is an oddball who sends letters and emails with hidden messages in them, okay?"

"I promise."

"Are you going to read it?"

For some reason I don't tell her about the last hidden message, the wedding song. I don't tell her that another letter arrived today either, so I've actually got two to read. Or that yesterday's envelope bore a command. I know it's just an immature gripe from a frustrated writer, but I also don't want to worry Donna. She'll just panic text Tony again. And I don't need that.

"I don't know. I've messaged and emailed Jenni, so I'll probably just continue to send them to her. I followed her request and told him to email any submissions, so if he ignores that then he has no one to blame but himself if we just blank his post from now on."

"Oh yeah, I know what I meant to ask you actually. About Jenni. What was with her having those baby wipes in her bag the other day?"

"Is it really that strange?"

"Does she *have* a baby?"

"No."

"Then... facial wipes, fine. But baby wipes are very specific. Is she still... you know..."

"I think she's still struggling. Who wouldn't? She had to deliver stillborn. Remember?"

"I know. Surely though she wouldn't want any reminder of babies around her."

"Maybe having a small token, whatever it is, is how she deals. Maybe it's a left-over pack that she bought when she was pregnant - people bulk buy stuff in advance don't they."

"I guess. If it was me though I don't think I would want a reminder of what I'd lost every time I opened my purse."

"I get a reminder of what I lost every time I open *my* purse, too."

The sentence hovers somewhere within the 1s and 0s between our laptops: not grieving, not emotional, just there. A fact.

"I don't think you can ever really know how you'll deal with something like that until you've been through it. I don't think we can judge anyone for how they cope with something as traumatic as death, however it happens."

Again, no judgement. Just an opinion. I can almost hear Donna thinking.

"You're right," she sighs, "you're totally right. I know I bitch about her, but I do feel sorry for her. Your whole family have been through so much. In a way, what she went through makes me understand her choice on abortion. How *could* you agree to it when you've lost a baby?"

There's a silence. I look away from the screen for a second.

"Okay, this is getting too heavy even for me now. I can handle #youknowme but that's about it for abortion talk."

"What's that?"

"And you call yourself a feminist! It's an online movement. Women use the hashtag to let their followers know they had an abortion. It's meant to reduce the stigma of it I suppose. The idea that we all know at least one person who has had one. We all think it's this sordid thing that happens in alleyways illegally when actually the woman you've followed online for years, just liking her shoes or whatever, had an abortion and isn't as filter perfect as you think she is."

"Isn't perfect?"

"That came out wrong. This *is* heavy." A pause. "Let's just talk about boys again."

"She's been good to me. Jenni, I mean. Better than my own *mother*. You know I rang her the other night and she didn't even recognise my voice?" I turn away from the laptop to clear away my cup but can hear Donna's various expletives. That's a new topic for her to get her teeth into. "Well," I say, "it is what is it. She won't change now will she?"

"No but I thought that after Billy… if anything would make her try more…" We leave the sentiment there, both knowing it's pointless to try and make a positive out of something that never has been there.

A few minutes of more aimless chat and we say goodnight. Donna even kisses the screen before logging off. "Love you Sherry."

-

Donna is crazy, Billy says.

Crazy in a good way, though, I say.

Yes. Life would be... quieter without her around, that's for sure, Billy says.

Do you want a quiet life?, I say.

Billy just shakes his head.

-

Before I head up to bed I stop at the foot of the stairs and pick up the two unopened envelopes from Andy. I decide to read them and get them out of the way before I go to sleep, and then I'll email him, copying in Jenni, with a fresh head in the morning. I'll just say that although his writing is good and interesting in parts, I must insist that all further communication must go through the proper channels from now on as previously requested. That's fair, I decide. If I was as cutthroat as he seemed to think all editors and publishers were, I wouldn't bother even reading them, would I?

-

LETTER FOUR

I read an article once about a study carried out at a university in America. Those leading the study asked a wide range of men and women what their greatest fear and concern was.

I brought this up during a seminar. We had been studying various Margaret Atwood novels such as 'Alias Grace', 'The Handmaid's Tale' and 'Oryx and Crake', and in our discussion about feminism I thought this article and study seemed relevant. I don't usually speak up in seminars, so my lecturer happily let me have the floor for a minute. I told the group that the study's results revealed just how different men and women are from each other, and how different the social experiences were between men of different backgrounds, too. The number one fear of women in the study, no matter their colour, age or sexuality, was sexual assault and sexual harassment. Gay men said homophobic abuse. Black men and women in the study also referenced the police.

"And do you know what the top concern was from white males in the study?" I asked the group. They didn't reply. "Ridicule."

I let that hang in the air for a moment. Sexual assault. Sexual harassment. Homophobic abuse. Police brutality. And being *ridiculed*. No one in the group made much of a response. One or two girls nodded. One guy laughed. I thought it made sense in relation to the books we had been reading. Clearly no one else did. My lecturer could tell that the temperature of the room wasn't too hot for my, I presume they felt, potentially aggressive view of men. Maybe he didn't like the hot potato topic I had dared to introduce: the powerless place of women in society. I mean, how on earth did that relate to the works of Atwood? Silly me. He just thanked me for my contribution and moved straight on.

I didn't tend to go out at university. Out, as in nights out. Maybe that's because my greatest concern as a young woman was more serious than being *ridiculed*. Jesus Christ. To be honest, I never find clubs and bars that interesting and, also, the girls in my house rarely invited me. I hated that phrase when I heard it: The Girls. It instantly conjured up this image of a coven, some collective group of giggles that would only exist to wear makeup, go to clubs and flirt. I oversimplify of course but I just dislike any term that groups women together like that: the girls, my ladies, 'I'm out with the girls.' It makes my stomach churn inside. Why couldn't these idiots that I lived with do anything independently? Why did they have to be surrounded by their other clones in order to go to a bar, go shopping, even go to the toilet? It felt like it was socially unacceptable for girls to do anything on their own: American sororities, where the whole point seems to be to degrade young girls into 'wanting' to get into a house; girl groups on stage flaunting their bodies; women used as props in boxing matches; only white, thin, blonde women shown on the front of magazines, mouth slightly open to be sexually suggestive at all times. It was everywhere, it was infiltrating how men viewed women, how men felt they could treat women and how women thought they could treat themselves and others. Girls have a pack mentality, which parts of society create. Women shame other women and don't realise they are being manipulated to do so.

The girls I lived with embodied all of this, and I hated them for it.

It was a usual Saturday evening. The gaggle were pruning themselves in the bathrooms dotted around the house. I avoided the hallways, fearing running into any of the girls who would look at me like I was some sort of freakshow oddity: something to be pitied, feared and mocked in equal measure. I could see myself performing for them, but where a freakshow act would be something like an 'Armless Anita' balancing beach balls on her chest, or 'Four-Eared Francis' showing off her superhuman hearing, my performance would just be reading a book, highlighting a passage, a Pot Noodle in bed, an early night... any badly applied makeup would probably add to my freakish sideshow look. I could hear the laughing, the guffawing, the sarcastic clapping. They made me feel like an outcast, all of them. Some sort of freakishly awful girl than belonged in one of their diary entries, an anecdote to be made fun of again years later. Maybe my was greatest fear *was* ridicule after all.

Music was blaring out from all bedrooms. It seemed to me that over the years we had lived together, and perhaps with a lingering memory of housemates gone by, the house was constantly covered in a smog of perfume, hairspray and sticky fake tan that appeared to leak from the walls through cracks, like blood in a horror film. The trapped bodies inside these walls were the bodies of free thought and intelligence, empty vessels made of scent and material that girls traded in for dancing and boys at the weekend.

I was sat in my room when it happened, flicking through a newspaper, and over the yelps of laughter and squeals and battering music I heard it, clear as a bell: a knock on my bedroom door. It never happened. It took me by surprise. One of the girls, I can't remember her name (let's call her Elizabeth or Lizzie), smiled at me. I smiled back, what I could muster anyway. I thought that she'd probably just be wanting to borrow something, a phone charger.

"Hey, are you doing anything tonight?"

"Me?" I said, stupidly. Who else was here? The Ghost of University Experience's Past, perhaps.

"The girls and I were thinking, if you were free, would you like to come out with us tonight? It might be fun. I mean, it might be nice for us to do something together for once. You never really get involved in stuff we do."

Instinctively, I felt my ankle buzz. It seemed to invite me to scratch it out of irritation at what she'd just said. So much of it irked me: "The girls"; "might be fun" with the raised intonation of a question that had soaked into her from the American TV she watched; "You never really get involved" - because you never ask me, you stupid bitch.

Before I could reply though, she continued: "It's just... we're coming to the end of term and exams and everything and... I'd like you to come out with us just once," then she held her hands up as if to protect me from the night of debauchery they had planned, "even if just for one drink (raised intonation here again). Just something to say goodbye. It's not likely that we'll ever see each other again, is it?"

I looked at her for a moment and was surprised at how genuine she seemed. She said exactly what we all knew; that never in a million years would those girls want to see me again in the future, and vice versa. Why would we? 'Unless they wanted help with a job application maybe' I thought. I stopped myself, realising that I was being just as cruel in my own thoughts as I felt they were to me. Lizzie was at least trying to be kind, even if just once.

"Sure," I said. "Why not?"

I stood in front of the mirror, dried my hair and put on lipstick. It felt like the reversal of a demasking process, where I was putting one on rather than taking it off. The powder felt heavy on my skin, the colours clashed with the pale flesh they were painted across, my hair seemed to limp into a shape rather than be confidently held in one. I hated myself for enjoying it though. I hated myself for revelling in the process of making myself pretty.

The first bar we went into was rammed. It took forever to get a drink, but I tried to smile and laugh along with the few jokes I understood and even those that I didn't. The look on some of the girls' faces when I walked down the stairs to meet them at the front door was priceless: a mixture of shock to see me out of my room, surprise that I knew what makeup was, and mostly disgust that I was actually going out with them. Lizzie took my arm and guided me from the house to the taxi to the bar. She didn't really speak to me much, but at least she didn't just leave me alone like the rest did. It was as if we had never met, me and these girls, that I was a foreign exchange student tagging along for the night, and they couldn't be bothered to make conversation with me because they knew that for one: I wouldn't understand them and, two: we'd soon never see each again anyway, so what was the point? I can't say I disagreed.

I had forgotten how bright the lights of bars and clubs were at night, and how smoky they were, as if the sweat and desperation to flirt intermingled into the suffocating mist that drifted from body to body and mouth to mouth. We went from bar to bar, them all tottering in high heels, clutched together to keep warm against the chill of the evening in the slips they were wearing. I can't remember how many different bars we jumped between but somewhere between the third and sixth, I set myself a challenge: I will stay out until the end of the night. I will prove to the girls that I can be just as sociable as they are, that I can drink and dance until they surrender to fatigue. I had nothing to lose, and I didn't really care if they were impressed or not, but I wanted to have at least one night that you were *meant* to have at university... just one night when you got drunk and forgot about everything else.

I put the writing to one side. I had no idea where this was going.

The extract was again, it seemed, out of chronological order.

But what was the message here? That girls need to be nicer to other girls? That we are manipulated into wearing makeup? Not to judge a book by its cover? The danger of peer pressure?

I felt a strange sense of foreboding - that this girl's night out would not end well.

LETTER FOUR

… just one night when you got drunk and forgot about everything else. So, I bought drinks and shots, I talked to people I didn't know – my housemates and/or other girls in a bar, I couldn't tell them apart- I danced, I sweated, I refreshed my lipstick in a slanted mirror with other girls in a damp bathroom. What was I doing?

I checked my phone and the time blared up at me. I couldn't remember the last time I had seen that hour of the night- or was it morning?

"Hey, we're going to go and get some food. Do you want to -"

Before Lizzie could finish, her drink seemed to fly out of her hand and spill right across my top. She looked embarrassed, then guilty, then laughed. I laughed too. I was too drunk to be annoyed. A couple of people behind her apologised for tripping into us and quickly scurried away to another part of the club.

"Shit. I'm so sorry. My girlfriend is so bloody clumsy. Even worse when she's had a drink."

I was too busy wiping myself with tissues from my handbag to realise that Lizzie was no longer next to me. I was stood on the edge of the dancefloor by myself.

"Do you need anything?"

It took me a moment to link the voice to the person who was now stood beside me. I didn't recognise him. But then again, I hadn't recognised anyone all night, even the girls I lived with.

"Erm, no thank you. I just need to find my…" I was turning my head to try and spot someone, knowing it was pointless as I had no idea where or who the other girls really were, "… friends," I finished, pathetically.

"Can you call them?"

"Yeah, yeah. I can do." I made to go outside but almost immediately slipped on the floor, now covered in a greasy film of spilt drinks and sweat.

"Come on, I'll help you to the door. It's the least I can do."

"But *your* friends…"

"They'll be fine. I'm the sober one for night. It's my girlfriend's birthday so my gift to her is to buy her and her girlfriends all the drinks and fried food they want. And drive them safely home later. They're too cheap for a taxi."

He hooked his arm around mine and guided me to the front double doors. The chill air hit me like a wave and my stomach instantly recoiled painfully, leaving me with an awful need to vomit. Seasick and nauseous, I grabbed onto the wall.

"Hey, hey," he lowered me slowly to the steps, "there you go. Sit other there. Hey, I'll go and get you some water. You ring your friends. I'll be back in a minute… what's your name?" I muttered something and let my head loll against the wall. I had never felt so awful in my entire life. At least when I got drunk in my bedroom I was already in bed, so could comfortably slip into a drunken, warm sleep. Here, I was freezing and tired, my face felt stiff with melted and reapplied makeup. I felt exposed. I had no sense of time, and after what could have been thirty swirling seconds or thirty dozing minutes I felt a hand on my back, rubbing the top of my spine and shoulders and saw a plastic cup of water being held in front of me. I sipped at it, trying not to vomit. I remember thinking to myself that there was a reason that girls like me don't go out on nights like this.

I had come back downstairs, reading the whole time whilst making a cup of coffee. I felt like I was reading a confession or warning of some sort. What was going to happen to this girl? Or was that the point; are we so programmed to think the worst of drinks and girls and men and the horror this combination might lead to? Would this story buck the trend and have a modern-day knight in shining armour help this poor girl?

I flicked through the pages I had left to read, trying to skim and see the outcome. I didn't want this girl to come to harm. Sure, she was flawed and a little self-righteous, but she was innocent. I didn't want anything to happen to her. I wanted to know that she was protected. Safe.

Whatever my thoughts were about the writer, he had me invested.

LETTER FOUR

I remember thinking to myself that there was a reason that girls like me don't go out on nights like this. All my life I have felt like that one last crossword clue that you cannot seem to solve: an irritation, but a problem that can easily be screwed up, thrown away and forgotten about. Even now, when I'm reflecting on that night and everything that happened afterwards... I wished I had just listened to myself and realised that this was a world I didn't belong in. Drinks and dancing and trying to be part of a group.

After that night, the girls in the house went back to ignoring me. Lizzie, or whatever she was called, acted as if I didn't exist, and what she said when she invited me out turned out to be true; we never saw each other again, not even whilst we still lived under the same roof. Sometimes I wonder if it was all a set-up, if it was all part of some joke to get me drunk to have a boy talk to me, to let me know once and for all how out of place I was in that world. Deep down I know that's not the case, I tell myself that that isn't what happened because if it is... if it was... I don't I think would ever trust anyone again.

It comes back to me in snapshots, like a camera reel that has several photographs missing. Throughout the whole thing - what else do I call it? Do I give it a name? I feel that if I *do* then that almost gives what happened a power over me, an entity that continues to be real. As it was happening, I remember thinking about where Lizzie went to, how bad I felt that she'd probably had such a rubbish night with me being there. Maybe it was just a way for me ignore what was happening, but I told myself that I had to get through it so I could see her again and apologise to her for ruining her night.

I never knew his name, the boy who took me outside. I never found out if it was him who folded my jumper under my head and left me on that bench, just down the street from the club. I didn't know, as he pushed me against the wall behind the club, if the water he'd brought me had something in it. I didn't know, as he forced me down onto my back on the floor of the alley, if he really had a group of friends to look after or if he just patrolled bars for drunken girls whom he could charm. I can't remember, as he pulled my dress down, my underwear down, let me keep my shoes on for some reason, if he whispered my name or something more disgusting in my ear. I can't remember, as he dragged me back up to a standing position and led me to the front of the bar, how he passed if off to passers-by: drunken girl, him the knight caring for me; girlfriend had one too many, him the boyfriend dealing with it yet again; trashed youth asking for it, him the man whose right it was to take what was on offer.

I left my body, I think, as it happened. I was in a drunken haze of vodka fumes and sweat and the acid scent of vomit still on my top and in my mouth and I remember standing to the side of him, outside of my own body, in the alleyway, and cringed at how my lips and tongue must have tasted and smelt as he forced himself in and around me. That's what I was embarrassed about: how *my* body was possibly offending *him*.

I imagined seeing myself as part of a circus act, one of those girls who gets cut up into pieces and shoved around into smaller and smaller parts inside boxes. It's all a trick of light and sleight of hand and I hoped, prayed to myself and for myself as I watched helplessly, that this was all an illusion too, it was all a storey and a trick that I would snap out of. That I would wake up and it would be nothing but a dream. For the nights and nights and months and months that followed, every time I closed my eyes I would see rotating boxes, body parts being cut and sliced and moved around from one square to another, my body, not whole but now torn and ripped, being transferred and shipped off against its will to somewhere else, for someone else to use. My mind would drift away in the middle of conversations and lectures and phone calls as I replayed that night over and over and stacked boxes upon colourful boxes and imagined seeing my naked body separated into the many parts that that man had cut me into.

I could never be whole again.

When I got home no one seemed to have even noticed that I hadn't been with them at the end of the night. The house was quiet, silent with hangovers. I crept into bed, my arms and hands still dirty from what I could only imagine was the filth of the alley floor, my back feeling as though it was laced with cuts from the rough concrete or the stiff wooden bench I had been left on. Over what felt like hours, I ran my hands slowly, gingerly, over my body. I felt clumps of grit under each fingernail. I flinched at bruises in between my thighs. I nauseously swallowed, clenched my teeth, at the dried blood inside my underwear. Each of these parts of my body were just that: parts. In the shower I scrubbed at one box, my legs, then another box, my privates, another box, my arms, another box, my breasts and so on... until I looked in the mirror, squares of glass, and saw a body blown apart, boxed off into separate pieces of flesh.

I never told the friends I didn't have. I couldn't tell my parents. My housemates never asked. I was too ashamed to speak out about it.

Anna

-

I have to stop there.

So many thoughts rush through my mind. I shower to give myself a break, have a breather from what I've just read. I have images dashing around inside my head - jagged, cold thoughts. Some from the story - some from... It's too much right now. As I get up, I knock my cup of coffee over. It's stone cold as it seeps into the carpet. It must be past midnight by now but I feel that I need to read the final section and then in the morning I can decide what to do next. Do I contact Jenni again? Email Andy back? Wait and see if something else drops through my front door?

I can't face the next letter just yet.

But the reality of the text is that it is describing something that happens to women, *and* men, every single day. I realise that this book could be important, could raise a real issue of women supporting women, of women feeling ashamed of the abuse they suffer. Part of me though feels uneasy, seeing this writing as being something to be sold. Isn't that what Andy was trying to say, that the media we buy into just perpetuates the horrors we do to each other? It dawns on me that I just took for granted it was a *man*, Andrew - but what if it is a woman, and this is not just *a* story but *her* story. This is her truth that she wants people to know about. These are her letters, her cries for help that may have been ignored for... years?

Before starting the next letter, I get out the notes I have made when reading so far. I read over the list of errors and the phrases they have created:

Here be liars.

Read each name.

Babies are lives too.

Can't help falling in love.

It is the third that now strikes me in the gut: *Babies are lives too*. I spread the fourth letter out on the bed, and I see the handwritten note on the envelope: *Email me back*. Perhaps it wasn't a childish moan at all, but a cry for help... a reply just to show that someone has listened to them. I swallow hard against an uncomfortable feeling that this poor girl, who might have turned what happened to her in real life into a narrative, a warning story, didn't feel she could tell anyone at the time but, when she felt ready to open up about it, was ignored time and time again by publisher after publisher. Her diary entries, her stream of consciousness, her truths... tossed into a bin and not even acknowledged. I remember something from the first email: *It begins to feel pretty empty*. I worry I was too hasty to see only the bad in what this person was trying to do.

I skim through the fourth letter a few times and find the familiar simple errors, and write them out:

I never find clubs and bars that interesting, should be *found*; the tense was wrong for the sentence.

I'm the sober one for night and *Sit other there*, both spoken by the boy in the club; *the* was missing and *other* should be *over*.

Found the over or, *Find the other*.

Neither made sense so far. I reread the last section and found:

it was all a storey, which needed to be corrected to the homophone *story*.

Find the other story.

"Find the other story."

I say this out loud. Was it something that would come later in *this* story? Was the girl, Andy, the writer, referring to another story they had written? She mentioned in her email that she'd written short stories... was one of them connected to this?

I pick up the letter that arrived yesterday, given how late it was now, and open it. Only one sheet this time. As much as I was engaged in the writing and invested now in the character, the possibility that this was based on a real event, that the writer was revealing something that had happened to them, made me uneasy about wanting to read more.

I unfold the single piece of paper.

LETTER FIVE

Of all the boxes I cut myself into, there was one that I didn't find until a few weeks after that night. My dreams were plagued with pictures of bloody saws and blood-stained wooden crates, parts of my body slashed and ripped and crammed into each one. It was now less of a harmless circus act, a fantasy that I had created during that moment to see me through it as safely as possible: it was now violent and cruel and aggressive. I sketched image after image of limbs torn from each other, doodling all over my lecture notes with bloody body parts. God knows what anyone would have thought if they had seen it. I don't really care if they did.

It wasn't until I realised I hadn't had my period that what happened that night wasn't over. I had another box inside of me that I hadn't been able to reach and scrub at, hadn't even known was there; a box that I hadn't separated myself into as I had tried to compartmentalise the rest of my body. A box I had had no choice over.

Abortion literally sucks the life out of you. It kills your whole day. A little guillotine humour there – but, what else can you do at a time like that?

Everything about it is sterile. The nurses try to be kind but just make you feel worse. The rooms smell of bleach. The walls are the colour of illness, a dull yellowy cream that looks like they have a permanent cover of grease. The waiting room, the aftercare room, the hallways... I flicked through magazines, tried to complete a half-finished crossword. Ironically one of the answers was *pregnancy*: 'One across, nine letters. A nine-month gestation period for women'.

In the waiting room women smile at each other in the vague hope that someone will hold their hand and tell them that what they are doing is right. But no one said that to me, nor I to them. The air is heavy with shame. We breathe each other's guilt.

The flight back home was unbearable. I hated myself for having the gall to even *try* to take my mind off what I done with magazines and airport coffee. I saw the 'Anything to Declare' desk and wanted to scream and shout and yell about what I had just put my body through.

What *I* had put *my* body through. Not him and what he had done to me and my body. Not him and what he had made happen inside my body.

What *I* had put *my* body through.

I didn't see the ugliness inside that thought for many years. It haunts me still.

My life before that day seems to be stuck in amber, it is a memory and passage of time that I have no real connection to. Like the circus act I fantasied about, my life was cut into different sections. Before and after. Pre and post. Then and what happened next.

I hate myself now so much that I actually use the date as my phone's passcode. Some people have birthdays or anniversaries. I use the date of my abortion.

It's self-harm every time I swipe.

Tri deug, a naoi.

Annabel.

-

I am numb. I stare at the pages before me. I hear nothing. My mind rolls around emptily. I try to make myself believe that this isn't possible. I feel my eyes start to wander around my bedroom as if searching for an answer, an explanation... anything that I can hold onto. A grasp on reality.

I don't need to scan through this letter for the hidden message. I know it straight away.

Tri deug and *a naoi*. The Gaelic for *thirteen* and *nine*.

Thirteenth of September.

The date of the girl's abortion.

And mine.

-

We can try again. Whenever we feel ready. Whenever you do, Billy says.

Maybe it's a sign, I say.

Don't say that, Billy says.

I kill every plant I buy. Why would I be able to keep a kid alive? I say.

Billy makes to take a step towards me, but seems to think better of it, and stays still.

-

I stumble, dazed, room to room. My eyes are tired from reading, from tears, from something else... I can't tell. My head is heavy. The inside of it hurts but not with a headache or impending migraine, but with a feeling I know all too well. I should try to brace myself for what's coming. But I can't. I don't have the energy to. I have no idea how many minutes pass, how long I wander from kitchen to living room to hallway to the foot of the stairs and back around again, looping, looping like a mobius strip of confused thoughts. Trapped. I stand in the middle of the kitchen and cry.

I just cry.

They turn into sobs, loud and ugly, and then transform in silent open-mouthed choking. A broken mannequin, bent out of shape, thin and twisted. Everything seems to slow down, a freeze frame: my eyes blink slowly, my mouth opens and closes as if filled with quicksand, my shoulders are stooped forward, my head lolls, pulled down with weights.

-

Are you ready? We need to leave in twenty minutes or so, Billy says.

I'm just jumping into the shower, I say.

Hurry up! The taxi's booked so that we get to the party on time. Traffic is a nightmare this time of night, Billy says.

I just need to stand under the water for a minute or two, I say.

Billy closes the bedroom door.

-

I find myself in the bathroom. I stand sideways to the mirror, pull up my top. I run my hand over the lower part of my stomach, just above the top of my trousers, and rub my palm from side to side. I cup my hand where there is now a slight pouch, I can feel it and I can see it. I'm disgusting. I am hideous. *'You're fat. You're fucking fat and you're in your thirties. How on earth do you think life will ever get better for you? You had a chance at a family and you blew it. That's why he died. He knew.* He knew what you did you dirty fucking whore and now you have to live with the guilt that he did because of the shame you brought on him and your relationship by killing what you killed. And someone knows. I bet it's him. He knows what you never told him. He knows and then everyone will know what they've always known about you and this will confirm it for them: that you are cruel and selfish and useless and pathetic and sick and filthy and a waste of everyone's time.'* I can sense my head shaking from side to side and but I can't bring myself to look into the mirror again. My head is bowed down to the floor, my eyes closing and opening, opening and closing, seeing my hand cradling the fat spread where a baby once was. My baby. Our baby. And my free hand is shaking, I can feel it – shaking away from my body as though afraid to touch it, rippling towards the phone or maybe a razor or probably the wine rack where I knowingly keep the temptation close so that I can give into it, not to prevent it, not to keep my enemies closer, but to give into it, to drink and forget and feel bad about myself because hating myself is easier than trying to feel better. My head is dull and wet, full of cotton wool, sodden. I turn around, then back again. I catch sight of myself in the mirror and I see something that can't possibly be me; the eyes red and long, pulled down and out of their sockets; my hair limp. Without thinking, before I realise what I am doing, both of my hands are reaching down into my underwear. I stand in the bathroom in front of the mirror and touch myself. It's urgent and angry and feels like a punishment, that doing this to myself is just another reason, another example of how wrong I am, but I allow it to happen, I will it: my thoughts darting from image to image, from Tony to a bloody mess covering a floor, to a hospital bed, to a guy I remember looking at during the last counselling meeting, to suddenly Anne and Ann or whoever she is and the night she described, the man she was with, the crushing feeling of him over her, pushing her down, inside her, taking her, and her being cut in half and sliced in half and in boxes and cutting myself with love letter papercuts with sharp lines, diagonal hearts, and what I am doing and what I am feeling is wrong and sick and disgusting but it's what I am, it's what I always have been, it's what I did and it's why he left me and it's why he died and -

PART TWO

The night moved on.

Stars shone from the heavens, eyes looking for diamonds in the earth, hidden. The seemingly endless tunnel of night was sweltering, the warm air unusual for this time of year. Insects flew in unison into the beams of car lights, radio signals filtering through space like tightrope wires giving news. Songs on a journey. A ringing is echoing from somewhere.

This is a dream. I see him. I see my husband.

Life is a trapeze act between lanes, roads growing quiet and towns sleeping through the night as your lone car rumbles towards home. Phantoms of a childhood, yellowed from years gone by, spark up in erratic thoughts: did that happen, did he say that, did he love me, did I ever win at that game, did I really cut myself like that?

Did you know that a girl was once drugged in this town? Outside a bar, yeah. She was found the next morning covered in grit on a bench nearby.

She cut herself into pieces.

Somewhere, a mother cries for a baby she did not have. Somewhere, an envelope opens and a black heart is beating where the letter should be. It oozes black blood, Black ink.

A phone, screen smashed, is on the floor.

Beside the road, a rabbit hops back into its warren with food for its young. It bleats with new-born hunger. Steam rises from the tarmac and lingers over cars like a question mark. Steam transforms into a rain cloud.

This is a dream. I see her. I see my sister. But she's not really my sister, is she?

As children we think we are unstoppable, that sleep is merely a curtain and interval before the act of the next day. The year of Billy's birthday floats inside the grey clouds. Raining numbers. Four digits I will never forget.

By nightfall. By nightfall, we all hope the wrongs of the day will dissipate. By nightfall, before daybreak, all will be well again.

This is a dream. But I see her. And I see him. Pouring drinks down my throat. In this dream I am drowning.

-

What could be hours later, I wake up on the bathroom floor. Freezing cold.

My head throbs. I hold it.

Then it throbs back to the letter.

I think I can hear my phone ringing from somewhere. Distant.

My mind throbs sideways to the bottle of wine that is touching my feet.

'You're sick. And everyone knows', my voice tells me.

And I know it's true.

-

You woke up today.

-

How are you feeling today? I made you some coffee, Billy says.

Yeah. Okay, I say.

We need to talk about what happened, Billy says.

Yeah. Okay, I say.

Billy opens his mouth but doesn't speak.

I watch people coming and going. It feels better just to be out of the house and around people. Safer somehow. I run a forefinger around the rim of my coffee cup, knowing I could cry at any minute, just the slightest shift in my thought pattern and tears would crumble down my face. Shame. It was so shameful. What did I think I was doing? What did I give into? What does it say about me that I... that I thought about...

I know that these questions will roll around in my head for days to come, attacking me first thing in the morning from underneath my pillow, appearing in the suds of my shower crème, swirling around and looking up at me inside the milk of tea and coffee. I'll make myself pay for this, I know I will, just like I always do. When the meltdowns come, thick and fast like last night... I told Donna once that it's like having a metal plate melted down and poured into your head as liquid: hot, heavy and crushing. It stays there, lies on top of your brain like a fog, a mist descending. Then, as quickly as it comes, it can dissipate and evaporate away, always leaving evidence of burnt ground behind. Debris as memory. Hours later, it's still hovering there on the periphery, a low thud just underneath my scalp. I've showered and eaten and managed to get dressed. I have been able to walk to a café, remembered to pack my laptop and ordered a coffee. I paid with the correct change. I can still function.

The dull ebb of a dream sits behind my eyes. I close them and see a car and rain... a rabbit. I see my husband drifting inside steam. In the eyes of the rabbit I see Jenni, twice. I think I remember seeing a baby in the middle of a road. Was Tony there? I think I heard Donna crying... somewhere, somewhere I remember hearing a woman sob.

My fingers hover over my laptop, unsure of what to write. I have decided today to contact Leesha, an old editing friend and colleague of mine. She freelanced for me a few years ago. We worked well together, our styles and tastes matched. My hands are reluctant to start typing though - what do I say? How do I broach whatever this is? I have no idea what word would best describe this situation I've suddenly found myself in. As I was getting ready to leave the house I checked my phone; I panicked that I might have called Jenni in a drunken rage about these extracts that keep appearing at my door. Luckily, there was nothing in my phone's history. I sent her a text letting her know I had received another letter but didn't go into detail about what it said. She'll read them anyway. Telling her the exact details makes it feel too real. Maybe talking to someone neutral might be easier. Might even help me.

I use my personal email rather than my work email.

From: michellebookworm@livemail.com

To: leeshaweathers1@livemail.co.uk

Subject: A favour

Dear Leesha,

I hope you are well! I am so sorry that it has been such a long time since I have been in contact. I have been really busy with lots of different things but that's no excuse, I should have emailed or called before now.

I hope you've continued to freelance and write. I'd love to read something of yours, maybe something new, if you have anything? I'm hoping to return to work soon and you always have such a good eye and ear for new trends!

If you are free anytime soon, I'd love to meet up. I could do with a favour actually. I have been receiving parts of a manuscript from a writer and I'd like to get your thoughts and feedback on it.

Also, can you remember ever having read a story whilst with us at Rose and Thorn about a circus act or a girl in circus show? An odd question I know.

Thanks in advance,

Michelle.

-

I hit send. It feels good to be in contact with an old friend. Just like it did when I first started to message Jenni. At moments like this I always tell myself that I need to be more sociable, see more people, talk to more people. It always makes me feel better afterwards, no matter how uncomfortable I am leading up to it. I tell myself this despite knowing that I will most likely ignore it.

Part of me even hopes, secretly, that she doesn't respond.

-

You started to write down some memories of him.

-

The office space that my husband and I rented, we never really used. At first it started off as a status symbol of sorts; we thought it maybe sounded more professional if we had an address different to our own to collect mail and enquiries; that, technically, we had an office space in which to meet clients and have meetings. In reality, it was a very small room. Billy said it was like a lock up that serial killers would rent to hide bodies... but, it had a city postcode and would be our headquarters: *Rose and Thorn*, Office 6 (Flat 6), Billsbury House. When writing that on an envelope, sending off a prospective manuscript to a publisher, we felt it might sound more professional than just a random street number and house. Billy liked the fact, more than anything, that his name was part of the property's title.

"It'll make people think we own the whole complex or something!" he said.

I'd rolled my eyes at him.

Initially, we started having scripts sent to our house but found it irksome after a while that we couldn't leave home and work separate from each other. The office was cheap, it was nearby, it was convenient. We still hold the lease. *I* still hold the lease.

The first time we walked into the room we both laughed. The first time we got a manuscript delivered there we clapped and patted each other on the back. The first time we met a prospective client there we wiped and shuffled and filled it with flowers and candles and stacks of books and magazines, left our laptops open and phones glowing to create the atmosphere of a hectic, busy workplace. But it was our business, our little world together. It was where he spent a lot more time after the baby died. I know, deep down, that he wasn't doing that to punish me or make me feel guilty but to give me my space, to let me, and let himself, try to come to terms with losing this part of us. He spent so much time there that his aftershave became part of the air there, his pens and pencils and papers became the stationary we gave away to impress a potential author. I went for meetings, he went to work. It was because we started to split our time up that way that we added our home address back onto our website: that way we wouldn't miss anything important. And two business properties (technically) looked grander than one, surely? Soon I stopped going to the office altogether.

It was there that I first told Billy... *Billy*... his name still takes my breath away... that I first told him I was pregnant. The news seemed to fill the room and seep into every crease and crack of the framework. This little room was becoming our business, our haven, or future - our professional life that was now providing for our family life together, our baby. I bought two pairs of baby boots that same afternoon and hung them, alternately blue and pink, above the tiny window. We wanted a happy, healthy baby and weren't concerned with gender or whatever they would choose to become in life. But when I lost the baby I began to see them everywhere inside that space: the umbilical cord that wrapped around their neck looked just like the pull chord on the window shutters; letters being pushed through the tiny post-box sent shuddering visions through my brain of their little head, trapped between my thighs and struggling to breathe; the pitter patter of water from a leaking pipe in the floorboards above us sounded like the tiny feet that would never walk, would never wear the knitted boots I'd bought and hung months before. The room that once held such potential, such hope, turned into an empty nest, an empty nursery. And I couldn't stand being there.

I was told I had postnatal depression, but I didn't want to believe it. I was told that drinking after something like that was understandable, but I didn't want my actions to be explained. I was told that grief counselling would help, but I wasn't interested. I was told that getting pregnant again soon after could be both a blessing and a curse, a hope and a reminder – I'm not sure who told me that, maybe no one did.

History was inside that room. I knew that, perhaps, answers to some of the questions bouncing around inside of me might be found there, but I didn't know if I was ready to go back. I knew Jenni would have straightened things up and tidied some papers, but I wasn't sure what I would find, what small horrors might rear up at me from inside a drawer or behind a chair. I hadn't been back since he died and before that, well, hardly ever once I had found out about the baby... and knew what my decision would have to be.

-

Even with my eyes closed, I know where it is. I pull it out of the top drawer beside me and bring it to my chin, then my nose. Slowly, I pull the t-shirt over me. I breathe him in: his scent that covers every inch of the shirt he would always wear to bed.

-

You found the clock you used to hang in the hallway. You can put it up tomorrow. One thing at a time.

As if forcing me to socialise, Leesha emailed back almost instantly - she was indeed free to meet.

Sitting in the same café as when I had met Donna a few days earlier, it seemed bizarre to me that so much had happened in such a short space of time: the emails, the letters, the short story that the correspondence had turned into. Was I drinking again? Was I bruising my wrists again? Had I ruined things with Tony? And what about Mrs Lullin? These questions twisted and circled around my head and within the rising steam of coffees and hot drinks peppered throughout the café. I was early. Her email seemed happy, eager to see how I was. It surprised me. I expected that a friendship not been tended to would just wilt. Perhaps that was just my own negative thought spiral. I found myself smiling as Leesha arrived in a blur of scarves and hugs. I remember that she always orders two coffees at the same time because it's a pet peeve or hers to stop a conversation to go back to the counter.

We chat for a while about the last year or so since we've seen each other. She tells me how her company is doing, what their latest big seller is. I say that I've seen it advertised but haven't read it yet. She tells me not to bother reading it but to buy it to give her more money. She's joking, I think. Her laugh reverberates around the café. People look out of annoyance, or possible envy. I can't tell which.

"So, tell me about this new manuscript. Is it good?"

"Are you on the lookout for your next bestseller?"

"Always. You know what this business is like. We ignore most of the stuff we're sent: 99% isn't even read, and the other 1% we fight over with other publishers. So, what's up with this one?"

It's the first time during our talk that I hesitate.

"Well I told you in the email that I'd been receiving parts of a manuscript?"

"Yeah. What's it like? Good?"

I always liked her short and to the point sentences. She is the complete opposite to me. "It's... interesting." I stress the word. "They're always sent by post, not through email. We've corresponded through email though, and I've requested that any further contact is electronic only."

"Why?"

"I... I can't put my finger on it. There's just... something." This time Leesha doesn't speak or ask another question. She waits for me to continue. "Some parts of it I swear echo my life. I know that sounds crazy but the things the girl, the narrator, describes are so similar to me: smells, songs, even a bloody saying on a fridge magnet. It's just a bit too close for comfort. I don't know... maybe I'm just sensitive after everything that has happened over the last year but... the last extract was so brutal and cold and real and... did we ever have a short story about a circus act?"

"What? Sorry, you've lost me."

"God, sorry. Sorry Leesha. I... I've not really spoken to anyone about this. Jenni has told me to let her know if anything more happens."

"Jenni?"

"Billy's sister. She's helped out with the business since... over the last few months. She's been a big help."

"Yeah, yeah. I remember hearing about her from Billy. I read in your email about the circus short story... but what about it?"

"Oh... I know it's a long shot, but the last part of the manuscript made these gruesome comparisons between a circus act going wrong and an assault. I mean, it was gruelling to read it. But it gripped me."

"What is the writer like in the emails?"

"Passionate. Angry. He seems angry that he hasn't been taken seriously as a writer. He, or she maybe now... I don't know... wants to write an epistolary novel I think. Wants to subvert the current genre trend of women on the edge."

Leesha taps her fingers on the table. "Have you heard from them before? This writer? What's their name?"

"The writer is called Andrew, Andy. The narrator is Anne. Or Annie. The name changes."

"And have you heard from this writer before?"

"What do you mean? Before now?"

"Yeah. You just said that you felt anger coming from them in their emails about not being published. Is that directed at you? At your company?"

I hadn't thought of that. Was she right? Was Andy - if that's even their name - contacting me with such venom out of annoyance and spite that *I* had rebuffed a previous effort of theirs? It hadn't occurred to me. We hadn't published many books, not enough that I would forget any, but I had read countless short stories and essays over the years; I still do from time to time for my freelance work. Maybe I *had* read something of theirs then? And the circus part of the story *did* register with me somewhere...

"I'm not sure. I can't say yes or no for certain, but it feels like... as if... part of the writing is similar even if the writer isn't. I know that makes no sense."

"What, like, someone is copying someone else's work?"

"Maybe? I don't know. I can't explain it."

"Okay. Look. Email me the contact you've had so far and scan over the manuscripts too. I'll have a glance over everything and let you know what I think... both in terms of the writing and if I can sense something, you know, off." Leesha was calming and organised, the two qualities I liked best in her.

"Off?" I laughed.

"Yes." She didn't laugh. "Look, if you're concerned that someone is trying to scare or threaten you..."

"Hang on a minute," I interrupted, "I never said *that*." I emphasised *that* in a way that attempted to make the whole discussion seem ridiculous; that I wasn't concerned after all. But I wasn't convinced, and neither was Leesha.

"Michelle," Leesha looked at me dead on, "would you have contacted me if there *wasn't* something about this that had been unsettling for you? Ignore the catching up and seeing how each other are – no complaints from me though, it's great seeing you, and I've not been as good as I should've been at keeping in contact either – but would you have emailed me about the story if it was just a potential good read, or if something else was going on here?"

This time it was me who tapped my fingers. "No," I admitted, not meeting her eyeline.

"And that's okay. Listen, this does happen. A disgruntled writer, singer, artist, whatever, decides they've had enough, they're pissed off, feel rejected and that their talent hasn't been seen properly, so decide to take their frustrations out on those they feel have neglected them or rebuffed them. It's not right but it does happen."

"Yeah. You're right. You are."

"I'm not saying this to scare you. Just think carefully back to any scripts you've read or essays you've skimmed over, emails you've not replied to. I'm not giving this man a reason, but there might be a motive. And..."

It was unusual for Leesha to not finish a sentence. This worried me more than anything she'd said so far. "What?" I prompted.

"And... you said that some parts of the story felt like they drew comparisons to you?"

"Yes. So?"

"Well, what have you thought about it? About that?"

"About those comparisons?"

"Yes. You mentioned it, so it must be something you're aware of."

I run my hands through my hair.

"I know how this sounds. I sound like..." I turn my head to the window, look out onto the busy main road. From here I can see the road I take down to the care home; I can see Tony's bar, the sign waving in the wind; I can make out the corner shop that I go into to test my resolve to not buy any alcohol; I can see the tree I cross under when I walk to my group meetings, and I can visualise the pavement to the left that would eventually take me to the town's cemetery; I can feel the bend in the road, just a few yards from where I am sat, towards my own home. These different parts of my life mapped out in such a small part of the world, these threads that seem at once to both loop back over and into each other but are also separate and distant and sheltered and different – they all feel changed somehow, as if they each hold a secret, as if they each know something about the other, about me. A secret that I don't yet understand.

"I sound like a mad woman."

"You sound like a woman who has been through a terrible ordeal. You sound like a woman who is vulnerable."

"Are you saying I'm like one of these fragile women in one of these bloody books of ours?"

In perfectly timed irony, a bus drives past promoting a current bestseller that Leesha's company handled. It's even due to be turned into a film by the end of the year. We both laugh.

"No, honey. Not at all. What I am saying is that you might be reading too much into something that isn't there. Maybe it is just good writing, as you said. But I would still take stock of previous communication you've had with potential writers and clients. You're a small enough business so it shouldn't take long." She smirked. "And I don't say that to be bitchy." She leaned over and put her hands on mine. "If this is someone taking the piss and trying to freak you out then they have a certain advantage. They know your company name, they know you, they may even have met with you. They may think Billy is still in the picture."

"Is that bad? If they think... he's still alive?"

"No. It just means there are two people for them to be angry at. Has Billy had any mail? Does he still have an email account?"

"Nothing to the house no. Nothing apart from the usual hangover of bills and credit card applications and stuff. That all still comes in dribs and drabs. It's like walking on glass every time I see an envelope addressed to him."

"Do you open them?"

"I did. I just keep them in the little set of drawers near the front door now. I haven't checked his emails once."

"Okay. This is what we'll do." Leesha sat up, all business like. "Send me everything over and I'll check it. Email me anything you have on your work laptop or memory stick or whatever. I'll have a good scour for you. Sometimes fresh eyes can see things that you don't."

"Really Leesha? That's a lot of work. You don't mind?"

"I'm offering, aren't I?" She smiles, comforting me. "When you can, look through any post that has come for Billy and just check that he hasn't had any manuscripts sent to him too. And his emails if you can. If this guy feels he's been ignored by Billy too than that will just add to his irritation, won't it? If he has been contacted, then it's up you how you handle that. You might want to let this Andy person know about Billy. It might appeal to his human side and perhaps he'll leave you alone if, and it's a big *if*, he's a problem. We still need to assume he is just an over eager writer, yeah? I'd also make sure you pass any further communication you have with him to Jenni. She seems to have your back. And, as she is kind of the manager at the moment, she should know about it anyway."

I removed one of my hands from under hers and placed it on top. "Thank you, so much. You talk total sense. I'll do all that. I think I've just been... caught up and tired and... maybe I have been reading too much into everything."

Tri deug, a naoi.

I shake my head and look back out at the main road. Another bus goes by. Then, 'The Bride on the Balcony' flashes past on the side of a taxi. Another of Leesha's money makers.

Thirteen. Nine.

The little voice appears again and tells me that everything Leesha has told me is useless - kind, well meaning, believable, but useless. *Of course it's someone with a vendetta against you. How on earth else would they know your wedding song and when you murdered your baby you stupid bitch?*

"Michelle? Are you okay?"

Thirteenth of September.

"Hmm? Yeah. Yes. Sorry. Just thinking. It's been a lot to digest."

Tell her. Why don't you tell her? Because you're ashamed. As you should be. And someone has found out. Someone knows what you killed and why Billy is dead.

This voice repeats and reverberates inside my head as I hug and say goodbye to Leesha, tell her I'll speak to her soon; this voice repeats and loops inside my head as I walk past Tony's bar and remember crying in front of him; this voice repeats and circles inside my head as I stop to check for something inside my bag when really I am deciding whether to go into the corner shop and buy a bottle of wine; this voice repeats and echoes inside my head as I walk back home and grip my wrist tighter and tighter, to ignore the urge to go back to the corner shop after all.

-

I made myself a to-do list.

It's what I always do when I feel the need to get some control back in my life. It's an easy win so I can feel good about myself; if I tick something off then I have achieved. I can be an adult. I am successful. The only problem with tick-lists and to-do lists is that they can be never ending. It is easy to add something else then something else then another idea or task that must completed and if you don't do it then you're just as useless and shit as you've always thought you were. The little voice inside whines at you again. You wait for it like one of Pavlov's dogs.

I circle round and round these thoughts in the hallway of my house. It takes me five minutes to decide whether to take my coat off first or my shoes, write another to-do list, or pull out the envelopes to Billy I have hoarded away. This constant second guessing and uncertainty and anxiety, it's... exhausting.

My grief counsellor said it's something I can retrain. I can unlearn. *Keep going, keep going,* I tell myself: a mantra, a cycle, keep going like spokes on a wheel.

But I'm not so sure. I'm not certain that the guilt I feel over what I've done will ever go away.

Eventually I make it up to bed. I make a to-do list on my phone:

- Check Billy's emails
- Check post to Billy
- Email Jenni
- Email Leesha
- Visit office space
- Email Andy back

Before I go to bed I want to do one of the jobs. It will make me feel less of a pointless person. I am a functioning adult because I can complete a task I have set for myself. I tap the internet icon on my phone screen and type in the website of the email account my husband and I use. I try to ignore the word 'husband' that stabs inside my mind. I need to distance myself from that part of my life for the next few minutes. I don't know what I might find. For the next few minutes, he just needs to be an electronic account.

Typing in his email address and remembering his password comes surprisingly easy. I have held both in my mind for so long; like perfume hanging around after a party has finished. Fingers tiring at the edge of a cliff. For a second, I worry that the account will have been frozen or deleted, that somehow the internet will have found out about his death, that even his online life will have ended too. But after mere seconds, I am taken to his inbox.

Thousands of unread emails clutter the screen. Bold titles and subject lines. Times ranging across the twenty-four-hour clock. Dates that stretch to two months ago, and that's just from the first page of scrolling. It feels as though I have accessed a hidden world, as though the afterlife we all wonder about *is* here – electronic and hovering behind a glass screen - because surely, if someone can still receive an email about a holiday special offer or deals from a ticket company, then that person must be alive. Right?

We could go on a last-minute trip to Greece. Or Spain, Billy says.

With what money? We have the office still to pay for, I say.

It's these emails. They work on me. They make me want to book trips away with you, Billy says.

That's the point. They want to rob you blind, I say.

Billy closes his laptop, kisses the top of my head.

I run over page after page of requests and suggestions and the electric vignettes of a life. I stab at the top of the email list and for a moment contemplate deleting everything: every email that will now never be read by him. My thumb hovers over the screen. But if they are gone, then another part of him will be gone too. Maybe keeping him alive in the ether keeps him alive too. An electronic stasis. I wonder how Bily would react to these thoughts rumbling around my head. How Donna might. How Jenni would feel if I deleted an entire section of her brother's life for good.

My iPad lights up from across the room.

I tap Andy's email address into the search bar. I wait for a minute or so as his email handle is searched for in Billy's email history. It comes up empty. I am somewhat relieved. It now means that this writer hasn't been targeting both of us. Maybe he is just a passionate writer after all. But part of me feels a bit deflated. Because now, a bigger story doesn't exist. A chance to spend more time with Billy has been taken away before it even started. My mind jumps to Billy's unopened mail downstairs. Maybe I could find something in there tonight before I go to bed?

I flick back to the to-do list and put a line through one job. I decide to quickly forward on the emails between Andy and myself to Leesha. I resend them to Jenni as well just in case I have missed forwarding any to her. I can complete basic tasks because I am not a failure. I close my eyes and say this to myself twice.

I can complete basic tasks because I am not a failure.

Because I am not a complete failure, I also send Jenni a text message.

Jenni, I am thinking of going to the office space soon. I need to look through some old papers and manuscripts. I'd like to start getting back into the swing of work. If you're free and would like to meet me there it might be useful to have a helping hand. Let me know when suits you.

Because I am a successful person, I also send a quick message to Donna asking about her day because that is what I used to do and what I can still do because I can have a functioning life. I consider doing the same with Tony but don't feel quite that confident just yet. I put my phone on standby. I tell myself that I *can* function as an adult and as a friend. I *can* do all this and stave off inner voices and pangs of guilt and desires to drink and the pull of tears behind my eyes because I am a grown woman. I *can* just get on with things.

The iPad lights up again on the floor near the window. I'll check it before I go to sleep. I log back into my emails on my laptop and start to tap out a response to Andy. I want to let him know I have read his latest extract before he thinks I have ignored it or him. If he *is* a crazy and bitter jilted writer or stalker it is probably best to keep on his good side. This would amuse Donna. I wonder too what Leesha would make of this if it turned out to be true, thinking that she'd steal it as a plot for her next bestseller. *The Woman and the Writer. The Girl on the Internet.* Both sound ludicrous. Both I could see on the shelves of supermarkets.

-

To: caprahircus@livemail.com

Re: Latest extract

Dear Andrew,

I am just emailing to let you know that have I received and read your latest extract.

It felt very different to the previous instalments. I say this not as a negative, but more as a query and interest about where the story will go. I am intrigued if the story will follow, or already is using, a nonlinear narrative. Certain sections seem to jump or leave gaps where further details could be added. Perhaps they will, and I, as you say, will have to wait to find the information out. Like any successful fragmented narrative and epistolary text, the reader is left wanting to know what happens next and almost cast in the role of a detective to put the missing pieces together. I would hope this is what you want your writing to begin doing. Working on this style can be part of an editing process too if whomever takes your work on also feels this way.

I also feel that your writing and topic of choice, writing in role as a woman struggling with relationships with not just men but also women, is something which is currently in the public sphere. The place of women in the workplace, in social hierarchies, their treatment by men and even their female peers is an odd hot potato at the moment; by this I mean that it is an issue that many people are discussing but are almost afraid to. Perhaps, in your writing, you could bear this in mind. Playing into current debates and news cycles will make your novel (if this develops into an extended piece?) relevant and therefore potentially more 'sellable' for an agent and publisher.

Although I am not yet able to offer you a working relationship or contract, I am still happy to read your work and offer something akin to freelance comments or suggestions if that would interest you. I empathise with your frustrations about being ignored by publishers, so am happy to help in any way I can, even if I personally don't see your work through to publication.

-

I pause for a moment and read over the email so far. I think to myself whether to push further with this. How much do I really want to communicate with this person? How much do I want to poke the beast. I decide to hide my intentions with praise, as best I can. I continue typing.

-

I would be interested to know more about the inspirations behind the story. Many parts of the writing appear rooted in everyday circumstances, such as the references to songs and smells and places, which is what a good writer will do – they will use situations that place their reader in a realistic world and scenario.

I am, again, intrigued by the errors I have come across in your writing. I presume these are purposeful as they appear to spell out certain phrases. Either this is pure coincidence or I have been dragged fully into your manuscript and have, as I said earlier, become part detective in figuring out how the story will end.

-

Out of nowhere I consider asking him to meet. If we met… then the mystery would end. If we met, then this odd narrative I seem to have constructed for myself will be complete. The next chapter can begin. I decide to take the bull by the horns. I decide to be brave.

-

If you would be willing to meet in person, we could perhaps look over your writing in more detail. It would be a good chance for me to ask certain questions and get your response face to face and therefore get more of a handle on where you want your narrator and narrative to be coming from and going. This is up to you. As I say, I can't offer you any formal support but am willing to lend an experienced eye and ear.

Please continue to contact me through my work email only.

Ms Thorn.

-

After I have hit send, I worry that I shouldn't have suggested we meet. Then I realise that they may not even want to, and that I can always just cancel a proposed meeting if I want to. I question too whether *I* should have included a hidden message of errors myself, to test him as I feel he has tested me. *Next time,* I think… *if there needs to be a next time.*

I go back to my to-do list and put a line through another job. Not bad going. I ease myself down into bed, feeling calmer.

Again, the iPad lights up.

I leave the warmth of my bed and unplug it, click the button at the bottom of the screen. I nearly drop it.

From: billygoat@livemail.com

The email address glares up at me from inside a bubble in the centre of the screen. I stare at it. Shaking, I slide my finger across the screen. Billy?

The bubble expands:

From: billygoat@livemail.com
Re: Security Check

I click on it. My bubble bursts.

Dear Personal Contact,

You have received this email because we have identified some unusual activity on the account of:
billygoat@livemail.com

When an account has not been accessed in more than ninety days, when it is next opened, we automatically email both the Account Holder and their chosen Personal Contact. You are listed as the Personal Contact of the Account Holder at:
billygoat@livemail.com

If you know of any reason that this activity might be suspicious, please do not hesitate to contact either the Account Holder themselves or us at customer service.

Thank you for your understanding,
The Livemail Team.

-

I switch off the iPad and stand with the dark screen in my hand. I stand there in darkness. My mind does not swirl, does not bounce from worry to anxiety to panic. Instead, I feel blank - what I imagine the inside of a cloud to be: plain, weightless, hollow. I have no questions, no words, just...

Even with my eyes closed I know where it is. I open the top drawer of the bureau next to my bed and reach in, immediately feeling the soft cotton. I pull it out and bring it close to my mouth, then my nose. Slowly, like a child taking their time eating a dessert, I pull the t-shirt over my head and I breathe him in. His scent, the mixture of sweet and salty sweat that covers every inch of this, his favourite shirt to wear to bed. I told my counselling group once that my greatest fear is that the t-shirt will be washed one day and that I will lose him forever, that once this smell is gone then he will be gone too. Now I realise he still exists in another way, in another world; through cables and lights his life still goes on, with companies still emailing him, with offers cluttering up his inbox.

In a way, he is still alive.

-

You tried to call your mother.

-

It's not until I'm awake for a few seconds that I realise it was only a dream.

I run my right index finger over the scar on my left thumb. If it was Billy's index finger he would leave a trail of black ink on my skin.

In my dream my finger was bleeding. In the dream, I knew it was an injury from a childhood accident. Falling from a swing perhaps. The incident wasn't in the dream itself, but the bleeding, the sharp pain and metallic smell was real and palpable. When I woke up, I was holding my hand, as though to try and stem the bleeding. Looking down at my hand, I realise the blood was just a sensation, a memory - even if the scar is still real. The shatter of glass echoes through my head and for a moment, like the dream, I think it must be real too, that something has just been broken, somewhere downstairs or in the bathroom... but it's just a memory, a muscle memory, with the pain slowly throbbing away into the distance, back under the covers, back into a drunken sleep.

I sense him in the t-shirt I am still wearing. Waking up with him so close to me just exacerbates the empty hours ahead of me when he won't be there.

The ceiling above me is blank. Nothing to come but hours of loneliness, the long hours of keeping busy. I imagine flicking my hand up towards the ceiling and covering the white paint with speckles of my dreamt red blood. They'd shine above me like dying stars. The image of my cut flesh shoots through my mind's eye and I remember the tipping of the wine glass, the slice of skin, the dripping blood, the crying and wailing of not knowing if I should go to the emergency room or if I could even drive with how much I had drank. It's amazing how quickly pain sobers you. Instead, I wrapped it up in several tea towels and kept on drinking. 'Who cares if I bleed out?', I remember thinking, 'Everything I care about is already dead.'

A flash of the circus girl tears through my brain.

I bolt up in bed.

I don't want to think about that letter or about that writing today. I rub my head into the palms of my hands, let out a quiet groan. I can't read another page of it until I figure out what or *who* it is. If it's even anything to be concerned about. I raise my head, bleary eyed, and sigh. Another day.

Jenni has agreed to help me look through some papers at the old office. Her text message, which I awoke to this morning was, as always, was polite and to the point. I'm relieved - not that I particularly *want* to spend the day in a room that reminds me of him, but at least there will be a few hours when I am not on my own. And I'd rather get this done today than wait. The weekends are the worst. That time, unfilled and unplanned, is like hefting a suitcase upon your back, one which gradually gets heavier and heavier with invisible items thrown in minute after hour - reminding you how alone and forgettable and silent you are: young enough to start again if you wanted to but old enough to pack it all in, until the weight of an invisible anxiety and guilt crushes you to the floor. I never felt this way before he died. I never felt this way before we couldn't get pregnant again.

On the way out of my front door, I remember that I was going to look through some of Billy's letters this morning. The tick-list I wrote on my phone hovers before me like Macbeth's dagger. The phantom email from Billy's account rears up in front of me too, and I decide to face it all another day. If I don't look at any of the letters or manuscripts sent to him then it lets me keep another part of his life with me, another puzzle piece for me to hold on to. If I look and find nothing of interest nor anything to explain this mystery, then I worry it's just another fragment of him that I won't have anymore. Part of me hopes this is all part of some elaborate hoax or gaslighting against me – that someone, somewhere has a secret about me, a vendetta against either me or Billy or someone in my life. Then, at least that way, I have a reason to keep thinking about him, to protect him, to look after the memory of us together. If there is a motive for all this, then there is something tangible I can work with and discover. Like the plot in one of the books I used to edit, if there is a problem then there is a crisis to be solved with backstory and exposition and, ultimately, a conclusion. I just don't want that conclusion to come too quickly. Is that wrong? Am I some sort of sadist?

'Yes'. The voice stabs me – quick, fast, knowing.

What truly scares me is that there is no story, that there is no mystery to solve at all. That this is all in my head. I try not to reach for my wrist. I reach for my phone by the bed but it isn't there. I look under the covers, in the bathroom. I check my bag. Coat pockets. I haven't been into the living room or kitchen this morning, but I look just in case - and there it is, face down by the empty wine rack. It is empty because one wine bottle is standing, open, next to the phone. I can't remember coming in here last night. I can't remember leaving my phone in the kitchen. I can't remember opening a bottle of wine. I pick up the phone and type in Billy's birthday. The passcode isn't recognised... but it's something else that makes me nearly drop it... Acidic bile rises slowly up into my throat. I put the phone down. I step away. It's not just the passcode that has changed.

My home screen image, which used to be a picture of Billy and I on our wedding day, is now a picture of my baby scan.

-

Walking to the office, I do my best to focus on the here and now. I try to tell myself there is an explanation for my phone, even though I can't come up with anything logical. I *don't* think of the email as I cross the street and smell coffee from one of the many cafes. I *don't* remember the bleeding hand in my dream as a gust of wind sends shivers of leaves down the road. I *don't* see the girl from the story on her back, pinned down, cut into a magician's box of tricks as I pass by Tony's bar, serving students a hangover breakfasts. I *don't* feel anxious about not finding a link between these emails and these letters and my life and Billy still being alive somehow and the inexplicable changes on my phone because he can't be alive because he died coming to see me after what I had done to him, to us, to –

I am grabbing my wrist. I am rubbing it – I am spiralling back into the thoughts I have worked so hard to avoid.

'No,' I tell myself, *'just press the traffic light button, just stand and wait, just cross the road, just get to the office and meet Jenni.'*

That's all I have to do for the next few minutes. Nothing else. Just that. I pause and listen to my breathing. All of this can and will be explained away.

I can't help falling in love with you.

I stop.

I.

But I've already stopped walking, haven't I?

can't

I'm already standing still. I am. I think I am.

help

My head spins, following the sound. A car. A car slowing down at the traffic lights. The radio.

in love

Someone knows everything about my life, everything about Billy, everything about our careers, everything about what I've done.

with you.

I can't stand here, I can't wait, I can't hear that song again and that line again and again.

I can't help falling in love with you.

I dash across the road, away, away from the car and the radio and the song and Billy and our wedding and a horn that sounds somewhere behind me. What feels like both seconds and hours later, I'm outside our office space. I'm out of breath and I can feel sweat beneath my top. I take a moment to lean against the front door. I feel the buttons of the intercom press into my back. I run my hands through my hair. I breathe. In and out. In and out. I close my eyes. Slowly, slowly, the memories fade, the song ebbs away. The girl's dorm room flashes behind my eyes. Then a trapeze wire. I open my eyes again, look up at the office window. There's no light on in there as far as I can see. Hopefully Jenni hasn't arrived yet. That way, I can take a few minutes to centre myself, appear normal, sort a few things out, tidy some papers. Cool down. Get myself ready for a conversation. And for whatever I might find.

I can't believe it! I can't believe we own this place. This is going to be where we work and run the world, Billy says.

Don't get too ahead of yourself, I say.

We need to think big! You don't get anywhere by thinking small, Billy says.

You need to stop reading fridge magnets and posts on Facebook, I say.

Billy sniggers and hugs me.

My key turns in the lock. The door opens easily with a gentle push. I'm not sure what I was expecting, perhaps the creak and cobweb of a Dickens novel, the door needing to be forced open after years of being closed, keeping whatever had been inside at bay. Trapped. But the sounds I expected are replaced by something much more human. Jenni is already standing the middle of the room, and although her back is turned away from me, I can immediately tell she is crying. It is the hunch of her shoulders, the way both arms are sloping inward as if hugging herself, how one knee is bent to support the quivering other. For a second the moment hovers - I watch, unsure whether to step back outside and not break the inertia of the room. I hold my hand on the door, not letting it close just yet, keeping the silence as it is. Jenni turns around. Her eyes are wet, glistening. Her arms are crossed over her stomach, a weak cradle. There's something in one her hands, enclosed in a fist. Something blue.

"Jenni, I... sorry, I didn't know you were already here."

She makes to wipe her eyes before replying. "Oh, Michelle. No, it's fine. Sorry, I should have waited and met you downstairs. I'm just used to letting myself in."

Files were open on the desk. I could tell from the line of dust that the computer had been moved. The room itself needs a good clean. Maybe she only ever dashed in and out. It would make sense; I wouldn't want to spend much time in here either.

"Are you okay? Has something happened?"

Something on her face told me she briefly flirted with trying to play innocent, to deny that she was clearly upset. It was how her eyes moved from my face, how she started to move her arms. I wouldn't have pressed it if that was what she chose to do, but she faltered, crossed her arms again, squeezing her fist a little tighter.

"It's nothing really. I... went to open the window over there," she motioned to the dusty window with her shoulder, "and I just spotted this behind the radiator."

I take a step forward and she opens her hand like a reluctant child, unsure whether to present their plunder, whether they should have it or not. She coughs and opens her fist, revealing a small cotton boot. A blue boot for a baby. I blink, feel myself nod. I meet her gaze and see her eyes starting to water again.

"God, I forgot we hung those up in here."

"Billy was so excited. Do you remember?"

"Do I remember?" I almost laughed. "He pretty much burst with the anticipation of waiting to tell everyone. Anyone he met."

"He told me what he was going to do in here," Jenni says. "His plan was to make it a family friendly space."

"And you *let* him?"

"Do you think he wouldn't have done it even if I'd said not to?"

"No," I smiled, "I don't think it would've made a difference, would it?"

I look around the small office space and let my memory paint what Billy had done for me, for us: pink window blinds and a bunting of baby boots that hung from one light to another; a 'congratulations' banner that was slightly askew on the wall above the desk; a plant pot in the shape of a crib full of pink and blue roses. At the time I didn't have the heart to tell him that it was slightly overkill, that we needed to get to the second trimester before getting so ahead of ourselves. But he was so thrilled, so happy that we had managed to get pregnant. I remember laughing at the banner, not sure who was being congratulated, him or me. He told me that he had gone for a mixture of pink and blue as he wasn't bothered about the sex of the baby just as along as it was healthy. No one even saw the office apart from us, and a few potential clients who smiled a *Jesus Christ* smile when they came in -they were probably expecting a hive of tapping and typing and page turning, rather than an explosion of pregnancy excitement.

When the baby died the room seemed to wilt alongside it. The flower crib dried up, the rose petals falling to the floor like unformed eyelashes; the banner half fell down and folded over itself, almost mimicking the split between Billy and I, - that we weren't one straight line anymore, but something bent out of shape; the bunting was taken down one boot at a time, dangling the footsteps that would never be taken.

"I thought he'd tidied everything away."

"He just missed this, I guess. The rest is at your place, isn't it?"

"Yes. It's in the attic. He wanted to keep it all. I… I would've thrown it all out."

"Why? Why would you get rid of everything?"

I couldn't tell if she was she annoyed at me for getting rid of her brother's handiwork - that she felt I was being disrespectful to the baby perhaps - or whether she was just curious. Her face was blank, unreadable. Did it make me a bad mother for wanting to erase the visual presence of the child I would never have, or was it just survival? It felt that way at the time. I also couldn't stand seeing Billy's face whenever we came across something that we had bought or prepared for the baby: a premature menagerie of toys; the cards of congratulations upon the mantlepiece at home from the one or two friends we'd told; the positive test that we kept by the bathroom sink. In the days after I lost the baby that positive cross appeared behind my eyes whenever I blinked. I wanted everything that could remind me of the baby gone. My body had betrayed me, and I wanted nothing to do with being a mother. Looking at Jenni now I couldn't begin to imagine how she would react, how she would feel if she ever found out what I did. What I did to Billy.

"I… it was too hard to see. Even to know it was in the same space as me. But Billy wanted to keep it, said it would be used again one day if we ever… so I agreed as long as it was out of sight. It's where a lot of his stuff is too. Some photographs. Letters he wrote to me. I still have some of his clothes." I pause, wondering whether to reveal this about myself to her, unsure how close we are. "You'd think I was crazy if I told you some of things I did. That I still do. Some of the things I keep." She doesn't speak, just looks me, silently inviting me to continue. "Last night I wore his t-shirt to bed. It makes me feel he's there next to me." She nods, understanding. Again, her nonverbal reply means it's up to me how much I care to disclose. "I worry that... if his clothes ever get washed, like if I ever bundled that shirt into the wash with mine by accident, that then he'd really be gone. That having his smell means he's still alive somehow. It hurts having those things in the attic, but it keeps him near me too."

After a few seconds she turned away from me. She bent forward and seemed to fold over into herself. I could tell she was crying again but this time it was more like sobs, sudden and harsh, the kind that are silent apart from a painful intake of air. I moved to put a hand on her shoulder, left my palm hovering for a second, unsure whether it would soothe or irritate, then placed it on the top of her arm and walked to her front.

"Jenni, what is it? Look, I'm okay. I'm actually glad that I kept everything now. I'm sorry, I didn't mean to upset you."

"It's not that. Really it's not you. It's... I can't..."

We had never really spoken about the fact both of us had lost a child. Strange considering we were family, but we just had never discussed it. It's the social taboo that no one wants to broach: how do you talk about being a failure as a woman? What are you if you can't mother a child? Despite myself, I found the featureless face of my would-be writer floating before me, his feminist rantings being fuelled even further by this inner debate I was having around the role of motherhood.

"Jenni, what is it?"

She took a deep breath. "I can't have children. We found out a few weeks ago. After our first was stillborn and my second miscarriage months ago?" - she raised her intonation here into a question, as though hoping for a different answer to the one she must have been dealt - "It revealed something more serious. About me, I guess. The tests we had and bloods and... whatever..." here she sighed, exhausted with the story, the fate handed to her, "we just... can't."

"Oh Jenni. I'm sorry. I'm so sorry." I tilted my head below hers, trying to check she was breathing. Her body had stiffened. "How *is* Sampson? How did he take it?"

"Yeah," she coughed, almost gagging on a bitter laugh, "well, he's not here with me at the moment. He needed some time *away*. Read into that whatever you want to."

"Jesus, Jenni. Really? I would never have thought that of him."

Another choked laugh. "Me neither. That's why I've been down here so much. Seeing my parents, you know? I just need to be around people."

I straightened her up and ran my hands down her arms. I waited for her to meet my eyeline.

"God. I just can't help thinking how lucky some parents are. And the kids they love. There's nothing worse than being an unwanted child. And I just want one so... so... It just makes me feel like an outcast... from... all of them, you know... mothers. What a woman is meant to be. We're meant to have children, aren't we?"

I didn't know what to say, worried I'd say the wrong thing. Or say something about myself that I shouldn't... but Jenni speaks, almost to herself.

"I see them in cafes and the library and... everywhere. I just feel like some sort of freak who belongs in a museum, something to be studied and poked at: a woman who can't have children. A woman who can't do the one thing we're meant to be able to do."

"You should've come to me. I know we aren't that close, but you *should* have and *can* come to me. I mean it. You've been so good to me since Billy. And it's *my* turn now. We're going to get each other through all this... *bullshit*."

I shocked myself with the volume and petulant venom with which I swore. Unlike her previous laughter, the one that came now was genuine and, like my own, surprised.

"Well, that's one way of putting it. *Bullshit*. We can be – what? – socially unacceptable non-mothers together, huh?"

We laughed again, then hugged. We pulled apart and took a moment to breathe the room in.

"Come on. Let's just get what we need from here and go have some lunch. Okay?"

Jenni sniffed, smiled weakly, and nodded her head. "Right, so what are we looking for again?" She turned to the desk and started moving a few files around. She turned the laptop on. I was surprised it didn't emit a sigh of dust as it powered up.

"Well, just any unanswered mail. Perhaps look for packages first, ones that might have a manuscript in. There's just something about this guy that's... I can't put my finger on it."

"What?" Jenni was tapping into the computer now, the password presumably.

"I'm just certain I've heard from him before, or he's written to us before. Or it might still be a female writer. *Andy*. Leesha, an old colleague of mine, thinks they might be annoyed that we ignored them. That's why he's got such anger in all his correspondence so far. He's pissed that the publishers, as he sees it, just fling his work to one side."

"Him and about a thousand other people every day."

"Yeah, I might not say that to him though. I don't think he'd respond well to sarcasm."

"Who's being sarcastic?" She was now pulling open the desk drawers, pulling out some random papers from inside. "Seriously, does he or she or whoever this is not know how these places work? No one gets contacted back. Hardly ever. It's a tough bloody business. He needs to not take things so personally."

"Another phrase I probably won't be replying to him with. I don't want to piss him off any more than he already seems to be." I was looking through some drawers by the window. I could only see what looked like files full of bills, various meetings we'd organised and taken minutes of. We had run a good little business here. I tried not to dwell on it. Maybe I could come back to it all one day. "Keep an eye out for that short story too. You know the one I mentioned?"

"Which? The circus act one about the girl getting cut up? You think he wrote a story you rejected? That that's the one?"

"Maybe. Maybe just one of them. I really don't know." I closed one drawer shut and pulled open another, standing on tip toe to see inside.

Jenni kept her eyes on the computer screen. "This is slow going," she said, pointing at the laptop. "How about I check some desk drawers, give this time to load up - have you looked in here yet?" She motioned to a desk behind her.

"No, no I haven't yet. God, this might all be a fool's errand. Hopefully it is."

"Hopefully? Do you mean that?" She shut one desk drawer and pulled open another. I saw her grimace at what might have been inside; I imagined a tissue, crusty with snot from one of Billy's hay fever sneezing fits.

"I don't know. Part of me is interested to see what this is all about. I mean, does this guy know me or Billy and is pissed we rejected his work? Then again, it's a bit scary if..."

"...if he is pissed off and is stalking you now."

"You sound like Donna."

"Don't ever say that!" I turned to see her holding up her hands in mock innocence; "I know, I know... I know she's your friend. But she doesn't like me much, does she?"

"How can you tell?"

She slammed one drawer and yanked open another. The laptop let out a pinging sound. It must have finally loaded up. I laughed uncomfortably. I couldn't hide that Jenni wasn't a million miles away from the truth. Luckily, she smiled. "Let's just say I don't see her winning any poker games soon."

Trying to lighten the mood, I joke that Donna has what some would call a "Resting bitch face," and then try to change the topic of conversation: "Find anything?"

"Maybe." I hear a click and see Jenni removing a pen drive from the computer. "It'll be easier to do this at home or at my office. Less stuffy. And cold."

"And much less miserable," I add.

"Do you know what this is though?" She was holding what looked like a shoebox. "It was just here in the bottom drawer. Do you want me to open it?" I nodded and closed the drawer that I had been rummaging in. I walk over and cough from the dust that Jenni blows from the lid of the shoebox. It's battered looking, browned and crumpled around the edges. I hear the rustle of papers inside it as her hand rifles through the contents.

"They look like letters. Maybe notes. Editing notes perhaps?" She passes the box and its contents to me. "Take it with you and have a look through it when you can. No need to rush it now. I'll," she held up the pen drive and then slipped it into her bag, "let you know if I find anything on this."

We stood for a moment in silence. Just looking. Both thinking about what this place once held, might once have held.

"Should I sell this office space?"

"Maybe. It depends if you plan to come back and start working again." There's a short beat before she speaks again. "I'm sorry, Michelle. That sounded heartless. You should take whatever time you need."

"No, no. Come on, we're both being open and honest this afternoon, aren't we? It's true. I need something. I can't work at the care home forever."

Jenni closed the laptop down and straightened up a few piles of files on the desk. "Come on," she said, "we need to go have something to drink."

-

I can only imagine what Donna would think if she saw me here with Jenni, coffees and cakes between us, laughing and actually enjoying each other's company. Would Donna be jealous? Most likely. Curious and wanting to know the gossip straight away? Definitely. Being with Jenni, even if just for an hour or two this afternoon, has, despite the obvious memories and flashbacks it creates being around her (his eyes, his voice, his neck, his fingernails), has made me feel the calmest, most centred I've felt in a while.

"It was always his hair that stood out the most for me. That bit, that quiff, you know, at the front of his head that would never stick down."

"His front cow lick?" I laughed.

"Yes. Yes. Exactly."

"It was his fingernails for me. His hands. How he'd open a bottle of wine, write with a pen, tear a package open at the office, leave his fingerprints all over the place from his endless crosswords. He was obsessed with them. It was all so creative and arty and manly at the same time."

"Shall we get some wine over here?" Her arm went up to signal a waiter, and then, realising, her hand faltered, and fell back to her side. "Sorry. I wasn't thinking."

"No, it's okay. I know that Billy worried... I'm fine. You can. If you want to."

"No. No. I'm just... I'm having a nice time with you."

"Yeah. Me too."

"Surprised?"

"Yes!"

We both laughed, comfortable enough to know that we knew how bizarre this encounter seemed. We had always been a little bristly with each other, and now it was positively balmy.

"And *manly*? Billy?"

"He was! I always thought he was so handsome." I ran my fingertips around the edge of my coffee cup. "I was only talking about this the other day."

"Who to?"

"Just a lady at work. A lady I care..." I pause, and correct myself, "*cared* for. She passed away just the other day."

"Is that the lady who fell?"

"Yes." I couldn't hide the surprise in my voice. "How did you know?"

"Local radio. I heard about it."

I picked up my cup. "I wasn't aware that the care home had released a statement. I didn't think anyone would care enough to be honest - not about an old persons' home. Anyway, it was an accident."

"That's what the radio said. An accident during the night?"

"She was so lovely. So many stories. She liked hearing about romances and marriages and telling me about her own. She showed me a photograph of her husband and then I showed her one of Billy. Actually," I reached into my handbag and took out my purse, pulled out the photograph I had shown Mrs Lullin, "it was this one here." I couldn't believe how much had happened in the few days since I had shown the picture to her. There we all were: Billy and I, most of his family. Jenni. All smiles.

"That's a great picture. We look so young there. Hold on." She took out her phone and took a picture of it. "I'd like to have a copy of my own."

I held it between us a little longer.

Jenni said: "What about your parents? Do you hear much from them?"

"Did Billy ever tell you about them?" I fold the picture away, return it to my bag.

"No. Nothing. Did he know much about them? Meet them, I mean?"

"No. Not really. We're not too close. After..." I paused. I was worried that I'd let something slip, that being on familiar terms with Jenni now might mean I'd say something she didn't know, and I didn't want her to know. It felt strange starting to feel comfortable with someone, someone other than Donna. And Billy, of course. An image of Tony popped into my mind. I shook it away. "After we lost the baby I hoped it might change things, that they might reach out and be supportive but... nothing. They almost didn't come to the wedding."

"Really? Why?"

"They were never happy I didn't follow through on what they wanted me to do at university. They had ambitions of me being a doctor like them. Or something in medicine at least. Creative writing, literature and the arts... all seemed lesser to them. Below me. And Billy, well... he was artistic and bookish and therefore as equally disappointing as I was. I'll always remember what my mother said to me when I told her we'd gotten engaged." Jenni sat listening. "She said that we'd be poor and that writers never get anywhere in life."

Jenni leaned back and folded her arms. For a moment I wasn't sure if she was annoyed, amused, shocked... but then she said, "Are you sure this freak who's writing to you isn't your mother? Provoking you the only way she knows how, through the medium of literature?"

I could tell by her grin that she was joking, but it wasn't the response I had expected. It wasn't something I had even considered myself. Why would I? My parents weren't *warm*... but they weren't vindictive; critical at times, yes, but even this bullying would be beyond them.

"Funny. But no. I don't think my parents even have email."

The shudder of a bus going past made me look outside and, seeing the darkening sky, realise how long we'd been in the café. I watched Jenni for a moment as she swiped something on her phone and tapped away on the screen. I had known this woman for years, off and on, and in the space of one afternoon she had gone from cold and aloof and someone who I really only knew through my husband, to someone who had shared with me their personal tragedies - and now, some of my own too. An odd sensation wriggled in my stomach. I wasn't quite sure what it was.

"Right," she said, snapping her phone case shut - the snapping sound jolted me back to my kitchen that morning... my phone, my password, the screensaver - "I've got to head off. But... this has been really nice. Really good, actually. We'd should meet up more often. Look," she paused, moved her empty coffee cup around on the saucer, "I know I said about you coming back to work but maybe we could look into carrying the business on together? I mean, I know the accounts and the money side of things. That's all ticking over, but it won't last forever. You need to choose and edit and publish something. You'll need the money eventually. We could do it together. Just... think it over. Let me know."

The feeling in my stomach was still there, a soft rippling of water, of waves moving over a current. It felt warm, almost like my stomach was bloating a little. It was a positive sensation, it and told me that Jenni was someone I could perhaps now count on too.

"You know what Jenni, I definitely will. I *really* will. God, I can only imagine what Billy would say if saw us together now, laughing and arranging to meet up again. I wonder what one of Billy's crossword clues would be for this!"

"Did he do those with you as well?" I ask.

"He told me that he used to do it to annoy you. I thought it was funny. Sweet."

"Funny? No. But sweet? Yes."

Outside, we briefly hug and pull up our jackets against the early evening chill. The traffic had picked up. Another bus went past with the same advert for the best-selling novel I saw when with Leesha. I wonder if she's managed to find anything of interest yet.

"So, I will get looking through these files and stories that I saved from the laptop. I'll let you know if I come across that circus story, too. Why *does* that one stand out? You never said."

The girl's body flashes before my eyes. Her being cut and bent out of shape in the alley. My drunken heavy head from the morning after suddenly crashes in and weighs down on my shoulders. Out of nowhere I feel the impulse to grab my wrist. *'Because you're a freak just like her'* it says, viciously breaking through.

"It's just something he mentioned in one of his letters. It's probably nothing."

"Okay," I could hear a little scepticism in her voice, but she didn't push it. "I'll let you know, okay?"

"Yes. And thank you. For today. For being so helpful."

"Thank *you* for listening. And please don't tell anyone about what's happening with… you know…" she waved her hand to represent her relationship with Sampson. Maybe it was too hard to verbalise twice in one day.

"Of course."

"Right. I'm away for a few days now but I'll message you when I'm back. We can meet up again."

"Great. I'd like that. Well, actually, I've somehow managed to lock myself out of my phone, so it might take me a while to reply!"

"What? How do you *accidentally* do that?"

"I really don't know. And…" I can't tell her about the background image though, can I? *No, because then you'd have to explain more, wouldn't you?* it says. "But listen," I move on, "what you said before, about feeling like some kind of freak? That you're not a woman? There are other things that make you *you*. You don't lose who you are just because you can't have children."

I think maybe I was saying that to myself, too. Jenni looked away for a moment. She wiped her cheek. Maybe I said too much.

"You're right. I know you are. It's just tough. Really tough." She coughs. "Anyway, maybe *you* should pass by *Tony's* on the way home. Just to, you know, say hello." She smirks at me, playing.

"Oh god, you and Donna are as bad as each other! That's twice today you two have crossed paths with ideas!"

"He's cute. That's allowed. I saw how he'd look at you, even when you were with Billy. He liked you."

I sighed, stuttered the start of my sentence. "I... He's.... Yes, he's nice but that's *it*. Really I'm not interested in anything like that. *And*," I refused to let Jenni leave without a jive back at her, "seen as you must have met him, like, twice in our life, *you* must've been looking at *him* pretty hard to see him supposedly looking at *me*!"

And with that, we hugged a final time, smiling, and walked in opposite directions down the street.

-

You spoke to him and didn't want to jump into oncoming traffic.

-

On the way home, I decide to stop ignoring it.

Mrs Lullin telling me to write down memories, parts of conversations with Billy, made more sense to me than most other suggestions that people have made over the year. Well-meaning ideas like... visit your honeymoon spot again, frame old pictures of you both, start an evening class. But writing down short memories are easier to do, less painful. And I can commit to it as much or as little as I want. And today with Jenni also spurs me on. A feeling, a need to tangibly, somehow, keep his voice alive. Something inside me wants to just face it, to face up to what I pass by nearly every day and wish wasn't there. That shouldn't *have* to be there.

I can sense it across the street from me, an invisible hand that is tethered to me somehow, an umbilical cord that can reach and pull and drag. It is a churn and grind that turns inside me like a corkscrew each time I walk down the street to work, from work, to home, to the store, to see Tony or Donna or – and I pause. I *know* what I am doing. I am making my mind drift so I can ignore the inevitable. Standing on the curb I realise that I could just carry on home, carry on walking and cross the street and open my gate, then the front door, then take off my coat, go into the kitchen, click the kettle on, look at the bottle of wine I may open and smell later on that evening, run a bath, forget about the cup of tea, scroll through my iPad, look for an email or a message or a hidden account that might open up the truth of – and I stop. Again.

I shake my head. I am doing it again: the distraction. It's how I get by most days, with to-do lists and things I can say I have done, in baby steps, to survive the almost constant barrage of thoughts and questions. I feel my wrist being squeezed. I let it linger, just let the sharp Chinese burn ripple through my skin, along my veins. It always wakes me, snaps me back to the present.

Be positive. Go.

This doesn't have to be negative anymore. It commemorates him. You *want* to keep him alive, remember. I turn and try to be more confident than I feel. I walk towards the wall and the plaque.

It is nailed onto the brick wall of the building not too far along from Tony's place. It's invisible and unimportant to nearly every person who will walk past it. Several words stand out, the letters jutting out from marble in raised font. Billy's name. His birth date. The date of the accident. There is a carving of a dove below. I remember when a local community group contacted me about wanting to put something up in his memory. Billy's death had been in local newspapers and on the radio for days afterwards. The tragic accident of a husband rushing to the hospital to see his sick wife. Killed on the way. I declined the offer of course, but they insisted and wanted to pay for it and let the community know that solidarity overcomes grief and... and... and...

I'd looked at it once. Just once before now. The day it was put up I stood with Donna, holding her hand, her arm around me. It didn't rain. It was warm, sunny. I remember feeling sweaty and hot and ugly. My stomach was sore. The whirlpool of grief and guilt and anger seized me, washed over me in a wave of nausea. It was everything I could do to not vomit on the street.

It was a kind gesture from the community group, but I didn't want it.

I had gone to the hospital for an abortion. There had been a complication. The hospital had contacted Billy. I had told them not to tell him the reason I was having to stay in hospital overnight. I'd make something up. He didn't know I was pregnant again. And he had been killed whilst rushing to see me. The killing of my baby killed my husband. Some might say that was karma, divine intervention. Revenge. Maybe it was just a series of tragic events.

I place my hand onto the plaque and run my fingers along each letter, then the dove. It's like a second grave, but I imagine it's where his soul is rather than where his body is. Where his soul is trapped. A slight breeze moves along my neck, shifts the back of my hair. And that invisible pull I felt, that I feel whenever I walk past this sign, I realise is *him* – pulling me back to the spot where I lost him, where I caused him to lose me. To lose us.

-

Back home, I put the shoebox found by Jenni at the foot of the stairs, then I look in the drawers by the front door. I can't put it off any longer. Especially after today. Electricity runs through my body as I pull out the letters and mail addressed to Billy that I have hoarded away over the months, not daring to open them; the electricity sparks again at possibly finding something I don't want to see. Having his unopened mail just out of reach keeps him alive somehow, keeps the ever-fading possibility of his returning to me a little clearer, rather than being invisible forever. I think to take a photograph of all the letters before I open them, as they are in their current condition. Held. Trapping his essence. Then, I remember I'm still locked out of my phone - another twist in this tale I've found myself in. I try his birthday again. Nothing. A few variations just in case. I'm almost too exhausted to care.

I spread the envelopes over the kitchen table, letting my fingers hover over each one, just long enough to feel like I am taking something from them: something of Billy, something of us being together. A number of them are addressed to us both. My stomach twists with the sudden panic of bills and overdrafts that I should have opened as soon as they arrived. Maybe leaving them was a bad idea. Maybe opening them now *is* a bad idea... Can ignorance really be bliss? No. I steel myself and rip open one letter, quickly, like tearing off a plaster. A credit card statement - we paid these through monthly direct debit so it's okay that I ignored that one. The next is a letter to Billy offering life insurance. The irony doesn't evade me. Letter after letter moves from the mundane to the mundane: bank statement, store card offer, upgrading a mobile phone that neither of us owned, some magazine subscriptions, a subscription to a crossword and puzzle magazine. The only letter that raises my eyebrows is a headed piece of paper from another publishing agency, suggesting a meeting to merge our companies. I've never heard of them. I add it to the pile beside me.

There are only a few left and as I flip through useless finding after useless finding, suddenly I can't catch my breath.

One envelope, square, reveals a sympathy card. The front is covered in flowers, circled into a wreath-like shape. Gold lettering offers me condolences. I open the card slowly at arm's length. There is no 'Dear', no extended message inside apart from the vaguely polite comment already printed inside. Below is a name signed, 'Sam', and several kisses. I let out a sigh. 'Sam' doesn't register with me, and I find it a relief that it doesn't. If it was a close friend, a family member, the pain might have been stronger, too much. An ambiguous well-wisher leaves just emptiness. But then... *Sam*. The *Sam* that Mrs Lullin mentioned? No, how could it be?

I look over the mound of papers and torn envelopes, the odd stamp strewn over the table. It looks like a battleground, the fallen letters representing the dying embers of Billy, the final parts of him I had to hold onto. Numb, I stare at them, unsure whether leaving them unread would actually have been the better thing - because then, I would still have had something to look forward to. A lie that I could have kept hoping was a truth.

I wander upstairs, carrying with me the shoebox of notes that Jenni found at the office. I place it down on the bedroom floor. I run a bath. In the filling water I see papers and laptops and baby clothes, all floating. I think about how I haven't received a letter or email back from Andy yet today. I'm not sure how I feel about it... relief or dread, I can't decide. I see Jenni's hair drifting before me in the water. I think about her: how she had kept her fertility problems quiet, how much I had disliked her in the past only to now feel an odd connection with her. How I had felt a strange twinge of grief when she had mentioned Mrs Lullin. The guilt I felt for not thinking of *her* pain over Billy.

I look over at the shoebox on the floor at the foot of my bed. I sit on the floor and, opening the lid, run a hand through the pieces of paper inside. I notice something - the handwriting on all the notes is the same but it's not a style I recognise. It's certainly not Billy's. His looping cursive I would know anywhere. I read a few words that send shivers through me, cold ice down into my stomach.

Love. Us. Can't wait. Together. Tell her. Came.

Blood is rushing in my ears, getting louder and louder with each note I unfold, with each crumpled piece of paper I can find.

When. You. Hard. Wet.

Words jump out me in a staccato of knife-like jabs from the pages, each word a pinprick on my skin.

Forever. Hidden. Are you. Inside. Hotel. Sam.

I bolt up, realising that the rushing I hear isn't just the pumping of blood in my head but the overflowing bathtub. I dash through a cloud of steam and turn off the taps just as the water laps the edge of the tub. Silence - drip, drip, drips of water from my skin and hair, damp from the hot steam. The rushing of my blood is now a deep thump and thud that aches across my scalp.

I don't know what to do. I don't know what to think or say. I can't face looking at the shoebox again but I can't stand ignoring it either. This pandora's box just feet away from me. My hands are shaking, still gripping the bath taps. Through the steam I walk back into the bedroom and perch on the end of the bed. I look at the writing littered over the floor.

Billy. When. Cock. Again. Pleasure. Sam.

They are love letters.

Sam.

Secret love letters written to my husband.

Sam.

That was the name Mrs Lullin mentioned to me.

Sam.

The name of the person she said had been in her room just days before she had died.

Sam.

The condolence card.

Sam.

One handwritten line sends a dagger through my heart. The black ink might as well be poison:

Nine across, two then six letters. When two people cheat.

I take Billy's t-shirt from the top drawer and scream into it as loud as I can.

Nine across, two then six letters. When two people cheat.

An affair.

Nine across, two then six letters. When two people cheat.

Billy had been having an affair.

Sam.

The crossword puzzle. The crossword puzzle guts me.

He'd even had an affair in how he'd spoken with me.

-

Somehow, I arrive at work early the next morning. Something was pulsing through my veins. A mixture of anger and excitement. Nervousness and thrill. Something was happening. Something was going on. I knew it. I could feel it. I *wasn't* just imagining that there was a bigger story going on around me, or that I had been reading into moments and events and misunderstandings or coincidences. The card and notes from 'Sam' clarified this for me. This name, their sudden presence dropped into my life seemingly out of nowhere, meant something. It had to. I imagine telling Mrs Lullin about this - hadn't she suggested I write down loving memories of my husband? I wonder how she'd react to the irony of my finding those loving memories, only for them to have been written by someone else entirely

This morning, I studied the envelope and card and notes over and over. I ran my fingertips over the handwriting as if trying to find a vein, a road, anything within the ink that would lead me to who this person was. *Could* it be the same Sam that had visited Mrs Lullin? And if it was, what was the connection between us? I couldn't believe that my husband had been having an affair. I just couldn't bring myself to picture it. How could I have not known?

But you did. You had an affair. You fucked around on him.

I had never even heard of a *Sam* before. Thoughts rolled around in my head, down hills and into streams. Could it be Mrs Lullin's son, or a daughter? Perhaps he had a middle name? Maybe Jenni would find a link to a Sam somewhere in the emails she'd taken from our work computer.

You had an affair. Maybe he did too.

Before I managed to sleep last night, I had sat with my laptop open in front of me for what felt like hours. I had no idea what to write to this 'Andy' now in my life. Where *they* Sam? What on earth did I ask? What did I let them know? It felt rational at the time, to go out on a limb and email my writer, Andy, and see if I could get some kind of reaction out of him. It had been over a day since I had received an email or envelope, and up until finding the card and those letters I was glad of it, especially after the mild threat that had been scrawled on the back of the previous one. And to think I'd been starting to feel sympathetic for them. Now this. It all *had* to be connected somehow. And now I wanted answers. I needed to know who this person was. I needed to know who I had been communicating with.

-

To: caprahircus@hotmail.com

Re: Your manuscript

Dear Andy/i,

After receiving your latest extract, and the rather terse addition on the back of the envelope which enclosed your script, I am writing just to let you know that from now on, all communication regarding your manuscript (and any future works) should be sent directly to the current manager of Tulip and Thorn.

At present I am on sabbatical and, whilst I enjoy looking at some promising shorter works in my spare time, texts that appear to require more dedicated time, such as yours, are best handled by someone more senior in the agency.

Again, I would like to thank you for your interest in Tulip and Thorn and wish you all the best with your future writing. I am sure that my colleague will be happy to pick up our communication and continue to work with you as required if they choose to take your work further. I have passed your extracts so far onto them to look over. It would be best to wait for them to contact you, rather than you contact us again in the sam vein in which you have corresponded with me thus far.

Thank you again,

Ms Thorn.

-

My finger hovered over the 'send' button. I was worried it came across as too blunt, too cruel, too... exactly what they seemed to loathe publishing companies for in the first place. I had to remind myself that the sympathies I had been feeling were for the girl in the story, not the angry writer. I had to do something; I needed to try and coax them out and reveal some truth about what was really going on. I was counting on them picking up on my deliberate error.

Instead, I saved the email in my outbox, deciding that I would send it later today depending on what I managed to find out at work. I was at work on the pretence of carrying on as normal after Mrs Lullin's death. Just wanting to busy. What I really wanted though was to find some answers.

Lizzie was on the front desk, tapping away at her phone rather than answering the one that was ringing next to her. I picked it up, directed the call to elsewhere in the building, and smiled at Lizzie as she guiltily put her phone away.

"Sorry. I was just responding to my Dad."

"It's okay. It's not like I'm the boss or anything. Just don't get caught." I smiled again. "How's it been this morning?"

"Fine. Breakfast was breakfast. Morning classes have just started. Do you want the shift rota for the week?" Lizzie pulled a drawer open under the desk and handed me a clip chart, the names and dates and hours for shifts that week covering an A3 sheet. "Hey, you're in early. You don't start until 11."

"I know. I just thought that after what happened to Mrs Lullin I might as well come in a bit earlier and try to tidy up her things. I didn't manage to sort it all out the other day. Her room will most likely be taken in a day or so won't it? That's how it works around here."

"Yeah. One in and one out."

"It's better that someone gets to use the space though." I paused. I believed what I said; this *was* an important place for people to have access to. It was a luxury that younger people, including myself, took for granted: that when you grow older you will have someone to care for you, have somewhere to go and be looked after. This wasn't always the case. For someone like me, with no partner, no child, no one close in my family, what would happen when I grew old and infirm? Who would care for me if I needed it? "If someone needs caring for then they should have the room, right?"

"Definitely. I'm surprised it hasn't happened already. I mean twenty-four hours is a long time here. Usually, it happens the same day. You know how it is around here, as soon as one room becomes empty..."

"Have the police been back?"

"No. Not that I know of. But it's not being treated as a crime scene. Mark said they don't believe anything suspicious happened to Mrs Lullin. They might come back for some follow up questions if needed or if the son pushes it, but they're happy for staff to go into the room."

"I see. And is her room still full of her things?"

"Some. Her son came by last night to pack a few items up. I think he's just going to leave most it and donate it here actually. Clothes and things. He seemed to mostly want photographs and jewellery, you know, sentimental stuff."

Stuff. Such a throwaway term about objects accumulated during a life. "Am I okay to go into her room? I'd like a last look in before... you know..."

Unexpectedly, Lizzie reached over and placed her hand upon mine. Her sudden change from flippancy to empathy threw me. "Yes of course. And you can check if there's anything else to keep or move out?"

"Listen," I said, patting her hand before pulling mine away, "could you do me a simple favour? Could you look at the visitor records over the last few weeks? I'm trying to locate a visitor that Mrs Lullin mentioned."

"I can try. What's the name?"

"I only have a first name. Sam."

"No last name will make it trickier, but I'll see what I can find."

"Can you also get me the number of the son? Of Mrs Lullin's son?"

"We're not really meant to hand over information like that. Unless it's, you know, an emergency."

"Yes. I'd just like to just pass on my condolences. I worked with his mother for months. She was a terrific lady. I never got to say goodbye to her, and I didn't get to meet him. It's just something I'd like to do." It wasn't a lie.

She nodded. "Sure." She placed the rota clipboard back into the drawer and opened another, pulling out several files. "Check back in with me later."

"Thanks Lizzie. I really appreciate it."

-

You watered the tulips in the hallway this morning. Buying the flowers reminded you of Billy, and that is okay.

-

I make my way down the main corridor to where Mrs Lullin's room was. I can't think about it being *her* room now though I tell myself. I need to see it as a space where people stay, move into and move on from. Relationships with death are complicated, intertwined with people and places and memories and the forever not knowing who will be around, until when. Yet it isn't as simple as turning her room into a vacant, available space, for as soon as I put my hand on the door handle I am pulled back into thoughts of her.

"What do you mean his fingernails? Who misses someone's fingernails?"

I smile at the memory of her. And of Billy.

Her room is pretty much empty. The bed has been made up with new sheets and I can smell the laundry detergent, the scent trapped in the room like a breath being held. One at a time I look inside the drawers, all bare. The cupboard is also vacant of clothing and shoes. The cabinet behind the bathroom mirror presents only a few loose cotton earbuds. I even kneel and look under the bed, only to find a single slipper - not one I recognise as hers. I wonder what else I never got to find out about her, other stories she hadn't told me or had *forgotten* to tell as the years started to erase her memory, as the dementia slowly began to seep into her brain and clog the pictures she held.

"Are you Michelle?"

I turn around to find an old man standing in the doorway, one hand on the handle, the other on a walking stick.

"Are you Michelle? Did you know Mrs Lullin?"

"Yes. I mean, yes my name is Michelle and yes, I knew her. Meredith."

"Awful what happened to her."

"Were you a friend of her?"

"Not really. I'm up on the top floor and my bones aren't what they used to be. Even with the stairlift I mainly just stayed upstairs in my room." He shuffles inside, just a few steps. He seems uncomfortable. "She did mention you though. We sometimes played bingo together and we'd trade stories about the orderlies and workers here. Well, all the old folks here do that. We do like a good gossip." He chuckles a little, and the gentle sound reminds me of her. "Of course, she gave you a very good review. Not like some of them here. I mean…" he manages, despite his fragile looking body, to lean backwards and look down the corridor, and then point with his thumb in the same direction, "that girl on the reception desk. Thick as two short planks if you ask me."

I stifle a laugh. I can tell why Mrs Lullin would have liked him and I tell him this. He tells me his name is Nathan.

"So, are you moving in here? Into her room?"

He takes a few steps back, lowering his head. "Yes. I hope that's not too difficult for you. I presume you'll stay looking after me in here too. I don't know how it works when patients move. Do you stay attached to a room or a patient?"

...a room or a patient. That sends a chill down my spine. How awful to think of yourself like that: a place or an illness. I don't know whether it was what Nathan said, or being in her room, perhaps a mixture of everything else going at the moment, but I started to cry, just a little. I could feel it coming and couldn't stop it. I clutched the slipper to my chest, choked on an intake of air, desperate not to make a fool of myself.

"Oh dear, oh no. I'm sorry. I shouldn't have come and said anything to you." I wave my hand at him to signal it's not his fault. "Doddering old fool that I am. I'm sorry dear."

"No, no," I croak out, "it's not you. You should have this room. And I'd be happy to work with you. Honestly." I smile at him, he still looks concerned. "I guess... what happened to her was a shock. You get more acquainted with the people you care for than you realise, you know?"

He nods. He smiles at me again, kindly. "Well, there's no reason *we* shouldn't get on, is there? There's nothing I like more than talking."

"Do you have family? To visit you, I mean."

"Some. They come when they can. They're busy with the grandchildren and school clubs and ballet and well, you must know what it's like."

I nod. Now probably isn't the best time to unload.

"Would you like to see a photo? I have a phone. A mobile!"

I can't help but laugh. He produces a small phone from his pocket with such relish that the obvious pride he has in having one, something modern, is very endearing.

"I can use most of the bits and bobs on it. My daughter in law got it for me. It's so much easier to keep in contact with everyone back home. I can call and text and send pictures," he runs this off, like a child proud of a school achievement, "but these other things like *Snapgram* or whatever. Well, not a clue."

I walk over and see one photograph he has loaded up on the screen. It shows a man and woman, his son and the daughter-in-law I presume, in an embrace. He moves the screen onto a picture of some children. Then what looks like a party. Then a photograph of himself with a woman.

"That's Natalie. She passed away a while ago now." He smiles at the screen for a few seconds, and then puts it away in his pocket. "That's why I moved in here. I couldn't look after myself as well as she did for me." He looks up at me and I see Mrs Lullin in his face. In his skin I see part of each elderly person that we care for: in his forehead wrinkles I see the weddings; in his crows' feet I see the births of children and grandchildren; in the creases by his nose I see the deaths of loved ones; in his folds of skin by his neck I see the worries of not getting to see next week, or tomorrow. A loved one.

I think again of Mrs Lullin and her advice about stories, about my memories. *'But they're not just your memories now are they? He fucked someone else. Didn't he.'* Suddenly, it cuts in - unbidden and sharp like a papercut.

"Would you like to see some of my pictures, Nathan? Of my family?"

"You see," he wags his finger at me, "that's why Meredith liked you. You talk to us oldies here like we're actual people. I bet most of the staff don't even know our names."

We sit down on the bed, me helping him with his walking stick, and I pull out my phone. Instinctively, I tap in the passcode, Billy's birthday, and it works. I'd forgotten that just yesterday I'd been locked out of my phone altogether. And that's not all that changed: the screensaver is back to my old photograph. Did I imagine the whole thing?

"Are you okay dear?"

"Yes... yes. Sorry, I...."

I try not to dwell on it - whatever I did or didn't do - but a sharp sensation, like a scalpel on skin, skims my heart when I see Billy's face glowing back up at me from the screen. I could swear that I took that picture just yesterday. That we were just at that family dinner last night.

"That's your husband?" Nathan asks.

"Yes. Yes, that's Billy."

Nathan's eyes close in on the picture. It's as if he's really straining to see the screen.

"Can you see? Do you need your glasses or anything?"

"Oh no. I can see just fine. I don't wear glasses dear. Your husband, he... has one of those faces. He seems familiar. Smiley. He looks happy." A beat. "Please, go on!"

"Sure, if you're interested." I show him some more photos, one after the other: Billy behind his desk in our publishing office, some random pictures inside our house such as of our new sofa, one of my father waving. I eventually come to a picture of our wedding day.

"You made a beautiful bride."

"Thank you. I'm sure your wife did too."

I swipe through a few more pictures and realise that I am probably boring him now. "No, not at all," he says, "I'd love to have chats like this with more people. Come on, show me just one or two more and then you can get on working."

"Well, this is our collective family I guess you could say." I point out my parents, Billy's parents, Jenni, some cousins that were in the background. I made up one of their names as I couldn't remember it.

"This is your wedding reception?"

"Yeah. I look so young there. And thinner." Nathan knocks into me, as though to tell me I look fine now too. "Him and his sister look alike, don't they?" I say.

"They really do." Again, he appears to be straining to see the picture.

"Most people say it's..."

"Their eyes." Nathan cuts me off before I finish my own comparison. But he's right. The eyes.

"Yes. The eyes. They seem to run in the family. Just look at their mother." I place the tip of my finger just under her chin in the picture.

"If you cut her hair or gave him longer hair, well... they'd almost be the same person. Are they not twins?"

"No. No, not at all. But they do look similar. Everyone said so."

"I could swear..." Nathan holds his sentence there in mid-air, almost a whisper. He continues to look at the photograph on my phone until it fades to standby.

"Do you recognise someone? Maybe a relative or guest in the background?" It's not implausible. It's not a large town and we did get married near here.

"No... him. I could have sworn I saw him *here*."

"*Billy*? When?" I can't bring myself to tell him why that would be impossible.

"Must be my old age. People start to look the same and faces merge together." He taps his head, implying someone forgetful. "Like I said," he pats my hand now, "your husband has one of those faces. Some people do, don't they?"

I help him to his feet, tell him I'll be on hand if needed to help move his things down from his room. He shakes my hand.

"Thank you. It's been nice to meet you, Michelle. I feel a little bit better now about moving. I'm looking forward to it."

And with that, he leaves me in Meredith's room, alone. I place the slipper I found back on the floor at the foot of the bed. Billy's face floats up before my eyes. Billy was never here. There's no way he could have been here. Is there? Nathan is just a forgetful, old man. Billy is not alive. How could he be?

I close the door behind me. I am grabbing my wrist.

-

During lunch, Lizzie came to find me.

"So, I got you his contact number. It's his mobile. Can you make something up when you call him? Cover for me? I don't want to get into trouble."

"I will," I said as I took the piece of paper from her, "I'll tell him I got his number myself if he asks. Don't worry. Thank you."

"But I couldn't find anything to do with a 'Sam'. I found a *Samantha* but that was just the lady who filled in to run the Bingo a few weeks ago when the regular person called in sick. No *Samuel* or any other name I could find that was similar. Nothing else, I'm sorry."

"You've done more than enough. Honestly, thank you."

-

I decide to call him from a café on the way home. I hung my finger over the call button for a few moments after typing in the number, running through some of the things I would say to him to make sure the conversation went as smoothly as possible, to not arise any suspicions.

He picked up on the third ring.

"Hello?"

"Afternoon. Is this the son of Mrs Lullin?"

"Can I ask who is calling?"

"Sorry, yes of course. I worked at the care home where your mother was living. My name is Michelle. I cared for your mother."

There was a pause. I wasn't sure whether to continue speaking, immediately worrying that I had made a mistake, that he was going to hang up and call to make a complaint that his number had been given out to a member of staff. Then he said: "She mentioned a Michelle. Did you work with her long?"

"She was one of my main patients actually." I shiver at using the word by accident. "I don't like the word *patient* but you get used to saying it unfortunately. She was a wonderful lady." I'm nervous.

"Thank you. Is everything okay? Has something else happened?"

"No. Not at all. Sorry for the call. I hope this doesn't cause you any further distress. I just wanted to pass on my condolences. It didn't seem right to approach you the morning that the police were here, but I wanted to just try and contact you to let you know how sorry I was, I am, for what happened to your mother. She was a lovely person to get to know. I loved taking care of her."

"That's very kind of you to say. She, er, she was one of a kind."

I laughed, thinking I could hear something like a smile through the words he spoke. "Yes she was. She had wonderful stories."

"To tell you the truth, I worried constantly about whether I had made the right decision to place her in a home. Assisted living. But whatever I tried it never seemed like the right solution for her. And us."

"I'm sure it's not an easy decision. It never seems to be, from my experiences working here."

"I wanted her to come and live with me and my family, but she didn't want to leave where she had been with my father. I understand that. Understood, I should say, I guess. But my wife didn't want to move and our son is only a year old so... it didn't seem right or easy to just... well..."

"I didn't know you had a son, that Mrs Lullin had a grandson."

"They had only met each other once or twice. But mum was starting to forget things and become difficult at times and... it wasn't always an easy task explaining to her who he was. Who we were."

It seemed pathetic to say 'I'm sorry' so I didn't. I just listened.

"Well, I've chatted mindlessly at you for a couple of minutes now. I do apologise." Formality returned to his voice again. "But I must be going. Thank you, though, for your call. It's good to know she had company where she was."

"She did. She was popular here, I promise you that."

I couldn't ask him about a 'Sam' – it didn't seem right. I was invading his time of grief. We traded a few more short pleasantries and ended the call. I think about Mrs Lullin and how her changes in mood and memory loss must have been happening, creeping in, for some time. It upset me, the idea of her not understanding who her grandson was; of her son explaining things that seem so basic and human to me – knowing who your blood was. I feel guilty too that I suspected him of being caught up in these odd events somehow; of being a careless son. But, I'm back now to square one about whoever this Sam is, if I was ever past a square at all.

I take out my phone, find the email I composed last night in my draft folder. I hit 'send'.

If we had a kid what would call it? Billy says.

Well, not 'it' that's for sure, I say.

Like the clown, Billy says.

To be fair, giving birth does seem like a fucking horror show, I say.

Billy sniggers.

As suspected, it didn't take long for me to get a reply.

EMAIL TWO

From: caprahircus@hotmail.com

Re: Re: Your manuscript

Dear Ms Thorn,

Thank you for your email. I must admit that I am a little downhearted after reading your recent message. I understand though that my previous letter may have seemed somewhat intimidating and I can only apologise for that. Sadly, my interest and passion in my projects often gets the better of me and patience is not my strongest virtue. I hope that I have not burnt this bridge as, until now, I have not been lucky enough to have even the slightest dialogue with an editor, publisher or anyone in the industry and would hate for that to now come to an end. I do appreciate though your offer to pass my manuscript onto a fellow colleague.

I wonder though if I could ask two favours. As I type this I realise how I don't really have the right to ask but I suppose I have nothing else to lose!

First of all, I would like to explain to you my passion for my writing and where my ideas for the text come from. Have you ever taken a moment to look at literature, film, art, religion, history and think about how women have been represented? Are continually represented? You yourself, in previous correspondence with me, highlighted that the place of women in modern society is akin to a 'hot potato' topic, that women trying to speak up for themselves is deemed taboo, as wrong and inappropriate. If you recognise that this is a serious issue still plaguing women in the 21st century then I have to ask why, as a woman, as an educated person, as someone involved in the publishing world with the potential power to print and send out meaningful words, why would you then ignore this topic within a piece of writing such as my own?

I recently went to a gallery where on display there was a painting named The Birth of Pandora, foreboding her cursed box. The more I looked at it the more my mind wandered to just how many times and ways women have been blamed, chastised, cast out for causing ruin, disease, famine and whatever other crime that men can point towards the opposite sex. The 'lesser' sex. I found myself asking why this was the case, why this has always been the case. Eve was blamed for Adam being flung out of heaven, tempted by the devil, the snake, the phallus that seemingly no woman can ignore. Women caused the fall of mankind. Not men. Not the men who rape and pillage and cause war and terrorism and the sublimation of the female sex. Women, if we are to believe all we are shown, are to blame for their own downfall too.

But how can we possibly deny this fact when we are constantly bombarded with images of how women should look, should act, should smell, should eat, yet are similarly torn apart by their peers for being too confident, too thin, too sexual, too nonconformist? The catch 22, the vicious cycle of historical sexism angered me. It angers me now.

But I am sure you are thinking what on earth this has to do with my writing and the manuscript I have been sending to you. Well, just think about it for a moment: do you see any recently published books containing a female lead in which the protagonist is not in some way fallible or depressed or addicted or violent or overtly sexual or abused in some way? They are alcoholics who have lost children and husbands, self-harmers with a history of family mental illness, girls who have to kill for survival, women constricted to one room or one house, one role to be a birthing machine, twentysomethings with drug addled twins who disappear. No wonder misogyny still exists. We perpetuate it by not realising that what we hail as modern women, these characters who 'take back the night' only act to actually degrade women further. They become their own antagonists.

And then they become films.

Or plays. Or television shows. And women who are beaten and drunk and vulnerable are viewed by millions who ignorantly accept that the only way a woman can be powerful and strong is by battling through fight after shout after battering time and time again. And how do they cope? A man helps them with a break in. A man calls someone who knows someone who worked with someone on the police force. A man sleeps with them despite their puffy, bloated, sin filled body. And the men are then the heroes of her story. There's a reason it's known as history.

Have you read the Ten Commandments in the Bible? I studied these at university and found myself asking why it is seen as a sin to 'covet thy neighbour's wife', which immediately implies that a) a woman has to be married and cannot be single b) a woman belongs to a man, implied by the possessive apostrophe c) neither a man nor woman can be gay d) no one would covet a female neighbour's husband (...why is that, exactly?) and finally, e) woman are made to be wanted, seemingly against their will or choice.

Do you see what I am getting at here? There is a real, tangible reason our world, culture, life has a history and never a herstory. Woman have been written out of the past, even in religion.

There's a reason it's known as history.

Do you know just how many countries still follow the laws of arranged marriages? Or that Saudi Arabia only allowed women to drive in 2018? That women have only been able to hold the role of Bishop in the Church of England since 2014? That in countries around the world, even places as close as Ireland up until 2018, women still cannot choose to have an abortion? Women are dying for the same treatment and chances that men have always had, a freedom of choice they simply take for granted.

And it makes me angry.

So - I wanted to write a story, a herstory I suppose, where a woman doesn't turn to a man to be saved, where she doesn't shy away from her problems but embraces them; where she accepts the fact that she doesn't deserve to be treated badly by a man because that is what time and history dictates should happen. I realise that the extracts you have received so far perhaps do not fully show that yet, but the novel as whole works towards showing women as being worthy without men having to be there to act as a white knight. I promise you this.

My second request then, is that you allow me to send just one or two more extracts, hopefully bringing my argument and passion to light. I know that this is a big ask, I understand I don't necessarily deserve the sam patience you have shown me so far.

There is no need for you to reply to this email at all; you have, quite rightly, made it clear that all communication should now go through other channels and I should wait to hear from your colleague. However, unless I hear from you requesting not to receive a final few extracts I will at least send them to you, whether they be read or not.

Yours Sincerely,

Ant.

-

The word I'd hoped to see pulses up at me from the screen. He took the bait and responded. *I understand I don't necessarily deserve the sam patience you have shown me so far.* He knows what I know. Or think I know. The duplicity between us is oddly invigorating and draws me in despite wanting nothing more to do with this person, their story. Whoever they are. And now they're going by the name of *Ant*? I rub my temples, trying to massage away the thoughts and questions and worries and bizarre throbbing thrill that rushes around my head. It's not until I open my eyes and see my reflection across from me in the bedroom mirror that I realise my other hand is raised too, gripping the wrist of the hand rubbing my forehead. I lower my arms but keep my hand and wrist as they are, linked and grasped, and watch my wrist become redder and redder, feel the pinch of twisted skin, before I snap out of it, from under a spell.

I wander down to the kitchen. I don't know what to do next. I want to reply but am fearful to. There has been a shift now. Whoever this *A* is, they know that I am aware of something amiss, some mystery. I find myself looking through my kitchen window and out into the black night. I feel that I am in a glass box waiting for a stone to be thrown and to shatter it. Panic and electricity jolt through my body. What am I wanting? What am I hoping to find?

I find my gaze drawn to the wine rack and the single bottle. I want to do more than merely open it and smell its contents, so I make my hands do anything else. They tap the counter. They tie up my hair. They push around some papers on the kitchen table. But the pull is there, from bottle to finger, that rotting umbilical cord not yet cut between mother and child – it is fleshy, pulpy, and it throbs with something more than blood.

From birth to after birth.

-

You showered.

-

I imagine sometimes that my child didn't die. He comes to me in dreams, and I wake up suddenly, urgently grabbing at the air above me. Other times, she appears in a daydream, floating past me on the street. Times like that, I don't always realise what I'm imagining for a couple of seconds, until the blinding pain hits. The guilt. I never know whether it would have been a boy or girl, so each vision, each false memory is slightly different: blue eyes, brown hair; narrow green eyes, misty, with blonde locks. In my dream last night, first she was sitting at the end of my bed, then I was perched at the end of hers. She turned away from me. I couldn't see her face. She had flecks of light hair along her arms, teenage and young. A few freckles covered her skin like a map. There was a vase of tulips on the windowsill, and she told me that her father had bought them for her to celebrate an anniversary. She told me to leave, to get out of her room, *Just leave mum, just leave me alone,* and I knew that's what she needed but I'd already let her go once and I didn't know how to for a second time. When the baby comes to me as a boy, I never fully see his face. He's only ever in profile – nose long, pointed, artistic looking like a brush bent in half. With my daughter I only ever see the back of her head, hearing how angry she is with me.

-

I wake from the dream, bedsheets wrapped around me. I dread going downstairs. I don't want to see the bottle and what I worry I have done. I reach for my phone and tap in my password, grateful that this morning it doesn't have any unwanted surprises for me. Turning down the glare, I make a to-do list for the day:

- Donna for coffee at 10
- Must tidy house – don't put off vacuuming again
- Meeting at 8 – fortnightly group
- Text Jenni re: email
- Write new post-it note. Positive.

I breathe in, feeling a familiar sense of calm in having a to do list. It centres everything for the day. It makes the vast expanse of time, of the day ahead, slightly less daunting, less submerged in silence - I have things to fill the void.

-

That evening, I go to my group meeting. I just listened. I don't interact in every session unless prompted or asked to. One lady speaks about the death of her mother. It hangs before all of us, the visceral feeling that grief creates, permeates into a room when it occurs. I thought once about trying to bottle it, what it would look like, smell like. I decided on burnt toast. New perfume – 'Charred Black'.

My mind drifts and most of what the lady talks about moves over and around me in waves, words that hold no meaning for me: I understand what she *says*, I can understand what she is feeling in terms of her reaction to grief, but I don't feel anything *for* her, towards her. I look at her and imagine how my eyes must seem glazed and hollow, unfeeling. I sometimes wonder if this what grief has done to me, leaving me without emotions, as though that is my penance.

The latest email from him, her, Andy, whoever, slides into my thoughts and I visualise them typing away at me, electric sparks from the screen, angry that I am allowing myself as a woman to feel guilt for what has happened *to* me and not *by* me, what I had a right to do *to* my body and not dictated *for* my body. Oddly, it's comforting to know that they would understand. For a moment I imagine that they are my baby, grown up far too quickly against the laws of time, and are as sexless and genderless as my dreams make them be. I want something to hold onto.

The lady continues to talk. She is putting a tissue to her eyes now in that annoying way that women do, as if dabbing the tiny corner of tissue to your eye will prevent the tears that are forming. I want to tell her to rub her goddamn eye properly. People on either side of her are putting a hand here and there. Like before, what she says registers in meaning but not in emotion. I make sure to nod and tilt my head to feign empathy.

You're so fucking cruel. You aren't emotionless. You're just heartless, it says. It's probably right. This is what it feels like to be drunk. To wander randomly from thought to thought in a stream of consciousness that lilts and drifts aimlessly like life itself: finite but endless.

I remember opening the bottle of wine last night. I remember wanting more than to just smell the drink inside. Did I put the bottle to my lips? I feel my fingers tracing my bottom lip, see red wine dripping from my forefinger's nail as if blood, colouring my mouth as though I have feasted on flesh or some bloody cluster of grapes crushed underfoot, mashed into wine, into drink, into alcohol. Into my mouth. I can't remember. I can't remember. My hand is still pressed to my lips, and it scares me... my lack of memory scares me

Philip motions for someone else to speak now. No one volunteers, so instead he asks me a question directly.

"Michelle, are you still writing yourself positive notes?"

"Yes."

"Good. Tell me."

"I am. I am Philip, honestly. Most days, anyway."

The short happy notes were his idea. I hated it at first. But I do it. As often as I feel I deserve to.

"And are you keeping them? I know you question these ideas of mine, I know you find it 'fluffy' to quote your own description." I can't help but smile, like a naughty child found out at school. "But being kind to yourself is important. It's *so* important, Michelle."

"I am. I promise. Each morning, I write myself a short email and send it to myself, or the post-its I write I leave by the front door and then put them in a little pot to the side. Just like you told me to do." I nod at him, reassuring him that I am good student. "God, if anyone ever hacked my emails I would look fucking mental."

"Why do you say that?"

This is why Philip is so annoying. And, also, so good at his job. He always questions your wording, questions your reactions to everything. If you are made to explain your words rather than have them numbly accepted by someone, only then do you start to realise what you said maybe isn't really what you mean. He's wonderful - but irritating.

"I just mean... it makes me feel sad."

"Why?"

Because it's never going to get better, is it? You know it and so does everyone else.

"At my age. Writing myself post-it notes and emails telling myself... what a good job I did on something that day or will do that day... it seems... like I should be *normal* by now. Over all of this." My hands open and close, grasping for something, finding nothing.

"Michelle, you are normal. Maybe not how you want to be right now, not the okay where you feel you're good enough - Jesus, no one ever feels that. You're doing well just to be here. Trust me."

Pathetic little notes and emails. You sad bitch. Don't listen to him. He doesn't know what you did.

"Trust me."

Someone near me puts their hand on my shoulder. I want to scream. Their words melt into the stagnant air of the room. From the fist that I didn't even realised I had clenched, I slowly uncoil one finger for each thing I can remember from last night. I try my hardest to hold off the voice that is eager to strike at me like a dagger.

One finger – the email. One finger – wanting to smell the wine, just to sate my need to drink. One finger – the dreams of him, or her. One finger – seeing Donna this morning and keeping to an engagement, even though it was the last thing I wanted to do. One finger – I tidied the bathroom, the bedroom, I vacuumed, I dusted and mopped. I kept busy.

I nod my head to appear engaged in whatever this person is saying to me - I really *should* be trying to listen to this person who is also grieving and whom I could maybe learn from if I tried to, if I stayed positive and in the moment rather than drift and ignore and shut out what is or could be or, or, or and if, if, if...

Tony's face appears in front of me.

Oops. One finger needs to go back down. Tony, Tony, Tony!

I curl one finger back down. The voice is right. I don't deserve to feel good about myself.

I look directly at the person talking now, focus and breathe in what they say. I hear words such as *they* and *miss* and *wanted* and *milk* and suddenly I am back with Donna that morning.

"Bloody hell. Now I understand why she voted against abortion back home."

"What do you mean?"

"Well, she isn't exactly going to be supportive of it is she? Why would she be?"

"Aren't you? Supportive of it, I mean?"

"I don't mind what people do. I'd always let someone choose what they want to do with their own body. I mean, luckily, I've never had to make that choice but... yeah, I can see why she voted it down."

"Are you on her side now?"

"What? Michelle no... I just. Well, surely you can see where she's coming from?"

"Yes. Yeah. I do. Of course I do."

"I can't believe she said you can be *non-mothers* together. That's a bit weird."

"So, you're back to disliking her then."

"Mate, have I missed something here? What's gotten you so riled up?"

How could I ever tell her? About what I had done? *Have* done. Tell Donna, or Jenni, or our families, or... There's nothing I can say that would explain what happened. What I caused to happen. And yes, I tell myself, I understand what Jenni voted for, what she believes in, which only makes my own choices and actions hurt even more. It makes her kindness towards me even more painful. It makes our relationship drown in even more guilt.

I leave the group meeting early. 'At least I went', I tell myself, I haven't been a complete failure today. Back home I look at the bottle of wine in the kitchen. It's still full. I need to message Donna and apologise for being abrupt. I need to email Leesha to chase up on her finding any stories for me. I remember that on my to do list was to also contact Jenni. I text her about any progress on finding something on the office computer. I also ask her to look for any links to a 'Sam'. I half expect her to just ignore me, fed up with my paranoid questions to find this and look for that. A random story that might not even exist. A random name. Just a few minutes later though my phone buzzes:

Hi, nothing to report yet on the circus story. But I'll keep looking. I've got a long train journey back up north tomorrow so I'll spend most of the time doing that! I can try and search for a Sam too... any reason why? J x

I wasn't sure what to explain over a text message, so I just typed that I might have found another connection to who had been emailing me. She texts back a simple *Okay* and *Keep busy* and *I'll see you in a few days*. Her words bounce around inside me like a ricocheting bullet. I don't know how I can get through keeping in contact with her, knowing what she has been through. I text a vague apology to Donna. I leave messaging Leesha until the morning, adding it to tomorrow's currently empty to do list.

I get into bed with the iPad. I spend a few minutes mulling over whether to waste time on gossip sites or news or downloading a film. Before I can decide, a notification pops up:

To: michellebookworm@gmail.com

From: caprahircus@hotmail.com

Re: re: re: Your manuscript

It takes me by surprise. I hadn't emailed back, so didn't expect another email from them quite so soon. Then again, they did say that they'd take silence rather than an emailed refusal, as an invitation to send more material. The *Re: re: re:* makes me feel like I'm stuck in Groundhog Day, a loop, destined to reply reply reply to an unknown black hole. A boy then a girl then the back of a head sparks before my eyes, then withers away into smoke. I worry that tonight she will come back into my dreams and be angry with me again. I tap the notification and read the email.

EMAIL THREE

Dear Mum,

It feels strange writing this to you but hopefully it will give me some peace at last.

I realise it might come as a little bit of a shock hearing from me after all these years, but there probably would never have been, will never be, a perfect time - so why not now?

I've read enough books and seen plenty of films to know that a sudden letter like this can easily unbalance the status quo of a previously happy life - something like Desperate Housewives, only without the thinning waistlines year after year. I don't know how often you have thought about me, but I have thought about you every day for years. It really has been that long. I would know.

I'm not sure where to start really, so it's probably just best to tell you a little about myself. I know that you gave me up. Don't worry, I'm not mad. It happens. I know that people have lots of reasons for doing what they do as parents, in relationships, with jobs. It's fine. I only really started to think about my life and who my mother would have been, who my father might have been, when I started at university last year.

There was a rally on abortion near my lecture building on campus and a few of my classmates wanted to go along and show their support. I don't know if you maybe heard about it on the news. It was over a girl who had been raped on a night out with her friends, the boy was never caught (not that the university tried to help her, not really) and the main reason it seemed to make the press was that the girl had had an abortion afterwards. And people were fucking vicious. I mean, can you imagine? Being violated like that and then having the consequences of that terrible event splashed over social media and local news? As if that was the crime and not the rape itself? After all, we're living in a time where the most powerful man in the world can brag about sexual assault, so I guess anything goes. I don't think I realised how this issue made me feel, what my reaction would be to it, until I was right there in the melee. There were placards and chants and banners and people of all ages and genders and sizes and races and backgrounds together, shouting and demanding and supporting. It was amazing. It really was.

It was later that night that I lay in bed and found myself wondering about the baby. The baby that had been aborted. I didn't for one second judge the girl. I mean, I have no idea what I would have done in that situation, so I couldn't possibly cast aspersions on her. We live in a #metoo world now, don't we? But my mind kept drifting to the baby in their crib, crying, or taking their first steps. Still, even days and weeks later, I'd suddenly think about this kid as a teenager and their first kiss, or passing school exams, meeting a boy, bunches of roses and tulips and daisies, all manifesting into that perfect first date. Taking a road trip across America down Route 66. Making mistakes. Cheating. Marrying someone. Having a son or daughter of their own.

I decided that the best thing to do would be use these thoughts and feelings and put them into my writing. I study English Literature by the way mum, and a few of the courses test our own creative skills: poetry and short story, that kind of thing. I started writing from the child's point of view, a mini mystery with this teenager trying to solve who their parents were and how they disappeared: conspiracy, kidnapping, maybe they weren't alive anymore, or did their parents simply not want to be found? One passage linked their own birth to the downfall of their parents, as though them being born caused their parents' pain. Her birth birthed their struggle somehow. A problematic child Eve, and the blaming parent of Adam.

You know mum, there is nothing worse than being an unwanted child.

'She imagined her birth like a painting of Pandora and her ill-fated box. Demons and fiery hell spilled from her mother's womb in her place. She wasn't born a baby, she wasn't born at all. It was just slick red blood, pumping like red wine from a broken bottle, down into an abyss between her legs, between valleys that tried to close up to prevent black smoke and wet cold mist from smothering all. Where hands should have come down to pick her up and swaddle her and bathe her and love her, there were knives shooting down from the ashen sky like props being tossed in a circus show. Knife and throw and hit and knife and throw and hit and... she didn't stand a chance. She didn't stand a chance of being wanted.'

That paragraph caused a bit of a stink in my seminar. Some liked the imagery, likening a metaphorical birth to the physical and emotional hell it can be for women, and mirroring a womb with Pandora's box. One student (a boy, obviously) said it made him feel queasy. One girl said it was a clear "fuck you" to how women have been blamed for everything since time began. My lecturer said he thought it had "potential" but that with the recent student campaigns and rallies he didn't think it would be "prudent" to be published in that term's newsletter which usually promotes up and coming talented students across the university.

Fine. Play it safe, I told myself. Fine. Publish a poem or short story about a bored student in class who mindlessly links paperclips together - an allegory for the Mexican wall, or something. Fine.

I hope you liked it though. Or can at least understand where it came from. I needed to delve into the thoughts and feelings and possibilities of this child and use it, somehow, to work through my own questions. I knew what it felt like to be unwanted, to be the product of a mistake.

I know what it means when people say that actions have consequences. Because I am one.

I think that's maybe why I drift into so many stories and characters, try and feel what other people feel. I can be whoever I want in those tales, I can change how I look and speak and act. I can become someone other than myself. We all love an unreliable narrator, don't we?

I've left my contact details on the back of the envelope, so if you want to meet up then we can. You might not want to. Maybe you'll call me and we'll both just pretend it's a wrong number. It might be easier that way.

Maybe it's all too much too soon, or rather, too little too late. Maybe you've forgotten about me. Maybe this is just an inconvenience. Maybe this will dredge up memories of that night, when my would-be father reduced you to imagining sliced up boxes of flesh as he fucked you against your will. At least there's a plaque there now. At least something has been commemorated and acknowledged out of all this.

You know how I said that there's nothing worse than being an unwanted child? Scrap that. There's nothing worse than being an abortion.

And I'm yours,

Antony.

-

The bin by my bed smells of vomit in the morning. I vomited as soon as I finished the email. I vomited again as I read it the second time, then third, then fourth... until I couldn't face it anymore. My wrist aches.

This time the letter wasn't just an exercise in writing, it wasn't an excerpt from a manuscript from some random eccentric writer. There were no mistakes this time. No hidden message. Because the message was clear.

They knew who I was. They knew what I had done. They knew about Billy. They knew about my child. None of this was a coincidence.

They know so much about my life and I have no idea *how*. Or *who* they are.

Antony was always the name that Billy said we would have for our first son. And for a girl, any name with an *A*.

My wrist is burning.

I run water from the bath tap into the bin. The noise and splashing of the water is a welcome distraction. I should have known from the very first letter.

A... A... A...

They want to meet up, that much is clear. But I don't know who they are. My wrist is throbbing.

I'll make myself a list about them - a whodunnit of whoever they could be. A list is what I am good at. It's what I always do when I feel the need to get some control back. If I tick something off then I have achieved. The only problem with tick-lists and to-do lists is that they can be never ending and I have no idea where to start or who to ask or turn to or why why why they would do this and my wrist aches aches aches and I want a drink I want a drink I want a drink.

What if it's not someone you know at all? What if this is all inside your own drunken head and swollen belly? it says.

I realise something.

They didn't email me at my work account.

They'd contacted me directly.

PART THREE

I called Leesha and I called Jenni and I called Donna I can't remember in what order I didn't contact Tony - their conversations were so heated and protective and angry and maybe I shouldn't have called them one after the other because when I got into bed that night every word seemed to melt into another, each conversation drip into the other - I lay in bed and their faces swam above me like I was in a drunken haze, that swirling sensation of being drunk which loops and loops and loops around you as though are on a rollercoaster and I didn't contact Tony - they all said "You need to report this to the police now because if you want to meet him then it would have to be in daylight and I think I've found some pieces possibly linked to what you've asked me to look out for but simply ignoring this isn't going to work they got into your fucking email account so I could be there too and sit a few tables away and at least get a good look at them if nothing else so I'll send them over sit tight and keep safe" and I didn't contact Tony but Billy had an affair he had an affair even with how to spoke to me and I found the evidence and I found the love letters and I fell into a drunken sleep

-

If this doesn't start to get better, know that you can still end it.

-

I wake up to Tony's name flashing up at me on my phone screen. Last night plunges down upon me like water from a showerhead. My eyes open and close erratically. My breathing is in short bursts. Once again, I can't remember drinking last night but I must have done because this feeling in my head, my bones, is more than just the stress of yesterday. My dry and stale mouth is another sign.

It's a text message. He wants to know if I'm okay and to stop by for breakfast before I go to work. I don't know if it's because of our last conversation, if Donna has told him I'm off the rails again, whether he's just being kind. Maybe it's a reply to a call or message from me. I close my eyes, hope to the God I don't believe in that my outbox is empty. Thankfully it is. There are a few messages to Jenni and Donna. There are outgoing calls from last night.

Jenni has text me too, asking for details of when I am meeting the 'writer'. That she'll make sure she's nearby just in case. I check my emails. There is just that same email from Andy or Antony or whoever the hell they are. And now I am pissed. I am lying in bed and I am hungover, and I shouldn't be hungover and I should be with my husband and I should have a husband and I should have a baby and there should not be these hot tears streaming down my bloated wine soiled face and my wrist should not be throbbing like a fucking wisdom tooth that needs to be pulled.

In my outbox I see all the pathetic emails that I write but never send, the emails that I write to myself. I open one at random: *You showered.* I turn my face into my pillow, scrunch my eyes, open my mouth to bellow into it. I open my mouth to scream but nothing comes out. This is what my life has come to... writing emails to myself to remind me how much progress I am making. That I am deserving. That I don't need to be lonely. That it is okay to feel feelings. Fucking Philip. It's the kind of thing Donna would laugh at other people doing. It's the kind of thing I can imagine Jenni doing though, in the middle of a fucking yoga class or juice cleanse. It's the kind of thing I'd expect to be included in these letters I'm getting from someone who somehow knows *everything* about me. And it's the kind of thing I didn't even know about, need to even think of, before Billy left me. Before I killed him. Us.

No. *No* I tell myself.

Be angry. Be fucking angry.

Get up get up *get up.*

-

The smell of coffee takes some of the hangover throb away. I feel a little more human. I get a text from Donna telling me to take the day off. Jenni emails me from her conference and says she will be back tomorrow; she's coming back early so she can be here when I meet up with Antony or whoever this person is. I feel bad for mocking her. It's when I feel the natural gravitational pull of hand to wrist that I realise I need to, for once, go easy on myself. If I want to moan about someone in my head that I can. Especially on a day like today, after a night like last night.

I took Donna's advice and called into work, said I had a stomach bug. I didn't want to get any of the old folks ill. I sit at the kitchen table and look over the various screens and papers around me. I am working and trying and starting to piece something together; some jigsaw that will end up forming a picture of who this person is. Reading email after letter after threat and drinking coffee after coffee and resisting the urge to grab my wrist - I am surprised by my resolve. I am surprised by my lack of a meltdown. It's only been a few hours, but it's a start I guess. The anger of the morning has subsided slightly. Philip would want me to write a happy email or post-it to myself. Instead, I continue to work through what I know so far. I read over the hidden sentences that I managed to decode. I write down all the names this person has used so far. The letters delivered to my house can be explained away - my house address may have accidentally been up on the *Rose and Thorn* website - but my personal email account? That's something I can't rationalise in my head yet. I can't make it go away. This person knows me. They know things that I have never told anyone, things that even Billy didn't know... *especially* things that he didn't know.

I decide to go for a walk and clear my head. As I open the front door, I see a post-it of mine on the wall: *If this doesn't start to get better, know that you can still end it.*

If I can email, leave post-its and to do lists for myself, then what would prevent me, in a drunken or anxiety riddled moment, from writing these *letters* to myself too? How well *do* I *really* know myself?

I know what it means when people say that actions have consequences. Because I am one.

-

We read to escape, Billy says.

That's what I did. As a kid I mean. I don't know if I knew it at the time though, I say.

With your mother I'm not surprised mate, Billy says.

I'm being serious Billy, I say.

Billy tells me that he is too.

-

As a child I always loved being able to lose myself in page after page and be somewhere else. I looked forward to being able to travel to a different country, meet new people, hear exotic languages. Writing itself though was never really for me. I dabbled in poetry and short stories but nothing of any note. It was Billy who was the creative one. The letters he wrote to me when we first got together, and the love notes he would leave for me around the house. Anyone who read them would have wanted to vomit but it was just how he was, and it worked for us. Those letters from Billy are one thing that this 'A' figure hasn't referred to yet, perhaps haven't managed to find out about. There's some hope there, I guess. A small bright light. They haven't mentioned either the affair notes that I found – if that's what they even are. I really don't want to believe he would ever have done that to me. Surely not?

When my parents would argue I would just sit in my room and read book after book. I held conversations in my head with characters and would miss them after the final page. At university I did write one poem that I was proud of. Most of what I wrote during my Creative Writing course was just one terrible draft after another, trying to write anything that wasn't an acrostic – "Is there a less impressive or more simplistic form of poetry?" my professor mocked, knowing full well that that had been my submission the previous week - but there was one that got the attention of the class and my lecturer. It was about how a book is like a timeline, a lifespan running out, with each page like the passing of time. You want to rush and get to the next chapter, the next plot twist, the next dramatic scene, and before you know it you've got twenty, ten, five pages left and... it's gone. Transitory. Finite. A book ends and so does life. I've not written anything for a long time, certainly not since Billy's death. And the soppy self-help emails and post its and trite magazine articles do not count.

The thought crosses my mind again: what if I am so grief stricken, so full of guilt, that I *am* writing again? *I'm* writing to myself *about* myself and getting everything I have done wrong in my life out onto a page? Failing at university. Not following in the footsteps of my parents. Marrying a man with no financial security. The troubles with getting pregnant. The drinking. The affair. The abortion - *'killing your husband, sleeping with -'*

My hand is clutching my wrist. I look at my face in the café window. My eyes are red and damp. I know what I need to do. I just can't decide what to write and how to phrase everything that needs to be said. What do I agree to? What do I suggest? *'Offer to sleep with him. That seems to work for you.'* And that voice, that fucking voice, is so hard to ignore. It's so strong, and so raw and so painful – and sometimes I worry that it's *right* in everything it says about me. About Billy. About my life. About all that I have done.

I need to fight it.

I need to fight whoever and whatever this is that has come into my life and try, try to move on. If this were one of the bestsellers Leesha or I would try to peddle out to the masses, I'd be the main protagonist *'More like the antagonist and villain and rotting old crone who deserves to die at the end and-'*

I open my laptop. This has to be done. Today. Now. I type their email address. I start composing. I decide to test the relationship by leaving another hint of my own. Whatever my lecturer might have thought, a simple acrostic can hold an important message.

-

To: caprahircus@hotmail.com

From: michellebookworm@gmail.com

Re: Meeting

Dear A, (I am not sure which of your many names to use),

I received your latest email and have to say, like the other instalments, it did intrigue me.

Knowing that you want to write a true feminist piece, I can hear the passion in your prose.

Nothing is tougher than being rejected by publishers, so please don't be downhearted.

Only thing to do is to believe in your own writing.

What no one can take away from you are your ideas, your characters and your vision.

That being said, I hold true to my previous emails and correspondence with you.

Having a back and forth conversation like this is not, I feel, helpful or professional.

After some consideration, I feel it might be best to meet in person and talk face to face.

That way, we could find out if we could work well together on this project of yours.

You are local I presume, so I suggest we meet somewhere we will both know.

One place that appears frequently in your text is the campus where your character studies.

Usually I wouldn't meet someone I don't know, so I hope a public place is okay with you.

Knightsbridge Café is by the English department on campus, so we could meet there.

Not that I'm paranoid, but you do hear of internet dating horror stories, don't you?

One or half past one tomorrow would be good for me if that suits you.

Won't it be fantastic if we get along, and I can take your text to my publishing partner?

Feel free to just turn up tomorrow. Or email me back. I will be there. I'm looking forward to meeting this mysterious writer. I feel like 'The Woman in the Lift', just about to find out who the mysterious communicator is.

I really wish I'd written that, don't you? I'd be a millionaire by now!

Michelle.

\-

I feel like signing off with 'Fuck you, Michelle' instead.

As I sit and look again at my reflection in the café window, eyes now a little less red, I realise how often I visit this place. The staff know me by name and usually predict my order. I remember once saying to Billy that if it ever got to the stage that the barista told me my drink before I had the chance to order, then it was a clear sign I needed to either drink less coffee or just start going to a new coffee shop. Maybe I really *am* stuck in Groundhog Day. Looking around I understand why so many people come to cafes to write. They offer a pool of ideas and stimulus: people rushing around, possibly late for a secret rendezvous; friends gossiping or lovers whispering; awkward first encounters between internet daters; frequent loners, early thirties, trying to ignore that they are running out of time to turn their lives around. My brother would call anyone who writes in a café pretentious. I would say they are researchers. Billy's smile drifts in front of me like steam from the coffee machine. Somewhere, in the recesses of my mind, something about his name suddenly flickers – I can't quite get to what it is... his name, a meaning in it, something I used to call him. *Billy, Billy Goat* I hear myself saying to him. But why I'm remembering this I can't place a finger on... I can't reach it... and then the flame is snuffed out.

Less than five minutes after sending my email, I feel a buzz from my phone and hear a notification from my laptop.

'A' has emailed me back.

EMAIL FOUR

To: michellebookworm@gmail.com

From: caprahircus@hotmail.com

Re: re: Meeting

Dear Michelle,

Glad to hear you enjoyed my latest extract. I hope it's better than 'The Woman in the Lift'.

Only someone in publishing would think to meet by an English department building!

On the other hand, it might make me feel even older now that I am no longer of student age!

Don't worry about offending me - meeting in public is fine with me. Half past one it is.

Yours,

-

No name. No sign-off. There didn't need to be. Message received loud and clear: GOOD.

The word repeats itself, loops in my mind.

Good, something is starting to happen. Good, we are on the same wavelength. Good, that I feel, for the first time, in control. Good, I need to let Jenni know that I have reached out to this person and have arranged a meeting. Good, this feels *good*. Across from me, someone knocks a cup over. It clatters noisily to the floor. I text Jenni the arrangements. She texts back almost immediately that she knows the café and will arrive soon after half one and just sit and watch what happens. I text back to say thank you. I could tell her I'm nervous but that seems pointless. I think we both are.

-

Billy was going away on a conference for four days. He was so excited about it. He was always good at networking and talking to new people. This was an opportunity to meet industry experts and other publishers and aspiring writers and perhaps to gather new business. Our agency had been up and running for a few years and we were doing fairly well; we hadn't had the bestseller successes that lined the aisle of supermarkets and stood in bookstore windows, but we were able to take on a few clients, sell books, make a living.

"I'll come back with the next big thing. I promise you. I'll find the next bestseller."

He was the most positive person I had ever met. He always believed something good was going to happen, whether next week or next year - and that any awful patch, any time of anger or pain or illness would be replaced by good news. All it took was belief.

When he left for the conference I had been sober for months. When he left for the conference he still thought I had been taking my hormone injections, trying to get pregnant again. When he left for the conference I loved him still, more than anyone on earth. When he left for the conference I was nearly two months pregnant. When he left for the conference I had scheduled to have an abortion.

Tri deug, a naoi. Thirteenth of September.

I thought that I would be able to go in, have the procedure, recover at home, and he would never have to know. Never have to know what I had to hide what I had done behind his back. Lies upon lies. When he was leaving to catch his train, calling from the front door to say goodbye, I remember looking at myself in the bathroom mirror, wanting to run downstairs and tell him and apologise and beg him to understand and come with me and hold my hand. In the days leading up to his absence and my operation – what else *do* you call what I chose to do? - I thought about telling him everything. Blaming it on drink. Even claiming that the baby was his. But I knew I couldn't do that; I knew, even that morning when I looked at my hollow face in the mirror, hearing him running up the stairs to kiss me goodbye, I couldn't do that to him. There was no way that I could lie to him about a child. So, I did what I thought was best.

There was a complication. There was bleeding. I needed surgery. In the blind panic and fear of the situation I asked a nurse to contact my husband.

He rushed back. He got knocked over on a main road as he ran from the train station to the hospital. He died.

And the worse thing, despite knowing that because of my actions he suffered an injury that he never recovered from, is knowing that all he wanted was to get to me - to comfort me, to love me, completely unaware, as he was dashing to see me, why I was in the hospital to begin with. I had asked the nurse to just let him know *where* I was, and not *why*. I still thought, naively, cowardly, scared in the stress of my surgery, that I could somehow still cover it up.

I told Donna that I had had a miscarriage. I told our parents I was in hospital due to the severe bleeding from it. I slept through the funeral arrangements. I allowed Jenni to comfort me. No one knew the truth behind the two people I was grieving. I let Billy's parents console me and offer me a place to stay if I needed it. I even cried down the phone to my mother when she eventually called, slurring my words which she replied to monosyllabically.

This person knows me.

This writer, my *auto-biographer* of sorts, knows me and knows what I have done. I wonder if Billy knew everything – if he told a friend, kept a diary, wrote me a Dear John letter. If he did tell someone, maybe this is them trying to avenge him for what I did.

We can always try again. Another time, Billy says.

What if I don't want to, I say.

I know that you feel that way now, but…, Billy says.

I can't see it happening, I say.

Billy doesn't say anything.

At home, I'm waiting for Donna to come over. Jenni is also going to call so we can all talk at the same time. About my decision to meet whoever this. I am hoping they will understand my need for closure. I can sense a precipice of some kind, as though I am about to get an answer, as though I am about to see something in a clearer light. I can't help but let my mind wander to tomorrow's meeting and hope that I'll see Billy walking towards me, laughing, smiling, letting me know that this has all been one big ruse; that with Jenni and Donna and Tony, this has been nothing but an elaborate joke, a test to see how much I love him and know him and can remember about us - as a couple, as parents in waiting. I allow the vision to linger a little longer than I should.

There is a knock at the door. Suddenly, I am covered by the silence of my house, of being alone in my house. Of the darkness of night. Donna's joke about changing the locks rears in my mind. I stand for a moment, waiting. I wonder if I imagined the knock or whether something has fallen over upstairs. Another knock. This time it's louder and harder. Then, two knocks, quick and hard on wood. My natural instinct is to turn down the lights, creep to the front window and peer out to check if I can see anyone. Who would knock like that? Donna would just call through the letterbox to annoy me on purpose. Three knocks now. Short and rapid but just as loud. I walk from the kitchen to the hallway where I can see the front door. I can just make out the shape of a figure through the glass beside the doorframe. It doesn't seem to move as I approach. I brace myself for another series of knocks but step by step, by the eerie light of night, another knock does not come. Can they see me? Have they decided to come and visit me now tonight, rather than wait? My wrist is hurting from being squeezed but I can't help it - right now I need it to ground me, to feel something real. From the wilting tulips on the table by the door, a single petal falls to the floor.

There, in the white light, looking as if made from moonshine, is an envelope at the foot of the door. It looks ghostly against the darkness of the surrounding hallway. Silently, I creep forward, pick it up, cast a glance through the glass pane and, seeing nothing now, almost run back to the kitchen. My heart is pounding as I look at the front of the envelope: my name and address in the handwriting I have now come to recognise.

My mouth feels dry, and my eyes are being pulled towards the wine bottle near the sink by an invisible line. Hastily, needing answers, I tear open the envelope.

I pull out the letter inside.

LETTER FIVE

During the first month I moved into the house the girls set me a challenge. It was like a scavenger hunt and I had to find four things that were around the house. They said it was a typical initiation for anyone new living with them. I doubted this, but I went along with it anyway.

Looking back, I should have just said no. Did I really want to be a part of this group, this ridiculous gaggle of girls? No. But I needed somewhere to live, and I needed my parents to believe I was doing well at university. It made me feel so ashamed when they would call and ask about friends and parties and what I was getting involved with. I told them I'd been to pub quizzes and on midnight walks for charities, taken part in fresher drinking games, seen the various museums and galleries that the city had to offer. Well, that last one was true at least, even if it was something I did on my own. So, when offered a place to move into, even if it felt a little like a pity offer, a freakshow act the prettier girls could look at to feel better about themselves, I decided to take part. Why not? What's the worst that could happen? Of course, if I had known then what would happen on a night out with them a year later, then… But it's impossible to ever know something that awful could happen to someone. To you. And despite myself and my feminist protestations, how I loathed these girls and the lives they represented, I secretly wanted *in*. I wanted to be liked. Who doesn't? My dad's voice of reason echoed through my head, telling me to just keep my "chin up" and get on.

"So," one of the girls said to me, both enthusiastically and unnecessarily loud, "you need to find four things. Four items. It will show how much you know us and paid attention to your interview questions. Okay?"

Shit. I couldn't remember anything from that day. It was all I could do at the time to put a few words together into a sentence and answer. The urge to rub my shoe against my ankle, to feel that painful distraction, rippled through my body.

I nodded at her and took the piece of paper she thrust towards me. On it were the four things I needed to find:

- My favourite stuffed toy
- The name of Sam's boyfriend
- The ONLY drink acceptable to have whilst watching *Real Housewives*
- The flowers banned from this household #badboyfriend

I nearly laughed at how ridiculous this was. I wanted to smack them for taking themselves so seriously. Who hashtags their own treasure hunt - a treasure hunt aimed at poking fun at the new girl?

I sighed, read over the list two more times, and nodded my head, resolute that I would complete the mission. Some of the girls giggled and waved me off, clearly thrilled to send me on this fool's errand.

I decided to do them in order. It made just as much as sense as randomly looking around the house for them. The first one was easy. I went straight up to Meredith's room (I think that's her name, I couldn't tell them apart) and pushed her door open. Seeing as this was part of the game I didn't think I had to ask to enter.

She hadn't been joking at the interview; her room was covered in stuffed toys. Pink unicorns and *Disney* characters, pillows in the shape of cartoon heads and various mythical creatures seemed to cover nearly ever surface of the room: bed, desk, shelves, wardrobe, even hanging around her mirror. She was stuck in a fairyland, waiting for a Prince Charming. It was easy to find the toy needed for the list though. It was placed in prize position on the pillow at the head of her bed. Surely the one closest to her when she slept would be the toy she held most dearly. I scribbled it down on the list and crossed it off.

- ~~My favourite stuffed toy~~
- The name of Sam's boyfriend

I knew Sam was on my floor as it was her terrible music that I could hear banging through the wall night after night. Her door was covered in all kinds of positive quotes and inspirational phrases that any idiot can get from the internet. Each time I walked past her door I wanted to get a red pen and correct all of the spelling and punctuation errors that littered the pictures. It irked me that she hadn't even bothered to read them properly - that, or she just didn't know how to spell. *'You're only one sleep away from tomorrow!'* What does that even mean? I steeled myself and knocked on her door. No answer. She wasn't with the girls downstairs, so she must be out of the house - not at a lecture, that would be asking too much, probably shopping or posing for pictures she can upload later. Her door creaked slightly when pushed and I was instantly hit by the smell of incense. My eyes were drawn to the chest of drawers near her bed. It was covered with cards, showing me that it had just been her birthday. I closed the bedroom door and a calendar swung gently, pinned onto the back. Several dates had been circled and scribbled over, including her own birthday, just two days earlier, stars and love hearts drawn around the date. I had a brief pang of jealousy, of loneliness, that I had been left out, that I had had no idea it was her birthday. For a moment I questioned whether part of the issue with the girls *was* me; maybe I needed to make an effort, too. How can I expect to be accepted by them if I don't even take the time to know their birthdays? Then I remember why I am in this room in the first place, and the bitter taste of this initiation repeats itself in my mouth. *No.* I don't want to be a part of this world that badly. I walk over to the drawers and quickly open card after card, seeing notes from her parents, brother, a few friends, all the girls in the house (including one collective card from them all, larger than the rest) and finally I pick up one shaped like a heart. Inside is a typed note, generic to any 'gorgeous girlfriend' and then signed below with *'Your the one that I want, J.K xoxo'*

I roll my eyes. How can a girl be impressed by a birthday card that contains a prewritten message, a scribbled spelling mistake and a reference to a musical by someone who doesn't even share the namesake of the character they're referencing? Perhaps I am giving *J.K* too much credit, him not realising his attempt at romance is even from *Grease*. He probably doesn't even know the song comes from the film. I cross off the second task on the list.

- ~~My favourite stuffed toy~~
- ~~The name of Sam's boyfriend~~

Still in Sam's room, I put a line through the third one without even having to think about it:

- ~~The ONLY drink acceptable to have whilst watching *Real Housewives*~~

Red wine. The house pretty much has it coming out of the taps. How these girls' faces aren't bloated from alcohol poisoning I'll never know. Getting through the dining room and kitchen is like playing bowling, where you're the ball and the flotsam and jetsam of wine bottles are the pins you try not to knock over for fear of spilling any left-over wine. Unlikely.

I look at the last of the four challenges:

- The flowers banned from this household #badboyfriend

This one stumps me more than the first three. I walk back downstairs and am hit by an oddly damp smell that I didn't notice before. The sweet incense of Sam's room make this putrid smell more apparent. One of the girls comes out from the living room to check on my progress. "Can you smell that? It smells like dirty water or something," I say, as I hand her the list with my answers so far.

- ~~My favourite stuffed toy~~ - *Goat*
- ~~The name of Sam's boyfriend~~ - *J.K*
- ~~The ONLY drink acceptable to have whilst watching *Real Housewives*~~ - *Red wine*

She ignores my question. "Good girl! You've done that much faster than we thought you would!"

I can't tell if she is being genuine or sarcastic. None of the other girls come out to see, so I presume they've lost interested or even forgotten what I am doing. Or that I am here.

"Remember the rules!" I want to remind her that she neglected to inform me of any rules prior to starting this, but I bite my tongue. "You've already moved in I know, but this is just for fun. We all did it!" I doubt that. "But you're not allowed to ask any of us for help. And you have until after-lecture-drinks-time to solve the clues. So, like, 5 o'clock." Now I know why they never get any work done of an evening if that's when they start drinking. And why they hardly ever make it to lectures in the morning.

"Just one more to go! I'll give you a hint – you're on the right floor of the house." She grins and scuttles back into the living room, closing the door behind her. I ignore the urge to let her know that she has just contradicted her own 'no help' rule.

The hallway feels empty despite the various posters stuck up, the clothes hanging over chairs. No one seems to clean up. Maybe I can do that. Maybe it will make them like me. I become aware of a burning sensation on my ankle and realise that I am rubbing the sole of my shoe on it. Was I doing this when I was talking? *No wonder they make you do this stupid ritual you're like a walking target to be made fun of you can't even make friends you have to win your way in you ugly thick stupid loner b-*

The voice comes, unbidden. I have worked so hard to keep it at bay. I know that rubbing my ankle is a painful and short-term remedy, but it feels like the lesser of two evils. The ache in my ankle is muscle memory; it takes me back to the flashing light outside my halls room; graduation, and scratching away the disappointment I wanted to hide from my parents; the cut and slice and attack where I could only focus on the tiny separate parts of my body in order to survive and get through what was happening - and finally, to the rip, pull and bloody tear of my baby away from me.

The guilt is a patch of dried skin on my ankle that I need to itch away, red and pulsing and throbbing burning shame.

I am at once looking down at this messy stretch of wine-stained carpet and seeing how, years later, people don't change, people continue to lie and test and tease me. Like the serpent shaped broken light, lies continue to slither in and out of my life, and will continue to do so long after I have written my story - people biting me like the broken glass that littered the floor of that corridor. I am at once there and here, in both a memory and the present. If only we could see how our actions ripple and replicate and have consequences beyond the initial action, however small, however secretive we think they may be. If only people knew what their behaviours did to others.

It's then that I realise the final clue is right in front of me. The damp smell comes from a flower vase on the floor, empty and propped up against the wall. I say it's empty, but when I get closer I see that it contains some greenish water. The flowers must be dead, in the bin I presume. I pick up the vase and pour its contents into the kitchen sink. I look in the pedal bin and see several wilted petals staring up from the various bottles and wrappers they are surrounded by. I pick them up, ignoring the mushy and dripping stems. Tulips. The flower heads are brown and bent out of shape. In the middle of the dried-out petals there is a card. On one side is the name of the florist and on the other a short message, handwritten: *To Jennifer, Happy Valentine's Day, Love Tony.*

I drop the letter to the floor. My stomach reels at each clue and its answer:

- My favourite stuffed toy - *Goat*
- The name of Sam's boyfriend – *J.K*
- The ONLY drink acceptable to have whilst watching *Real Housewives* – *Red wine*
- The flowers banned from this household #badboyfriend – *Tulips, Tony*

Goat, J.K, Red wine, Tulips, Tony.

These are all things and pieces of information that could be found in and around my own home. Names and people that could be found in my life.

This person knows me. This girl is me. Her house is mine.

But J.K... this I *don't* recognise. The two letters hover before me, threatening. This is the final twist, I am sure of it ... whatever, whoever, this J.K is.

I wait for another bang on the front door. It feels as though I have found the edge of the cliff and at any moment will be pushed over and drop into an abyss. Slowly, I bend down and pick up the letter. I know there is more to read.

LETTER FIVE

The girls feign interest in my completed list. I think they are a little disappointed that I solved them all so quickly. I presume it's Jennifer who starts sniffing when I ask about Tony. I am told by Sam that he "fucked some medical slut" the day after he sent the Valentine's flowers. I pretend to look concerned for who I, again, presume Jennifer is. Sam then tells me she hopes I didn't move anything in her room.

I feel my ankle bleeding from where I have been rubbing it.

The silent threat of violent knock hangs in the air. Everything feels cold. They knew I was home. They were outside, watching and waiting. I want to move, to pace, to run - but I just stand. I am too scared to move.

To Jennifer, Happy Valentine's Day, Love Tony.

Jenni. It's too much of a coincidence. I need to let her know that this doesn't just concern me now. This person knows about people in my life. And *Tony*. What do I tell him? How on earth do I let these people know what I have done… how it affects them now too? How - after all this time?

Questions bullet around my brain, mirroring the erratic order in which this bizarre story has been sent to me. Why chop and change from event to event and time to time? Are they purposefully confusing their reader, me? Are they playing with their reader, me, letting them know that they, the writer, are in charge of what happens and when? Are they letting me know that anything from my past can come out next - in any order and at any time? A void opens up in front me, vast and black. A dizzy, sickly sensation washes over me, and I grab onto the nearest chair.

I sit. I breathe. In and out. In and out. I close my eyes. I listen to my breathing. In and out.

I turn over the letter and read two sections again. It only adds to the nauseous feeling in my stomach.

People don't change, people continue to lie and test and tease me.

If only we could see how our actions ripple and replicate and have consequences beyond the initial action, however small, however secretive we think they may be. If only people knew what their behaviours did to others.

This is my test. I am being challenged by someone who knows my lies. By someone I have lied to? But who? I have lied to so many people: Donna, my parents, Billy's parents, Jenni, Tony, even people at work. The goddam group who raised money for the commemorative plaque. To myself. But who would do this to me? Surely no one I know would enjoy putting me through this much pain? No one, no matter how badly I have acted, would want to get revenge this way… would want to ruin me this way… Maybe I am imagining it, but the scent of red wine seems to waft over me. It is warm, welcoming. I lick my lips.

And then, my eyes shoot to the fridge. My eyes focus on the magnets. I stumble over and take the ceramic Billy Goat magnet from the fridge. Something clicks into place – Billy Goat, my Billy, and the email address of the writer.

I grab my phone from the kitchen table and type in *caprahircus*, stabbing at the screen. It glares up at me, brash and knowing.

'Capra hircus' is the Latin for 'Male Goat'.

Billy Goat. Billy Goat's Gruff.

My Billy.

My nickname for Billy.

The goat.

The fucking stuffed toy in the fucking story.

If only people knew what their behaviours did to others.

I know what it means when people say that actions have consequences. Because I am one.

-

You got out of bed.

I walk to Donna's, but I struggle to put one foot in front of the other. I keep checking my bag - that I've got my keys, that I have my phone. I close the bag. I reopen it and check that my purse is inside because that's all I need now if I've lost that and someone steals it and uses my bank cards and I go bankrupt and have to move because I can't afford the mortgage anymore and there's no money in the business anyway and working at the retirement home doesn't pay shit but I can't go home I just can't - I snap the bag shut again and manage a few steps before taking the purse out once more to check my credit card is definitely still there.

Pause. Breathe.

I close the bag again and turn my hands into fists to stop myself from checking my phone is on standby and therefore isn't accidentally calling someone but what if I'm locked out again I still don't even know how that happened and I button up my coat even though I can't remember putting it on and then I open one button because I might get too warm but then I button it up again because I catch my reflection in a store window and having some buttons open and some closed looks odd.

Stop.

I blink... shake my head... try to stop the looping thoughts that rattle away incessantly just so I don't have to think about the goat and Billy and the story and the letter and his affair and I check my bag again and –

"Watch where you're fucking going! Jesus!"

A cyclist swears at me as, without even looking, I step out on the road. His words rush away with him. I stumble back and the palms of my hands feel a brick wall behind me. I heave deeply, painfully. My hand goes up to my mouth and I stifle a sob. My chest aches from the sudden, panicked intakes of breath.

"Oh God. Fuck," I stutter. A choked breath.

I see the cyclist appear again in front of me but this time he isn't just an angry blur. This time he is bloodied. He isn't wearing a helmet. He isn't wearing helmet because half of his head is crushed, the helmet is shattered, cracked on the road beside him. The tyres of his bike are still rotating as the bike lies sideways, half up on the pavement. They spin at different speeds. His bloody hand reaches out towards me and it is Billy's hand with broken fingers and it is Billy's leg snapped out of shape and it's Billy's neck that looks like a gallows rope, twisted round itself and round and round and round and...

"Christ. Stop."

I try to inhale more desperate air. I rub both hands over my face, turn from the road to the wall and close my eyes. I know people are walking past me, wondering what I am doing but I don't care.

I run my right forefinger over the palm of my left hand, along each finger to the tip, down and up, along and around.

Billy is not on the road. The cyclist is not Billy. Billy is not behind me. I unbutton my coat and turn around.

-

"Here. Drink this. It's okay."

Donna rubs my back, and steam from a cup of tea drifts in front of me.

"It was so real Donna. It was so real." I can hear the crack in my voice. "He just rushed past me and I wasn't looking where I was going, and I saw him there. Just blood *everywhere*."

"It's okay." Her hand moves in circles on my spine. I try to focus on my breathing. "You're bound to be spooked by cyclists. It's not unusual mate, really. I'm glad you came to see me. It's okay."

There is so much I want to tell her. So much I need to say.

"I thought I was coming to you? Why were you in such a rush to get here? Your text sounded so panicked." I can't even remember sending her a message. "Has something happened?"

I look up at her and she takes the seat next to me. Our knees touch as we face each other at her breakfast bar. Memories flash before me of drunken mornings eating toast, hungover at this very spot; the sound of her old coffee machine spluttering; hearing Billy call from the living room asking where her remote control is so he can watch TV while we chat. It feels like there are an ocean's worth of memories in this one room, washing around my feet and rising, attempting to drown me in black, liquid guilt. I let out of long, heavy sigh. It feels like an iceberg is on my shoulders, ready to melt and add to the increasing rising waters ebbing at my chest, my neck, my bottom lip.

"Donna... I need to... There's something I..."

Her look of sympathy kills me. I can't meet her eyes. The shame is too strong.

"Is it this book, this guy or whoever that keeps messaging you? Has something bad happened? Is it Tony? What? You can tell me anything. I just want to help."

"You've helped me so..." I sob, my voice catches as I speak, "...so much already."

"Oh, Michelle. Come here."

I sink into her warm arms and I feel my tears wetting her jumper. I feel her breathing, the rise and fall of her chest. I smell her perfume. "I'm so sorry."

I feel the vibrations from her shaking her head, silently telling me *'No, you have nothing to be sorry for...'* because that's what friends do, that's what friends like Donna do.

I come up for air and try to speak again.

"I imagine sometimes what Billy would say to me if he could see me now. If he knew me now."

"And what do you think he'd say?" Donna asks.

That he hates you, it says.

"I think... I think he'd say that he hates me."

There's a pause. "Why? Why would he say that?"

Because of what you've done, it says.

"Because of what I've done."

There's another pause, but this time she doesn't speak. She lets me continue.

"I think, somehow, he knows. Maybe he knew before he died. I keep thinking that he knew why I was really in hospital and what happened to put me there. What choice I'd made without him. Why I couldn't tell him the truth. But he knows now what I did to him. What I did to us. What I did to... to the baby and, and..." A deep guttural gasp echoes from inside my throat. It aches. Everything aches. "And I go around and around in my head and all I want to do - all I want to do is speak to my mum and have her tell me I'm not a fucking disappointment but..."

Donna takes me into her arms again and buries my head into her shoulder. She lets me just cry into her for what feels like an age. I didn't know I had that much water inside of me; odd images of empty wells and misfiring water guns bounce back and forth inside my head. The darkness inside my eyes spins, a soothing blackness that eventually helps me breathe. When Donna holds me away from her, lovingly, gently, it is her that speaks first. She doesn't stutter once, doesn't falter. She only coughs once to clear her throat.

"Listen to me. Something awful happened to you. Something that should never happen to anyone. You lost someone that you loved in the most cruel and terrible way. It's something that many people don't ever have to go through and are lucky to never have to experience, to never have to explain and try to rationalise every single day. I have seen you be so strong over the last year and I have seen you break and pick yourself back up. I have wanted to help more but knew I needed to step back and do less. I've not known if I should just leave you be or push you to speak more. But you have been so brave. I can't even imagine the pain you've suffered with losing a baby and Billy and everything you thought you had that was safe and was secure. I watched as I worried you drank too much. I hated myself for judging you for drinking when you were trying to get pregnant again. I felt sick for so long after I spoke to you about it, like I was just making you feel even worse about something that was ruining your life. I also know you and Billy loved each other. I also know you became distant. I think I knew something had happened. And I can understand *why* it happened. I also think I know and understand what you've just told me. And deep down I think I knew, anyway. And it has haunted me that I have never asked you about it, not because I think it's wrong or shameful, but because I didn't know how and I didn't want to upset or offend you. But I know, I *know*, you are not a bad person, you do not deserve to feel this way about yourself. You did not mean for any of this to happen. You would go back and change things if you could. You would never have done certain things if you had been in your right mind at the time. You did not kill Billy, and I know that Billy, even if he knew or knows all of this, still loves you."

A few seconds pass before I nod, very slowly.

"Then everything is out in the open. Everything is good. We can handle all of this now. Okay?"

I nod again.

"And nothing, nothing you ever do or have done, would ever change how much I love you. Or how much you meant to your husband. Okay?"

I nod a final time.

"Then here's what we're going to do. I am going to take you home. I'll let Jenni know not to call tonight. I am going to run you a bath. Then we are going to have dinner together and we are going to talk about anything and everything that has *nothing* to do with books or family, men or work. And definitely *not* about bloody emails." She takes a breath. "You are going to get a good night's sleep in your own bed, and in the morning, I'll bring you breakfast and coffee and anything else you want. And then, and only if you want to, we will figure out what to do with these emails and this person contacting you. But there will be no talk of that tonight. Okay?"

I don't nod my head this time. I don't need to.

-

When I'm asleep I dream of Billy. His fingernails. His hands. How he held his pen to write, to cross out and make changes to the manuscripts we received. The ink fingerprints he left all over the office and house, a little map of his day. In my dream, at least at the start, all is calm. Everything seems white and pure. In this dream I allow myself to believe that everything will be fine, that everything will work itself out. I know I am dreaming but I let myself seep into this mattress of gentle belief, these pillows of hopeful clouds. But in this dream, like all others, I can't see his face. It's the back of his head I can see and where once was hair is now just a bloody clump, his neck full of holes, shot through with grit and gravel, his left shoulder crumpled up, the other crushed down - bent out of shape like a freakshow act. And each time I think I am about to see him, his true face, his death mask, I wake up just before his face moves from a grotesquely crooked profile to –

"Hey. Sorry. Did I wake you up?" Donna.

"No. No don't worry. I was just laying here."

231

"I made you some tea." She speaks from the bedroom door, slightly ajar. "How did you sleep?"

"Well," I say. Despite the dream.

"Good." She comes over and places the tea on the bedside table, sits on the edge of the bed. "How are you feeling? After last night?"

"I'm okay. I think I needed to just," I sigh, as though continuing the exorcism of guilt started the evening before, "let it all out. Thank you."

"You don't need to thank me for anything. I need to apologise to you." I am taken aback. I open my mouth to say something but don't. I can tell from her reaction that she expected me to respond that way. "No, I do." She puts one hand on mine. "What you told me last night, about Billy and the baby and everything you've been through. The guilt that I can only imagine has been plaguing you ever since... I should have done something sooner. I should have spoken to you about it. And I am so sorry. I am so very sorry." Her voices breaks slightly. This is unusual, seeing Donna get upset. She gets angry and frustrated, often with comic results, but never this. It breaks my heart that I have made her feel this way. She's right, I do feel guilty. All the time, and especially now. "And I should not have been so fucking pushy with Tony. Jesus. God how could I do that to you? I was just trying to..."

"It's okay. I didn't take any of it to heart. I know you were just trying to help me move on."

She smiles a little, then says, "How is it that you are the one comforting *me*? We're so messed up, aren't we?"

"Well, *I* am. But that's nothing new."

We sit in comfortable silence for a few minutes. There is something to be said for a friend with whom you know that no words are need, that you both know what the other is thinking, wants or doesn't want to talk about. As she gives a half-hearted smile and sips her own tea, I can see in her eyes that she knows everything, that perhaps she always did even before my outpourings last night – about the baby, about the hospital – and I can also see in her eyes that she does not judge me for any of it. She just wants me to be okay.

"Thank you," I say.

She squeezes my hand by way of reply.

"Whoever this person is though Donna, they know everything. Everything about me. They knew my address and they know where I work. Who Jenni is. They know about Billy and the pregnancy. Tony." A beat. "I'm sure they know every secret I've got hidden inside of me."

"How though? How would anyone know that? You only told me last night."

"I don't know. I keep thinking who it could be. Who would want to do this to me and why."

"Well, what are the reasons? Why would someone want to hound you with emails and a story they've written that outs your mistakes?"

"Someone who knew Billy? Who knew about the abortion? About my cheating? Or, maybe, someone who blames me for his accident."

"Who could it be? How many people do you both know that could hold this grudge against you?"

"That's just it though... anyone we both knew are people I just can't see doing this. I mean... you, Jenni, Tony, our parents? Come on." I pause for a moment. "In one of the letters there were initials: *J.K.* I don't know anyone with that name though. Do you?"

"No. No sorry, I don't." She looks away for a second. "So it *might* just be a pissed off writer that you'd snubbed too many times?"

"Maybe. But how would they know so many details of my life?"

"What *do* they know? I mean, could any of it be purely coincidental? Just a horrible, horrible coincidence? Is there *any* chance?"

I think about the fridge magnet and the wedding song. I think about what Phillip said and the proof he showed me about both of those. I think about the motif of the circus act gone wrong that appears in the writing, the feeling I have that I've read that piece before. Maybe this is just a disgruntled artist. But then I remember the email address, the hidden clues in the last piece I read and... and...

"They knew the date I had the abortion. In their writing, in their story, the character has their abortion on the same date. And they include names as well that just show they know too much about me for it to not be personal."

"Whose names?"

"Tony." I try not to look at her. "Names beginning with the letter 'A', which Billy and I had planned for a baby. Jennifer. Lizzie from work. And a Sam."

"Sam? Who's Sam?

"I was looking through some old mail of Billy's and there was a card that I'd left unopened, a bereavement card from someone called Sam. And in the last piece of writing I got sent one the girls was called Sam. And something Mrs Lullin said too."

"What?"

"The night she had to be calmed down. Remember me telling you about it?" Donna nods. "She said a man who came into her room, which no one believed, of which there was no evidence, was called Sam."

"Do you think that is who is doing all this? *Sam*?" I know I need to tell Donna about the letters I found between Sam and Billy too, but I don't think I can face that just now. "What is it? Is there something else?"

"I have no idea. I didn't think I even knew a Sam. I even looked up Mrs Lullin's son, but it's not him."

"*Didn't* think you knew a Sam? What aren't you telling me?"

I honestly don't know where to start: the shoebox, the email address, the open bottle of wine. How I think someone might even have gotten into my house to mess with the settings on my phone. This is all too much for a friend to handle; how could it not be? I breathe, swallow, and reach under the bed and pull out the shoebox. Donna looks completely bemused when I hand it to her. I just nod, letting her know it's okay to open it. I watch as her face changes from confused to shocked, from upset to angry. Her eyes quickly scan the writing. I can see words jumping out and stabbing her in the same painful way they did me.

Get rid. Deep. Next week. Forget. Billy. Fuck. Love. Sam.

Eventually she pushes the box away from us across the bed, as though a mousetrap, precarious, which could snap shut at the slightest touch. It takes a few moments for her eyes to reach mine and when they do, the stoicism I love her for covers her face, again revealing her support for me rather than her own pain, her own frustration.

"What do you want to do?"

"About the letters? I have no idea. I don't even know where to start with those."

"What about this guy who's emailing you. Do you think this Andy and Sam could be the same person? Or maybe they know each other?"

"Well," I start, slowly, "we emailed yesterday and have agreed to meet up today. I guess one way or another I'll find out soon enough. I think that's what's got me so freaked out."

"Fuck Michelle! You're meeting this guy *today*? And you're just telling me this now?" She gets up from the bed and starts to pace, her hand on her forehead. "Where? Who with? Do you know how dangerous this could be?"

"It's the middle of the day. It's a café on the university campus. Jenni will be there too."

"Jenni? What's she got to do with this?"

"She's just going to be nearby in case anything happens. In case he's-"

"*Dangerous*? Yeah, I just said that Michelle. I can't believe you're seeing him today and you didn't tell me."

"It's last minute. It happened yesterday after all the... before I came here."

She puts her hands on her hips and I can tell she is trying incredibly hard not to get angry. I understand why she is.

"Okay." She holds up in one hand in my direction. "Okay. You go and meet them. Go and find out whatever shit is actually going on. But the *minute* you feel uncomfortable or scared... you leave. Right? Right?" She practically shouts it the second time. "And Jenni better fucking be there."

"She will. She's as confused about all this as I am. As we are."

"I bet."

"What do you mean?"

Donna turns to me. "I don't know. I don't know. I just... I feel so helpless. I just wish..."

"Donna. It's okay. By the end of today... it might all be sorted out. Listen – *I'm* being the optimistic one for a change."

"Don't. I'm allowed to be pissed off with you for a few minutes." She walks over to the window, looks out at the morning traffic. I watch her breathing. It breaks my heart that I am causing so much pain for so many of the people that I love. "How well do you know Jenni? Really? I mean, she'd be the first one to condemn you for having the abortion."

The meaning behind what she's said hangs between us momentarily and then drops, shatters to the bedroom floor.

"That's cruel. Even for you. Do you know what you've just accused her of?"

Donna keeps her back to me, her front to the window. She lowers her head. "I know." A deep intake of breath. "I *know*. It sounded ridiculous as soon as I said it. I know." She turns to face me. Her eyes are red and damp. "Just *please* be careful."

-

I'll get the first drink, Billy says.

Of course you will, I say.

You're not a feminist then, Billy says.

I'm a feminist who forgot her purse on purpose, I say.

Billy licks his lips.

Billy is sitting opposite me. He is trying not to spill his pint every time he takes another nervous sip. We are on our third date and at the stage where we both know we like each other enough to graze knees under the table and make flirtatious comments - a little bit more obviously than before.

I can feel him. I can smell him.

The *Knight and Day* pub has flocks of students coming in and out of its doors. Being on the university campus again feels like I have stepped back in time. Seeing the pub still standing where Donna and I, Billy and I, friends from lectures I have never seen again, drank and got drunk, creates an odd sensation in my stomach. I don't know whether I can call it nostalgia. I had spent less time preparing for the third date than I had for the first. It was years later that he told me the reason he was so nervous on that date, more than any other, was because he had planned on asking me back to his flat (which he had prepared with candles and flowers) and thought that it was when we would sleep together for the first time. He was terrified I would decline his invite and even more terrified that I would accept it. Tulips littered the dining room table, the kitchen island and his bed. When I told Donna the next day, she just laughed and mocked Billy for being "A: Presumptuous and B: Pretentious and C: Weird. Who chooses tulips over roses?"

I am torn between wanting to walk inside, have a drink, breathe in the scents and sounds that would bring part of him back, that time of my life - but part of me wants to run away and forget that I ever spent time here. How can those moments that defined so much of me, of Billy, of us, simply not be here anymore? How can our memories be plastered over with the new laughter and drunken kisses of other people, younger students, those yet to age and experience loss? I feel invisible here, an old woman stood in the busy crowd of youth, all obsessed with the only thing they know - themselves. I can't judge them though, I was the same at that age. We all are.

My phones buzzes, taking me out of my reverie.

"Hi Michelle. You okay? Where are you?" Jenni.

"Thank you again for doing this. I really appreciate it."

"It's fine. I want to know who the hell this guy is just as much as you do. Where are you?"

"I'm on my way there now." I move to avoid several students, already mid-afternoon drunk, from blindly crashing into me. "I'm not far."

"Okay. I'll get there twenty minutes or so after you. I'll just sit somewhere nearby. That sound good?"

"Yes. Thank you. I know you had to cancel meetings for this."

"Michelle it was a dull meeting that could easily be done over email. I just told them my dad wasn't feeling well. A white lie but..."

"So, I will sit and wait and see what happens?" I wasn't sure why I phrased it as a question. I don't know what I'm doing. Maybe Donna was right to say this is dangerous. "What if nothing happens?"

"Then nothing happens. What do you *want* to happen?"

"To be honest I'm terrified if they do turn up and terrified if they don't." Just like Billy felt on our third date. "I don't know what I would say to them. What would I ask them? I don't even know what they look like." I feel the impulse to grab my wrist shoot through my body. I feel the impulse to graze my shoe against my ankle as well. Maybe I'm morphing into this character I'm about to meet. Maybe, maybe, maybe.

"It's the middle of the day. It's a public place. I'll be there as well. Nothing will go wrong. You never know it might be an extremely *attractive* stalker."

"Jenni - I genuinely think that's the first time you have ever told a joke in bad taste." I laugh despite how nervous I feel.

"Sorry, my guillotine humour again."

"Gallows."

"What?"

"Never mind. I'll see you soon. Thanks again for this."

Before moving on, I nod at the pub. I know that that time has gone. I mouth the word 'reverie' to myself, realising it was the wrong word for what I've been experiencing standing here. It wasn't a daydream at all because it really happened. Billy happened here. Billy and I did fall in love here. It was a memory. It *was* nostalgia, after all.

When I was a student here the café was called *The Coffee Cup,* and the most impressive drink was hot chocolate. Now, it's the *Knightsbridge Café*, with sofas everywhere that don't match, potted plants and vegan versions of everything. Again, I imagine my brother in here, reeling off passive aggressive comments about "Instagram idiots" and stressing about this being "...our next fucking generation." I take a seat near a window and place my hands firmly down on the table. I see a young man, maybe twenty, flicking through a textbook with a highlighter. I see a group of girls showing each other pictures on their phones. I see the waitress behind the counter looking a little flushed, casting glances at the four-person deep queue. I see two people leave and three more people enter.

I have no idea who this person is that I am about to meet. But they know who I am. They know what I look like. They know where I live. Where I work. They know me. And I know nothing about them at all. A thin layer of sweat forms between my palms and the table. I am nervous. Now that I am here I really, truly am.

I take a pen from my bag and grab a napkin from the table behind me. I always make myself a to-do list. It's what I always do when I feel the need to get some control back in my life. I am early, I have a few minutes to gather my thoughts. I make a list of what this person knows about me and what I know about them.

- The pregnancy

Seeing it written down jolts me. I can't bring myself to write the word *abortion*, but writing 'pregnancy' still makes me catch my breath. How much must this person hate me? I force myself to write.

- The affair
- Tulips
- Drink
- Wedding song

My mind is straining back through all the letters and emails. It feels like I am being weighed down in print. I look at my arm, imagine that my veins are filled with ink rather than blood.

- Sam
- Fridge magnet
- Billy
- Names of people I know
- J.K?
- Disappointing my parents
- Scratching

What is this? A maudlin greatest hits? A depressing bucket list? Is this all my life has been?

- Shame

I put the pen down and fold the napkin in half. I push it away across the table. I check the time on my phone. I glance at my emails to see if they have cancelled or sent a mocking email, enjoying the fact they can see me and I can't see them.

Suddenly, I become aware of everyone with a phone. The student has put his highlighter down and is texting someone. Is he about to call me? Someone in the queue is swiping their screen. Are they looking at photos of me taken when I was asleep, at work, walking home? The group of girls are all buried in their phones rather than talking to each other. Could it be one of them? Maybe a friend of Billy I didn't know? Did he have a long-lost sister, angry that her brother died before she could get to know him? Was he dating a girl on campus? Was he sleeping with some ingénue creative writing student? Is she the final twist in this story?

The crumpled napkin catches my eye and my mind shoots back to something written in one of the first emails I received. They were trying to explain why they were writing to me with short extracts, one at a time:

It leaves you wanting more, wanting to get the next letter as though you are the powerless recipient of whatever the postman delivers.

A book cover hovers in front of me. I can see my face on it - drawn, pale, dark rings around my eyes. One of the generic titles scrawled below my haggard appearance: *'The Lady with the Letters'. 'The Woman Being Watched'. 'Girl, Stalked'.* My stories.

"Fuck." *I* am one of the women in those books: manipulated, flawed, irritable, easy to dislike. This is what I have become. This is what Andy or Ann or whoever has done to me. They have made me a character for them to play with. The café starts to feel off kilter. Suddenly the angles feel wrong, out of sync with each other, off centre. One wall looks longer than another, the corners of the room seem to slant in opposite directions. The floor feels like it's on an incline and decline at the same time. Like in Meredith's room, I have the same sickly sensation of being seasick. Warm and nauseous. Ill.

I need to leave. I want to leave. I don't need to know who this is. I can ignore it. I can blank them out. I can just delete every email and put each letter in the trash and quit my job and move home and leave the area and start again and not see Donna again and Jenni will understand and –

The café door opens, the bell rings. I feel the familiar burn of my hand gripping my wrist. I close my eyes and make myself breathe. I try to picture one of the many notes I have written to myself over the last few months. Something positive, something helpful, something brave.

You told yourself not to feel bad about yourself.

I open my eyes. I can do this. I just need to wait. The café door opens again. The bell rings again. In walks Jenni. She scours the room for me, sees me, nods and widens her eyes as if to say "Anything?" and I just shake my head. She walks over to the counter like any other customer. We pick up on each other's nerves. Neither of us want to spook the potential visitor. We don't want them to know they are being watched. Jenni chances another look back at me and then around the café - she could just be a casual diner looking for a friend, for a seat. There is a buzz from my phone. Jenni has messaged asking if I have seen anyone or heard anything yet. I message back *no, not yet*. I don't type that I am nervous, that I am not hopeful, that I am worried in case they don't turn up and worried if they do. I turn my phone over, screen down.

Time seems to slow, the muggy air stifled by steam from the cups and hot drinks being passed around. I can feel sweat forming on my forehead now, the back of my neck, underneath my armpits. All my senses seem heightened, and I can hear every word being spoken, feel each draft of air as the door opens and closes, smell each coffee bean ground down and liquefied. My phone vibrates again. The brief sleepy calm jolts back into present panic. An email glares up at me from the screen:

From: caprahircus@hotmail.com

Re: Meeting

I run my finger across the screen, leaving a trail of sweat behind, glistening.

EMAIL FIVE

Dear Michelle,

I apologise for the late message. I know we were due to meet today. I thought it only polite to let you know however that I won't be able to meet you after all.

To be honest, I never intended to come and meet you in the first place.

I cannot tell you how happy it has made me to know you went through with this though, and have been sitting waiting for me. I imagine this will only make you distrust me even further and I do not blame you in the least. It irks me though, and I am sure you can appreciate this, that you felt the need to bring a friend with you.

What do you think I am? What did you envisage me doing? Attacking you in broad daylight like the girl in my story was? I am not the villain here Michelle. I am not the murderer. Only you have that blood on your hands and until recently you thought that only you could see and smell that blood.

Not anymore.

I am still that postman and you, the reader, are waiting for the next instalment. You are in my story now. And the very fact you have figured out my riddles and even come to meet me at a secret rendezvous, shows just how desperate you are for the final reveal and twist.

It's coming. Don't worry.

One thing you should know though is that there are no red herrings. I find red herrings so awfully dull, especially in these carbon copy supermarket commercial fodder books, so I will at least relieve you of that.

Everything I have written has meaning. There are no empty words. No empty threats.

Oh, and I don't know why you chose to meet in a café that holds no real attachment for you rather than the pub where you had your third date with Billy. The Billy goat himself.

No need to reply. I'll be in... what would Billy say? 'Four down, five letters. One of the five senses':

touch.

You can come up with my name this time:

A_____.

-

Michelle?

What are you doing here?

I know this isn't our usual spot but I knew I'd find you in here.

Oh god. I don't even know where to start. Honestly, I didn't mean for any of this to happen.

It's fine. Truly. It's all one big misunderstanding. I'm okay, I'm here.

It feels so…. I can't tell you how good this feels. To have your arms around me again! But how? How are you here?

Because this is me. It's always been me. I needed to know how much you loved me and how much our love could withstand.

But why? Why wouldn't you just tell me that you were safe? That you were always here?

Come on Michelle. I mean, you haven't been exactly perfect, have you?

I…

Don't worry. I know. I know the baby wasn't mine. I know all about the hospital ruse. Just like you know that I rushed to see you in the hospital only to get hit by a bike and crushed by a car. I know that that kills you. Each. And. Every. Day.

Billy? I…

Look. Look at what you've done. Look at this dead baby. Look at the blood all over my body. Look. Look at the blood on your hands smeared all over –

"Michelle? Michelle what's happened?"

I am standing in front of Billy. He is holding our dead baby in his hands.

"Sit down. Come on."

I can smell blood, slowly dripping from his stomach. He's holding a baby, tiny feet and hands curled up, touching. Red.

"I think this is hers. She dropped it. Is she okay?"

"It's alright Michelle, come on. It's okay."

Billy please. Please don't go. Please don't leave me.

You know what you've done, and you need to tell him. He deserves to know you don't regret fucking him when you were married to me because you were lonely or whatever bullshit reason you want to give both of us. He deserves to know you sucked his baby out from inside of you like the whore you are. Everyone knows and you know they know and this is why women travel out of the country and write signs and march and Instagram #youknowme to make them feel better for killing a baby they say is a mistake when they and you are all -

"Does she need anything?"

"No. No. We're okay. We're just leaving."

I know Billy isn't really here. But he was here. He was standing right there. Was he here? Right in the coffee shop. Holding my dead baby. Knowing that I had an abortion. Knowing that the baby was never his in the first place.

-whores, Michelle.

-

Sit in the sadness if you need to.

-

The breeze is trying in vain to cool to my skin. It feels like fire.

"Michelle, what happened in there?"

This is purgatory. I don't deserve to be in hell.

"Did they show? Did you see him?"

Limbo is my punishment. Realising that Billy died knowing my secret.

"Here, you dropped this on the floor. I'm sorry - the screen's a little smashed."

That his last action was to rush to me. To love me. Despite what I had done.

"Please, Michelle. You need to say something."

And I can never be forgiven.

"Here." I manage to say. "Read it. It's what he, she, whoever this is sent... sent to me just now. They..." I pause, swallow, almost choke. "They knew I was there. They knew you were there."

It takes me three times to sign into the phone. I mistype the password three times. It's Billy's birthday. I am forgetting him. Silence whilst Jenni reads the email. The anger, the threat, the intelligence behind this writing. How could someone hate me this much? How could someone put so much effort into hurting someone else? How long has someone been plotting this?

this is why women travel out of the country

"Jesus. This is... I don't even know what to say."

and write signs

"Neither do I."

"Did you see anyone though? I mean he must've been close enough to see you. To see me."

and march

"Maybe... maybe he was... maybe he was..." I can feel my mind slowing down, covered in miniature weights dangling from each thought, tugging, "...outside? Looking in?"

244

and Instagram #youknowme

"What do you want to do? Do you want to go to the police? We can show them these emails. There's got to be something they can do and work with."

"I don't know. I don't want to have to explain everything."

"Explain what? You haven't done anything wrong. This is some freakshow making stuff up about you. And about Billy. Someone who, I don't know, had an affair with Billy or whose writing you ignored or something. I'm clutching at straws here. I can't make sense of it. I mean come on, just think about what this freak is saying…"

She taps in my password and runs her finger down over the screen and email again, reading some parts aloud:

"'I am not the murderer. Only you have that blood on your hands and until recently you thought that only you could see and smell that blood. Not anymore.' You need to show this the police. You can get a restraining order."

"Against who?"

"What about Sam?"

I take the phone from Jenni, and I read out loud to her now: " *'…I am the postman…'* They have literally put me into one of their books. Whoever this is knows me. They know Billy. They know all of us and the mistakes we've made."

"What mistakes? Neither of you did anything that would warrant this. Jesus, no one deserves this." She takes the phone from back from me, unlocks it again, scanning over the email once more.

"Can I look at the others? I know you've sent them to me but it might jog something in my memory if I skim through them now."

to make them feel better for killing a baby that's a mistake

I close my eyes and nod. Images rush in and out, vicious and cruel. My head jolts from Donna to my mother, to the hospital to the office space, from a wine bottle and my iPad, to Mrs Lullin's room, my baby scan.

And then, something clicks in my head.

because they and you are all

"Can I have my phone back for a second?"

whores, Michelle.

Jenni hands it back. "How did you know my password?"

"What? On your phone?"

"I didn't open my phone for you. Just now, I mean. You just got into my emails without me opening my phone for you."

She meets my look dead on. "I just saw you tap it in, I guess. Eight nine down, one two across. Right?"

Something in my stomach drops.

"I'm sorry, I should've asked to you open it."

I look down at my phone; the home screen back to an image of me and Billy. Suddenly, a name flashes up and a shrill ringtone blares out.

"Hi. Is this a good time?" Leesha.

"Yes. No. Sorry, sure - what's wrong?" I try not to look at Jenni.

"I found it! I found the story. The circus short story."

"Really?" I try to keep my voice neutral. "Where?"

"After hours of trawling through your manuscripts and stuff you sent to me. Honestly you owe me."

"So, what's it like?"

"It's about a woman who suffers an accident when a circus act goes wrong, all in front of a live audience. I didn't manage to read the whole thing but it's interesting enough. It's by someone called S. J. Keane. Don't know if the name rings a bell?"

Somehow, the sweat that has started to flood my palms doesn't cause me to drop the phone. I put one hand to my stomach. I try not to vomit.

"Anyway. I'll send it over to you right now. I'm not surprised you refused to publish it even if it is quite good. It's full of mistakes."

"What?"

"Yeah. Loads of them. Stupid things like referring to guillotine humour, unless it's a poor attempt at a pun for what happens in the story. But it doesn't read like that."

It takes everything in me not to be sick. It takes everything in me not to scream.

"Okay. Thank you, Leesha, really." I hang up.

"Everything okay?" Jenni asks.

"Yes. Yeah. I've been called into work. I need to cover a few hours."

"Are you sure you are okay to go in? After today?"

I stand up, though I don't know how I'm able to. "Yes. It will make me feel better. Keep my mind busy."

I manage to walk away in a straight line until I reach the end of the road and turn the corner.

I bend over and vomit into the grass.

PART FOUR

There is an odd sense of calm that often appears when in the midst of the most stressful situations.

When my parents announced their divorce, I remember feeling nothing, just a relief that the years of shouting, seeing my father belittled day after day, would finally come to an end. When I was told the difficulties getting pregnant were more likely due to a problem with me, with my body, I felt happy that it wasn't Billy, that I didn't have to worry about his guilt and the shame *he* would feel for letting *me* down. Now, as I wait for Leesha to arrive with the story, these once innocuous pages that now possibly hold the answer to so many questions and secrets, I find myself breathing steadily. The final calm before the final storm.

In our bedroom, I look at the iPad which offered a ghostly feeling of company when his email address flickered up just days ago; to the chest of drawers by my bed where I keep his t shirt, and have imagined time and time again just wrapping myself inside it, inside his smell, his scent; to the box of letters that opened a Pandora's box of deceit and possible years of betrayal. But they are not the proof of an affair. It sickens me to think that I ever contemplated that Billy would have done that to me. To us. There was only ever one cheat in our relationship. These inflammatory declarations of love, of lust, of secrets... these aren't Billy. They never were. These aren't even from a lover. These pages are forgeries, lies to make me pay for what I have done. From someone who holds a grudge against me for hurting Billy, for taking something precious away from them and from this world.

My inner demon and enemy, the scratches on my wrist, would tell me yes – this is what I have had coming since I first looked at another man, since I went behind Billy's back, since I destroyed that life. But the me that leaves goodwill notes around the house is telling me *No*. The me that goes to counselling is telling me *No*. The me that tries, tries, tries to be a good person is telling me *No. This is not your fault. You may have made mistakes but this not something you deserve. No. This is not your doing.*

Leesha should be here any minute.

Donna is coming after she's finished work. "Who the hell is S. J. Keane?"

"I'll hopefully know more, know for sure after I've read these pages.". I promised to keep her updated. "I'll let you know."

I feel like I am on a precipice. That this might really be over soon. A knock at the door seems ominous – I know it's Leesha, I can tell through the frosted glass – but it jolts me. She hugs me and hands me the pages. She knows I won't want to wait.

"What are these?" she asks, looking at the letters to Billy scattered over the kitchen table.

"These," I sigh, "are part of the whole narrative. Just like this is," I say, waving the short story. "Honestly, you wouldn't believe me if I told you." Leesha looks at me, silently waiting for the mystery to be explained. "Someone has plotted all of this. The emails, the extracts from some sort of book, these letters to Billy. The visits to where I work. Even being in my house."

"Letters to Billy? This madman has been in your *home*?"

"I'm not sure it is a man."

It takes Leesha a moment to process everything. I don't blame her. It's been rolling around inside my own head for long enough and I'm yet to fully comprehend the whole picture.

"When have they been here? Did you call the police?"

"I only *think* they have been. I've just noticed a few things - things that I know I haven't done myself." I wonder whether I know Leesha well enough to tell her these things, then realise that she is here to help me after all. She wants this finished just as much as I do. "Like... a bottle of wine being left open that I know I didn't drink. My phone screen changed from a picture of Billy and I and then back again. I've heard knocks on the front door. Black inky smudges where Billy used to leave them around the house when he'd done his crosswords for the day... all these little things that when put together..." - a beat - "...tell a story. Someone has been putting this together, on purpose, for some time. And I need to know why."

Leesha moves closer and puts a hand on my shoulder. "Then I hope reading this helps catch them. You take your time and I'll... what can possibly be useful at a time like this?" She smiles at me, nervously. "Tea? Coffee? Takeaway? I've never done this before."

"You mean you've never scoured through old manuscripts to find something that might link a friend to a potential stalker?"

"Well, not this week. No."

I laugh, weakly. "Tea. Tea would be fine."

I unfold the pages one by one. I can see that there are multiple errors, crossings out and corrections. No wonder I didn't pay much attention to this the first time I saw it; it would have made a terrible first impression. No editor or publisher would have read this if they received it in such a sorry, unprofessional state.

And then I see it for myself: at the very bottom of the last page is a signature, dated: *S. J. Keane, Oct. 2016.* The name leaps off the page - a warning, a shock. The date matches up too.

I know who this is. I just need to read the story before I allow myself to be certain.

The opening line stirs something in me immediately. A memory.

I begin.

THE CIRCUS ACTCIDENT

Amite City, Louisiana

1942

This was her last chance. As a group, they had travelled around the country in and out of states - sometimes chased out of towns and cities. And it came to this – her final show.

Signs were often seen on roads outside of ~~the~~ towns for a few weeks before the show arrived. Cheaply made and tattered banners promoting and promising *The Bearded Lady, Six Limbed Steve, Dolphin Girl* or *The Tragic Twins*. Grotesque cartoon figures would loom down from these posters at cars that drove by, at people who passed underneath them and would look up in ~~a~~ disgust~~ed awe~~, only to turn away and shake their heads. No one wanted them in their town. No one wanted to be around their kind.

Town meetings would be held in advance, asking questions such as "Can they be stopped?", "Can't we blockade the roads?", "What if they do something to the children?" But there was no law against a circus act travelling through a town. There was no law, yet, against a group of performers settling into an out-of-town field for a few weeks and offering a show for local punters to come and see. It was up to them to come and see the performance or not, wasn't it? What harm did it do to those who chose *not* to go? But that was not how most people felt.

The first night that Madame Annie's troupe took their residence in the swampy fields outside Amite City, Louisiana, one of their caravans was set on fire. Six Limbed Steve awoke to an acrid scent of burning and managed to cough through smoke to the ~~plastic~~ flimsy door and out into the cold, dark night. His friends -the acts feared so much, such as Armless Anita, The Half-Headed Boy and Shandy the Clown – all came to his rescue. "~~Was~~ Is this really happening *again*?" they asked, "Are we really hated that much?" Sadly, the answer seemed to be *yes*.

In the days leading up to the first show there were protests at the entrance to the field, people putting makeshift barriers across the dirt track. Each night there would be a line of torches and candles flickering under the moonlight. The people of Amite City wanted to scare and intimidate the freaks out of their town. But 'freaks' are very difficult to scare and intimidate. Sitting around their campfire, listening to the names being shouted across the field, the colleagues laughed off the comments being tossed their way through the wind. How do you scare and intimidate those who have been outcasts since birth? How do you scare and intimidate those who do exactly ~~the same~~ that to others by just existing? You can't. You can try but you can't.

"I just want to get through this week," Madame Annie told her collective, "and then we can have a break. For a while at least." The eyes of her congregation fell to her hand, which was rubbing her belly. No one would have known that she was pregnant if not for her own admission of the fact. She could feel the life inside of her kicking, swimming around. In bed at night, she would whisper to it, wondering what life they would have together. Would raising a child in this environment be good for them? Could she do as her own mother had done and travel a family around the country from show to show, from town to town, field to field? "It will be Contortionist Annie's last twist," she told her friends, "I can't keep doing bends and backflips with this little one inside of me."

"What about 'The Incredible Pregnant Lady'?" one person asked, joking.

"Or, 'The Immaculate Conception'. People would come to see that!" offered another.

"No one is going to pay to see a pregnant woman stand on a stage. This actually makes me the least freakish of us all. Even though I am now, technically, a body with eight limbs instead of four, two heads instead of one, two hearts instead of one. An alien growth is inside me some might say but… I am though, oddly, the most normal here. Whatever 'normal' really means." Madame Annie sighed. Her eyes went up to the heavens. She clapped her hands. "This is why I get so frustrated with these imbeciles who berate us, holding their placards and fire; a person's body is *unique*, not freakish. My mother's mission was to promote that message to as many people as possible; that freaks should be respected, revered, applauded. Being different. Being a break from the mundane norm. Being special. That is what each of you are. That is what we will continue to tell people here – both in our final shows and in the new acts and performances to come!"

Her hand continued to protectively, lovingly, rub her stomach – a promise to her friends, her baby, and her mother: the original *Mistress Annette and her Circus of Freaks*.

-

"How is it so far?" Leesha places a cup of tea in front of me. "I didn't read it all myself, but it fits the bill, right? A story about a circus act?"

I think before replying, unsure of what to say. "Yeah, yeah it does. It's about a travelling freak show in America. People being bullied for how they look and act. It's not terrible but... you can see the mistakes and all the corrections. No wonder I didn't give it much thought. Who would, looking like that?" I turn the pages over, each blank on the other side. "Maybe that was the point though. Judging a book a by its cover."

"You think the mistakes are on purpose?"

"Perhaps. They certainly have been in the letters and pieces I've been receiving. Maybe I'm giving them too much credit."

"Well, I hope the title is a pun and not just a mistake that they forgot to correct."

"Yeah. It's a little too obvious. 'The Actcident'. Something's going to go wrong in the show, the final performance... before a woman has a baby."

"Bloody hell, Michelle. That sounds awful. I'll read it. You don't have to. This doesn't seem right." Leesha looks at the pages warily, almost like a spectator keeping distance from the freak show acts in the story. "You don't have to put yourself through this just to placate some..."

"...freak?" I say. "I want to know how the story ends."

THE CIRCUS ACTCIDENT

Her hand continued to protectively, lovingly, rub her stomach – a promise to her friends, her baby, and her mother: the original *Mistress Annette and her Circus of Freaks*. She would continue her mother's work. Her child, whether son, daughter, freakshow performer or Hollywood star, would be proud of this family. This group. This troupe. These freaks that belonged together.

Her mother, long ago, had said that she wanted her ashes to be scattered in the surrounding woods or fields of wherever their current, or her last, show was. On a tree, just outside of Minnesota, Annie had scratched her mother's name alongside the dates of her birth and death. And below, *'Her absence is a silent grief.'* This, Annette said, was what had been on each tombstone or carving of members of their family for generations. Annie could picture it on her own gravestone, too.

A few mornings later, the sun shone down on the ~~swampy~~ boggy fields outside of Amite City. Bird calls and dog barks could be heard for miles around. The main road in and out of the city was covered in ~~a~~ its usual mixture of dust and car fumes. The acts were rehearsing their tricks, both on the main stage in the Big Top and outside in the bleached grass. Everything ran like clockwork, these performances having been practiced and changed and perfected and improved over years: Shandy the Clown pulled flowers from every orifice; Armless Anita balanced beach balls, suitcases, porcelain vases ~~after~~ upon her forehead one after the other, increasing in weight and size; Madame Annie, a little more tentatively than usual, rehearsed her bends and twists ~~one final time~~. Tonight was her final show. She looked out across the ~~dried land at her feet, the~~ sun ~~having~~ burnt ~~the~~ grass, and was already sketching new costume designs and banners for the circus in her mind's eye – she would, until the baby was born at least, become more of a designer and promoter for the circus, as well as ~~the~~ manager ~~and current performer~~. She would enjoy watching from the side lines. She was ready to be out of the spotlight.

Despite the hatred that the circus act received from the locals over the years, most evenings were always nearly sell outs; people coming to give life to their morbid curiosities, laugh and jeer, shriek and be shocked at they what they ~~see~~ saw. A few would bring signs, ignorant slogans (often misspelt) scrawled over cardboard. The favourite moment of each evening for Madame Annie was watching from the wings of the stage and catching sight of one, even if just one, patron in whose face she could see a change: where there was disgust, or an expectation of something hideous, there became a look of empathy, sympathy, some ~~kind of~~ respect. It always surprised her who this person was in each audience, never the same from one night to another: a mother and wife, angry at having been dragged along; a teenage boy, initially laughing and pointing, sneering at the stage; a twenty-something guy, no longer swearing and swigging beer ~~and snorting it out of his nose at the first, generally tame, act~~.

Later that evening, and the time had come. Four Eared Frannie had gone to each dressing room to let everyone know that it was nearly time for curtain. Madame Annie had just finished powdering her face. She blinked at her reflection in the mirror, its surface cracked with years of travel. In a moment, as was tradition, they would stand in a circle outside the Big Top, listen to the murmurs of the crowd inside, hold hands and say a prayer. An old Native Indian prayer, the people of the land, persecuted, much like themselves. The promotional banners for the show that stretched the highways of America included a small drawing of a totem pole covered with goat carvings, a nod to the Haida tribe, a distant family relation of Madame Annie and her mother; "Our ancestors associated goats with the sky, so that's what we aim for." Not that many of the people who came tonight will have noticed that; too busy being offended by the weird and wonderful that they loved to hate. ~~Before she went to join the others,~~ Now, Madame Annie also had her own ritual, something she'd started only since realising she was with child. What a miracle it was, swimming around inside of her. Her own little goat kid, kicking and bucking, ready for the world. The truth was, calling herself 'The Immaculate Conception' or some such name wouldn't have been so ridiculous – she genuinely did not know how she was pregnant – but still, she was. Doctors had told her that, when her own mother had died from ovarian cancer years earlier, her own chances of conceiving were low if at all. But somehow here she was: her last show before a fresh start with a new life.

This was her last chance. As a group, they had travelled around the country in and out of states - sometimes chased out of towns and cities. And it came to this – her final show. The troupe would go on ~~too~~ after a month's break ~~or so~~, and she would work from the side lines, but she was looking forward to ~~a break~~, a pause, a breath. But this was her last chance to look out into that crowd and again find just one person who had been changed for the better by this traveling groups of misfits she loved so very much.

She smiled to herself in the mirror. She stroked her belly and the life inside and whispered a prayer. She stepped out into the bright lights of ~~the~~ showtime, ~~awaiting~~.

"Do you want to answer it?"

I hadn't even heard the phone ringing. It was my mobile, rattling on the table. The tea Leesha had made for me was cold.

"I can just tell whoever it is that you're in the bathroom or something."

I looked at the name on the screen. It was Jenni. I didn't know what to say to her. The last thing I wanted was to upset her.

"No, it's okay. It's only Jenni. She's probably just checking in from earlier. I was with her when you called. I bailed on her without explaining."

"Okay. I'll give Donna a call and let her know we're still here. Do you want me to order in some food? You need to eat. What would you like?"

"Anything, honestly. You choose. I probably won't be thinking about it enough to taste it anyway." I wait until Leesha had gone out of the kitchen before I answer Jenni's call.

"Michelle!" She sounded relieved. "Are you okay? You left so suddenly before I was worried I had done something. Has something turned up?"

I pause. Take a breath. "Actually yeah. The short story we were looking for, the circus story... Leesha found it. She found it amongst some of our archived stories from the office. She's spent hours trawling through our records."

"I thought we looked in the office. There was nothing there."

"We did, but we must have missed it in one of the old filing cabinets. Anyway, Leesha found it and brought it over for me to read."

"How is it? Anything useful?"

"Interesting. It's covered in scribbles and mistakes. No wonder we didn't take it any further at the time; a scribbled draft doesn't really have the makings of a best seller, does it?"

"I wouldn't say that to your possible writer-stalker if you make contact with them again."

I pause. "Why do you say that?"

"Well, isn't that their whole point? They're fed up with agents literally judging a book by its cover. Draft or no draft, scribbles or no scribbles, if a story is good it shouldn't matter how it's presented, should it?"

I hold the first page up in front of me, up to the fading light of the evening through the kitchen window. "You're right. It would annoy him."

There's a noise on the end of the line like it's been dropped. "Any clues about who this is? Is there a name?"

"I'm not sure yet. I'll call you if I find anything for sure. Is that okay?"

"Of course. As long as you're alright?"

"Leesha is here with me." I crane my head. I can hear her ordering food from somewhere down the street. "And I'm fine. And I'm sorry for dashing off before. It was rude of me."

"It's fine. Don't apologise. There's… a lot going on. I'll call you later?"

"That'd be good. Thank you, Jenni. I mean it. You've been so good to me the last few days. It makes me wish…" and I realise before say it that I truly do mean it - this isn't just family lip-service - "we'd been closer for longer."

When she replies I think she is crying. "Me too, Michelle. Me too. I wish a lot of things had been different." She hangs up.

As if on cue, Leesha reappears. "How was she?"

"Just wanted to know if I had found anything. In the story."

"Well, I'm going to get out of your hair for a little while. Let you finish reading it in peace. I'm going to pick up some food for us. Donna said she'll be here soon too. She's just leaving work. You okay on your own for a bit?"

"Yeah. Yes, of course. I'll be able to talk more when you come back. I'll have finished by then."

"Okay. Do you know who this S.J Keane is yet?"

"Yes. I think I do." I pause. "But I'll need to finish this first."

She takes her coat from the chair opposite me. "I just hope we can sort this all out sooner rather than later." She pauses as she puts on her coat. "You're sure you're okay for an hour or so?"

"Yes. Yes. Honestly, go. And thank you."

She squeezes my shoulder. I hear her close the front door behind her.

The silence seeps in and covers me. It is oddly relaxing, considering the potential bomb I am holding. These paper bullets. I am afraid to say out loud what I think - and for it to be right. I am also nervous to be wrong and to have to start all over again. Or that I have just been paranoid all along… that this is nothing more than a story I have concocted in my head.

But no. I *know* something is amiss here.

THE CIRCUS ACTCIDENT

She smiled to herself in the mirror. She stroked her belly and the life inside and whispered a prayer. She stepped out into the bright lights of ~~the~~ showtime, ~~awaiting~~.

Inside the tent, the scents of popcorn, beer and smoke, damp grass crushed underfoot, candy floss and sweat, all mingled together to make a heady mixture only found around the circus lifestyle. Madame Annie breathed it in, deeply, lovingly taking it into her lungs, the smell she knew so well filling her body. The warmth was like a hand welcoming her onto the stage.

~~Now, f~~ From the wings, she motioned to one of the stage hands to turn the lights down, and get the spotlight ready.

"Good evening, friends."

Her voice, although loud through the speakers, was soft, gentle; a quality she hoped would welcome punters, not scare them away before the show even started. First impressions were everything, and she wanted the audience to feel nervous excitement rather than fear - especially any children. "Fear is a wonderful thing." Annie remembered her mother speaking to her from ~~the~~ this very stage, teaching the tricks of the trade. How to win an audience. How to keep them enraptured. "But the key is ~~to~~ holding them in the middle ground between terror and interest, between horror and thrill. *That* is where the magic is."

"We are so happy to welcome you to our show this evening. We thank you for making the journey and we hope we do not disappoint. We've never had any complaints before. Well…" a dramatic pause, a little tension ~~never did any harm~~, "not anyone you'd be able to ~~ever~~ hear from ~~about~~ again anyway."

A nervous titter.

There were a few empty seats but not many. A good turnout.

"Before we begin, I would like make a few things clear to you our esteemed guests. Nothing you see here tonight is fake. Yes, we perform tricks and have various methods up our sequined sleeves, but we do so honestly and with the upmost respect for the performance and art that is the circus. Whilst applause is welcomed, any booing, any type of negative comment will however *not* be tolerated. It has never has been. At any performance. We are here to provide entertainment, not to be mocked. If you have any problem with this then I suggest you leave now."

Only once had a family left at that moment; it later turned out that they actually watched from the back, popping their heads into the tent every so often so as to not miss out completely ~~on everything, just the parts the children didn't like~~.

"So then," her voice boomed, "let the show begin."

-

Backstage, Madame Annie stood with the other performers listening to the whoops and cheers, the intakes of breath from the audience. That was the magic her mother had spoken of. The awe of the spectator that you could hear and could almost taste in the air.

"My turn. ~~You ready for your last show for a while Annie?~~" Armless Anita beamed up at her. "I'm so proud to be in this show~~, you know~~."

"I'm proud to have you here. My mother would be too." Madame Annie put a hand on her colleague's shoulder. "~~And yes, I'm fine. Thank you for asking.~~ Now go and warm up the stage for me! I'm on after you!"

"Break a leg! That's what they say isn't it?" Armless Anita asked. "That's what they call guillotine humour, right?"

"Not quite. But thank you. Now hurry up! Don't keep our audience waiting!"

Madame Annie took a seat nearby. She closed her eyes. She had performed her contortionist tricks hundreds of times, but this last act needed to be good. Perfect. Rubbing her hand over her belly, sensing the tiny life swimming inside, she just *knew* it would be a performance to remember.

There's only one page left. Parts of the story are coming back to me. I know that I've read this story before. I remember some character names. The pregnancy. How I was certain the writer was, somehow, trying to forge a metaphor about motherhood and preparing for a performance; the circus itself being the real baby that Annie and her own mother had parented for so long. I remember disliking some of the writing, finding it a little clumsy.

Now, it stands before me as something so much more... it has a weight to it, a hidden meaning.

Now, I cannot ignore the names of the women: Annie, Annette, Anita. All names beginning with the 'A' Billy and I always said we would use to name our first daughter.

The tribal reference to goats.

The guillotine humour error.

This is someone I know. I am almost certain of it now – and that I know who S. J. Keane is.

I pick up the final page.

THE CIRCUS ACTCIDENT

Madame Annie was lying down in the contortionist's box. The wood felt cool against her skin. She ran her hands along the inside and felt the marks she had made over the years twisting her arms and legs, her toes scratching the sides. Even though her eyes were closed, even though it was pitch-black inside, she could see the smiling faces of the audience. She had chanced a glimpse as she walked from the backstage area to the side of the stage. There, through the curtains, she saw faces aghast, laughing, gulping, eyes aglow with the thrill of the act before them. Armless Anita did not disappoint. And there, two rows back on the right-hand side, Madame Annie saw a little girl, her arms wrapped around a stuffed toy won at one of the fete stalls outside, gripping it out of both fear and joy. She bounced lightly on her mother's lap. She was smiling, she was happy. She was what Madame Annie always took the time to find in every ~~show's~~ audience: the one person who viewed the performers as special and not as freaks. Inside the box, Madame Annie held that little girl's face in her mind's eye, keeping one hand over her stomach, picturing her own child one day inspiring future generations of little children ~~to come~~.

"Hey, Annie. You good to go?"

"Yes Shandy. Let's put on a good final show."

The buzz of the chainsaw shuddered over the box. "Okie dokie! Let's do this!"

Madame Annie could hear the music change, signalling her introduction. If Shandy the Clown's shrill voiceover didn't chill the audience into silence then the sudden tearing sound of his chainsaw, wielded madly above his head certainly did.

~~Two~~ The two of them had the performance down to an art: a knock on the top left hand of the lid meant Madame Annie moved one way; a knock on the underside bottom right meant another. By now, the grinding teeth of the chainsaw were rather soothing.

Tap one: bend left knee. Tap two: lift right arm. The chainsaw ~~passes~~ passed through with ease. Yelps from the audience.

Tap three: head turned to the left. Tap four: stomach sucked in. Madame Annie imagined seeing her baby making a face, displeased at being squeezed, upset perhaps at the loud noises.

Tap five: left elbow lifted. She tapped her belly, whispered something soothing.

Tap six: she tapped her belly in time to the clapping outside. She smiled at the thought of her baby contorting in unison inside her. Her own little performer.

Tap seven: both feet lifted.

"Argh!"

A piercing pain shot through her body. Instantly, she could smell the metallic scent of blood, her own blood.

Tap eight: keep both feet lifted. *Yes, keep both feet lifted.*

"Urgh! Shandy!"

Something was wrong. Had she miscounted the taps? Had she got distracted?

"Shandy! Shandy! Stop ~~for a moment~~!"

Surely he would hear her? He was only ever mere centimetres away from her whichever side of the box he was ~~on~~ at: and... he'd be on her... *left* side now. Right?

Tap nine: shift to the right.

No. He wasn't.

The blades cut deep into her back. The metal teeth ground against bone, her spine cracking against the rotating motion of the saw. She heard screaming but wasn't sure if it was her own. She heard blood gush but tried to believe it was just a prop. She heard feet pounding, fists slamming, but didn't know who they belonged to.

She left her body as it happened. She stood to the side of the horror, outside of her own body. She imagined watching the circus act, watching as a performer got cut up into pieces and shoved around in smaller and smaller ~~pieces~~ boxes. She saw the show, rather than being in it herself. *It's all a trick of light and sleight of hand* she prayed, as she watched helplessly - willing herself to believe that it was all an illusion, a trick that she would snap out of. She would wake up and it would be nothing but a bad dream.

Instead of the feeling the pain, she tried to imagine her body in separate boxes: her arms, her head, her legs, her stomach; her baby, unborn but shielded, floating in ~~the~~ a balloon-like womb inside another box. Safe. Then, like a jigsaw, a beautiful mosaic, she would be put back together and slotted back into the shape of a woman. She would be handed her new-born baby, both crying, but alive.

I have another box inside of me, she thought, *the most precious gift. This box needs to be protected...*

But the trick was now a bloody reality. Outside of the horror, outside of the terror, outside of the screams, she willed herself to believe that this last performance of hers was in fact her giving birth: that the spotlights were from a glaring hospital lamp; that her yells were from exhaustion, from pushing and birthing... ready to meet her child.

But, she realised, fading... fading... *I will never be whole again.*

Before Leesha returns, I take myself to the bathroom. I turn on the tap. I don't want her to hear me crying.

This is a story of a woman who lost her child, taken from her in the most cruel and horrific way. I hold my stomach, and like Madame Annie in the story, I cradle where my baby used to be. The sobs come in waves; I stop and breathe, and then cry again - wracked with a sea of emotions washing over me. I know there's nothing I can do to change what I have done. There's nothing I can say. But this story, I realise now, is more than the metaphor I thought of it as being at first - motherhood being a performance, preparing for a new role - it's about how women are made to feel day in day out: cut up, separated, judged, in spotlight. Less than a person if they're not a mother. And if they can't have children, or lose a baby, or abort their baby... they might as well be in a freakshow. I remember Donna in the café... even *mothers* are mocked, seen as inconveniences with prams.

Women, mothers or not, are constantly training for a role they cannot ever do justice, because society won't let them.

I sit down on the edge of the bathtub. Feel cool porcelain. I close my eyes. Extracts from my anonymous author float in the darkness around me.

...there's a reason it's known as <u>his</u>tory.

...I wanted to write a story, a herstory...

I know what I need to do.

Back in the kitchen I tidy up the teas made by Leesha. I straighten things out on the table. I put my phone in my pocket. I collect the short story and go upstairs. I place it in the box with the love letters supposedly to and from Billy. These are all parts of one big story; all chapters of a novel in which I have been made the protagonist, the antagonist, the villain. I find Billy's t-shirt and hold it close to me. His scent is still there, lingering, holding on. Distant but there. I say his name.

As calmly as possible, I take out my phone and dial.

They pick up.

"Hello?"

"I need to speak to an S. J. Keane, please. I'm calling about a short story they sent to us here at Tulip and Thorn. I used to run the company. The submitted piece is called 'The Circus Actident', or, *Accident*, I presume. I'd very much like it if we could arrange a meeting."

Instantly the line goes dead.

What if that was the wrong thing to do? Foolish?

I panic.

I think to call Donna and Leesha, even Tony, until –

there's a knock at the front door.

They're here.

-

The day of Billy's funeral the weather could not decide what it wanted to do.

One minute it was raining, the next sunny. At times there was a breeze and then nothing, our grief just left to dangle in stale air. His father spoke during the service. Only at the wake did I manage to say a few words, and even then it was through stops and starts of tears and the utter, choking shame I had clogging my veins. People I didn't even know came up to me and offered their support and condolences; sent cards, sent flowers, appeared with food in the desert of days after the funeral. It was a blur. A black and white blur that mixed together into a swirl of grey that became a cloud that became fog that became a blanket I couldn't and didn't want to get out from under.

I remember my mother sitting on the same pew as me in the church. Not once did she put her hand on mine. *I know you know,* I wanted to say, *I know you know what I've done. And why Billy is here.* But please, I wanted to beg, *please just tell me it will be okay.*

Dressed in black. Statuesque and stoic. Aloof.

Jenni had always been so distant that I naturally assumed it was due to some dislike of me, that I had done something early in my relationship with Billy that upset her. That unimpressed her.

I had no idea of the pain she was in - the pain to be a mother, to be a wife. To be what a woman was expected to be.

And I stood before her in that church, responsible for the death of her brother and his child.

Another knock.

I stand at the foot of the stairs and see an outline through the frosted glass of the front door. I know that if I open the door I can never go back. But whatever happens now, I have to do this for myself. For Billy. For the family we should have had.

I open the door.

"Michelle."

-

Okay, so you've met my mum and dad. Most people are here now, Billy says.

Billy, don't worry. Family gatherings don't bother me, I say.

They stress the fuck out of me, Billy says.

I don't know why. Your mother is actually nice, I say.

Billy sees someone I've not yet met and waves them over.

"So, you know then."

"I figured it out. Eventually. S. J. Keane."

"When did you realise?"

"Come inside, Jenni. We can talk inside."

She hovered for a moment on the threshold, seemingly, like myself, scared to cross over - to make this real, to turn this work of fiction into nonfiction, to make this story into something. I close the door behind us. We walk in silence to the kitchen. We sit down opposite one another.

"Can I get you anything?"

"Like a bottle of wine? Or will you just open one to smell?"

"It *was* you."

"Who moved the wine bottle around, making you think you'd been drinking in the night? Yes."

"Why Jenni? Why have you gone to such lengths to torment me?"

She held my stare for a moment. "You know. If you've figured out that this has been me all along, then you know why. Don't embarrass yourself by making me explain. Don't insult me like that. You know what you've done to make me act this way."

"You're right. I do." Pause. "But I'm not sure what you want from me."

"First of all, tell me how you figured it out. When did you realise it was me?"

"I should have known earlier. But it was what you said just after we had been to the café at the University. When you unlocked my phone. You spoke like Billy did when he spoke in his crossword riddles. And you being at the café when I got the email was just too convenient a cover. You were very clever." I spoke calmly. The release I felt, the relief from being able to say all of this *and* know I was right, was overwhelming. "The guillotine humour reference in your story - you'd said that to me only a few days beforehand. Did you mean to drop these little hints during our chats together? Was it all part of building your narrative around me?"

"I was tired of being invisible. I couldn't write. I couldn't get published anywhere. What was the point of that stupid Creative Writing degree I'd done? I was stuck in some stupid business office job I hated. Even my own flesh and blood's publishing agency wouldn't accept my writing. Perhaps I shouldn't have used a pseudonym. Maybe then you'd have taken it seriously."

"S. J. Keane. Sampson Jennifer Keane. Your name. Your husband's name. His surname."

"Well done."

"You've been Sam all along?"

"Yes. And Andy. Andi with an *i*. Ann with an *e*. Ann. Annie. A. All of them."

"But why?"

"I knew you were always going to call your baby a name with an A. That's what Billy wanted. Until," she leaned forward, her face coming closer to mine across the table, "you slept with Tony behind Billy's back. Had an abortion. And got Billy killed."

It's like a gunshot to the stomach. I can't deny it. I can't ignore what is true. But it winds me to hear it said out loud.

"How did you find out?"

She runs her hands over the table and places them together, as if in prayer. "Billy mentioned to me that he thought something had happened between you and Tony. He said you'd been having problems with getting pregnant. He was worried about your drinking and that he and Donna had spoken to you about it. He'd seen you, he felt, flirting with Tony on nights out." She claps her hands together. "It's amazing what men tell you when they're in bed with you."

For a moment I don't understand and just look at her, waiting for her to continue. But then another piece of the puzzle clicks into place. "*Samantha*. You're the Samantha that Tony mentioned to me."

"Sam. Samantha. Sampson. One name that's really so useful. And yes, it's amazing how drink makes a man spill his guilt. Of course, he didn't know I knew you. He had no idea who Billy's sister was. He told me *everything*. I didn't take long... how he was in love with someone he couldn't be with. He didn't want to pressure her when she was grieving. How he still struggled with the guilt of sleeping with her when she was at a low point in her marriage. He's actually a good guy. Another one you've fucked over."

"Tony never loved me."

"That's not what he told me."

"Why should I believe anything you say? Our entire friendship has been a lie. Every conversation has just been part of your story, this fantasy to punish me. Even the letters you led me to in the office. You planted them there. You've been playing with me all along!"

She leans back in her chair away from me and folds her arms. "I wanted you to hurt. To hurt like you hurt Billy."

"How can I believe you when you say that Billy knew about Tony? You've lied about so much."

"*I've* lied?" Suddenly, Jenni stood up, kicking the chair back behind her. Her eyes flared. They looked red in the growing darkness of the evening that was creeping into the house. I didn't know what to say... what would provoke her further. "I've lied? What about you? What about your wedding vows? What about your wedding song and how you fucked that that the moment you made eyes with Tony across the street? How do you think that made Billy feel, seeing you flirt with a friend when you were both struggling with not being able to get pregnant? When Billy was stressed and upset and needing support from you, you just went off with someone else! You destroyed him. You destroyed the life you could've had with him."

"But one thing I don't get Jenni,"- she is still standing, her hands now palm down on the table, and I remain sitting, keeping her eyeline - "is why, when all your writing is about your disgust for how women-shaming current literature seems to be, how men have *history* and women have nothing, how every book on sale these days seems to be about a drunk woman, a flawed woman, a woman with a secret which is her own fault and cross to bear, a woman beaten down by a man... then why, *why*, have you done nothing but shame *me*? Why have you spent so much of your own energy and time and pain in bringing my shame out into the world? Why shame yet another woman?"

"Because you killed *everything*! Everything I ever wanted. Everything I never got to have." A pause. A rising of her chest. "That's why."

Jenni turns away from me. I chance a look at my phone. The screen is blank. Donna and Leesha don't know anything has happened, but I wonder if maybe Jenni has intercepted them somehow.

"Listen Jenni, my friends will be here soon. You don't want them coming in and finding you like this. Let me call them and tell them that I'm going to bed or not feeling well. That way we can keep talking and get to the bottom of this. Surely you want to talk this through together, now that we know the truth."

"We? Together? Talk? Michelle you're too late. The truth killed Billy long ago. I don't care what you've got to say."

I make to stand up, but she turns and moves quickly around the table towards me.

"No. No I don't think so."

"Donna and Leesha!" I yell their names as though trying to invoke their presence. "They know to come here. They won't be long. We won't be alone for long."

"Michelle. If you think I haven't already called them and told them to go elsewhere to meet us about a *very* important find related to this whole scenario, then you clearly haven't read many of these recent popular thriller novels, have you? I mean this is *exactly* what happens in nearly every single one of those stupid books you all keep peddling." She takes a step closer. I am frozen to my seat. "And yet, for some reason, nothing I wrote was good enough."

It all happens in a blur.

I feel Jenni grab my hair, yank back my head.

Then all I know is blackness and blankness and the dark.

-

I dream of Tony.

I see him holding a baby, rocking it back and forth in his arms. He turns, and now I see Billy who, like Tony, is beaming and holding a child. They turn in profile, and I can see both their heads, back-to-back, both babies writhing and snuggling into their father's arms. Father… the word rolls around inside my head, inside this dream, like a snowball racing and racing downhill, getting bigger and bigger, heavier and heavier until it blinds my vision, until I can't see anything else outside of the white snow. The blizzard. Flecks of ice ricochet off and away and around this snow globe I find I myself in. Trapped.

I hear voices, muffled through the thick glass. I hear a whirring sound, a sloshing sound. Perhaps the snow is melting.

I think I hear someone say my name.

-

"Michelle. Michelle? Come on Michelle."

I open my eyes and a face swims before me. The eyes remind of Billy. It's Billy. Billy is here with me.

"Come on. Wake up. I didn't hit you that hard."

"What? Where's Billy?"

"Billy? He wouldn't be here even if he was alive. He'd have left you by now. Although, a *part* of him is nearby I guess you could say."

The whirring sound from my dream is pounding inside my head now. It sounds like a whirlpool swishing in slow motion.

"You really have no idea what you've done do you? To so many people."

She is sat on the floor just in front of me, her back resting on the kitchen table. I am sat with my back against the fridge, the cold metal sending shivers down my spine. It is dark outside. Jenni hasn't turned on any of the kitchen lights, so the only way I can see her is by the light coming from the street behind my house, and the glare of various electrical lights in the room: the microwave timer, the fridge's temperature gauge, the... I realise that the turning sound I have been hearing is the washing machine.

"Then tell me. Please, Jenni. Tell me. I want to know. I want to help."

"Help? You can't help. I mean you could have done, but you can't now." In the red flashing light of the washing machine, I see her look above my head, before continuing to talk to the space above me. "After I lost the baby... babies... one after the other..." I hear her swallow. "I had no idea what to do with my life. I had no plan. What do you do when you want to be a mother and you can't? What do you do when your husband doesn't support you through that? Through the emptiness. The hollow, intangible pain. It's all consuming, the loss of a baby. I tried counselling. Grief therapy groups. I talked to Billy. I shopped. I exercised. Nothing. Then one day I read an article in a magazine about a woman, around my age, who had had miscarriages one after the other. She wrote so clearly, so passionately, so bravely, about how she used her writing to grieve, to understand what her body had gone through. What her mind couldn't make sense of."

I remembered something: a torn page from a magazine in Mrs Lullin's room.

"You left that article in the room of the lady I cared for. You ransacked her room. She *said* a Sam had been in her room. That was you too... you... I can't believe you've been doing *all* of this."

"What have I written many times now Michelle? I am the postman, and you are simply left to wait for the next piece of the puzzle to arrive. Teasing Mrs Lullin was an enjoyable subplot. Her death was unexpected I'll admit, but it helped to add another layer of confusion to the story. Bless her, she was quite sweet to talk to. She had no idea who I was, but she believed whatever I told her."

"Please tell me you didn't hurt her. Please tell me that what happened to her was an accident."

"I admit that I messed up her room a bit. That was easy. That girl on the front desk is useless by the way. But no. I didn't harm her. *I* don't hurt innocent people."

"So why send me these pieces of writing? Why torture me with threats and details of my own life? If you wanted to bully me, shame me, you could have just come to me face to face. Or told Donna. Or told Tony about the baby. Why do all this?"

"I wanted you to know what it feels like to be betrayed. To be hurt by someone who is meant to love you."

Silence covered us for a minute, or it could have been an hour. I was too tired to speak. Too confused. Too angry. Too ashamed of what I had let happen. The only sound was the repetitive cycle of the washing machine, something thudding inside.

"So I decided to write. To use my writing degree for something other than a useless student loan I was still paying off. I wrote some shitty poems. I tried a diary, but I couldn't stand the selfish feeling it gave me, writing about yourself. How narcissistic it felt. And then I thought about a short story. An analogy. *Those* I had been good at. I dug out some of my old pieces and read through them, remembering what I loved about writing and why I wanted to do it for a career in the first place. You and Billy had already set up your business; it was small, but it was a start. I thought that if anyone would take on a story of mine it would be you two. So, I worked on a short story about a pregnant lady. A pregnant circus performer. A freakshow. How could a freak survive in such a judgemental world? How could a woman survive in a world where the one thing she is *meant* to do she can't provide…? What kind of freak is she? Me, that's the kind of freak. So, I wrote the story of a woman whose future and whose hopes are destroyed irrevocably and horrifically, leaving her forever scarred, forever empty. Cut into pieces of what a woman should be."

"And that's what happened to the other girl too," I say. "The girl in the letters. She imagined herself in separate boxes when she was attacked. That's how she viewed herself."

"Because that's what society does to us. Men tell us what to do. Women who are attacked are told it's because they wore a short skirt, or drank, or sent a flirtatious text message. Women judge each other for how they look. Mothers are mocked for giving up who they used to be before motherhood. Single and childless women though are viewed as ugly Miss Havisham spinsters. We are splintered off into boxes that are easier to digest and easier to ignore. But whichever we choose we can't win." She takes a breath. Exhales slowly. "But it was story no one was interested in. No one wants to publish a story about a woman with an actual message. With a meaning. People only want to read about women when they are victims, when they are abused. Abused for entertainment."

"We didn't know it was your story. Jenni, we might have read it differently if we'd known."

"Yeah, context adds a lot to a story, doesn't it? What did you think when you first read it? Something gross, something disgusting that no one would want to read? Some pathetic effort at metaphor? I thought I would send it to you without my real name, just to see how it would do without that pressure, that added embarrassment if you still didn't like it. Or if you published it just *because* it was mine."

"Then you couldn't win, could you? And we couldn't either. Whether we published it knowing it was yours or we didn't... you'd almost accepted that it wouldn't work out."

"Don't try to twist this around on me now, Michelle. I tried to deal with my grief in a creative, positive way... and everyone shit all over it. And then, *you*."

She said "you" with absolute venom.

"You did what you did. You killed something I would have given everything for. You killed a marriage. You killed a baby. You killed a husband. You didn't know, you *still* don't know, how lucky you were."

My head lolls back against the cold fridge. I know I am not tied down, my legs and arms are free, but I am too tired to move. To try and get up, to get away from her. The washing machine beeps, and the swirling sound of water comes to a stop. In the dim light of the kitchen, I can make out something white inside the washing machine.

Suddenly, my throat constricts. I feel my heart drop to my stomach.

"What did you mean when you said part of Billy is nearby?" I don't want to know the answer.

"Remember how you told me that you always keep him near you? Something to keep him alive? You told me during our heart to heart in your office. Just before I gave you the box full of affair-soiled letters."

It's everything I can do to not be sick.

I crawl over the kitchen floor. My hands slip on the tiles, grasp the washing machine door handle. I pull it open, almost ripping it off its hinges, and delve inside.

I feel it, damp and freezing cold. But I can't feel *him* anymore. And I can't smell him anymore. The t-shirt isn't Billy's anymore.

I pull it out and cradle it in my arms like a baby. He's gone. Now he's really gone.

I let my tears drop down onto the t-shirt, adding to the water that has already washed away any remaining memory of him.

"This is all I had left of him," I choke through tears. "I don't have anything else."

"Neither do I."

"Are you going to kill me?" My voice sounds pathetic in the darkness.

"Michelle." Her eyes glare at me. I can't tell if they are shining with adrenaline, tears or both. "I was wrong before. You *have* read some of those fucking novels."

That seemed to go well, Billy says.

I hope so, I say.

And my sister liked you. I think you'll get on, Billy says.

Jenni? Yeah, I guess so, I say.

Billy nods, rubs my arm.

-

I don't know how long we sat there in the dark.

I could make out Jenni's figure across the kitchen. She was at the table, hands together, head down, perhaps waiting for me to speak or move. Perhaps she was waiting for me to explain, apologise, say something to justify my actions or her own... whatever this was that were engaged in. I was on the floor, my back to the washing machine. The light was no longer flashing but was static red, a tiny display of anger. Jenni's hatred of me was more like a torch, flaming and hot, scorching to the touch. I imagined her standing opposite me, lantern and pitchfork in hand, charging at me: the beast, the freak, the adulterer, the baby killer.

"You know, our marriage wasn't perfect."

It takes Jenni almost a minute to respond. I'm almost convinced she's asleep.

"What do you mean?" she sounds tired.

"No marriage is perfect, Jenni."

"Yes," her reply is quicker this time, "I'm sure being married to Billy was an awful situation to be in. Loving, caring, worked hard, wanted a family. Faithful." On the last word she raised her head and looked directly at me.

"It was also full of anxiety, uncertainty. Failure." I look her in the eye as I speak. Billy's t-shirt, that no longer smells of him, is in my lap. "We couldn't get pregnant. I wasn't working as much as him. I felt that he and Donna were overreacting about my drinking. I felt guilty all the time that the reason we couldn't conceive was down to me and my body. That what I was built to do was the one thing I couldn't. So I drank more. And I saw Tony."

"Is this meant to be an excuse Michelle? I don't care how sad you were. You had everything going for you and you just abandoned it all."

"I'm not asking for forgiveness, Jenni. This isn't an excuse. It's... I guess I'm trying to explain." I change my position on the floor, blood rushing along one leg giving me pins and needles. The painful rush of blood reminds me I am still alive. "What I'm saying is that it happened and I can't go back. These awful things happened. I slept with Tony once. That is the truth. Billy and I had argued. When I found out I was pregnant... for a second, just a *second*... I considered keeping it, letting Billy think it was his. But I couldn't. I knew there was no way I could do that to him. So, Jenni, I made a plan. Not a good one. Not a sensible one perhaps. Not a plan I would have had to make if I hadn't made so many bad choices beforehand, but I made a plan. I did what I felt I needed to do. I can apologise until I have no air left in my lungs, but that won't do any good." I look down at the t-shirt. I put both my hands on top of it. "I can only explain. There's nothing left for me to do now."

Jenni is looking above me again, focussing on something above my head. Out of nowhere, a conversation with my father floats into my mind. I am due to give a presentation to classmates at school the next day. He tells me to find something to look at just above the classmates I am speaking to: a picture, a mark on a wall, a crack in a windowpane. If I focussed on that enough then I wouldn't see everyone in front of me. I could just think about my speech and nothing else. It occurs me to that it's something we never stop doing; finding a spot, a small mark to look at, to work towards, to rely on, so that we can avoid any unpleasantness around us. Mine has been my wrist, or maybe the notes I leave for myself. For Jenni, it has been me. I have been that mark on the wall so that she could avoid the pain in her life: the loss of her marriage, the difficult pregnancies, the death of her brother. She has also been mine- or rather, finding out who the anonymous author has been. This has been a distraction from moving on with my life. From putting an end to grieving. To forgiving myself - because I don't believe I will ever deserve to be forgiven.

But maybe, I can *forgive* instead.

Jenni is looking above me so that she can control herself. She doesn't want to hurt me, not physically, she never did. She just wants me to be punished for what I have done. And I have been. I have punished myself. And by punishing me, she is also punishing herself.

"So, I made a plan." I continue. "I made an appointment at the hospital. I made sure Billy would be away with work. I went to hospital. I had the abortion. I didn't plan for a complication. I didn't plan for Billy to be contacted. I didn't plan for him to rush to see me, for him to get hit. I didn't plan for him to die because of my mistakes." Cold tears are rolling down my face, releasing all of the fret and agony and guilt I have been bottling up around Jenni for so long. "I am so sorry for all the pain I have caused you. I will never forgive myself for what I have done. But *you* don't need to hurt because of what *I* did. Don't stay so angry and so bitter just because I fucked up. It's my guilt. It's my shame. Not yours."

Jenni changes where she is looking. Her eyes move down to me.

"You keep saying, especially in your letters, that you don't want stories where women are victims anymore, where women are abused and shamed for mistakes in their lives. Where women keep the cycle of misogyny going by hurting each other when they should be helping each other." I think I can see her softening. I can feel her listening to my words, not just as sounds coming from my mouth. "Then let's stop that now. Us. Here. You can get up and leave. I won't say a word about this to anyone. We can together make some small step forward in preventing more women hurting other women."

She's silent.

"Jenni?" She blinks. "What do you say?"

My chest is heaving. I didn't realise how heavily I was breathing.

"Get up."

I look at her as she stands up from the table.

"Get up. Get the fuck up."

I'm not sure what to do.

"Now! Get up! Stand up!"

Before I can move, Jenni lunges at me with lightning speed. She grabs and pulls me up by my hair. Her other hand seizes my arm and suddenly I am being dragged through the kitchen, out into the hallway. I can feel the hard bumps of the staircase hitting my spine, the back of my head being bashed on step after step after step. I try to scream but any noise I make is beaten out of me by the seemingly non-stop hit upon hit of the stairs upon my back and neck, even my hands, which are being twisted and bent in all directions in my attempts to hold onto anything to prevent my being dragged and beaten. At the top of the stairs Jenni pauses briefly. I can't tell whether she is getting her breath back or simply deciding what to do with me next. Within seconds, I am being pulled on my back again, my legs kicking out, my arms and hands again desperately trying to latch onto anything to stop whatever Jenni is planning to do. I knock over a plant pot, seeing the soil spill across the carpet. I hear a crash, and vaguely make out splinters from a glass table embedding themselves in the rug just outside my bedroom. Jenni kicks open the bedroom door and before I know it, I am torn around the corner and feel the cold, slippery tiles of the bathroom floor on my skin.

In the moments that follow, I am certain that time slows. I raise my head. I hear my throat trying to swallow. I feel the blood pulsing through my veins. I see, lopsided, the bed where Billy and I slept, the cupboard where he hung his work clothes, the window where he would occasionally sit to read the morning newspaper. I swear I can see his inked fingerprints, black from his crosswords, on the windowsill. I can hear his voice: "Five along. A short-sleeved garment."

Somehow, amidst all the chaos, his t-shirt is still with me, crumpled up in one of my hands.

The room feels off kilter. Not just because I am on the floor, seeing the bathroom sideways, but more to do with the feel of the room itself; what is happening in here, what Jenni is doing. The angles feel off key, invaded. The floor seems tilted like a ship at sea. One edge of the floor looks longer than others, the corners where each tile meet seem slanted, at once both on an incline and decline. I have a sickly sensation déjà vu. Of being seasick. This painful, nauseous anxiety has been following me around for days. And now it is inside my own home.

"Do you know why I wrote those letters to you?"

I struggled to hear over the sickening feeling that was rippling through my body. I lift my head and instantly feel like I'm going to vomit. My neck aches. I smell blood, instantly feel a sharp pain on my forehead. My fingers explore the spot and show red - sticky and metallic. I couldn't remember hitting my head.

"Do you? I sat with them on my lap for days before I sent them to you. Wondering if it was worth it. Would you learn? Was I overreacting? Did I have any right to be so fucking angry with you? And that made me even more furious... that I felt *guilty* about wanting you to feel guilty. That's how fucked up we are as women. We can't just feel something for *ourselves*."

I opened my mouth. It took me several attempts to make a noise, to form a word. My tongue felt too big, my teeth seemed to shudder. An ache shot through my neck.

"Why did you send them?" I managed to splutter. "If you weren't sure, then why did you?"

"Because it was better than the alternative."

"Which was?"

I hear her turn on a tap in the bathtub. Droplets sparkle in the light coming through the bathroom window.

"Forgetting them. Billy. My baby." She turned on the other tap. "Your baby. Billy's child." She runs her hands over her thighs, grips her knees. "When I wrote that circus story it was to have some evidence, some proof, that I had been a mother. However briefly, however it had turned out, I wanted something to show, even if just to myself, that I had been pregnant. That's what no one ever thinks about. People offer their condolences, they feel sorry for you, they pity you, but there's nothing left behind. There's no funeral. No sympathy cards. What happens when you lose a baby? What is left behind to prove that there was ever a life inside of you? That a tiny person had existed?" One hand moves from her knee and drops into the bathtub. I hear her swill the rising water. "I had to have *something*. If you can't have children, what are you as a woman other than a freak? In today's world what are you, if not a walking freakshow?" She flicks some water down onto the floor. I don't dare try to sit up, unsure what she would do. "And those sideshow acts," she continued, "those people who were mocked and stared at, we still do the same today. Sure, we hide it behind hashtags and social media movements that make it *look* like we all accept each other and that things are progressing, but are they *really*? We still judge others for how they look and what they do. Women who aren't mothers. Women who aren't married. Women who wear hijabs. Women who drive badly. Women who work rather than be a stay at home mother. Women who dare to ask for equal pay. Women who have sex. Women who socialise with other mothers. I mean, even your friend Donna judges women for *that*."

My mind swims back to when I first bumped into Jenni. The café with Donna. Donna had just been openly criticising a group of mothers. Jenni had been there and heard every word. We'd practically given her an invitation to start hating us. To continue hating me.

"Jenni..." I don't know what to say. So I just say her name.

"And then," she speaks as if I haven't said anything, "one day I decided to put together this new narrative. I thought to myself, why not write something that doesn't just show how abused women are in today's society, how judged they are, how blamed... why not create the narrative in real life? Every book you read today, everything publishers like you churn out, show women that are unstable, flawed, sinful. It just perpetuates what the world already thinks about us. It just continues the circle of women being below men. And the funny thing is that it's women who buy that shit! It's women who listen to pop songs about sex and flaunting their bodies. It's women who buy trashy magazines which tell them how fat and ugly they are. It's women who watch television shows about how they need a man to mean something. It's as if The Bechdel Test never fucking happened." She turns, suddenly, and plunges both hands into the bathtub water. The warm water splashes out over the rim and onto the floor, splattering towards me. A small trickle, a little river, makes it way over the tiles and licks my hand. "So I decided to put you into a real life story. Make you part of a narrative where the female protagonist is not to blame. She hasn't done anything wrong. Where she has no reason to feel the guilt that society weighs her down with."

I am conscious of the water rising. I can hear the gushing of both taps. I see the renewed anger glaring in Jenni's eyes. Billy's shirt is still bundled up in one of my hands: he's still here with me, trying to give some last ounces of strength.

"But…" again, my voice falters, my neck searing with pain, "all you did *was* make me the victim. You *did* blame me, the woman. You didn't *change* anything. You didn't rewrite this cannon of work you seem so intent upon eradicating. You…" Blood from my forehead drips and mixes, like oil on a pavement, with water from the bath. "You just made *another* female suffer."

I know I have said the wrong thing, but I don't have anything left to lose. What else can she accuse me of? What else can she take from me?

"You fucking idiot." Jenni stands up, lightning fast, and with both hands gathers water and chucks it from the tub towards me. I am drenched, coughing. "You ignorant, arrogant, fucking idiot." Each word is spat at me. "You *aren't* the victim! You were *never* the fucking victim! Jesus *Christ*, have you not been listening to anything I've been saying?"

She walks over towards me, grabs me again by the hair, and lifts me up. I scream out, try to say something that isn't a garbled yelp.

"*She* is the victim! Anne. Annie. A. All the anonymous women who have been dumped or mocked or passed over or blamed for wearing makeup or told they asked for sex because they wore a short dress and are then made to feel ashamed that they were raped. All those anonymous women who can't have children, who can't do the one thing they are expected to do but aren't offered any kind of sympathy from this fucking medieval, patriarchal world that women like *you* help run!" She's dragging me towards to bath. I reach out for anything to hold onto: the toilet, the rug. My legs kick out at nothing. "You were *never* meant to be the victim!" She's screaming. She lifts my head, and I feel my chest crash painfully against porcelain. Water, now hot and steaming and still running from the taps, splashes me. "*You* are the fucking *enemy!*"

Jenni holds my head right above the water. I can taste the heat. I see blood from my head drop into the water, swirling like liquid steam.

"Do you remember what I wrote? That I know what it means when people say that actions have consequences? Because I am one?" I try to nod my head, to move against her vice like grip. "Well, guess what." She is whispering now. Her words hiss in my ear. "These letters are the consequence of your actions. This, *now*, is the consequence of your actions. And it's time you face up to them."

Bubbles erupt from my submerged screams. My hands pummel the sides of the bathtub. I am sure that the skin on knees is tearing, bloody on the tiled floor. Jenni pushes down on the base of my neck, forcing me deeper into the boiling water.

Sometimes, everything seems to fade away.

Try, try, try, Billy says.

Billy is here. He's talking to me. He's telling me not to worry.

But I'm scared, I say.

I don't think I can fight anymore. He is holding out a hand toward me. His mouth is moving. It doesn't make a sound, but I can lip read every word he says.

Try, try, try, Billy says.

I'm so sorry, I say.

His hand reaches out but just misses mine. We're under water. He's trying to swim towards me but he's drifting further away … that, or I'm being pulled away from him. I try to move my arms to reach out, but my arms are stuck, tied behind my back. Above me the water is black. A rippling shadow moves over the water's surface. I can't make out anything more than an inky shape, a splodge.

Billy is further away from me now… floating into the darkening distance, his hand still outstretched. His mouth continues to move and he's telling me to try, to try, to *try…*

Something floats past my hand. I flinch, thinking it must be some sort of creature. An eel. A white eel, electric, swimming in the water with us. It floats up and hovers before my face. It is twisting into a long thin line. White material.

Billy is holding something.

I open my eyes.

-

It all happens in a flash.

Somehow, I find the strength to push my hands and arms up and out of the water. I twist my body around, and through the water still running over my eyes and face, I see Jenni - shocked, dazzled, inches above me. I raise my hands behind her, over her and wrap Billy's t-shirt around her neck – quickly, before she can start to push me back under the water. Her eyes widen, still shocked, but are now threaded with fear, with panic. She tries to stagger backwards, pulling me up with her in the process. This tightens the noose around her neck, the white eel-like material of Billy's shirt. Protecting me but hurting her. Hurting his sister.

She continues to struggle, her mouth gaping like a fish, her hands clambering over my arms, up at my neck and hair. I turn my head away. The noises from her throat are guttural, pained. It turns my stomach. Can I do this? Can I hurt anymore people? In the darkness, in the milky light coming in from outside, the shirt around her neck looks like knotted hands, ghostly knuckles. I see Billy's hands around his own sister's throat.

Okay, so you've met my mum and dad and Jenni. Most people are here now, Billy says.

Billy, don't worry. Family gatherings don't bother me, I say.

They stress the fuck out of me, Billy says.

I don't know why. Your family are lovely, I say.

Billy kisses my forehead.

"Michelle!"

Whether I fall first or Jenni does, somehow we separate and coming crashing down to the floor. My head hits the toilet, pain breaking through my skull as though hit with a hammer. I try to straighten myself up and see that Jenni is face down on the watery tiles, her hands splayed trying to push herself up. Dripping, she looks like a nightmarish mermaid: her hair black seaweed, her clothes soggy and filthy. She pushes herself up onto all fours and her eyes latch onto mine, then travel down to the t-shirt I am still clutching – clutching like my life depends on it. It did.

"Michelle!"

The voice sounds panicked.

"Jenni?"

My throat aches.

I hear my name called out again, but it isn't from Jenni. She isn't speaking. She is just staring at Billy's t-shirt, immobile. Frozen.

"Michelle? Michelle are you up here?"

From somewhere I hear footsteps. Running. Doors being opened and slammed, feet stomping from room to room. In the steam of the bathroom, it feels as though I'm sleeping, drifting, dozing... soft thuds, a hammering of fists ... my eyes begin to close again... blood thumps through my head... I hear voices... Michelle! *Try...* Michelle! *Try...*

"Michelle? Oh my god. Michelle!"

I am pulled up. Two hands under my arms. Dragged from bathroom to bedroom. My vision swims. I make out a dark figure above me. Lights flash on. It blinds me. My eyes blink against the harshness of the bright light. I feel my face crease, and the pain from the cuts and bruises sears across my skin. I grimace again at the light from the ceiling. The bedroom. I am in my bedroom. I'm safe.

Am I?

"Michelle, are you okay? Can you hear me?"

"How... how did you get here?"

"It's Jenni. Leesha is with her. Don't worry, I'm here. Oh my god. I'm so sorry."

"Donna?"

-

You have friends.

I push myself up. I rest my back and my head on the side of the bed. Donna runs her hands over my face. She grabs a jumper from my drawer and starts to dab at the blood on my face and my neck. She tries to dry my hair.

"What happened? Are you okay? God, you've got so many cuts all over you."

"Jenni. Jenni, where is she?" I think I'm slurring my words.

"She's in the bathroom with Leesha. Don't worry."

I hear other footsteps. "Is she okay?" Leesha.

"Yeah. Disorientated."

"She was trying to drown her or something. The bath was fucking overflowing. There's water everywhere. She called and told us to go somewhere else tonight. She knew. She knew all along."

"Where is she?"

"She's just sitting on the floor. She's not saying anything."

"Leesha?" I think it's me speaking.

"Michelle don't worry. You're safe. We're here. You're safe now." She is kneeling in front of me. Like Donna, she runs a hand over my face. It's comforting. "God, I am so sorry. I should never have left you." I can hear tears in her voice. I try to smile.

"Thank you." I manage to speak louder now, more clearly, but it hurts. "Thank you for coming back for me."

They both put their arms around me. Their warmth seeps into me. I don't want them to let go. I can feel their tears on my neck.

"Thank you."

You need to listen to your friends. They care about you, Billy says.

I know, believe me. How much they care is etched across their faces, I say.

They just don't like seeing you so upset. They don't want to see you making yourself ill, Billy says.

Maybe I deserve it. Maybe I deserve to feel this way, I say.

Billy tells me that no one deserves to feel unhappy. No matter what they've done.

-

I used to be afraid of time.

I don't know how much time passes before I open my eyes again. I don't know how much time passes before Tony arrives, before I am helped downstairs. Before we decide what to do next. It occurs to me that time might have stopped altogether. It seems to ebb and flow slowly into one minute and then another - perhaps an hour has gone by, it could even be a whole day. A month. A year? A lifetime of changes and questions, of regrets.

Perhaps it has been a trick of time – perhaps a gap year, a lightyear, a leap year. Maybe I will understand in four years' time. Maybe forgiveness will be something I am only given once every four years. That might be what I deserve: a quarterly understanding, a twenty five percent chance of acceptance.

I see a clock melting in a painting somewhere - in a memory from school, from a trip abroad, from a poster in a university dorm room.

I don't know how much time has passed... but I do know that Billy is not speaking to me now. He's not here. He's no longer saying those words. His words are memories I will forever hold, will forever keep. But he's not here. He's not judging me. He's not disappointed in me. Not anymore.

I'd like to think he never was. Perhaps I'll get to fully believe that one day.

But I'm not afraid of time anymore.

-

"She's sitting in the living room."

Tony, Leesha and Donna are at the kitchen table.

"How did this happen? How did she manage to get in and do all of this?"

"Some of it I understand," I say to Tony, "some of it... I need to find out. I still need to ask her."

"That's what the police are for. That's what *jail* is for." Donna taps her fingers loudly on the table as she speaks.

"We need to call the police. We should have done that as soon as we arrived."

"We didn't know what we were walking into." Donna says to Leesha, but also to me. "We didn't know what to do." Despite her vigorous hand movements, her voice is fragile and high pitched. She can't seem to look at me. "We didn't know what we might find."

"Where did Jenni tell you to go?" Tony asked.

Leesha sighed. "She called both of us and asked us to meet her and Michelle at their office. She said she'd managed to figure out who was doing all of this, that she'd found something incriminating there and they needed our advice. She said she'd already called Michelle who was on her way." She bows her head, and I can see tears fall onto the surface of the kitchen table. "I should have just come back here to check. I'd only gone out for... I didn't know..."

I reach out my hand and put it on hers. I do the same to Donna.

"I wouldn't be here if not for you two. Don't you dare feel guilty. She's been fooling us all along."

Tony shifts uncomfortably in his seat. "What did you find in the office? I mean, had she left something there?"

Donna and Leesha share a look, then look at me. "It's okay," I say, "there's nothing that will shock any of us now." I even manage a smile. It hurts my neck and face to smile. I imagine how I must look, covered in bruises, blues and purples splashed over my skin. I close my eyes for a moment and breathe.

"It was a picture. Or, lots of pictures. The same picture."

"What do you mean? What picture?"

Donna quickly looks at Tony, then at me. She gets her phone from her pocket and hands it to me, careful to not let Tony see. It takes me a minute to get my eyes working, to look at something so bright up close. Then it clears and comes into focus. Tony's name is spelt out in a series of copies of my scan photograph, all over the floor of my office. And at the bottom of each picture, my surname -Billy's surname - is circled in a marker pen. Jenni certainly knows how to send a message.

I swallow. Even that hurts. I nod gently at Donna. She puts the phone away. Tony doesn't speak.

For a minute or two we just sit in silence. We drink tea as though nothing is amiss. As though we are friends just catching up over lunch, and I remember, when Donna and I sat in silence just a few days ago. A comfortable silence makes a friendship. Somehow, sitting here with the three of them, this *is* comfortable. It is a safe silence.

But I know what I need to do.

"Did she say anything to you when you brought her down?"

"No," Tony says. "She just sat down in the living room. She looked kind of blank. She didn't speak to me. She was just holding onto a shirt. I don't know why. She was drenched but wouldn't let me try and clean her up."

"Why would you want to? She doesn't deserve any kindness." Leesha almost spits in Tony's face, incredulous. "We need to call the police, quickly. Before she tries to run off."

"She won't do that." I push myself up, aching all over. The three of them, on instinct, make to get up and help me. I hold up a hand to show I can do it alone. "She won't try to run away. And we're not calling the police."

I walk around the table and towards the hallway. I know what they will be thinking and wanting to say. I can feel their eyes on my back.

"We're not calling the police," I repeat.

-

There's no point worrying about the future or the past. We can't stop either, Billy says.

I just keep thinking about getting older and how much older I look every day, I say.

But wrinkles show what's happened to us. Like a map of us on your face, Billy says.

You might want to rethink that compliment, I say.

Billy tells me that he can see our first date in my crow's feet.

She is in the living room. She is sat looking straight forward, a blank stare at nothing. Her hands are on her knees, feet flat on the floor. She looks like a broken China doll: pale, young, innocent, despite all that has transpired over the last few days. The floorboards creak under foot as I walk towards her. I sit beside her and, without expecting to, I start speaking straight away.

"Jenni. I don't know how to best move on from here. I don't know what you want. I don't know what to do. But - we're not going to call the police. I'm not interested in having them involved in this." She blinks. "On one hand... I don't know why you did you did, but then... I also understand it. I do." I run my hands over my thighs and knees, trying to muster more courage.

"I know how hurt you have been. And I can only imagine how I must have added to that - with what you have found out and believe I have done. But I need to you know that I loved Billy. More than anything in the world. I wanted a family with him more than anything. We tried and we couldn't. I couldn't handle that and... I ended up turning to anything *but* him for support. But I loved him." I feel myself starting to cry, tears running down the bruises over my face, my strangled neck. "And when I found out I was pregnant I did what I thought was best. I couldn't lie to Billy about a child that wasn't his. And Tony doesn't know. And it will be my decision as and when to tell him. You have to believe me that I didn't plan for any..." the words catch in my throat. "... for any of this to happen."

I look at Jenni. Her gaze is focussed on the wall opposite us, but like me she is crying. I don't see any anger in her tears, I no longer see hatred or blame, just sadness.

"When we finish talking here, you need to get up and leave and never come back. I won't tell anyone what has happened. I won't contact your parents. I won't report this to the police." Nervously, I take her hands in mine. I cradle them. "Because I know you won't do this again. Will you?"

She turns her head and looks at me. She is crying, sobbing now. And I am too.

"Will you," I repeat.

She shakes her head. "Thank you," she whispers, "thank you. I won't apologise but... thank you."

I manage a laugh through my tears. I cough through the pains that echo inside my neck and throat. "Okay. I can handle that."

"But why? Why won't you call you police?" She is still whispering. "I nearly killed you."

I look up at the ceiling and shake my head. I want to scream out loud that I don't know why. That I should. That I am crazy to not report her. But I don't. Instead, I say, "Because what you did... you have been in so much pain. And I know what that pain feels like. Do you remember what you said and wrote to me about consequences?" She just looks at me. "'I know what it means when people say that actions have consequences. Because I am one.' We're both consequences of grief, of a terrible mistake and a tragic accident. We don't need any further pain and anger in our lives. Okay?"

She nods. "Yes."

Bizarrely, we smile.

"So," I say, "it *was* you after all. The wine bottles in the night. Changing my phone screen. Leaving ink marks around the house. How did you know to do all of that?"

"I've known Billy my whole life. I've known you for years. You just have to watch people."

"And Mrs Lullin? You really had nothing to do with her accident?"

"No. I promise you that. I didn't. But I did see her, I did pay her a visit."

"Sam. That was you too." It's a statement not a question, even though I know I won't understand for some time exactly everything that has happened. All that Jenni has done. She must be able to read the look on my face.

"It's easy to make yourself look different," she says. "A hat to hide your hair. A jumper and baggy trousers. I was 'Sam', a volunteer care giver. I initially went to try and follow you around, but I heard an old lady mention your name and overheard her telling her friends how wonderful a carer you were. I followed her to her room. We chatted a little. She was sweet. And then I came back during the night and... well, you know what happened."

"But why? Why go to all that trouble? Why create 'Sam' who attacks random people and places?"

"Michelle, come on. Do you really not know by now how these stories work? You've read and published enough of them."

I pause. "Because there are always clues everywhere. Little hints throughout a story."

"Exactly." She nods, almost proud that I figured out another part of her narrative. "'Sam' was just another plot thread and plot device I needed to make you the character in my story. Remember what I said about being the postman who delivers the next part of the story?"

"Jesus." I lean away from her. A feeling of fear ripples back through me, ice cold. "I've been in this story all along. My friends, my work, my house. All these letters and notes. I have literally been acting out your book."

"But I never hurt anyone but you. I promise you that."

"But you went back afterwards? Another man saw you there. He took Meredith's room. Nathan."

"Yes. I went back a few days later just to see what had been taken. To see if what I'd left behind as clues had actually been collected by you."

"The note from Sam. The magazine clipping."

"Yes. All part of it."

"You really are a good writer. You really brought your story to life. All those mistakes you added in on purpose. You certainly know how to trick and engage a reader." As I say this, I don't know whether I am being sarcastic, feel disgusted or in awe of her. The churning in my stomach suggests it's a poisonous mixture of all three.

I don't know how much time passes. We sit for a while thinking, considering our next steps. I close my eyes and conjure Billy's face. He smiles at me. He's not judging me like I have judged myself. He's not disappointed in me like I have made myself believe he was.

"You say that you want to write a story where women don't hurt other women anymore? Where women aren't the victims of men or of each other? That you're sick of women being portrayed in that way?" Jenni doesn't say anything. My hands are still around her hands, and I grip them tightly. "Then leave," I say, "and never come back. I will let you go. We don't have to continue hating and harming one other like society dictates we have to. Like all these books which portray women as being weak and angry and hurting each other. Leave. I forgive you." I pause, then - "But *never* come back."

Jenni looks at me.

We embrace for a final time.

Then, without speaking, she stands up. Carefully, she folds Billy's t-shirt and places it on the side of the chair.

She turns and simply walks out of the room. I hear the gentle click of the front door. And I know she is gone.

I place one hand on Billy's t-shirt. It is still damp. I will myself to recognise his scent again in the fabric.

I wait for the voice to come, angry and cruel as always. I expect it.

But everything is silent.

And I'm not afraid anymore.

PART FIVE

We should have some dogs and cats around here, Billy says.

I'm allergic to cats? It'll have to be dogs I'm afraid, I say.

That's okay. I don't want us to become that crazy old couple with cats that scare children in the neighbourhood anyway, Billy says.

We can just have the dogs that bark at the postman. That'll be fun to watch, I say.

Billy laughs. He sips his tea and continues his crossword.

I put down my pen. I look at the pile of conversations I have written between Billy and I -
little A5 sized memories that I have collated over the past year. I pat them with my hand and
see Mrs Lullin, remember her telling me to get down on paper all these words, Billy's voice
and anecdotes, that I never want to forget. The phone rings.

"Are we still on for lunch?" Leesha.

"Yes. I am just putting the drafts together now. Well, the originals."

"Great. Bring them along so they can be photographed. They'll make a brilliant cover for the
book. Bring the post-its too."

"They're here." I place my hand on the post its I wrote to myself during my counselling, the
notes of confidence I would leave for myself around the house. "Everything I need is here.
And the emails are printed. I can't believe this is really happening."

"Well, it is! Believe it! The publisher is going to bring the first proof copy today so we can go
over it. And he loves the idea, as do I, of photographing the original notes you made about
all of this. Honestly, this book, this collection of memories, is going to touch so many
people."

She pauses, letting me take in what she's saying. This is real. I am going to be published. I
am going to, in some small way, help people who are going through grief, or have suffered
grief, like I have done. Through my memories of Billy, through my notes which encouraged
me to get up every single dark morning, perhaps someone, even just one person, might feel
better. Feel seen.

"And then," Leesha continues, "just wait for the book tour!"

We chat for a few minutes more. I promise to be on time. I place the notes in separate
envelopes and tape them shut. I hold them close to me. I don't know how I will feel handing
them over to someone I don't know. I will want them back. They're what makes me feel
closest to Billy now.

A text comes through from Donna, asking me if I still want her to come to the lunch
meeting. I reply yes; that I definitely still need her there for the moral support.

Before leaving to meet Leesha, Donna and the publisher, I open the bedroom wardrobe. So
much of my life is inside these clothes: the hat I wore to a family event years ago; my work
overalls from the care home even though I only volunteer with Nathan once a week now;
the dress I wore to the first meeting with the publishers and Leesha.

The voices still come, still unbidden, but not as viciously as they used to do. And not as
frequently. Now, the voices in my head are mostly conversations I choose to listen to and
recall, rather than have forced upon me in blaming shame cycles.

I run my hand down Billy's white t-shirt. It hangs there in the middle of my clothes. It no
longer smells of him, but when I hold it to my chest, I swear I can feel his heart beating
through the fabric.

-

Can't I give some of this stuff away? Half of this I don't even wear anymore, Billy says.

Sure thing. You knock yourself out and organise our closet, I say.

I'll do my stuff, sure. But I like seeing yours hanging there. It reminds of all the things we've done together, Billy says.

Don't you dare say a wrinkle in my clothes reminds you of something, like when you said the wrinkles in my face tell our story, I say.

Billy laughs, then holds up the shoes I wore on one of our first dates - all those years ago in a university pub.

The post has arrived. I don't have much time before I am due to meet Leesha, so I flick through the envelopes. A bill, an advert for some new restaurant across town, a catalogue. One envelope is handwritten. The letters curl in a style I instantly recognise. My pulse quickens.

It's been a year. A whole year with no contact.

My wrist throbs.

The envelope shakes in my hand.

I rip it open.

LETTER SEVEN

Dear Michelle,

I know I promised not to contact you again, but I felt that after a year I needed to at least reach out to you. It seemed fitting that I write to you rather than come and see you face to face. I don't think that would be a good idea. I'm sure you would agree that it's best we don't see each other again.

I cannot thank you enough for allowing me to leave that day. I still stand by what I said: I won't apologise for what I did, but I am grateful that you let me go. I will always remember your kindness - and am still genuinely grateful for it. It makes me hopeful that somewhere in the future, we as women *can* support each other and no longer look to hurt one another like we have done for so many years. Like society has made us do for centuries. Your understanding is a part of that change.

I remember posing the question to you in one of my emails, about whether every story has to end with a death: in a way, our story *started* with a death, and now... maybe we can both find a way to live again.

I do hope you are well and safe. I hope your friends are still caring for you. That is something I never really had and, thinking back to how protective they were of you, it is a testament to you as a person. It helps me understand why Billy loved you so much. And this, I think, perfectly represents the duality of how I feel towards you: at once I feel still so much betrayal at your hands – but also, I respect and admire the full life you have managed to create for yourself.

Perhaps I will put all this confusion into ink for my next book. I promise to leave you out of it this time though. Sorry, my guillotine humour again.

There is a reason though why I have written to you. After I left, I spent many days unsure about what to do and where to go. Obviously, I couldn't go back to running the business for you. I'm glad that the merger with Leesha has proved to be successful. It helps keep his memory alive, doesn't it? I couldn't go back to my own work either, just pretending that everything was normal. I couldn't go home. So, I decided to go and stay with my parents for a while. They decided to move back to Ireland and, mixed with all of the madness that I'd been through with you, I encouraged my parents to finally clean out some of Billy's things - especially before their big move. They still had clothes and books and all sorts of things that were only holding them in a constant state of grief, unable to move on. It was hard for all of us, but slowly we sorted and tidied his things one box at a time.

In his room I came across a letter. There were lots of letters and papers and documents and folders in his room that he'd kept over the years. Different bits from friends and from work. But one letter stood out.

It is dated the twelfth of September. It is addressed to you. It seems that he never sent it. I've enclosed it for you.

I think it's important that you read it. It's what Billy wanted to say. Everything he knew.

I hope you don't mind if I write to you again every now and then. I don't expect you to write back.

Yours,

Jenni.

I fold up Jenni's letter and place it back inside the envelope. Inside is another piece of paper.

I don't know what to do. Part of me wants to, automatically like muscle memory, look back through Jenni's letter for errors - purposeful mistakes showing me this is part of another plan: another game and narrative she is crafting for me.

Eventually, I take out the second letter. On the paper I can see black smudges. I can see the inky fingerprints Billy always left after he wrote. I can see the curve of his lettering through the folded paper. I almost feel his hand upon mine, see his fingertips and fingernails curled around the pen as he writes this letter to me.

It feels like an artefact. Something that has been dug up. A time capsule, hidden long ago.

I open the letter.

Printed in Great Britain
by Amazon